THE APPRENTICESHIP OF EBENEZER WELLS

LOUISE HARMON

ISBN: 979-8-9915313-2-0

Book Cover by David Provolo
Silhouettes by Lauren Muney, after William Bache (1771-1845)
Map by Owen Bruce McKenzie

HOT BRICK BOOKS

TABLE OF CONTENTS

DIXWELL AVENUE NEIGHBORHOOD
ELM STREET
YALE COLLEGE
DR. EBENEZER CABOT'S HOUSE
NEW HAVEN GREEN
NED HAINES'S HOUSE
CHAPEL STREET
CHURCH STREET
HAINES & HAINES
LONG WHARF
The City of NEW HAVEN

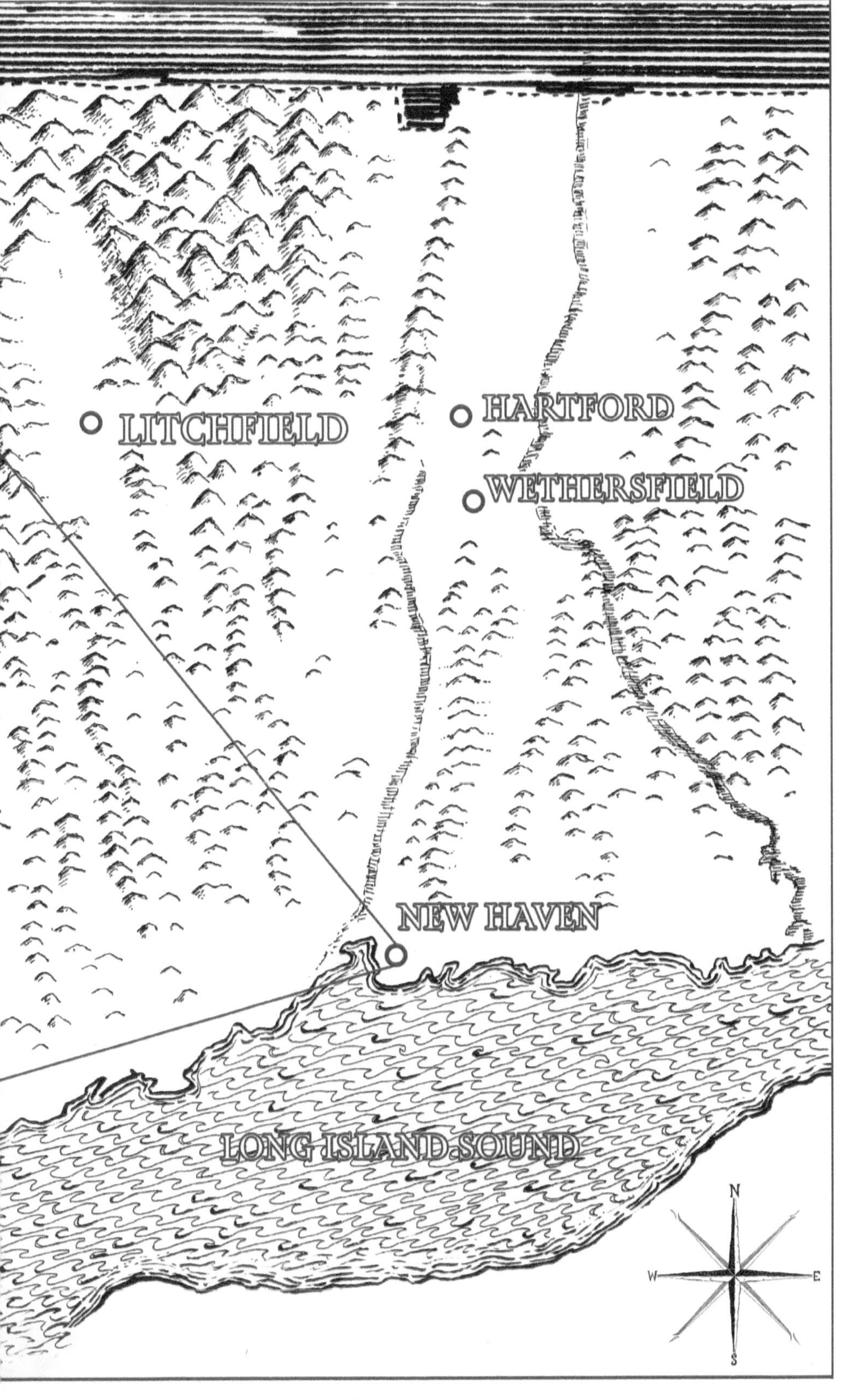

LITCHFIELD
HARTFORD
WETHERSFIELD
NEW HAVEN
LONG ISLAND SOUND
N
W
E
S

CHAPTER 1

Snow Drifts

"Someone's moving into your room next month." Mrs. Edwards sipped her tea by the fire in the kitchen of her boarding house. It was the first week of December 1820. The long, dark kitchen had been tidied up after breakfast, the dried dishes stacked on the table to be put away. She and her favorite lodger were alone, her two daughters on a morning walk, her servant, Maggie, down in the cellar, and her other boarders—law students and female academy students—off to class. A frugal older woman, Mrs. Edwards usually rationed her tea, but Eb Wells was leaving Litchfield on a stagecoach this morning. "A young woman from Poughkeepsie."

"That's good." Eb pushed his auburn hair back from his face, peering over at Mrs. Edwards through his gold-rimmed glasses. His face was handsome on a small scale. Everything about Eb Wells was on a small scale, at least physically. He had just finished his course at the Litchfield Law School, and an apprenticeship in New Haven awaited him. "I hope she's fond of cats." He dreaded leaving Sir

Winston, Mrs. Edwards's old orange-and-white cat, who had been his constant companion for the past year and a half. Sir Winston had not joined them on the hearth, having ventured out the back door to greet the frigid day.

"I did warn her there's a cat up there who keeps the mice at bay." Mrs. Edwards tucked a wisp of silvery hair into her white housekeeping cap. "The new lodger's a female academy student."

"Good for her," Eb said, sounding glum.

"I neglected to mention to her—the cat sleeps on the bed." Mrs. Edwards gave Eb an appraising look. He was dressed for travel in his brown wool suit. Eb Wells had arrived in Connecticut an insecure, ragged law student—a boy—but he was leaving town a well-tailored, well-groomed young man, perhaps not always confident, but more certain about his right to inhabit the world. Today, he looked doleful. "She made no mention of the cat in her reply."

"She'd better be kind to him." Before living at Mrs. Edwards's, Eb would have recoiled at the thought of a cat even entering the house. But now, how could he fall asleep without the familiar weight of Sir Winston at his feet?

"Your sister Malinda and her companion will be at your uncle's?" Mrs. Edwards tactfully changed the subject. She knew all about his family. Eb often lingered in her kitchen, wanting to gossip or seek advice. Did she think he needed a haircut? Which one—the brown or black suit for moot court? What kind of herbal tea is good for a sore throat? Might she sew on a button? And then there was Eb's love life, which was often in disarray. His mother had died in Savannah last year from yellow fever. With all her dithering, Mrs. Edwards had filled in some of the maternal gaps.

"Yes." Eb brightened at the mention of his sister and her companion. "My uncle will have a full house. I haven't seen Malinda or Susan since they came up north."

"And your apprenticeship? When does that start?"

"Right after the New Year." Eb's law practicum was with Haines & Haines, a commercial firm in New Haven. He had a family reputation to live up to. After the War of Independence, over thirty-five years ago, the senior partner, Mr. Ned Haines, and Eb's father, William Wells, had been law apprentices together in New Haven. Ned held Eb's father in high esteem. His older brother, John, who had a law practice in Charleston, was also well-regarded in legal circles. Eb's father had been dead for over two years, and his brother was far away, but Eb feared disappointing them—and Ned Haines.

"I'm nervous about it," Eb confessed. "I told Judge Reeve that last night." He had eaten a farewell dinner with his mentor, Judge Tapping Reeve, the founder of the Litchfield Law School, his wife Betsey, and their grandson, T.B.

"The renowned Eb Wells, nervous?" Mrs. Edwards teased. Eb had been at the top of his class in law school, a fierce competitor in moot court and oral exams. "I can't believe that."

"Truth to tell, Mrs. Edwards . . ." Eb shook his head. "I'm not very practical. Thomas is much better." Thomas Bradford, another boarder at Mrs. Edwards's, would apprentice with Eb's brother in Charleston. "He knows how to get things done."

"Well, you'll learn, Eb. That's the whole point of being an apprentice. You're supposed to learn."

"Yes, but my strength is in legal theory, not solving problems." After an unremarkable college career, except in the classics, Eb had discovered a passion for the law. As a law student, he spent hours daily in Judge Reeve's dark law library, relishing every minute of it. But practicality—in law and life—was not Eb's strong suit. His trepidation was justified. "I wish they didn't know about my reputation at the law school." Haines & Haines had vetted their new apprentice, and Judges Gould and Reeve had written glowing recommendations for him. "They're expecting some hotshot. Instead, they're getting me."

"You *are* a hotshot," Mrs. Edwards said affectionately, leaning over to poke the fire with an iron. A log fell, with a woosh of ash and a burst of flame. "Don't you worry, Eb. It's all going to work out fine." Her optimism was that of a mother—well-intended and baseless.

"Thanks, Mrs. Edwards." Eb looked over at the old woman, trying to memorize her face, warm smile, and wrinkles around her eyes and mouth. "I'm really going to miss you."

"And we'll miss you too." Mrs. Edwards straightened her cap. "Me and Sir Winston. But now you must get ready." She stood up abruptly and smoothed her apron. "Thomas already brought your trunks down before he went off to the lecture. Charles will be here any moment." Charles Godwin, Eb's best friend, had skipped the law lecture to help transport Eb's trunks down to the Green and say goodbye. "You've got to get going, lad."

Malinda Wells, Susan Graham, and Dr. Ebenezer Cabot lingered over breakfast in the chilly dining room on Elm Street. In the past two months, Malinda, Eb's older sister, and her companion, Susan, had settled into Dr. Cabot's elegant home, adjacent to the New Haven Green. Malinda and Susan helped out in his clinic, which was not open this morning.

Dr. Cabot was the older brother of Abigail Cabot Wells, the mother of John, Malinda, and Eb Wells. Abigail had died from yellow fever in Savannah the summer before. The epidemic continued to decimate Savannah, even into the autumn of 1820. Her two brothers insisted Malinda evacuate—to move in with John's family in Charleston or Dr. Cabot in New Haven. Malinda had chosen the latter, accompanied by the housekeeper's daughter, Susan. Eb would arrive soon to start his apprenticeship at Haines & Haines.

"You're beginning to convince me, Malinda." Dr. Ebenezer

Cabot was sixty years old, thick around the waist, bald and bespectacled, his ears too large for his head. But his face was kind.

"About getting a carriage?" Malinda Wells put down the newspaper. She was a compact woman of medium height, her straight dark hair pulled back in a bun, her face round and pretty, the beginnings of crow's feet around her eyes. Her accent bore the stamp of Savannah. Malinda had been lobbying her uncle to purchase a carriage for his clinic and private practice.

"Yes, for the clinic and you two girls as well."

Malinda smiled when her uncle referred to them as 'girls.' She was almost thirty, and Susan was twenty-four. Her mother used to do the same thing.

"I gave up our old carriage when Mother became ill," Dr. Cabot said. "She used it more than I did. I never go out much, as you know." He glanced up at his housekeeper, who had just entered the room. Esmeralda Smith was an elderly free Black woman who had been with the Cabot family for over forty years. "But you and Susan are young people. You should be going out. Eb too, although he might be working most of the time."

"I imagine he will." Malinda smiled, looking forward to her younger brother's arrival. "Is there any more tea?" She made eye contact with Esmeralda, who tidied up the mahogany sideboard. Esmeralda was light-skinned, dressed in a simple gray dress, white apron, and paisley turban. "Susan, do you want more tea?"

Susan had her nose in a book. "Sure," she said, not looking up. She was slightly taller than Malinda, with shoulder-length, light brown hair, big brown eyes, a long, sloping nose, and a wide mouth—a set of irregular features that made her look alternately cockeyed and alluring. Her body was curvaceous and flexible, ready to wrap her limbs any which way, often to accommodate her reading.

"Here's what I'm thinking," Dr. Cabot continued, wiping his mouth with a white linen napkin. "I should get the carriage house done up first. It's gone to ruin out there. I know they say not to put the cart before the horse, but one really ought to put the carriage house before the cart." He chuckled at his own joke.

"That makes sense." Malinda reached over for the last piece of bacon and put it on her plate. "Speaking of horses, are you thinking of one? Or maybe two?"

"I'm disinclined about the horses." Dr. Cabot shook his head. "It's not just the initial outlay. Horses must be fed, watered, groomed, have their shoes maintained, put to bed, and exercised. They generate manure. And when they're ill, you've got to call a horse doctor. My father hired a full-time man to do all that. He lived in the carriage house." Dr. Cabot offered his empty teacup to Esmeralda, who circled the table with the teapot. "Besides, we can rent a driver and two horses from William Lanson whenever needed." William Lanson was an acquaintance of Dr. Cabot's, a free Black man in New Haven, an entrepreneur who owned an establishment on Fleet Street, leasing carriages, horses, and drivers.

"Well, you know best, of course, Uncle." Malinda lifted the piece of bacon to her lips and chewed it thoughtfully. When she resumed speaking, her voice was lower, her accent suddenly more Southern. "That doesn't really address the problem of emergencies though, now does it?"

Malinda was referring to an incident the week before. One of their older private patients had fallen in his bedroom. Dr. Cabot could not leave the clinic, so Malinda and Susan were dispatched to assess the situation. It took over an hour to arrange a carriage, two horses, and a driver with William Lanson. By the time they arrived at the patient's home, his distressed wife had dragged her ailing husband up onto their four-poster bed, not a prudent maneuver since the injury was to his back—and it did her back no good either. Neither was harmed, but everyone agreed: Dr. Cabot's office had not responded in a timely fashion.

Malinda used the incident to bolster her case for a carriage—and horses. It would take just as much time to arrange for two horses and a driver as it would to arrange for a carriage, two horses, and a driver. A carriage in the carriage house, with no horses to pull it, did not solve the problem at hand. They also needed a driver, but Malinda instinctively knew to lobby her uncle for one thing at a time—carriage first, then horses, and finally a driver.

"Malinda makes a good point," Esmeralda interjected. The elderly housekeeper had known Ebenezer Cabot since his teens and felt free to interject herself into any conversation. Now that his niece had arrived, the two had formed a cabal, needling Dr. Cabot into making improvements—new fire screens in the bedrooms, fresh pillows for the beds, and the purchase of a rose-colored velvet settee for the library so that Malinda and Susan too could enjoy the fire's warm glow in the evening. Ebenezer Cabot was generous with his considerable wealth but did not like change. "What's the good of a carriage without horses?" Esmeralda muttered.

"She's right," Malinda said in a sweet, lilting voice. "We'd take up just as much time renting horses. And then there's the matter of a driver," she added, dipping her toe into the water.

"Yes, well . . ." Dr. Cabot muttered. His niece was almost always right, a trait that inspired his admiration—and irritation. "I suppose I could drive the carriage, but who would drive it if I weren't available?"

"Maybe Malinda or I could learn how." Susan looked up from her book. "How hard could it be to drive a carriage?" She gave Dr. Cabot a disarming smile, aware she might be shocking him.

"That wouldn't be proper." Dr. Cabot cast a dubious eye on Susan, who was even more outspoken than Malinda. Still, he always knew where he stood with Susan. Malinda's honeyed intonations might be subtly manipulating him. Susan Graham was not a woman for subtle manipulation, being forthright and frank. Sometimes, she dismayed him, but Dr. Cabot admired her spunk.

"It was just a suggestion." Susan shrugged.

"I'd never let a woman drive my carriage, even though I doubt there's little you couldn't do, Susan." Dr. Cabot gave her a wink. "And I'm leaning toward a 'no' on the horses," he added with a decisiveness that signaled the conversation was over.

"We can talk about it later," Malinda purred, keeping the door open a crack for further negotiations. "Let's see what happens when Eb gets here."

It was a frigid December day. The sky was a bluish gray, the sunlight pale and wintry. Charles Godwin and Eb Wells staggered down North Street, struggling with a wooden hand truck that held two trunks, one stacked precariously on top of the other, tied loosely together with a canvas strap. Charles had skipped the law lecture this morning to help Eb get his luggage to the station on the Litchfield Green. Eb's stagecoach to New Haven would arrive soon.

"You must be traveling with rocks," Charles panted. The air was so cold that the exhalation of his warm breath formed ephemeral clouds of condensation.

"Books and boots," Eb said in a halting voice, trying to avoid a pothole in the road. Charles had much longer legs, and Eb found it challenging to keep up with his side of the hand truck. "Could you please slow down a little? We're in good time."

Eb Wells and Charles Godwin had started at the Litchfield Law School together, both boarding at Mrs. Edwards's. Charles had been a shy, reluctant law student, an aspiring artist, but Eb had coaxed and wheedled him through law school for the better part of a year. The two friends had attended lectures, copied their notes in Judge Reeve's library, and studied together at night. In Charles's words, Eb's support made his experience in law school 'not as wretched as I expected.'

In the middle of the course, Eb and Charles had moved in opposite directions, with Eb becoming a moot court star and Charles dropping out of law school. Charles had suffered a bout of melancholy over a failure in love and had fallen gravely ill. Eventually, his health was restored to him, as was his fiancée, Martha Lewis. Worried about the welfare of their future children, Martha had pleaded with Charles to go back and finish law school. This past term, to please her, Charles Godwin had returned to his law studies, living in the studio behind the Lewis cottage on the outskirts of Litchfield, where he apprenticed part-time with Martha's father, a silhouette artist.

When Eb and Charles arrived at the station on the Green, the stagecoach had already arrived, the driver having disappeared into the tavern for sustenance. The assistant loaded Eb's trunks on top of the stagecoach. Eb and Charles faced each other for their farewell.

"Goodbye, Charles." Eb buried his face in Charles's skinny chest. It was like embracing a shorebird on long, spindly legs. Charles loomed more than a foot over Eb. Engulfed in Charles's woolen jacket, Eb took in the familiar smell of the Lewis portrait studio—paint, glue, and smoke from the wood-burning stove. "I could never have done this without you."

"Nor I you, Eb," Charles said solemnly. "I can't imagine law school—or Litchfield—without you. It makes my heart ache."

"You'll be fine. You've got Martha and the whole Lewis family." Eb looked up at his friend and smiled. Charles had undergone a transformation of his own. His face was fuller, his countenance more cheerful. Was it Eb's imagination, or had Charles's sandy-colored side-whiskers grown thicker? "I don't have to worry about you."

"Nor I you. You'll be with your family in New Haven. Will you go and visit my mother when you get home?" Charles's parents and two stepbrothers lived in New Haven near Eb's uncle's home.

"I will, of course, and you must keep your promises to Martha." Eb knew Charles still had lectures to make up. "Remember what she expects of you. To finish the law course, do an apprenticeship, be admitted to a bar."

"I'll do all those things. I promise." Charles gave his friend another hug. "I only wish Martha were here to say goodbye." Martha Lewis was spending a month in Wethersfield, Connecticut, with her best friend—and Eb Wells's love interest—Rebecca Harding. Martha and Rebecca had met at the Litchfield Female Academy the year before. Martha was still a student there, but Rebecca had moved to Wethersfield, where she was a tutoress in a private academy.

"Martha and I said our goodbyes before she left." Eb pulled away from Charles. "I got a letter from Rebecca yesterday. Martha's done some guest lectures in Rebecca's class on drawing maps." Eb grinned up at his friend. "Can you imagine the two of them? Rebecca and Martha, holding forth from a lectern?"

"Of course I can. Who better than our own to educate the next wave of young women?" Eb and Charles smiled at each other. Neither romance—Charles and Martha's nor Eb and Rebecca's—had gone smoothly last year. Even now, Eb and Rebecca were not on the same footing as Charles and Martha, who were engaged to be wed. Eb and Rebecca wrote often, but the future of their relationship remained hidden, even from each other—particularly from each other.

"Promise you'll write." Eb leaned over and picked up his satchel. "I want to hear all the news. About law school, Martha, your work with Mr. Lewis, your little cat Midnight, what Mrs. Reeve serves at the midday meal. No details spared."

"I promise." Charles put one hand on his chest, the other, shoulder high, facing front, in a gesture of oath-making. "Now it's time for you to go."

Eb gave Charles another hug and, with a boost from Charles, crawled up into the stagecoach. Settling in, he gave a small wave to the other passengers in the cabin. He took in the scent of leather from the worn coach seats. It smelled like travel. "Until we meet again, Litchfield," Eb said softly. He peered out the window to see the figure of Charles Godwin growing smaller and smaller on the Green, looking like a scarecrow dancing the tarantella, waving his long arms and calling out after him, "Goodbye, goodbye, my dear friend." Eb leaned back in his seat and breathed a sigh of relief. He had survived the farewells.

I'll dine with Uncle Ebenezer, Malinda, and Susan tonight, Eb thought. His older sister and her companion had been in New Haven since October. And I'll see Esmeralda and Mrs. Potts. Eb's thoughts drifted to his uncle's housekeeper and cook, wondering if the latter might, at this very moment, be baking an apple pie to welcome him home. One with extra cinnamon.

As a young mother in Savannah in the late 1790s, Abigail Cabot Wells refused to have enslaved domestic help, insisting she could manage the household on her own. But when the couple lost two little girls, one right after the other, a devastated Abigail could no longer cope. Even in these dire circumstances, purchasing another human being was out of the question. But she allowed her husband to hire a housekeeper, Lottie Graham, a destitute young Scotch-Irish immigrant, and recent widow.

Lottie Graham's wheelwright husband had dropped dead of a heart attack in his early thirties, leaving her with no means of support. She was taken in by the Savannah Female Asylum, along with her infant daughter, Susan. Lottie received vocational training and was soon hired out to the Wells family. Unfortunately, the Female Asylum would not release her baby girl until Lottie had proved herself. After completing a probationary year of employment, Abigail and William Wells had grown so fond of Lottie that they agreed to bring her daughter into their home. While Abigail was a generous woman, she was also thinking of her own new baby boy—little Ebenezer, or 'Eb,' as everyone called him.

The loss of the two little girls between Malinda and Eb had left a sorrowful gap in their family. Abigail worried that her baby boy was destined to become spoiled and lonely. Malinda was seven years older, John nine, so Eb was functionally an only child. Little Susan Graham would give him someone to play with. As a condition of her release, the Savannah Female Asylum insisted that the Wells family educate Susan, something Abigail readily assented to. She was already educating Malinda in their makeshift schoolroom on East York Street and had taught John, as she would teach Eb, until he enrolled at the boys' academy. Adding Susan to the mix was no problem.

Susan Graham was a bright, brown-eyed toddler when she entered the Wells household. Susan and Eb grew up like siblings. On rainy days, the two played together inside. On steamy, sunny days, they ran through the streets of Savannah, Susan striding up front, Eb trying to keep up. Eb was quiet and shy, Susan outspoken and bold. Teasing was their medium of expression, and their competition was fierce in the schoolroom. Eb lorded it over Susan in Latin and Greek, but Susan outperformed him in math and reading.

But Susan's academic prowess did not matter. Neither did it matter that Malinda too was a promising scholar. Beyond literacy, no one had any expectations for the girls on East York Street. For a fleeting moment, John had lobbied for his sister to attend the Litchfield Female Academy, but their father had nixed the idea— too expensive. When Susan Graham came of age, no one even mentioned a female academy. While William Wells loved Susan, she was, after all, the daughter of his housekeeper. The girls were lucky because Abigail had attended a female academy in New Haven and was an able teacher. And to keep Eb from failing at the boys' academy, William Wells was forced to hire extra tutors. Susan and

Malinda were permitted to sit in on those sessions, a benefit not planned for, but one they profited from.

By the time Eb matriculated at the boys' academy in Savannah, Susan was thirteen, on the threshold of womanhood. As often happens when childhood friends of opposite genders reach adolescence, Eb and Susan stopped playing together. Susan and Malinda, who was almost eighteen, became inseparable, forming a feminine conspiracy that excluded Eb. He began to roam the streets of Savannah on his own, making notes and drawings of birds, flowers, and trees in his commonplace book, *The Detritus*.

When it came time for college, William Wells refused to send Eb to Yale, insisting such a fine education would be wasted on him. Instead, Eb attended Franklin College, a public institution in Athens, Georgia. On his rare visits home, he barely noticed Susan Graham. Maybe this was due to arrested development, a circumstance not entirely his fault. Once in school, Eb only operated in masculine enclaves, at the boys' academy and later at college. Until his introduction to the students at the Litchfield Female Academy, he had no opportunity to meet young women. Feminine allure had eluded him. Perhaps too, Susan always had her nose in a book and did not command Eb's attention. More than likely, he regarded her like a sister. Susan was just one of several constant stars in his family constellation, with 'family' being the operative word.

But when Eb saw her on that first night at his uncle's home in New Haven, running down the stairs to greet him, all that was about to change.

"Did Charles ever make you a lavish, well-orchestrated proposal?" Rebecca and Martha were nestled into two red-and-white chintz Martha Washington chairs, warming their feet before the fire.

They were upstairs in Rebecca's bedroom in Mrs. Cox's stately, two-story brick house in Wethersfield. The house sat right on the Green, on Broad Street, behind a white picket fence. Wethersfield was a bustling commercial town and one of the oldest English settlements in the Connecticut River Valley.

This was Martha Lewis's first trip away from home. On a break from the Litchfield Female Academy, she was visiting Rebecca, who was in her first year of teaching and served as a companion for Mrs. Cox, a widow and grandmother of her childhood friend, Elizabeth Stafford. It was a cold, dark December night. Rebecca and Martha were in their nightclothes, their woolen shawls wrapped tightly around their shoulders, an embroidered pole screen behind them, retaining the heat. In winter evenings, Mrs. Cox saw no need to use wood for more than one fire upstairs. The three women had already listened to Rebecca read aloud a chapter of *The Antiquary*, sharing a pot of tea and the shortbread Martha had brought from Litchfield. Mrs. Cox had tottered down the long, dark hallway to her bedroom, a hot brick waiting at the bottom of her bed.

"I mean," Rebecca said, "did Charles ever kneel at your feet and ask you to marry him? Make a bold gesture?"

"No, not really." Martha tied her thick, coppery red hair in a knot, preparing for bed. The fire lit up her smooth skin and the spray of light freckles across her high cheekbones. "Charles isn't really inclined toward bold gestures. Or to orchestrate a lavish proposal. You know that."

"You're right. But was there ever a moment you can point to and say, 'Charles has asked me to marry him, and I have said yes'?"

"Good question." Martha gazed into the fire. "We talked about marriage before we broke up, but after we got back together, and he moved into the studio, it was just understood we would marry." Martha looked over at her friend. Rebecca was taller than Martha, but not by a lot. A slender brunette with an angular face and sharp, dark brown eyes, her beauty was more understated. Rebecca was pre-ternaturally pale, her hair usually parted down the middle and pulled back into a bun at the nape of her neck. Her only ornamentation was a gold chain and locket. "No big proposal," Martha added.

"That's what I thought."

"Should I be aggrieved by that?" When Martha first started at the female academy, Rebecca had been an assistant teacher, and Martha a naïve, boisterous local girl. Even though Martha's rough edges had smoothed out from her education, Rebecca's opinion still held sway. "By no dramatic proposal?"

"Of course not," Rebecca hastened to add, sensing anxiety in her friend's voice. "It's just that the proposal scene is so important in novels."

"That's true, isn't it?" Martha laughed. "You know that novel I just finished? It took hundreds of pages for the hero to finally ask her to marry him. And when he did, the heroine keeled over in a swoon, with much bodice-heaving and heart palpitations."

Rebecca grinned. "And then they fell into a passionate embrace, kissing with slightly parted lips—a kiss that 'went on forever.'" She too had read the same books. "No, wait, 'forever and ever.'"

"You got it." Martha nodded. "You wonder whether the women in these novels got any nutrition, with all that swooning and eternal kissing." She shrugged. "Anyhow, I can't feature my Charles in a proposal scene. He'd be too focused on his art, worried about some detail in a portrait like the lace on an old woman's cap."

"It's good to keep your expectations low." Rebecca reached over for the last piece of shortbread, settling back into her chair. "Better to love the man you've got than the one you're reading about."

"That's the most sensible thing I've ever heard you say, Rebecca Harding." Martha smiled, staring into the fire, which was beginning to die down. Having a fire in a bedroom was a luxury Martha had never encountered before. "And what about Eb? Could he play the part of the lovesick swain, kneeling at the feet of his beloved?"

"I can't feature it." Rebecca laughed. "Eb's fairly short to start with, so I don't think he'd do his cause much good by kneeling."

"Well, what are his letters like?" Martha cautiously needled her friend. The couple had only become an 'item' in Litchfield at the end of last summer, right before Rebecca left for Wethersfield. "Would you say they're romantic? Are they love letters?"

"They've been full of news about studying with Charles and Thomas, moot court, Mrs. Edwards, Sir Winston's bacon breath, his upcoming apprenticeship in New Haven." Rebecca paused. "He sends letters several times a week, but I'm not sure they're 'romantic.'"

"Does he tell you he loves you?" Martha had just received a letter from Charles that morning. While newsy, the letter had ended with unambiguous words of love and was sealed with a kiss. "The inclusion of an 'I love you madly' at the end is usually a good tip-off that it's a love letter. Not just a letter from a friend."

"No," Rebecca replied with an unintended sharpness. "He doesn't. Then again, I don't tell him I love him either. Madly or not." Rebecca chewed thoughtfully on Mrs. Lewis's shortbread. "He does start out the letter, though, 'Dearest Rebecca.'"

"Hmm . . ." Martha seemed unimpressed. "My brother Jack starts his letters out that way. How does Eb sign off?"

"'With affection.' What do you make of that?"

"Well, it's a step above 'Yours Truly.'" Martha frowned. She had been trying to match up Rebecca Harding with Eb Wells for over a year. Finally, Martha thought she had accomplished the task last summer, but now the couple seemed to be dancing around each other again. Their correspondence lacked the passion Martha had been hoping for. "But I wouldn't call 'with affection' very romantic."

"Maybe I've been waiting for Eb to make the first move. You know what I mean. To declare himself." Rebecca shook her head. "I'm not sure he's up to it."

"He made the first move in August." Martha referred to Eb and Rebecca's first kiss on a bench behind Mrs. Edwards's house, right before she left for Wethersfield—a meeting Martha herself had arranged. Eb had confidently executed that first kiss. And Rebecca had returned it, even though it had surprised her. At least, that was what Rebecca had told her.

"Yes. Eb did make the first move. But one kiss doesn't always lead to love. Even a lot of kisses. Remember Horse Face." Rebecca alluded to Oliver Hull, another student at the law school. Martha had walked out with Oliver during her embittered hiatus from Charles, bestowing upon him far more kisses than Charles could ever imagine—a fact Martha decided to keep from Charles after a lengthy discussion with Rebecca, who insisted no good would come from full disclosure.

"Yes, well, Oliver didn't count." Martha wavered. "But back to Eb. Why doesn't he say he loves you?"

"Maybe he's been waiting for me to set the tone."

"So, what about your letters to him? Equally newsy?"

"Mostly, I write about my quarrels with Mr. Hitchcock." Rebecca had been in a power struggle with the stern headmaster at the Wethersfield Academy over their expectations of female students. "I tell Eb everything about that. He's very supportive of my work." Rebecca gazed down at her hands. "That means a lot to me. He always encourages me, says I'm right to expect more from my girls."

"Well, that's good." Martha leaned over to pat her friend's hand. "I suppose those qualify as love letters of a sort." She took this as a good sign. If this romance were to succeed—or even get started, so it now seemed—Eb Wells must not be cavalier about Rebecca's teaching. "At least he takes you seriously."

"He does, and I love writing to Eb. We share everything about our work. I never feel alone." Rebecca was quiet for a while, staring into the fire's glowing embers. The only sound in the room was the tick-tock, tick-tock of the Regency bracket clock on the mantel and the occasional popping sound of the dying fire. Martha too was silent.

"But you know, Martha, I'm not certain I want to be in love." Rebecca emerged from her reverie. "All my life, I've had no control over what's happened to me. I lost my whole family. My little brothers, my mother, my father. I was forced to live with my relatives in Hartford. They meant well, I know, but it was a cold house in more ways than one. I was miserable and all alone, but I dug my way out of that hole. I decided to go to Miss Pierce's and become a teacher, and then I made that happen." Miss Pierce was the headmistress of the Litchfield Female Academy. Rebecca continued to stare into the fire. "That made me feel in control of my life."

Martha remained silent, knowing Rebecca might not finish her thoughts if interrupted. Miss Pierce was working with Martha to curb her tendency to jump in. She could be irrepressible.

"But when you fall in love," Rebecca finally said hesitantly, "you give up that control. You yield yourself to another human being."

"I like that part." Martha almost whispered, thinking how different her own life was. She had not struggled like Rebecca. She had grown up in a cozy cottage on the outskirts of Litchfield with her devoted parents and three older brothers—all of whom were very much alive. While her family was not rich, they could afford the female academy, with her brothers pitching in. At times, having all that support thwarted Martha's autonomy, but it made falling in love much easier. Martha was accustomed to relying on others who adored her. "Falling in love isn't all that scary, Rebecca," she said softly. "You do give up some freedom, I suppose, but the benefits of having a partner, a helpmate at your side who loves you—that can be wonderful."

"But inevitably that 'helpmate,' as you put it, turns into a husband. And having a husband would end my teaching career." Rebecca's voice had a tinge of impatience. "It's not just that. Shifting status from a *feme sole* to a *feme covert* means a tremendous loss of power.”

“I forget what 'covert' means.” Martha ceded to Rebecca's superior grasp of all subjects legal.

“A *feme covert* is a married woman who's in the state of coverture. When a *feme sole*—that's you and me right now—marries, she gives up her right to make contracts, to sue or be sued. Her husband obtains the use of all her property.” Rebecca shook her head. “Worst of all, she ceases to exist as a person. She merges into the person of her husband.” Rebecca looked up from the fire. “I don't like that.”

“But Rebecca,” Martha protested, unsure she understood, “what property do you have to lose? I thought you didn't have any.” When Rebecca did not answer, Martha assumed she had missed the point, which happened sometimes. She ventured a tentative question. “So, you keep Eb at bay?”

“I would keep Eb at bay,” Rebecca replied, “if I needed to. Remember, 'to bay' comes from the Old French for 'to bark.' A hunted dog—one who feels threatened—keeps its predators 'at bay' by barking. But Eb doesn't threaten me with words of love. Or burden me with his expectations. I'm not sure why, but he doesn't.”

“What French word are you talking about?” Martha grew vexed when Rebecca assumed her 'teacher voice.' Besides, Martha's French was improving and might even be better than Rebecca's.

“Forget the word derivation.” Rebecca laughed, picking up on her friend's irritation. “The fact is I'm not barking at Eb because he's not on the attack. No 'keeping at bay' here.”

“So, you're happy with things as they are?” Martha did not grasp either her friend's explanation or hesitation. Her love life was simpler than Rebecca's. She and Charles were in love and would be married within a year or two. While Martha wanted to make maps, she had no other aspirations, at least none that would stop her from marrying. She too might want to become a teacher, but not at the expense of losing Charles. “So, let me see if I understand.” Martha started up again. "You're not barking at Eb, but only because Eb isn't chasing you? I'm confused, Rebecca. What is it exactly you want?"

"Honestly, I don't know what I want." Rebecca shook her head. "That's the truth. Half the days, I wake up, and I want just what you do. To be in love, and to be loved. On those days, I'm frustrated that Eb's letters aren't more romantic. That he doesn't say he loves me. But on other mornings, I wake up, and I'm pleased with my quiet teacher's life. It's peaceful, forgetting about The Ogre Hitchcock for a moment. I feel calm and in control. Purposeful. So, I don't want to be in love on those days. It's too agitating."

"You're a complicated woman, Rebecca Harding." Martha gave her friend a gentle smile. "I hope you don't mind that I love you. I wouldn't want my love or friendship to burden you."

"Never." Rebecca poked at the fire, spreading the remaining logs around to ensure all the flames were out. "I don't know what I'd do without you and Lizzie." She smiled at the thought of her lifelong friend, Elizabeth Stafford, Mrs. Cox's granddaughter, studying at a female academy in Keene, New Hampshire. "You two keep me sane."

"Then we'll leave it at that, shall we? I want to turn in." Martha felt a sudden wave of exhaustion. "Tomorrow, I've got some research to do for a map."

"Good idea. I'm tired too," Rebecca conceded. "And I've got class in the morning." And with that, Martha gave her friend a quick kiss on the cheek and made her way to the chilly guestroom—to her own hot brick at the bottom of the bed.

"My father apologizes for not being here to greet you." Nathan Haines looked down his nose at Eb Wells, the new apprentice at Haines & Haines. Nathan's father, Ned Haines, had wanted to waive the customary letters of recommendation for Eb Wells. He was the son of William Wells. That was enough for Ned.

But for his son, it was not. As junior partner, Nathan supervised the apprentices and scriveners at Haines & Haines and would discharge his duties as he saw fit. Ignoring his father, Nathan wrote to Judges Tapping Reeve and James Gould, the proprietors of the Litchfield Law School, who both gave Eb Wells a glowing recommendation. He was not only an outstanding scholar, number one or two in his class, but also an excellent orator in moot court.

Nathan Haines gazed down at the short, nervous young man who stood before him. Unbeknownst to Eb, Nathan had a prejudice against apprentices from Litchfield. Last year, the law practice hired one who had not worked out. Nathan had also not attended the prestigious Litchfield Law School and wore a chip on his shoulder about those who had. Particularly ones with accolades and his father's warm support.

"My father's out on an arbitration in Poughkeepsie," Nathan explained to Eb in a flat, uninterested voice. In his mid-thirties, dressed in a black wool suit, Nathan Haines was of medium height and balding. This latter fact he attempted to disguise by sweeping his jet-black hair from the back of his neck and sides and repositioning it over the more deficient areas. The resulting construction was maintained with a pomade whose scent followed him everywhere. The effect was akin to a rigid helmet, and with his pale skin, it gave Nathan the look of a marmoreal bust of Julius Caesar without the laurel crown. "That's why he's not here."

"That's fine. That's fine." Eb chided himself for saying it twice. Senseless repetition was a bad habit that emerged when Eb was nervous. For years, Malinda had tried to break him of it. But this was his first day at work, and he wanted to make a good impression. Malinda had picked out his brown suit with a tan vest and asked Mr. Potts to shine his boots. His preparations were for naught. Nathan

Haines already seemed to dislike him—Eb must have failed some hidden test. "I'll be happy to meet Mr. Haines Sr. on his return." He bowed, sensing deference was indicated.

"This is where you'll work." Nathan led him down a narrow hallway with squeaky floorboards. They entered the scriveners' room, a large, cavernous room at the rear of the first-floor law office on Fleet Street, near Long Wharf, the epicenter of New Haven's booming maritime trade. Near the door, two oak scrivener's desks with slanting surfaces faced each other, with two more desks, in the same configuration, at the other end of the room. Three of the desks were occupied, one desk up front by a tall young man about Eb's age, in his mid-twenties, the other two in the back by men who might be in their thirties. All three were bent over their desks, busily copying documents. Each had an Argand oil lamp at his elbow, the two windows on the side of the room being so small and far away they shed almost no light. It was equally impossible to see out. Through the wavy glass, daylight could be discerned, but not much more. Eb noticed the remaining scrivener's desk was vacant.

"These are your compatriots in servitude." Nathan Haines clapped his hands in an imperious gesture. "Gentlemen, may I present to you Mr. Ebenezer Wells from the Litchfield Law School. He's here to do his practicum. He'll sit here." Nathan extended an open palm to the empty desk up front. "Those are our scriveners down there." Nathan nodded toward the two men at the end of the room. "And this is Samuel Taylor, our senior apprentice. Will you get him settled, Samuel? Show him the ropes?"

"Yes, sir," said the lanky young man who sat across the vacant desk. Like the scriveners, Samuel dressed casually, with his shirt sleeves rolled up, wearing a smudged white apron to absorb the inevitable ink spills. He was tall, with strong features and a shock of straight brown hair. "I'll take care of it."

Eb's heart sank. He was overdressed. For once, his sister Malinda had been wrong, urging him to dress like a 'real lawyer' for his first day at work. Now it appeared that Eb would spend his day sitting at a scrivener's desk, copying documents, awash in ink.

"I've other business to attend to." Nathan shook Eb's hand, leaning over in an exaggerated fashion, emphasizing their difference in height. "I'll leave you in Samuel's capable hands." He glanced over at Samuel. "You're still working on Watson's shipping contract?"

"Yes, sir. They'll be done today, all three copies."

"Well, start Mr. Wells on one of those, then. The one for the file."

"Yes, sir," Samuel said again, his face impassive. Nathan glanced down the room at the two scriveners, hunched over their desks. Adjusting to the darkness, Eb was surprised to discover they looked alike, one a smaller version of the other.

"Ted, Oliver, you boys having any trouble?" Nathan looked down at his nails for a moment as if he had just discovered a hangnail.

"No, sir," the smaller scrivener replied.

Boys? Eb thought, surprised. They were only a few years younger than Nathan Haines—not boys. They must be brothers, Eb guessed, surely not twins, but oddly alike, as if they had been cut from the same cookie cutter. Their round, apple-shaped heads, cropped brown hair, wide-set eyes, and trusting faces were the same. Definitely the same batch of dough. "We're doing just fine, sir."

"I meant about the contracts for Mr. Ruggles. Are the copies coming along?"

"We'll be done by tomorrow." The smaller scrivener did not make eye contact, adding a gratuitous, "Sir."

"Good." Nathan looked up from his hand. "I'll leave you to it then. I'll be in my office if you need me." He sailed out of the room, leaving the scent of pomade behind him. Eb stood alone on the threshold of the scriveners' room, feeling foolish for wearing a three-piece suit.

"Welcome." Samuel got up from his desk, extending his hand.

"I'm Samuel Taylor. These are our scriveners, the Redfield brothers, Oliver and Ted." The two brothers approached Eb to greet him, wiping their hands on their aprons. Oliver, the older but smaller of the two, shook Eb's hand. Ted, his younger, larger brother, stood behind him, looking timid, ready to offer his hand as soon as his brother was done.

"You're very welcome, Mr. Wells." Oliver Redfield had a warm tenor voice. "We're so glad you're here. We could surely use the help."

"Nice to meet you." Eb peered up at the two brothers. "And please call me 'Eb.' Everyone does." He squinted through his gold-rimmed glasses. "I'm sorry, but which one of you is Oliver? Or Ted?"

"That took me a while too." Samuel grabbed another white apron that hung on a peg on the wall. "Here's how I remember them. 'T is for Ted, who's Taller, O is for Oliver, who's Older.'" He grinned, exposing straight white teeth with a gap between the front two. For some reason, his dental defect made Eb instantly like him better. "The jingle only works if they're together, which mostly they are. You'll soon learn to tell them apart." He handed Eb the apron.

"Thanks." Eb took off his jacket and vest and hung them on the peg, rolling up his shirt sleeves as Samuel and the Redfields had done. This maneuver was familiar to Eb. Avoiding ink stains on his shirt was one of his professional strengths. The Redfield brothers settled back down at their desks. From a distance, sitting down, they looked the same to Eb. "I'm sure I'll get you straightened out in time," he muttered apologetically.

"Don't worry about it," Oliver said. "Everyone gets us confused. There're eight of us. We all resemble each other. But not like me and Ted."

"Eight of you?" Eb's eyebrows went up. "That sounds like a tribe."

"It is," said Ted, pleased to jump into the rushing current of the conversation, if only to assent to something.

"Ted and I are smack in the middle," Oliver explained, "surrounded by girls on either side. We're natural allies. We did our apprenticeship together."

"That's great. A brother by your side is a good idea." Eb was envious of the Redfield brothers, sitting amiably across from each other at their scrivener's desks like two peas in a pod. Eb respected his brother, but John was nine years older. Their world views clashed as well, with John owning house slaves in Charleston, and Eb an abolitionist.

"I want to hear all about your time at the Litchfield Law School." Samuel was retrieving a fresh quill pen, scrap paper for testing the ink flow, an inkwell, and a ponce for Eb's desk. He had already lit the oil lamp, which Ted Redfield had filled in anticipation of Eb's arrival. "But we'll have to leave it for a break. I promised Nathan we'd finish Watson's contracts by the end of today." Samuel looked down the room at the Redfield brothers. "Can you spare us an hour later today? We're going to need all four of us to proofread these contracts."

"No problem," Oliver replied. The copying of legal documents was always followed by a meticulous reading aloud of the original document, scrutinizing each copy for errors. The law practice of Haines & Haines maintained a reputation for having few, if any, scrivener's mistakes.

Samuel passed a completed page of a legal document and a piece of blank parchment to Eb. "This is the first page of the contract we're copying." Samuel pointed to the first paragraph, which included the date and names of the parties. "Watson's is a shipping company here in town—our client. We're making three copies of the contract from the original—an extra for Watson, one for the other party, and one for our files."

Eb briefly perused the document, an agreement between Watson's Shipping Company and a shoe factory in New Haven to transport three dozen containers of men's boots and ladies' shoes to Philadelphia. Eb felt a sudden thrill. For all his studies, he had never actually held a contract. So, this is what a contract feels like, Eb thought, rubbing the parchment lightly. He could feel the weave beneath his fingers, the paper made from linen rags. Eb wondered whether the copy constituted 'the' contract. Or does the term 'contract' refer only to the original document? Or perhaps to the agreement itself, with these various parchments—original or copies—constituting evidence of the 'contract'? These kinds of theoretical questions could keep Eb Wells up at night.

"I trust you have a good hand?" Samuel asked with hesitation. Haines & Haines's law practice was strict about its documents. The script must be legible, the spacing even, and the penmanship consistent, with no blots. "And can make a fair copy?"

"I do have a decent hand," Eb said modestly. Artful penmanship was emphasized in the South, and he had acquired an admirable script at the boys' academy in Savannah. His writing had always been a rare academic strong suit, a source of pride. His skill in penmanship was later honed at law school, crafting his leather-bound volumes of the common law. "At least, I think I do. I use a simple round hand, although I sometimes use Chancery," Eb added humbly, not knowing whether shipping contracts required a special script.

"A clear, round hand will suffice. Adopt my spacing, but you may use the hand that suits you best. You're doing the copy for the file, so accuracy matters more than form." Samuel handed Eb a quill pen.

"Goose feather?" Some people, Eb knew, preferred a turkey feather, but he was a goose feather man all the way.

"Only goose feather quills here. Nathan likes them. They're flexible and last a long time. He likes anything that saves money." Samuel sighed. "Personally, I'd like to try one of those new steel-nibbed pens, but Mr. Haines Sr. and Jr. are old-fashioned."

"Goose feather's perfect." Eb hesitated. "Is there someone here who mixes the ink, fills the ink well, sharpens and trims the quills?" He depended on someone else to manage the technical aspects of writing—like his study partner at law school, Charles Godwin, who loved complex technical processes. Eb could manage on his own and had done so when Charles was ill, but not with skill or enthusiasm. "I'm not so good with those details."

"Ted's your man," Oliver called out, pleased to toot his brother's horn. Eb would soon learn how indispensable Ted Redfield was. Unlike Oliver, who had ambitions to become an attorney, Ted was happy to remain a scrivener. Ted also drafted and copied Ned Haines's correspondence when he was in town. "My brother loves the mechanics of writing. Not only does he make the best copies, but he mixes our ink, fills the wells, sharpens the quills, affixes the seals to documents, and keeps the lamps going. Ted does it all. He even cleans up at the end of the day."

"Oliver's right. We couldn't run the office without Ted." Samuel smiled at the shy, tall man at the other end of the room. "Don't you worry. If your hand's good, you can write without interruption. Ted will provide you with anything your heart desires."

"That's good," Eb said. "I need that kind of support." He dipped the quill pen into the ink, tried a sample on the scrap paper, positioned the blank paper on his scrivener's desk, took a deep breath, and started to write at the top, 'State of Connecticut, City of New Haven, THIS CONTRACT, executed on this day of January 8, 1821, between Watson's Shipping Company, party of the first part and . . .' With that, he disappeared into his work.

As Eb worked, Samuel kept sneaking a peek to see how the new apprentice was faring. There he sat at his scrivener's desk, this Eb Wells from Savannah, a short man, wearing gold-rimmed glasses, with wavy auburn hair and small, neat hands. Just one hour into the job, he was carefully copying promises about the transportation of leather boots and shoes from New Haven to Philadelphia. Eb worked silently and did not look up, as if he were in a meditative state.

Samuel let out a long sigh. Things were going to be all right. He would have to forgive Eb his Southern accent, something Samuel associated with stupidity and slavery. Why do people from the South speak so slowly? And what if this Eb Wells comes from a family who owns slaves? Samuel spoke sternly to himself. Stop making assumptions. We desperately need someone solid at the desk.

Samuel Taylor was from Rhode Island, the oldest of six. His father was a master craftsman with a Providence jewelry manufacturer that made watches, clocks, and rolled gold-plated chains. His father hoped his son would become a professional, a lawyer, doctor, or minister. At great sacrifice, Samuel was the first in his family to attend college. Brown University was a liberal school, nominally Baptist, but it embraced other religious traditions. Founded by Moses Brown, a leader in the burgeoning abolitionist movement, its students were committed to social justice, advocating for public education and the eradication of slavery. Samuel Taylor acquired his progressive ideas at Brown.

Upon graduation, Samuel chose the law. He knew about the Litchfield Law School and would have preferred studying there like Eb Wells. After all, Eb would only need to apprentice for one year, unlike Samuel, who must put in three years. Eb did not have to read *Blackstone* and Lord Coke at night. His theoretical foundation had already been laid by completing a full-time, fourteen-month law school course. At Haines & Haines, Eb would learn the writs, the causes of action, the procedural nuts and bolts for bringing and defending lawsuits, and the practical aspects of transactional work— but he had already 'read the law.'

But Judge Tapping Reeve's law school in Litchfield was expensive, a training ground for the sons of the country's elite. Samuel Taylor's family depended solely on his father's weekly wages. His college education had already strained family resources, and Samuel had to set his sights lower. A traditional apprenticeship was all his family could afford. But apprenticeships were hard to come by. Family ties, friendships, commercial, and religious alliances were heavily relied upon to get a job. The Taylor family was not well-positioned to leverage those connections.

Nonetheless, Samuel Taylor obtained a highly coveted apprenticeship with Haines & Haines. Samuel was fortunate enough to be introduced to Ned Haines by Samuel's father's boss. Ned, who was swamped at work, had attended a Unitarian regional meeting in Providence. There, he met a jewelry manufacturer who recommended the son of one of his artisans, a Brown graduate. Ned took a chance on Samuel, and once at Haines & Haines, his sharp mind and admirable work ethic earned him the position of senior apprentice when Francis Hawkins left.

During Samuel's tenure, two other apprentices had been under Ned's tutelage: A self-aggrandizing Litchfield Law School graduate who had not lasted long, and Francis Hawkins. The former had considered copying beneath him, and when he did deign to pitch in, his scrivener's hand was almost illegible; his documents looked like a drunken chicken had soaked its toes in ink and danced across the page. Nathan had fired him within the month. The other apprentice, Francis Hawkins, was altogether different. For three years, he had been a respected and dedicated apprentice. Francis had studied Ned's volumes of *Blackstone* and Lord Coke, passed a bar exam, and was now building a practice in Haddam. With these two other apprentices gone, Samuel was on his own.

At first, Ned Haines had ably instructed his apprentices. Years back, Ned and Eb's father had been woefully neglected by their supervising attorney, Rufus Henderson. In his own law practice, Ned was determined to treat his apprentices responsibly. But his supervision came to an abrupt halt when Ned became an arbitrator in commercial cases. The death of his second wife occasioned this shift in his law practice.

Ned Haines was widowed twice. His first wife, Nathan's mother, had died of consumption after Nathan had graduated from Yale. His second, much younger wife, Fanny, died two years ago giving birth to a stillborn daughter, leaving Ned to raise their then five-year-old son. To distract himself from grief, Ned threw himself into arbitration. The senior Haines was now out of the office for weeks at a time, usually in upstate New York, Albany, Troy, or Poughkeepsie.

Even with his arbitrations, Ned kept a close eye on the law practice. At almost sixty, he still put in long hours when he returned, directing his son in difficult cases. Nathan was an able practitioner, organized, and hardworking. Not yet married, Nathan lived in lodgings near his father's house on Chapel Street, devoting his life to Haines & Haines. But Nathan lacked his father's legal acumen and ease with their clients. Ned Haines possessed an ineffable quality, a hidden charisma, which drew people to him. Nathan recognized that people did not like him for reasons he did not fully understand. Perhaps it was his lack of hair.

Nathan struggled to keep the law practice afloat in his father's absence. Their clients were unaware that Ned Haines was away doing arbitrations. The economic downturn was finally over. The shipping industry was expanding with new routes to the West Indies. With protective tariffs, their clients—manufacturers, retailers, shippers, and banks—regained confidence after the Panic of 1819. Business was booming, and their clients were busily entering into contracts, buying and selling real estate, and suing one another. Nathan did his best to keep up with the legal work, rightfully insisting that document production not lag behind. Samuel,

Oliver, and Ted had been tied to their scrivener's desks for months, barely keeping up with the demand.

The increased volume of work at the law firm, Ned's absences, and the departure of the other apprentices wreaked havoc on Samuel Taylor's apprenticeship. The job of an apprentice was to engage in legal research, help draft contracts, initiate and defend lawsuits, draw up wills—in short, learn how to practice law. Apprentices were not supposed to solely copy documents, serve papers, or collect debts. Samuel had been an apprentice at Haines & Haines for almost three years, and by all accounts, ought to be taking a bar exam. But by copying documents all day, or performing other ministerial tasks, Samuel was no longer learning any law. A volume of *Blackstone* that the absent Ned had lent him sat unopened next to his bed at his boarding house. Samuel's eyes were on stalks by the end of the day, too tired to do any reading on his own. How could he ever pass a bar exam?

For these reasons, Samuel Taylor had anxiously awaited the arrival of Eb Wells. Unlike Samuel, Eb came well-connected. His father had been a colleague of Ned's at Yale, and the two had apprenticed together. Both Eb's father and brother were lawyers, and his uncle was a prominent New Haven physician, also a colleague of Ned's from Yale. And Eb had been educated—and excelled— at the renowned Litchfield Law School. With such a privileged background, surely Nathan would be more circumspect about his assignments. At the very least, the apprentice Eb Wells would be accorded more respect. Some of that respect, Samuel hoped, would rub off on him.

*Letter to Eb Wells from Rebecca Harding, Wethersfield,
January 25, 1821*

Dearest Eb,

I finally received your last letter. So happy to hear about your apprenticeship. Now it's your turn to complain about work. After listening to me rant and rave about The Ogre, I owe you many hours of listening.

I trust you won't be copying and reading out documents all day long. It's a good way to learn about contract law, I suppose, to write down a contract's terms and contemplate its strengths and deficiencies. But Eb, you must learn the forms of action. I understand there's an intimate relationship between the writs and substantive law. The writ determines all—the contents of the declaration, the method of proof, the remedy, etc. As Judge Reeve told you, this knowledge can only be acquired from the practice of law, not its abstract study.

It was wonderful having Martha here. The house seems oddly quiet now without her endless, cheerful patter. Winter is upon us, although the weather in Wethersfield is much milder than in Litchfield. The Connecticut River exerts a warming influence, and we're at a lower elevation. I don't mind the cold as much as I did at Miss Pierce's. Of course, my little room on her third floor was unheated. Mrs. Cox has a much finer house built of brick, which holds in the heat from the sun. We practically live in our two bedrooms. She thinks it's unnecessary to heat the entire house. During the day, she has a fire going in her bedroom suite, and we take our evening meal up there. After supper, a servant makes a fire in my room. What a luxury having a fire of my own. Mrs. Cox comes to me each night to listen to me read. She's such a smart old lady. She too is worried about Elizabeth's attachment to this scoundrel, Mr. Townsend.

So happy you're making a friend of Samuel Taylor. It seems like everyone up north wants to know if your family owns slaves. Little does he know that you're infamous in Litchfield as a rabble-rousing abolitionist! Does he know yet that your brother owns house slaves? Or that his father-in-law owns a plantation with many slaves—perhaps hundreds? Don't judge Samuel too harshly for his attitude toward your Southern accent. When I first met the girls from the South at Miss Pierce's, I too assumed they were all stupid. In most cases, I was wrong, even though they wallowed in their vowels. Like swimming in molasses. It's a foolish prejudice, but one I understand. Do you think your Savannah accent will become diluted the longer you stay up north?

This week, my composition class is reading Mrs. Emma Willard's address to the New York State legislature in which she lays out a plan for female education. The girls will analyze her arguments, critique them, and build their vocabularies. Some struggle with Mrs. Willard's rhetoric, but the bright ones are challenged. The Ogre insists most of my girls are ineducable. I reject that, but frankly, a few do seem to have little interest in learning. They complain I'm too strict, preferring their embroidery—and they're outraged when I expect them not only to read, but to write. Still, a handful of my girls, Anna and Caroline in particular, are so eager to learn, sometimes I wonder if I can keep up with them.

Have you heard from Charles recently? Martha writes that Judge Reeve is no longer teaching. I know that saddens you, Eb, but he was getting quite forgetful.

You'll be amused by this gossip. Martha thinks Katherine Montgomery is walking out with Thomas Bradford again. You know how hard it is to tell in the winter months who's interested in whom, but Katherine managed to inveigle an invitation from Thomas to the annual sleigh ride—the one that Mrs. Edwards's boarding house co-sponsors. What do you think about that?

I do miss Litchfield, Eb, with its community of scholars, stimulating conversations, the recognition that a young woman might have something to say. Many people in Wethersfield—men mostly—are stuck in the eighteenth century as far as women are concerned. We're considered ornamental objects, much in need of male guidance and protection. I do have a cohort of educated women to talk to, Mrs. Johnson, Mrs. Cox, some of the mothers of my girls. They all read books and newspapers. That makes life much better.

I must go. It's getting late. Write again soon and tell me more about your work. I need to hear more about Elm Street, how Malinda and Susan are getting along, how you're managing to exist without a cat. All these important things, I need to know.

Yours with affection,

Rebecca

Eb Wells worried about his shyness around Susan Graham. Ever since his arrival in New Haven, he could not make eye contact with her or sit next to her. When others were around, in the dining room at breakfast and supper, Eb could chatter aimlessly in her presence, about the fierce cold, the clinic overflowing with patients, his frustrating work at the law office. In the library, after supper, when they all retired to read and share a pot of tea around the fire, Eb could sit in his wingback chair with ease, his uncle across from him, while Malinda and Susan curled up together on the new, velvet rose-colored settee. There too in the fire's glow, Eb could banter endlessly in Susan's presence, the furniture imposing a distance that kept him safe from physical closeness to her.

But proximity to Susan, and the intimacy of looking into her eyes, were more than Eb could bear. Certainly, he could not be alone with her. This was an unexpected, unprecedented, and inexplicable development in their lifelong relationship. Eb was afraid to examine the feelings beneath this new shyness—he was sure they were inappropriate. Susan was an honorary member of the Wells family. She was like a sister to him. He wrote daily letters to another woman in Wethersfield—someone with whom he exchanged kisses. Sitting next to Susan, looking at Susan, daydreaming about Susan, thinking about Susan all the time—everything about it seemed wrong.

Eb had no one to discuss this with. Charles Godwin, a Quaker at heart, might think it dishonorable for a man to be attracted to two women at once. And Eb would have to reveal his quandary in a letter. Every word written to Charles would inevitably be shared with Martha, who would inevitably share it with Rebecca. Neither could Eb confide his discomfort to Malinda, nor his uncle. Eb might have written to Thomas Bradford, who was more a man of the world than Charles, although he lacked Charles's keen moral sense. That was the point, Eb supposed. But Thomas Bradford was up in Litchfield and a poor correspondent.

Besides, Eb could not bring himself to put his feelings about Susan Graham into writing. He preferred them to roam wild and free in his imagination, even if they frightened him. To capture his feelings on paper, in a letter or the pages of *The Detritus*, would make them seem too real. Better to sound them out in the air, preferably in a dark, smoky environment like a tavern, over the din of men talking about politics and weather. But he was new in town and had no one to drink ale with. Maybe Eb could tell Samuel Taylor once they knew each other better. He needed someone to talk to.

At night, thoughts of Susan Graham flooded his mind. Her thick mane. Her dark brown eyes. Her smooth skin. The tantalizing cleavage at the neckline of her calico dress—a cleavage he had never noticed before. What would it be like, he wondered, to slide his hand down that neckline? To bury his nose between those breasts? Eb Wells was losing sleep.

"Why must you fill the girls' heads with ideas that do them no good?" Asa Hitchcock berated Rebecca Harding. In his late forties, dressed in black to give him an aura of authority, he looked like an old-fashioned minister. His hair was salt-and-pepper, and he sported a ferocious set of side whiskers that colonized most of his lower face. Asa Hitchcock wore spectacles, which Rebecca suspected he did not need. The glasses were a prop, a fruitless effort to lend him the air of a serious scholar, befitting the headmaster of the Wethersfield Academy. "Marie Chapman's been complaining again. You're working them too hard."

"I find it ironic Marie's the one to complain," Rebecca said. This interview took place in the headmaster's office in the Wethersfield Academy on the first floor of the two-story brick federal-style schoolhouse. Asa Hitchcock's was the largest office in the building, with a huge desk stacked high with files. An American flag hung limply in the corner on a rickety flagpole. He had summoned Rebecca from her office upstairs, a tiny closet, shared with the math tutoress, and on off-times, the teacher of navigation.

Rebecca stood in front of her headmaster, her hands clasped at her waist, giving the impression of a no-nonsense spinster. Her dark hair, as usual, was parted in the middle and pulled back in a bun, her dress a gray linen, without ornamentation, her only piece of jewelry a gold chain with a locket. "Marie's been doing next to no work," Rebecca said. "It's difficult to see how she can complain about being overtaxed." Marie Chapman was a lazy, whiny thirteen-year-old with a perennially drippy nose. Rebecca had been warned to censor any criticism of Marie—her father was a prosperous merchant in town who made liberal donations to the Wethersfield Academy.

"Marie's finding the reading difficult," Asa Hitchcock chided.

"She ought to try harder," Rebecca replied.

"Yes, well, that may be, Miss Harding," Mr. Hitchcock said curtly. "But we must take our students as we find them." Over the past few months, Asa Hitchcock had constantly chastised Rebecca for overly ambitious expectations of her female students.

"I would disagree with that, Mr. Hitchcock." Rebecca tried to keep her voice respectful. "Isn't that at the heart of being a teacher—*not* to take your students as you find them? If we weren't hoping for a change, some improvement, then why bother teaching them?" Rebecca instantly regretted her response. Engaging Asa Hitchcock on theories of pedagogy did no good. Abstract debate only exasperated him even more. Things went better if she just nodded at whatever he said, left the room, and went about teaching as she had before.

"Education must be tailored to the student, Miss Harding. Surely you learned that at your fancy female academy." Mr. Hitchcock drew a handkerchief out of his pocket and wiped his brow, even though it was a cold winter afternoon. These encounters with Miss Harding made him sweat. "A teacher must take into account a student's circumstances when setting expectations—his background, his natural abilities, his resources." Mr. Hitchcock taught only in the male division of the academy. "Where he's bound to go in life."

"And whether this hypothetical student is a 'he' or a 'she'?" Rebecca could not help herself. Asa Hitchcock got her hackles up.

"And why not? You and I both know our young women here in Wethersfield aren't going to any of those female academies. Or seminaries, whatever you call them. They're going to become wives and mothers. It's cruel to overeducate them. To make them want what they can't have." Mr. Hitchcock smoothed his hair back. How else might he find fault with Rebecca Harding? Marie Chapman had told him, amidst her sniffles, that Miss Harding's composition class was studying the 1819 testimony of Mrs. Emma Willard on female education before the New York State legislature. "And just what did you expect to accomplish with Mrs. Willard's tirade? You couldn't find anything from our own state to study?"

"If Emma Willard had appeared before the Connecticut legislature, I would surely have used that testimony." Rebecca bit her lower lip, struggling to keep her discourse civil. "But she testified in Albany."

"And what did you intend for your students to glean from this address?" Mr. Hitchcock rifled through the papers on his desk with agitation. "Could you explain that to me?"

"The girls are learning how to structure an argument from her testimony, how to use metaphor. It also builds vocabulary." Rebecca hoped to steer clear of the ideas embodied in Emma Willard's address. "From her address, the girls learned 'despotic,' 'orbit,' 'insinuate,' 'satellite,' 'pecuniary,' 'lethargic,' 'barbaric.'" She searched her memory for other vocabulary words. "It's always better to learn new words in context, don't you think?" Rebecca did not see how any serious educator could disagree with that.

"It depends upon the context," Mr. Hitchcock growled through clenched teeth. "If the context spreads pernicious ideas or feelings of despair in the students, then no, Miss Harding, vocabulary words in context aren't worth the risk."

"Mrs. Willard's ideas are not pernicious." Rebecca could not help herself. "She explains how educating women inures to the benefit of the whole nation. That our new experimental Republic depends on an educated citizenry. Women constitute an essential part of the body politic as educators of the young."

Mr. Hitchcock ignored Rebecca's exposition on Emma Willard, having never read her testimony. "Marie says you called her father a barbarian, and I quote, 'who has trodden the weaker sex beneath his feet.' Furthermore," he said with some alarm, his cheeks puffing out like a blowfish, making his prodigious side whiskers quiver, "Marie said you told her to throw off the shackles of her father's authority."

"She said that?" Rebecca pretended to be shocked, but inwardly, she was smiling. Little sniffling Marie Chapman had been listening after all.

"Yes, she did. How could you say that of Jabez Chapman?" Mr. Hitchcock was now sputtering. "You know what an important man Mr. Chapman is. He runs the largest dry goods store in town. He's in no way a barbarian. Marie should obey her father."

"I would never say anything against Mr. Chapman, sir," Rebecca snapped, her skin growing mottled from the neck up. "Nor would I suggest a student disobey her father. Marie conflates Emma Willard's indictment of societal patriarchy with her father's rightful authority over her. She is, after all, a child." Rebecca was thinking about how her students' fathers often *did* tread the weaker sex beneath their feet. Their fathers—and the headmasters of their schools.

"Be that as it may," grumbled Mr. Hitchcock, backing down slightly, "if you're going to introduce these radical ideas to our girls, don't be surprised when they come back to bite you." He shook his head with disapproval. "I'd really prefer you stick to the curriculum that was given to you, Miss Harding."

"I know that's your preference, sir." Rebecca drew herself up, ready to leave the room. "I do teach the curriculum, as you know, but I'll try to do better." She regarded Asa Hitchcock, who sat slumped in his large leather swivel chair—a chair bigger than the closet-sized office she shared upstairs. "But it's important to expose my students to ideas being discussed in the nation's legislatures—ideas that will impact their futures, and those of their daughters and granddaughters. We'll be studying Emma Willard as well." And with that, she left the room.

Mr. Hitchcock remained alone in his office for a while, stroking his side whiskers obsessively. This new young teacher from the

Litchfield Female Academy was not working out. She was too radical for Wethersfield and too intractable. He was grateful they had only settled on a one-year contract.

Rebecca Harding was thinking the same thing. But what if Asa Hitchcock gave her a bad reference? His disapprobation could bring her teaching career to an abrupt end. She could not wait to get home and write Eb a letter. Maybe she should also write to her mentor at the Litchfield Female Academy. Miss Pierce always gave good advice.

"Malinda!" Susan Graham stood at the library window on Elm Street. "Come and look at the snow coming down." The two women were waiting for a pot of tea and hot biscuits. Malinda sat with a book beside the roaring fire Mr. Potts had made for them. Mr. and Mrs. Potts did not live with Dr. Cabot but resided in the nearby free Black neighborhood around Dixwell Avenue. The couple had trudged through the blizzard to come to work. The storm had begun early that morning when everyone was snug in their beds. By mid-morning, more than twelve inches of heavy white snow blanketed the city. It was February in New Haven—a snowstorm was no surprise. But for Malinda and Susan, having spent their entire lives in Savannah, snow was a novelty.

"It's so beautiful." Susan watched as the snow tumbled out of the sky, creating a carpet of white, making the front yard indistinguishable from the road, were it not for the half-submerged wrought iron fence that separated them. The world had come to a halt. No elegant carriages moved up and down Elm Street on the urgent errands of the rich. No carts bearing fruits and vegetables passed by the window. No voices sang out, touting crisp lettuce, Wethersfield onions, or rhubarb just picked that morning. No invitations to sharpen knives, shine boots, haul trash, or purchase tinware sounded in the air. No preoccupied pedestrians rushed by, going to appointments or shopping, with parcels or leather satchels tucked under their arms.

Like us, Susan thought, probably everyone is at home sitting by a fire. The city's horses too must be chomping on hay in their stables, under blankets, taking a day off from the work of transporting humans and produce all over town, from pulling, sweating, and straining at the reins. And where would the city's stray dogs and cats find warmth and shelter? Elm Street was deserted, devoid of life. A soft, wet silence had descended upon New Haven.

"Oh my!" Malinda approached the window. "Would you look at that? It's just what Esmeralda predicted." The evening before, the elderly housekeeper had announced that a big snow was on the way. She could smell it. Dr. Cabot had so much faith in Esmeralda's sibylline pronouncements that he had affixed a sign to the clinic door. 'Closed due to weather. For emergencies, please knock at the front door.'

Early in the morning, Eb had taken off for Haines & Haines on Fleet Street with a bag slung over his shoulder. In it, Malinda had packed a change of linen, a clean shirt, a toothbrush, and comb, worried he would get stuck at work. The wind was picking up off the Long Island Sound. Even at six in the morning, the snow was beginning to drift. If it continued to fall, it would be impossible to navigate the city streets by the end of the workday.

Mr. Haines Sr. was out of town on another arbitration. Nathan Haines had announced the evening before that he would not come to the office the following day. He too seemed to have a nose for snow. Nonetheless, Nathan expected his staff of now four—two apprentices and two scriveners—to show up for work, bad weather notwithstanding. Their desks were piled high with documents to copy. But Nathan Haines was not without heart. If traveling home at the end of the day proved too daunting, Haines & Haines would pay for two rooms, and supper, at the tavern next door. Eb, Samuel, and the Redfield brothers could stay the night.

"I'm too cold." Malinda drew her woolen shawl around her shoulders, shivering from the perceptible draft at the window. "I'm going back to the fire." She settled into the wingback chair usually reserved for her uncle. Most days, Malinda wore her dark hair in a bun, but today it fell loosely upon her shoulders. No sense in fixing my hair, Malinda figured. No one except the family would see her today. Sitting in the orange glow of the fire, she looked soft and yielding, like a girl of eighteen.

Malinda slipped her stocking feet out of her shearling slippers, holding them up to the fire. It was such a treat to sit in her uncle's chair. Dr. Cabot was upstairs in bed, a hot brick wrapped in a cloth at his feet, reading Scottish history, waiting for his own pot of tea and hot biscuits. Staying in bed with a book was a luxury Ebenezer Cabot rarely afforded himself. It was his favorite way to spend what, to the great amusement of Malinda and Susan, everyone in the household called a 'snow day.'

Susan remained at the window. She could barely make out the Elm trees that lined the edges of the New Haven Green. They were so laden with snow that they blended into the wall of white, with only their dark trunks hinting at their presence. "Malinda, do you ever wonder if we're constitutionally suited for this weather?"

"All the time," Malinda groaned. "Honestly, what were we thinking? Sailing up north at the end of October, just in time for winter."

"If you remember, we were fleeing yellow fever." Susan and Malinda had nursed Malinda's mother through her illness and horrible death from 'Black Jack.' "Sometimes I miss Savannah."

"Me too." Malinda was silent for a while, thinking about last night's dream. She had dreamed of Savannah, where she and Susan had spent most of their lives. In her dream, she had been sitting on a wooden bench in Columbia Square, contemplating a Bird of Paradise plant, lifting its engorged, elongated purple head, with its outrageous spray of orange feathers, from the tangled jungle of long green leaves below. When she woke, Malinda wondered why she had not dreamed of her mother's noisette roses in the backyard of their house on East York Street. That would have been more fitting, given how much she mourned her mother.

But dream logic dictated a Bird of Paradise, and Malinda was not in her backyard, but on a wooden bench in Columbia Square. Bright yellow goldfinches flitted in and out of a purply pink azalea. The air was soft and warm. A slight breeze from the direction of the Savannah River bore a hint of brine. If Malinda had stayed asleep, her dream day would have turned hot and steamy. But now, Malinda Wells was wide awake in New Haven, warming her frigid feet by the fire in her uncle's library, made by a white-bearded free Black man named Anthony Potts. Outside, a bracing arctic cold front and a whirlwind of white snow bore down on them from Canada.

"Eb says we must be patient with Connecticut," Susan called out from the window, interrupting Malinda's reverie. "He insists the winter must be endured, but that spring will be lovely. And summer splendid." Susan returned to the fire, lowering herself down into the other wingback chair, the one Eb usually sat in. "He'd better be right."

"Eb took off early this morning. We assumed he'd be spending the night at the tavern." Malinda looked over at Susan. "I helped him pack his bag last night."

"It's a snowstorm. You'd think if the boss wasn't going to show up for work, he'd have let his employees stay home too," Susan grumbled. "He didn't set a very good example."

"Maybe he needed his staff to go in." Malinda was her younger brother's champion. In her opinion, Eb worked too hard at Haines & Haines, doing mundane scrivener work, and not enough substantive legal work. At the same time, she was sympathetic to Nathan

Haines's plight. "With the father absent all the time, Nathan's doing his best. It can't be easy running the law practice on his own. And he's putting them up at the inn tonight. Eb might even enjoy an evening down on Fleet Street."

"Do you think Eb's happy with the apprenticeship?" Susan asked. Eb had complained vocally at supper and around the fire about how many hours a day he spent copying documents. He yearned to do some legal research or draft a document on his own.

"I think when Mr. Haines Sr. is home, Eb's happy enough," Malinda replied. "Ned Haines comes into the scriveners' room and talks to Eb and Samuel about what they're copying. He explains this provision or that. But when he's gone, Nathan's just in a knot to get the work done. Eb and Samuel turn into scriveners."

"Wouldn't you like to meet these people?" Susan looked over at Malinda with a devious grin. She too wore her hair down today, but unlike Malinda, who sat upright in her uncle's chair with a studied elegance, Susan was curled up in a corner of Eb's chair like a cat. "I'd love to put a face to their names. See what they look like."

"A party for the people at Eb's work?"

"Well, no, perhaps not a party per se." Susan furrowed her brows, knowing Dr. Cabot loathed formal social occasions but was amenable to intimate suppers at home. This she knew from Eb's letters last year. "Maybe a small gathering for supper. Invite Mr. Haines Sr., his son, and Samuel, maybe the Redfield brothers." Susan lifted her feet toward the fire, noticing for the first time that her socks did not match. "That way, we could get a look at them. You know, size them up, assess the situation." She knew how much Malinda loved manipulating her younger brother's life, even from afar. Meeting the cast of characters would promote that endeavor. Give focus to her campaigns.

"I believe Uncle Ebenezer went to Yale with Ned Haines," Malinda mused. "Let's try the idea out on Esmeralda."

Right on cue, Esmeralda entered the room, carrying a tray bearing a fresh pot of tea, cream and sugar, a basket of biscuits wrapped in a red cotton napkin, a white tub of fresh butter, plates, napkins, butter knives, and a blue willow porcelain bowl of blackberry preserves. Esmeralda wore her usual gray dress and starched white apron, with a purple paisley turban wrapped around her head.

"Mrs. Potts sends these to you girls with her compliments," Esmeralda said briskly, with a hint of a West Indian accent left over from her mother. "It's a tradition here on Elm Street, from way back, to eat hot biscuits on a snow day. Mrs. Cabot always insisted on it."

Malinda made room on the table between them for the tray. "Tell Mrs. Potts thank you, Esmeralda." She hovered her hands over the red cotton napkin, hoping to warm them from the biscuit basket. "This looks lovely."

"Esmeralda," Susan asked, "does Dr. Cabot know Ned Haines from Yale?"

"I believe so. I remember the name. A whole lot of those boys went around together, before and after the war. Ebenezer, Ned, and later, your father." Esmeralda gestured toward Malinda.

"What do you think my uncle would say to a small party?" Malinda ventured. "We were thinking of inviting the staff of Haines & Haines for supper." She liked Susan's idea. A party would give her a project. Even with her work in the clinic, Malinda was bored. Winter wore on her more than she liked to admit, and unlike Susan, Malinda could not read all day. In the fall, she and Susan had taken some walks in their neighborhood, but now, with the advent of winter, it was too windy, too icy, too cold to go out. Dr. Cabot had not yet committed to buying a carriage, although renovations on the carriage house had begun. "Do you think he'd go for that idea?"

"Well, I don't know." Esmeralda shook her head. "Since Mrs. Cabot died, the social life here has come to a halt. He doesn't like to go out. But when your grandmother was alive, she often had small supper parties, and Dr. Cabot always enjoyed those. We had a few people over last winter when Eb was home. Your uncle liked that."

"What about Mrs. Potts?" Susan's mother had been the house-keeper for the Wells family in Savannah, so Susan was more attuned to the pressure a 'small supper party' could put on the cook. "Would it be too much for her?"

"No, child." Esmeralda gave a hearty laugh. "Mrs. Potts would be over the moon. She gets bored cooking for the likes of you who eat the same things all the time." She arranged the small plates for Susan and Malinda. "I think it's a fine idea. It'd be good for Dr. Cabot. He's become such a hermit." Esmeralda let out a sigh. "He misses his mother. We both do."

"I know how that feels," Malinda said softly. Some days, she could not bear living without her mother, but slowly, imperceptibly, she was learning how to. It was better to stay busy, though. Planning a supper party might be just what she needed. "How many guests could Mrs. Potts handle?"

"How many were you thinking?" Esmeralda looked back and forth from Malinda to Susan. Malinda sat on the edge of her chair, warming her hands over the biscuit basket, her eyes sparkling with the prospect of a project. Susan had settled back into Eb's chair and thrown her legs over the arm, dangling her mismatched feet in the air.

"Well, we'd have to wait for Mr. Haines Sr. to be in town, and then there's his son, Nathan, who I believe is unmarried." Malinda was calculating. "And Samuel Taylor, the other apprentice."

"So, three guests then?" Esmeralda counted them on her fingers, holding up her weathered hand.

"Well, it'd be rude not to invite the two Redfield brothers too," Malinda added. "They all work in the same room. Unmarried as well. So, five guests then."

"I love the idea." Esmeralda gave Malinda a huge grin. "But let's ask Mrs. Potts first, and maybe Mr. Potts too. If your uncle's going to protest, he'll say it's too much work for Mrs. Potts. And me." She gingerly peeled the red cotton napkin off the hot biscuits and offered them the basket. "Poor little old me." Esmeralda gave Malinda a wink. "Mrs. Potts will say 'yes,' I'm sure, and as for Mr. Potts, he'll do whatever Mrs. Potts tells him to."

"Thank you, Esmeralda." Malinda buttered her biscuit and dropped a dollop of blackberry preserve on it before settling back into her chair, balancing the plate beneath her chin. "This is a great idea, Susan."

"It is, isn't it?" Susan swung her long legs off the arm of the chair and righted herself, reaching for a biscuit. "What I'd really like to do is to invite that Rebecca Harding."

Around the table and before the fire, Eb had babbled on and on about Rebecca Harding. The entire household knew from her letters about her struggles with Asa Hitchcock, her holiday visit with Martha Lewis, and the books she read to Mrs. Cox. These recitals about Rebecca's everyday life in Wethersfield were a new chapter in Eb's story that had started the year before in Litchfield. From afar, through his chatty letters, Malinda and Susan had witnessed with fascination as Eb floundered on the threshold of a romance with Rebecca Harding, then blundered into a disastrous liaison with the Southern belle, Katherine Montgomery, and eventually found his way back to Rebecca. This was a narrative arc that Susan and Malinda were anxious to fill in with some much-needed character development. They both wanted to get the measure of Rebecca Harding. To see what she looked like. To talk to her. To test her mettle.

"Ah, yes, the elusive Miss Harding," Malinda mumbled through her mouthful of hot biscuit and blackberry preserve. "The unraveling of that mystery will have to wait. But I'll talk to Eb when he gets home. If he gets home." Malinda glanced over at the library window, snow swirling around the panes, filling the corners. "And maybe you, Esmeralda," Malinda added, "might feel out Mrs. Potts?"

"I'm on it, Miss Malinda." The elderly woman bowed, a gesture made more majestic in her paisley turban. "A supper party. I love the idea."

At what point does a young woman become a spinster? On this, the threshold of her thirtieth year, Malinda Wells had decided she qualified. At age eighteen, a casual stranger would never have predicted she would not marry. Malinda was a serious, well-educated young woman with her mother's pleasing, round face, carefully protected pale skin, and trim body with the requisite feminine contours. Her hair was shiny and black. Eb called her an 'owl' because of her dark, predatory eyes. Nothing that moved in Malinda's line of sight went unnoticed by her. Her spinsterhood was not due to any lack of natural attraction but to her unique circumstances—the most salient being that Malinda was the only surviving daughter of Abigail Cabot Wells.

When Abigail joined her husband in Savannah in 1789, she was a fish out of water. An inveterate Yankee with anti-slavery views, she never felt at home in Georgia. Typically, a church community would provide a social network, but Savannah had no Congregational church. And like her older brother in New Haven, Abigail did not enjoy going out. All her energy was spent inside their modest saltbox house on East York Street, creating a loving, comfortable home, insulated from the city they lived in.

Unlike Abigail, the men in the Wells family went out and about. Her husband was, by nature, gregarious. His law practice served merchants and shippers, requiring him to make daily trips down to the riverfront, the City Market, and the cotton warehouses.

Her two sons also ventured out into Savannah's society through the schools they attended. Malinda had no such opportunities, staying home most of the time with her mother. She belonged to no church, had no school to attend, no girlfriends with brothers to flirt with, no dances to go to, no way to meet any eligible bachelors. Besides, her mother's anti-slavery views were inculcated in Malinda, anathema to most Southern men she might encounter.

But Malinda was not lonely. In the schoolroom upstairs, she had the company of her mother and her brothers until they left home for school. Malinda was fiercely attached to her younger brother. Losing Eb to the boys' academy, later to Franklin College, and the Litchfield Law School, were painful separations for Malinda, but she took great pride in his accomplishments. She also became close friends with Susan Graham, the housekeeper's daughter, and it was Susan who finally dragged Malinda out of the house for what she called their 'expeditions.' With her arm linked through Susan's, Malinda learned to enjoy exploring their corner of Savannah. Susan was her ally, confidante, and 'partner in crime.' Malinda felt guilty for going out without her mother, but Abigail Cabot Wells would not leave the house.

When she was younger, Malinda's lack of marital prospects concerned her, but after her father's death, she gave up worrying about it. For reasons beyond her control, she had failed to jump onto the marriage carousel. Now it was too late. She accepted her status as an 'unclaimed jewel,' resigning herself to the roles of dutiful daughter and loving maiden aunt. She also became the self-appointed manager of the household. Malinda was, by nature, a controlling creature, endowed with a flair for organization. She ran the house on East York Street with an iron hand. Having a competent daughter suited her mother. The widow Abigail disappeared into her books and let her daughter take over.

But in the year 1820, Malinda's modest life plan crumbled. Her brother John's house burned to the ground in the Savannah fire, and he moved his family and law practice to Charleston. After the fire, Savannah was a pile of unsafe rubble. John begged his mother and sister to move in with them in the Charleston townhouse owned by his wife's parents. But Abigail refused to budge. She would not leave her home in Savannah. Neither would she tolerate being waited upon by enslaved people. Abigail's older brother, Dr. Ebenezer Cabot, offered an alternative haven, urging his sister and niece to visit him in New Haven. Again, Abigail refused to budge. Malinda's fate was tied to her mother. In the midst of this power struggle, Abigail died suddenly of yellow fever, and Malinda's close connection with her mother was torn asunder. Malinda went into mourning.

The timing was terrible. What was Malinda to do? Savannah was in ruins from the fire, and yellow fever was rampant throughout the city. The prospect of moving to Charleston held no appeal. She would have gladly gone to live with Eb and his hypothetical family, but Eb was not married yet. Neither had he settled into his career. But the men in her family—her brothers and her uncle—were pressuring her to leave Savannah. The latter's invitation was renewed, and Malinda agreed. An extended visit to New Haven solved the 'what to do with Malinda' problem.

New Haven beckoned. The house on East York Street in Savannah was heavy with sorrow, and Malinda needed a change of scene. The thought of a trip up north cheered her. She could finally see Connecticut for herself, a place she had heard about all her life—the Long Island Sound, the New Haven harbor and Long Wharf, the Green, the Yale campus, the blazing autumn leaves, and maybe snow. Eb planned to move in with their uncle during his apprenticeship, and she would be reunited with him. Malinda might work in Dr. Cabot's clinic, a distraction from her grief. Susan Graham would come with her as her companion. For the first time in her life, Malinda Wells packed a trunk of her own.

Once in New Haven, Malinda began to manage Dr. Cabot's clinic with the efficiency of a high-ranking military officer. She revamped his method for keeping appointments, had the clinic repainted, hired a carpenter to build more benches, and instituted a penalty system for patients who failed to show up. This latter policy caused some friction with her uncle, who did not like extracting even a few pennies from his impoverished patients. But Malinda held firm. If you charge a small fee for missing appointments, people will keep them.

Malinda was right. Indeed, she was almost always right. Dr. Cabot was averse to change, but acknowledged that the clinic ran more efficiently under her supervision. He had tremendous respect for his niece, but she both intimidated and exhausted him. Malinda seemed to believe she was the only person who knew how to run things, and she was always looking to improve him. Dr. Cabot's clothes, his diet, his habits, his clinic, the running of the household—everything was up for grabs.

Before her arrival, Dr. Cabot had worried that Malinda and his housekeeper, Esmeralda, would butt heads. After all, Esmeralda had run his life for more than forty years. But he had failed to anticipate their conspiracy, its sole purpose, in his opinion, to disrupt his life. When Malinda moved into Elm Street, the older woman instantly recognized a superior force of nature. But Malinda too appreciated the powerful sway of Esmeralda. Both women sized the other up, and without a single word exchanged, Malinda and Esmeralda formed a united front, an alliance to improve the household—and Dr. Cabot's life. Dr. Cabot was grateful for their efforts, but he also felt overwhelmed by all this feminine energy and upward movement. At times, like Eb, Ebenezer Cabot felt the need to rebel. To advocate for inertia and gravity.

"So, Samuel." Eb Wells lay flat on his back next to Samuel Taylor. The two apprentices shared a small, inadequate wood-framed bed in the tavern next to Haines & Haines on Fleet Street. Snow had poured out of the sky, unabated all day long. Over eighteen inches covered the streets of New Haven, and the drifts were even higher. 'No vacancy' signs hung from the entranceways of the many inns, taverns, saloons, and boarding houses near Long Wharf that housed sailors, dock workers, and maritime merchants on the move. Eb was grateful that Nathan had prepaid for their lodgings. As predicted, traveling home was impossible.

The Redfield brothers had promptly passed out next door. Through the planks of pine between them, Eb could hear two registers of snoring emanating from their room, a deep guttural intonation from Ted, a more sonorous tenor from Oliver. Both waves of sound were the even, regulated snores of two untroubled men who had worked hard all day. Neither Eb nor Samuel could fall asleep. In the dark, Eb stared up at the wooden beams of an unfamiliar ceiling.

"Have you ever been in love, Samuel?" Eb whispered.

"Yes," Samuel Taylor whispered back. "At least I thought I was. With a girl from my mother's church." A much taller man, Samuel was curled up on his right side, hanging onto the frame of the rickety bed, facing the wall.

Over the past two months, Eb and Samuel had laid the foundations for a friendship. Mostly, they moaned and groaned about work, but here in the dark, on this winter night, marooned at the tavern next to Haines & Haines, venturing into more personal topics seemed possible. The snowstorm, the howling wind outside, the delicious, steaming hot shepherd's pie, the pints of ale—all lubricated the conversation. Sounds from down below, faint music, muffled laughter, and the cheerful din of a tavern on a snowy night drifted up through the floorboards.

"What was her name?"

"Elizabeth," Samuel replied. "Elizabeth Wainwright."

"What happened to the romance?" Eb inferred failure. "Did you have a falling out?"

"Not exactly. Unless you call her finding someone else to marry a 'falling out.' We weren't officially courting or anything, but I thought we had an understanding." Samuel was quiet, and Eb did not know what to say. "But apparently," Samuel started up again, "we didn't because before you knew it, they announced her engagement from the pulpit. She married into a merchant family."

"Did you know the other man?"

"No. He went to my mother's church, but I didn't know him personally." Samuel paused. "I knew his family by reputation. They have a lot more money and a lot fewer children than we do. More social standing."

"Did Elizabeth tell you she was seeing him?"

"No," Samuel replied. "She did not. I almost fell out of the pew when the announcement was made. I asked her after the service what was going on. She claimed the engagement was all her parents' idea. They'd found this man for her to marry, and she was just going along with it, even though she didn't love him."

"But she did love you?" Eb persisted.

"Well, she said she did. She said she even loved me after she got engaged, but to my way of thinking, it couldn't have been real love. Not if she was willing to swap me out for some random fellow her parents picked out."

"Did you ever ask her to marry you?" Eb asked, trying to sort out how romance and marriage related to each other, a confounding subject no matter the century.

"I didn't." Samuel sighed. "I couldn't really. I was finishing up at Brown at the time and looking for an apprenticeship. It would be at least four years before I'd be admitted to a bar and get my own practice going, so I wasn't able to ask her." Samuel shifted his body, pulling the short woolen blanket over himself. "It takes wherewithal to get married, Eb. You can't bring a wife to a boarding house."

For a while, Eb was silent. He came from a prosperous family, at least on his mother's side, and his father's law practice had been successful. If not rich exactly, he was more than comfortable financially, particularly after inheriting from his parents. Eb recognized that Samuel's circumstances were different, and his relative wealth embarrassed him. "Well, this other guy, the one from the merchant family," Eb finally asked, his curiosity getting the better of him. "I take it he had the wherewithal?"

"He most certainly did. His family owns two large dry goods stores in Providence. Samuel manages one of them."

"You're kidding me! Did you say 'Samuel?'" Eb snorted. "His name was Samuel too?"

"Yes." Samuel erupted in a bitter laugh. "What are the chances of that? I told her she'd stumbled into the wrong Samuel when she met me. Another 'Samuel' was planned for her by divine providence, a scion of the dry goods trade—not the oldest son of a jewelry master whose overly large family subsists on weekly wages."

"And how did you know it was a romantic relationship? And not just a friendship?"

"Well . . ." Samuel smiled in the dark. "I think once you start kissing a girl in a closet, and you want to be alone with her whenever you can—which for us was almost never, her mother kept such a close eye on her. But the kisses made the difference, I think." He sighed. "Not difference enough though, I guess."

"Do you think she was kissing this other Samuel too? You know, at the same time?" Eb wanted to test Samuel's degree of moral outrage.

"She said she wasn't. I guess she has by now," Samuel grunted. "They have a baby. That's what my mother wrote in her last letter. Although let's face it, you could get one of those without love, or kisses for that matter, I suppose."

"Ah, yes," Eb said, unsure he understood Samuel's last comment. "Well, I'm sorry about your bad luck with Elizabeth. She picked the wrong 'Samuel,' to my way of thinking."

"Thank you," Samuel said softly. "I try not to think about it too much. And how about you? Have you ever been in love?"

"Well, I'm not certain." Eb sounded tentative. "I was definitely romantically involved with someone last year at school, a young woman from Charleston."

"You're sure now?" Samuel rolled over on his back and bent his knees, supporting his feet on the bottom of the bed frame. The ropes beneath the bed had not been pulled tight for some time, and the itchy tick mattress was sagging. He was too tall to easily fall asleep in this bed, even alone. With another person—one inclined to chatter—it was impossible. At least Eb was short. Samuel poked Eb in his ribs with his elbow. "How do you know this 'involvement' was a romance, not just a friendship? Did it involve any kissing?"

"Oh, yes." Eb was grateful it was too dark for Samuel to detect his blushing. "Plenty of kissing, but she broke it off."

"She broke it off with number one—or was it number two?—in his class at the Litchfield Law School." Samuel teased. "On what grounds?"

Eb hesitated. They had not yet delved into politics. Samuel had dropped occasional hints of curiosity about Eb's attitudes toward slavery, but Eb had not been forthcoming, worried that Samuel might reject him. He might be appalled, either by his family's involvement with slavery or by his abolitionist views. Even up in Connecticut, Eb's ideas on equality among the races upset many people.

"Well, Katherine Montgomery was the daughter of a wealthy plantation owner." Eb propped himself up on an elbow, launching into his explanation. "I was in a moot court about the American Colonialization Society, and my abolitionist views became public in that debate. Everyone in Litchfield knew where I stood."

"But you're from the South." Samuel knew little about the moot court tradition. "I'm surprised you took an anti-slavery position."

"You get assigned your side at moot court. You don't get to pick," Eb explained. "Besides, my circumstances are complicated. I may have grown up in Savannah, but my parents came from Connecticut. My mother was opposed to slavery, my father to a lesser extent. He had a law practice to protect, but I was influenced by my mother."

"So, your family didn't own slaves?" Samuel had danced around this question for two months.

"Not my mother and father," Eb replied. "But my brother John met a Southern planter's daughter at the female academy. There are many of them at Miss Pierce's. John and Eliza are married now and live in Charleston. They've got two little girls, my nieces." Eb took a deep breath. "But yes, Samuel, John owns three house slaves. Eliza brought them into the marriage as a wedding gift. And her father owns many more on his plantation. Their number might be in the hundreds. I don't know for sure." Eb hated to confess this last part to Samuel, but felt better once the facts were out. These realities about his family could not be changed.

"So, let me see if I understand." Samuel sifted through this information. "Is that why you're not apprenticing with your brother? Because of your anti-slavery views?"

"Yes," Eb answered quietly, still ashamed for disappointing his much-revered older brother. "I couldn't join his practice. His clients would never accept me."

"He didn't know your views before you went to law school?"

"My views got stronger when I came up north," Eb replied. "You know my friend from law school, Charles Godwin? He was raised by a Quaker, and he encouraged my abolitionist leanings. Judge Reeve too. And my uncle. He's a great supporter of the free Black community here in New Haven." Samuel lay on his back, saying nothing while Eb finished his story. "Anyhow, it wasn't just John.

My romance with Katherine couldn't be sustained either. Once I went public with my views, she broke it off."

"I understand." Samuel made no further comment. "So, when this Katherine broke it off," he finally asked, shifting the conversation to safer ground, "were you sad?"

"No, not really." Eb erupted in laughter. "I was immensely relieved. Katherine Montgomery was way more woman than I could handle."

"In what way?"

"Well, she was tall, blonde, and beautiful. Very smart, accomplished, fluent in French, and her Latin was outstanding. But my legal career became her ambition. Katherine didn't know where she ended, and I began." Eb laughed again. "She was determined to mold me into a powerful man—a hopeless endeavor, I assure you. It wasn't just that, though." Eb frowned, thinking about Katherine's cavalier attitude toward slavery, her disdain for Charles Godwin, her merciless attacks on *The Detritus*. "We didn't see the world in the same way."

"I understand," Samuel said again. "I couldn't marry someone who didn't share my abolitionist views." A short silence came after that pronouncement.

"You're an abolitionist?" Eb knew little about colleges up north. To him, a graduate of Brown University was the same as one of Yale, Harvard, or Columbia. He lacked any context to make accurate predictions.

"I am, but I don't mention it at work." Samuel had been discreet about his political views at Haines & Haines—for good reason. Ned and Nathan Haines insisted that the law firm remain politically neutral.

"I had no idea you were an abolitionist too." Eb found himself relieved. "How did you come by your views?"

"At Brown." Samuel shifted again to make himself more comfortable. "Privately, I don't know how either Haines feels about the peculiar institution. Ned professes to be a Unitarian, so he might share our views. But I don't know about Nathan or the Redfield brothers." A lull descended on the conversation. Finally, Samuel said, "But tell me this, Eb. Are you in love right now?"

Eb told Samuel all about his complicated relationship with Rebecca Harding, his dependence on her during his early days in law school, his respect for her intellect, how she had cut him off last winter to make way for Katherine Montgomery, her belief that marriage would end her teaching career, their newsy letters, their kisses last summer, satisfying but fleeting. He worried that she regretted those kisses. Eb told Samuel everything.

Almost. Eb did not tell Samuel about Susan Graham. How beautiful she was. How shy he felt around her. How he could not sit next to her, address her directly, or look her in the eye. How he thought about her all the time. He did not mention Susan Graham at all.

Eventually, Samuel drifted off, and Eb lay awake, listening to the sounds of the tavern down below. The distant hum of masculine conversation and muted music had ceased. The patrons had either trudged home through the snow or retreated upstairs to the tavern's uncomfortable beds. Through the floorboards, Eb heard a throaty meoorrrl of supplication from a cat. That must be the fat tabby from down below, begging for milk. Earlier in the evening, Eb had approached the cat, sitting on the hearth, soaking up warmth from the stones. She had demurely accepted a rub behind her ears. Feeling the soft, dark fur around her neck, Eb felt a sharp stab of loneliness for Sir Winston.

Eb missed a lot of things from Litchfield—Judge Reeve, Mrs. Reeve, Mrs. Edwards, Martha and Charles, the Lewis family, Thomas Bradford. But Eb missed more than people. He missed his law school classes, his hours of long, luxurious study in Judge Reeve's library, reading cases, distilling principles, writing them into his leather-bound volumes. He missed joking around with Thomas up in his attic room, pretending to study. He missed his long, meandering conversations with Charles. He missed walking up and down North and South Streets in Litchfield, between his boarding house and the law school, the autumn leaves crunching beneath his feet. He missed the noisy, delicious lunches at Judge Reeve's table, arguing about the niceties of the morning's lecture while slurping a hot chunky soup from an earthenware bowl. He missed Betsey Reeve's doggedly cheerful face and warm, fresh bread. Eb Wells missed his life as a law student.

It is a peculiar reverie only human beings are capable of—to miss an earlier period of one's own life. This genre of nostalgia is usually for a phase that is over and done with, completed, and sealed off, an earlier time that can never be returned to. Often, what we miss the most is the person we used to be. Eb Wells used to be a rising star at the Litchfield Law School, renting Mrs. Edwards's attic room, amidst the drying fruits and hanging meats, with the comforting weight of Sir Winston at his feet. Now, he was an overworked law apprentice in New Haven, living with his uncle, doing work he did not like, trying to get to sleep upstairs in a tavern during a fierce snowstorm, his colleagues from Haines & Haines all snoring within ten feet of him.

Again, Eb heard the cat's demand from downstairs. He imagined the tavern keeper's wife, bringing her pet a bowl of milk, setting it gingerly on the hearth, the cat's sand-papery pink tongue lapping the creamy white liquid up with feline tidiness and efficiency. Eb looked up at the beams of the tavern ceiling. I truly miss Sir Winston, he thought. I miss his broad orange face, his soft, padded paw at my knee, begging for a scrap from the table, bacon perhaps, or a small cube of cheese, his soft, gentle wheezing during the night. I even miss cat hair on my lapels.

Eb suddenly realized he needed a cat. That was what was missing from his life. And with that insight, Eb rolled over, his backbone aligned with Samuel Taylor's, and drifted off to sleep.

CHAPTER 2

Serving Notice

"Do you really think it's appropriate for us to serve notice?" Eb Wells and Samuel Taylor sat together on the seat of a hired hackney, traveling north to Whitneyville, almost to Haddam. "Isn't this something for Ted to do?" Eb grumbled.

"No, it's not appropriate." Samuel chewed on an apple he had pulled from his satchel for a snack. "Ted ought to do it, but he's swamped. I've served notice before. This is just your first one, that's all." Nathan Haines had requested the two apprentices to serve notice together on a debtor who lived in Whitneyville. In Nathan's words, 'It could be a rough neighborhood.'

To Eb and Samuel's way of thinking, this assignment was beneath their status, making them rank bill collectors. Eb also did not relish serving notice on a man in financial distress. It was one thing when two large companies sued one another—two giants rattling sabers. But Eb was uncomfortable harassing a person who had fallen on hard times.

It was early March in Connecticut. The morning sky was pale pink, and a few trees sprouted lime-green buds. The road north was wet and muddy, making the hackney sway unexpectedly as the driver avoided numerous ruts. Eb tried to keep his eyes on the scenery, ignoring his proximity to the hind end of a horse—and his fear of horses in motion.

Eb had been thinking about horses a lot lately. His uncle had finished the renovations on the carriage house on Elm Street. Malinda had won her campaign to procure two horses, not yet purchased, but agreed to. The question of a coachman was now on the table. Maybe they would not need one, Dr. Cabot suggested. Perhaps Eb could drive in the evenings? To this horrible suggestion, Eb put his foot down. He could not be a law apprentice and ferry Malinda and Susan all over town. He had professional obligations. Malinda backed Eb up. Their uncle's suggestion was not practical. She also knew Eb was terrified of driving a carriage, and regardless, Dr. Cabot should hire a coachman.

"At least it's a fine day." Samuel breathed deeply, taking in the morning's cool, moist air. "We can't really blame Nathan. The deeds for Mr. Hampton must be turned around today. You and I are no match for Ted at the desk, and Oliver's up to his ears as well. This notice has got to be served today, no matter what."

Samuel Taylor too was opposed to serving papers on an impoverished person, although to his mind, this was just a business debt. The debtor's name was Franz Mueller, a German, doing business as Mueller's Laundry. Franz Mueller had borrowed money from a New Haven bank to set up a laundry in Whitneyville and had defaulted on the loan. On the face of it, the story did not draw upon Samuel's well of compassion.

Franz Mueller and his wife Johanna had chosen Whitneyville for their laundry because it was full of workers in Eli Whitney's gun factory, many of whom were bachelors. It was a town with lots of dirty shirts and few women to wash them. The couple felt confident they could pay back the loan for the purchase of the building. Franz, Johanna, and their five-year-old son, Heinrich, or 'Henry' as he was called, had a cozy apartment inside Mueller's Laundry.

But Mueller's Laundry had fallen on hard times. Johanna, just thirty years old, had died last spring from burns she suffered in their backyard. She had been tending to the copper pot of boiling water over the fire, when her long skirt grazed the pot's bottom and set alight. In her panic to stamp out the flames, the pot tipped over on her, scalding her badly through her skirt from the waist down. The doctor could do little for Johanna except provide her with brandy and opium for the pain. She died a few days later of infection. With her death, the business floundered. Now that Franz Mueller was in arrears on the loan, the bank was moving to foreclose the mortgage.

Nathan Haines had relayed this to Eb and Samuel the evening before, adopting the same tone of voice he would have used to rattle off a list of office supplies. Their client was the bank. The bank was out their money. The building was collateral for the loan and must be sold. What had happened to Franz Mueller and his family was unfortunate, no doubt, but not their concern. The duty of Haines & Haines—to be carried out by Samuel and Eb—was to serve the foreclosure papers on Franz Mueller, doing business as Mueller's Laundry.

"I suppose he's got other creditors knocking on his door too." Eb sighed. "It's not only Mr. Mueller's business they're foreclosing on. It's his home. He lives there with his son. English law used to exempt a debtor's real property from creditors. Your home was sacred, something to pass on to your heirs. Personal property could be used to satisfy your debts, but your land enjoyed protection."

Samuel listened intently. For the past month, Eb Wells had taken on the position of de facto tutor within the scriveners' room, briefing Samuel on principles of law. His presentations were always clear, with an eye toward history. He made the dry and dated law in *Blackstone* come alive. Oliver Redfield too had started to arrive at the law office before business hours to attend Eb's lectures, with the slumbering gentle giant Ted in tow.

"The English Parliament passed The Debt Recovery Act in 1732 to apply in the colonies," Eb continued. "It got rid of the distinction between real and personal property for debtor's law. That meant a colonial judge could authorize the sale of a man's home—and turn the money over to the bank. This remedy wasn't available to creditors in England, where a man's home was exempt." Eb employed his newly developed 'professor voice.' "That's the way it ought to be."

"Go on." Samuel tossed his apple core into a passing bush.

"After the war, most states, including Connecticut, reenacted their own versions of The Debt Recovery Act. It was a very pro-creditor law. Slaves and land were up for grabs for banks to seize. The statutes promoted the free alienability of land, whereas, in England, the impetus was to keep land sacrosanct. To maintain power and wealth within the family. But Americans dislike anything that smacks of aristocracy. Most states considered English law feudal." Eb took a break and waited for Samuel to ask questions. Hearing none, he concluded. "So, that's why the bank, our client, can seize Franz Mueller's home. Throw him, and his son, out on the street. It's terrible, but legal."

"You're amazing, Eb." Samuel Taylor shook his head. "You know everything. How can you deliver an impromptu lecture on a hackney ride? Just like that." Samuel snapped his fingers. Eb smiled enigmatically. The truth was Eb had spent hours in the law library the night before, researching whether Franz Mueller's home could be taken from him.

"To me, Samuel, the law is unjust," Eb urged, forgetting his vanity. "To rob a poor man of his home when he's down and out."

"It does seem a cruel fate," Samuel mused. "First, Mueller loses his wife to a terrible accident, then he loses his business, and now he's going to lose his home."

"And he might lose his five-year-old son." Eb shook his head.

"What laws could be passed to prevent this from happening?" This was Samuel's signature response to an unjust law—how to make things better. Eb often remarked on how each of his study partners approached things differently. Charles Godwin made structural, systemic critiques. Thomas Bradford had a penchant for practical advice, and now Samuel Taylor wanted to legislate.

"There are different aspects of your question," Eb said thoughtfully. "First, how should the law deal with the loss of Mrs. Mueller? She was an integral part of the laundry business, but Mr. Mueller can't recoup from her unexpected death. Why not? Critical employees do sometimes die unexpectedly or become disabled. There ought to be a way to insure against their death or disability. To protect the business, not to mention their families from lost wages."

"I agree," Samuel said. "But it's trickier when a woman is the key player. To insure against her loss is to recognize the value of her labor. That won't happen soon."

"True, but we also need an enlightened law of bankruptcy, one that is pro-debtor. We need a real property exemption that protects a man's home from banks and bill collectors. Think about it, Samuel. How does society benefit from taking this man's home away?" Eb could feel himself on the verge of a rant. "To throw him out on the street? Or worse yet, into a debtor's prison? Why not help someone like Mr. Mueller get back on his feet? Or shift the risk of loss onto the banks. They've got the 'big bucks' and are better able to absorb it." Eb let out a heartfelt groan. "Honestly, I can't even bring myself to think about the boy's fate. Through no fault of his own, he'll become a ward of the state." The hackney began to enter the small town of Whitneyville, bringing Eb's critique to an end. The Mill River could be seen in the distance.

"We're almost here." Samuel looked around at the bustling neighborhood. "I can't believe Nathan insisted we go together today." Both Eb and Samuel observed the workers on a break. Most seemed to be Irish and German immigrants, and some free Blacks. They clustered around the food carts, trying to grab a bite before the factory whistle blew. "This is just a working man's neighborhood, Eb. There's nothing 'rough' about it." Samuel grinned at two men jockeying in line for bratwurst. "I grew up in a community like this in Providence, except our employer made plated gold and jewelry, not guns."

"Well . . ." Eb viewed the crowd of jostling, hungry men. "I'm grateful for your company anyway." Whitneyville was not a milieu that Eb Wells or Nathan Haines had been brought up in, an industrial hub, a factory town that manufactured guns, a company town full of big, burly laborers. Eb did not feel threatened, but not at ease either.

The defunct Mueller's Laundry was easy to find—on the west side of Whitney Avenue, not far from the Mill River, close to the boarding house for unmarried workers. The laundry building was unprepossessing, a two-story brick house with a small redbud tree in front of it, promising to bloom within the month. Beneath the tree, a little boy perched on a wooden stool, digging industriously. He was making a mud mountain. Eb and Samuel stepped down from the hackney, requesting the driver to return in an hour. Samuel's satchel contained an envelope with the notice of foreclosure papers.

"Hello," Eb called out to the boy, who was small for his age, with knobby knees, unkempt blond hair, and a precarious front tooth. "Is your father around?" Eb leaned over to inspect his mountain of mud.

"Yes," the boy answered with a slight lisp, absorbed in his geological creation. He nodded toward the brick house. "He's in there with Mrs. Tittles."

Eb and Samuel approached the slightly ajar front door. Samuel knocked lightly, and a German-accented, baritone voice called out, "Come in." Eb and Samuel crossed the threshold.

Eb braced himself to see a man and a woman, Franz Mueller and the aforementioned Mrs. Tittles, but instead, he saw a man in his mid-thirties, sitting in a rocker—with a cat on his lap. She was a calico. Like Sir Winston, she had a white underbelly and chest, but her upper markings were a mixture of black and orange. Her eyes were golden, her nose terracotta. Franz Mueller gently lowered the cat to the ground, stood up, and approached Eb and Samuel.

"May I help you gentlemen?"

"Are you Franz Mueller?" Eb extended his hand, not knowing the proper etiquette for serving papers. He had meant to ask Samuel, but forgot. The man nodded and took his hand warily. "I'm Eb Wells, and this is Samuel Taylor." Eb indicated to his right where Samuel too stood awkwardly. "We're from the law office of Haines & Haines."

"Law office?" Franz Mueller lifted his eyebrows. A tall, lean, muscular man of medium build, he had a shock of blond hair that defied gravity. It was clear the boy outside was his son. Franz's eyes were light blue, his features sharp. Eb was certain Malinda and Susan would call him 'rugged,' their favorite adjective for a man they deemed handsome.

"Yes, Haines & Haines," Eb repeated.

"On what business?" Franz was guarded.

"Our law practice represents the bank in New Haven that lent you money to purchase this laundry," Eb began. "You've been in default on that loan for over six months, and by the terms of the mortgage agreement, the bank is seeking to foreclose. We're serving papers on you today." Eb said all of this in a clear, steady voice.

"Here's the notice." Samuel passed the envelope containing the notice of foreclosure. "And a letter for you, explaining the proceedings."

"I see." Franz Mueller took the envelope from Samuel. "Thank you for bringing this to me. I've been expecting it." Samuel pulled a portable writing lap desk from his satchel and handed Frank Mueller a quill pen with enough ink in it for a signature. Franz signed the receipt. There was an excruciating silence in the room, broken only by a boy bursting through the front door.

"Papa," Henry said with a scolding cluck, the calico cat draped over his arm. Mrs. Tittles must have slipped out the front door while the men were talking. She was dangling, her white legs extended, having generously opted to fall limp like a rag doll in the boy's clumsy clutches. "We're not to let Mrs. Tittles out in the front. She might get run over. She's only to go out back." The boy put down the cat, who promptly shook herself, regaining her composure.

"I'm sorry, Henry." Franz Mueller smiled down at his son's mud-smudged face. "You're right. I was distracted." Mrs. Tittles wove between his legs on her way to the back of the kitchen. "She's fine, though."

"Who are these men, Papa?" Henry looked up at Samuel and Eb, boldly scrutinizing every detail of their faces, their dress, their slightly muddy boots, as only a five-year-old can do.

"These men work in a law office," Franz answered. "They've come to bring me some papers from the bank."

Henry's face clouded over. "The bank that's throwing us out of our home?" His voice had a sudden maturity to it, making him sound much older than five. "That bank, Papa?" He squeaked the last word.

"Yes, Henry." Franz sounded resigned, almost relieved, ready to yield to the inexorable forces of fate. Samuel was methodically packing up the writing lap desk, preparing to leave the house. Their notice of service mission was accomplished, but Eb grabbed the sleeve of Samuel's coat to slow him down.

"What are you going to do now, Mr. Mueller?" Eb asked. "Can you raise the money to pay the arrears?"

"No, sir." Franz shook his head. "I can't. I don't know what to do."

"Could you work in Mr. Whitney's gun factory?" Eb asked, desperately trying to come up with ways to dig Franz Mueller out of this hole.

"I could be hired," Franz admitted, "but I can't leave Henry alone all day. He's only five, and I can't afford a childminder. That would eat up most of my wages. Then there's food and wood for the fire. There'd be nothing left to pay the mortgage." Franz had considered his options in Whitneyville. "And I can't move into the unmarried workers' boarding house with a child." He let out a long sigh. "Or a cat."

"What other kind of work could you do?" Eb queried.

"I'm at a loss. Not with Henry to take care of." Franz looked down at the smaller of the two men from Haines & Haines, at Eb's well-tailored suit, his tall boots rimmed with mud, his gold-rimmed glasses, his auburn wavy hair, and above all, his kind face. "Would you gentlemen like a cup of tea before you head back?"

Samuel was about to respond with a 'No, thank you, we must go,' but Eb answered first. "Yes," Eb said, "we'd love to if it's no bother." He looked down at Henry and smiled. "We've got to wait for the hackney anyhow."

"Henry . . ." Franz put his arm around his son, who continued to stare at Eb and Samuel with suspicion. "Would you go to the breadbox and make up a nice plate of Lebkuchen while I put the kettle on?" Henry perked up at the mention of cookies. He followed Mrs. Tittles to the back of the kitchen. "Gentlemen?" Franz gestured toward the table, its wooden surface wiped clean. Indeed, the entire house was neat and tidy.

"Thank you." Eb settled onto the bench on the far side of the table, and Samuel obediently followed him. In Samuel's experience, staying for tea with the debtor had never been part of any delivery of service before. But he was willing to take Eb's lead.

Over tea, Eb learned that Henry had named Mrs. Tittles when he was a 'baby.' His mother had a friend named Mrs. Tuthill, and the cat was named after her. Henry mangled the pronunciation, and soon the cat became known as 'Mrs. Tittles.' Eb thought the name was undignified but had a sweet history. Franz was reticent at first, but once Eb plied him with questions about the cookies—Eb's first Lebkuchen—Franz opened up. The cookie was traditionally only served during the Christmas season, Franz explained, but the nearby German bakery took liberties. Eb was also introduced to another nutty cookie that tickled his nose, Pfeffernüsse, purchased for Henry as a special treat. Eb wondered whether Mrs. Potts would ever add pepper to cookie dough. He doubted it.

Franz told them a brief history of his life. He was not an immigrant but had been born into a German-speaking neighborhood in Philadelphia. Franz's father had come from Nuremberg as an indentured servant and worked as a blacksmith for five years to pay off his debt. Later, his father opened his own farrier business. An only child, Franz went to a German school for eight years and then worked in his father's farriery. He had grown up taking care of horses. Both his parents were dead. After he married Johanna, they moved to Connecticut.

Franz's idea was to open his own farriery, but Johanna had other plans. A determined young woman, she wanted to run a family business, to work side by side with her husband as an equal partner. It was Johanna's idea to locate the laundry in Whitneyville, with so many unmarried workers and grubby shirts. Franz agreed and took out a loan to purchase the brick building. Mueller's Laundry flourished until his wife died from the accident, leaving Franz to run the laundry all on his own.

But he lacked his wife's skill. Franz managed the washing, but wielding an iron baffled him. He kept burning collars and front plackets. Besides frying shirts, Franz fell behind, and the workers stopped using his services. Within the year, Mueller's Laundry had failed. Franz regretted not having hired a laundress to replace his wife, but grief had scorched his mind as well. He did not know what to do. The sale of the building would discharge the debt, but he needed work—and some way to care for Henry.

Before Eb and Samuel departed, Eb told Franz Mueller that he might know of an opportunity for him in New Haven. He gave him no details, wanting to discuss the matter first with his uncle. Eb's idea was to hire Franz as their coachman. Franz had handled horses all his life and seemed to be an honorable, responsible man—the perfect person to move into the newly renovated carriage house on Elm Street.

The problem was Henry. While the carriage house was capacious enough for a father and son, Eb's uncle had not expected to take on a motherless five-year-old boy. Henry Mueller needed to be looked after and eventually educated. Someone would have to watch him when Franz was driving the carriage, transporting patients to and from the clinic, or at night for medical emergencies. Dr. Cabot also intended for the carriage to be at Malinda and Susan's disposal. Indisputably, Henry's presence complicated things.

Still, Eb thought, spinning his argument, Henry could become a groomsman. The boy might know nothing about horses now, but Franz could train him. Eb would present them as a package deal—a father and son groomsman-stableboy-farrier-and-carriage driver duo. Taking in an employee's child was not a foreign concept to Eb Wells. That was how Susan Graham had come into his own family.

Mrs. Tittles was a further complication. The calico cat was part of the package deal. Franz Mueller had made that clear. Henry had lost his mother and could not lose Mrs. Tittles too. Eb also understood a cat as a family member. Personally, Mrs. Tittles's presence on Elm Street was more than tolerable for Eb—it was highly desirable. But he had doubts about how a cat would be received. He had been lobbying for a cat for some time, but his uncle was not interested, Malinda opposed, and Esmeralda had a downright aversion to cats, even a fear of them. Eb hoped Mrs. Tittles was a good mouser. That would help his campaign. For now, Mrs. Tittles need not be mentioned.

Samuel Taylor was quiet on the hackney ride home. He was impressed by how readily Franz Mueller had revealed his life story to the men who had just served him with foreclosure papers. But Eb's sincere interest in their welfare had coaxed the wary German out of his shell.

Samuel was also worried. What would Nathan Haines say if he learned Eb had agreed to have tea with the debtor? Or wanted to offer him a job?

Samuel's first instinct was to remind Eb that their client was the bank, not Franz Mueller. But he decided not to. It was not his job to monitor Eb Wells's behavior, and he suspected Eb would just shrug. Besides, Samuel had their friendship to protect—a friendship that meant far more to him than anything Nathan Haines had to offer.

*Letter to Eb Wells from Rebecca Harding, Wethersfield,
March 19, 1821*

Dearest Eb,

Thank you for your letter. I'm always glad to receive news from you. When more than five days go by with no letter, I worry.

How serendipitous the failed laundryman used to be a farrier. He sounds perfect for the job. How does your uncle feel about taking on a five-year-old boy? And how remarkable the Muellers come with a cat. Mrs. Tittles is an odd name. I wonder, Eb, does Mr. Haines know of your assistance to an opposing party? You represent the bank, don't you? Your good-hearted efforts may not be appreciated by your employer. Or your client. Is it possible your eagerness to take on a bankrupt German widower with a five-year-old son is motivated by getting a cat in the bargain? Perhaps it would be easier to hire one of Mr. Lanson's many relatives to drive the carriage—and get a cat of your own?

Mr. Hitchcock and I attended a town hall meeting last night. Our academy students are the children of successful people, doctors, lawyers, and some in trade. But many who live in Wethersfield can't afford to send their children to school. The town is trying to address their needs. Last night, the Committee on Education asked me to give a brief talk on the Lancastrian system, with its use of senior students as instructors for the younger ones. It's far more ambitious than the town leaders were looking for, but the core idea has great merit. I've spoken to you before of Joseph Lancaster, an English Quaker. Both Philadelphia and Baltimore have Lancaster schools now. It's a good way to educate large numbers of students when teaching resources are scarce.

My talk was met with great interest, but without Mr. Hitchcock's support—which I surely won't have—the idea will go nowhere. He didn't appreciate my addressing the Committee. It doesn't matter that I was asked to speak, or perhaps that galls him as well. His reception was chilly this morning. I'm sure The Ogre feels I undermine his authority by speaking in public—a mere woman and tutoress.

I'm trying out a modified version of the monitor model at school. Last week, I pulled my two best students aside, Anna White and Caroline Seymour, for special training. They'll spend one morning next week teaching the younger girls to read. *Qui docet, discit.* He who teaches, learns. (Is that correct? Your Latin is far better than mine.) I anticipated The Ogre's disapproval, so I approached their parents first. Permission was gladly given. Mrs. Seymour wants her daughter to attend a female academy.

I would be shocked if my one-year contract were renewed. Miss Pierce has advised me to look for a school better suited to my talents. So, here I am, one year down the road, seeking employment again. It's a little disheartening. Miss Pierce would take me on next year as an assistant teacher if need be, but that seems like a step backward. I'll be so sad to leave Mrs. Cox and the Johnsons. Penny is marrying her doctor this May. Our friend Elizabeth Stafford will be traveling to Wethersfield for the wedding and to visit her grandmother. I worry about her romance with this Mr. Townsend, but Lizzie refuses to heed our warnings.

Martha's suspicions were right. Thomas Bradford and Katherine are walking out with one another. It rankles me that a year and a half ago, Katherine dismissed him as unworthy, but now that Thomas is doing so well in law school, her interest is piqued. She's predictable, if nothing else. I told you Oliver Hull would never move to the South. When does Thomas leave to join your brother's law practice?

I must go and prepare for class. So glad Ned Haines will be back next week. Perhaps he should get better control of his office. To my mind, Haines & Haines needs, at a minimum, to hire another scrivener, to free up his apprentices to do the work you were hired for. That's what I think. Otherwise, your apprenticeship is hardly worth it.

Be well. I'll write later.

Yours with affection,

Rebecca

Eb had been at Haines & Haines long enough to learn about drafting contracts and wills, executing deeds, filing lawsuits, and complying with notice provisions. Nathan also invited the two apprentices to sit in on appointments, teaching them how to handle a client's expectations and justify legal fees. When Ned Haines was in the office, the two apprentices received substantive instruction. Rebecca's judgment was too harsh. Despite a surplus of scrivener's work and serving notices, no one could fairly say the apprenticeship was 'not worth it.' But Eb Wells was bored.

Teaching helped to combat his boredom. Eb got the idea from Samuel Taylor. While copying a lease for a client who was renting warehouse storage space, Samuel asked Eb how an 'Act of God' clause worked. Eb took to the law library. The next day, he lectured on the subject while Samuel took notes. Before long, Oliver joined them, and because the Redfield brothers arrived at the office together, Ted sat and listened, the sound of Eb's professorial voice lulling him to sleep.

Once Eb dug into the 'Act of God' research, he began to wonder where God's work ended, and a tenant's began. If lightning struck the warehouse and it burned down, that was obviously God's work—the tenant could break the lease. But what if the tenant carelessly stored flammable materials in the landlord's warehouse? God may have struck the first match with the lightning, but had he planned on such a huge conflagration?

Eb shuddered, remembering the Savannah fire. God had set the stage for that fire, with months of no rain and a high northwest wind. But when the small fire reached Market Square and encountered kegs of gunpowder, illegally stored in a warehouse, two explosions spread the fire all over town. God had created the conditions for the fire. God had started the small fire. But the tenant's carelessness in storing explosives was responsible for the scope of the fire, in that instance, for burning Savannah to the ground. Even a boilerplate 'Act of God' provision was rife with issues of causation—the kind of legal puzzle Eb Wells loved.

Eb's tutoring became a regular event, three times a week before the law office opened. He would choose a legal issue from the firm's practice and deliver a lecture on how the law worked, its history, and a critique. His lectures took effort, three hours of preparation for each hour of instruction. Eb waited until Nathan left the office to hunker down in the law library, a place he was happy to be. Since both apprentices had keys to the office, Eb often locked up.

Preparing for these lectures kept his mind active. The topics arose out of the practice of law, a far more dynamic environment than sitting in Tapping Reeve's law school, copying watered-down *Blackstone*. Teaching was intellectually stimulating—unlike most of the work at Haines & Haines. Eb rebelled against the nitty-gritty of law practice. He did not want to be staring at the ceiling at night, wondering which writ to file, how many days he had to appeal, or how to rustle up enough witnesses for the execution of a will.

Neither the questions nor the answers interested him. They represented the nuts and bolts of law practice, things every attorney needed to know. But Eb resented these niggling procedural minutiae. They intruded on his thoughts, clogged up his brain, and kept him from thinking about ideas. Eb wanted someone else to take care of the details. Someone steady and competent, like Ted Redfield. He wanted to be freed up to do what he liked to do—read, think, analyze, criticize, teach, daydream. And now to write.

Writing the article was also Samuel's idea. After their trip to Whitneyville, he urged Eb to commit his thoughts on Connecticut's Debt Recovery Act to writing. Eb was reluctant. His ideas were not original. Everything he had told Samuel on the hackney ride could be found in *Blackstone*—with some extrapolation to Connecticut. Samuel disagreed. Eb's originality was his ability to explain the law to others—its history, rationale, and in this instance, its unjustness.

Samuel Taylor read Eb's first draft, scrawled on six pages of *The Detritus*, and handed it back to him. Start from scratch, Samuel advised. What Eb had written was technically correct, but inaccessible. It sounded like an answer to an oral exam at the Litchfield Law School. Samuel understood it, but someone unfamiliar with the law would not. Aim to educate a layman, but be technically precise. Rewrite the article as if an interested, ignorant person were reading it—someone like your sister. Samuel rushed to clarify that he meant 'ignorant' in the Latin sense, as in 'not knowing.' He did not want to suggest Malinda Wells was ignorant. But she might be unfamiliar with the difference between real and personal property or what 'collateral' meant. Perhaps Samuel underestimated Malinda's grasp of legal language, but Eb understood his point. Samuel's other suggestion was to interject some human interest. While Franz Mueller's case was off-limits, Eb could craft a story about a hypothetical debtor who had fallen on hard times—something to bring the injustice alive. Eb grumbled but complied.

The second draft, Samuel insisted, was better, but too long-winded. Whittle it down. With each new unit of thought, insert a topic sentence. Write an introduction and a conclusion. Promise Malinda upfront what you are going to do, and then keep your promise. Eb grumbled even more. Unaccustomed to criticism, he secretly took pride in his writing, but he grudgingly accepted Samuel's authority over his prose. Writing the introduction caused him to hyperventilate. Topic sentences made his arms itch.

After the third draft, Samuel asked Eb's permission to edit the manuscript one last time. Eb groaned but agreed, and Samuel went quickly to work, cutting out extraneous words, propping up wobbly topic sentences, injecting vigor into the verbs, and adding color to the hypothetical debtor's story, which he moved up to the front. Eb was amazed by the improvement. From here on out, Eb promised himself, I'm going to use an editor.

On April 20, 1821, the New Haven *Connecticut Journal* published an article by Ebenezer Wells with the catchy title, *Debtor Relief Law: The Need for a Homestead Exemption.* The following week, the

Connecticut Courant in Hartford reprinted it. Both newspapers published letters of praise for the article, several from practicing attorneys, a Connecticut state legislator, and one from Judge Tapping Reeve, his mentor. Ned Haines also wrote Eb a personal note, lauding his efforts. Nathan Haines never mentioned the article. Malinda had the newspaper clipping framed.

"I spent a year in the Walnut Street jail." Franz Mueller met with Dr. Cabot and his niece, Malinda Wells, in the library on Elm Street. He sat erect between their wingback chairs on the edge of the rose-colored velvet settee. Esmeralda stood like a statue by the door, listening intently. Franz's son, Henry, leafed through a book Malinda had provided him, sitting on the floor next to the window. It was a gray morning in early spring, and no fire had been lit. The light was murky and dim.

It was Franz's second interview for the coachman's job. Dr. Cabot had met with him the week before and was impressed, but he wanted the approval of Malinda and Esmeralda. He also wanted Malinda to meet Henry. Franz had brought the boy to the first interview, having no one to watch him, and Henry had played quietly in the corner with a set of tiny tin soldiers his father had magically pulled out of his coat pocket. Dr. Cabot had a soft spot for children. It helped that Henry was well-behaved. Franz Mueller treated his son with a loving but firm hand.

Dr. Cabot wanted to explore how Henry might be cared for when Franz drove the carriage. If appropriate, the boy could accompany his father or stay behind in the house. An adult would always be present on Elm Street. When he was older, Henry would have to go to school. For now, Malinda had volunteered that either she or Susan would organize his education. But Dr. Cabot did not want

Henry's presence to burden his household staff. Esmeralda and Mrs. Potts would inevitably absorb some of the Henry-minding. While both women were fond of children, bringing one into the household, even a well-behaved one, was another matter. Mr. and Mrs. Potts had delegated their decision to Esmeralda. It was agreed that Esmeralda would give Malinda some sign at the end of the interview, voting in favor or against hiring Franz Mueller. It went without saying that Malinda too must approve.

Franz was troubled about his insolvency. The proceeds of the laundry's sale would go to the bank and his other creditors. He would start his employment debt-free but penniless. While the salary offered was sufficient, Franz worried about how to pay for Henry's education, having promised his dying wife to send him to a boys' academy. Dr. Cabot offered to revisit the issue next year, hinting that he might help with Henry's tuition. Franz was satisfied. These terms were far more generous than any apprenticeship he could have found for Henry. Besides, the boy was too young to learn a trade. This way, father and son could stay together.

"I assaulted a man in a tavern when I was twenty-one and broke his nose," Franz continued, wanting to lay his cards on the table. "He brought charges, and I was convicted." He looked shyly over at Malinda Wells. Her face was round and pretty, but her dark eyes were sharp and discerning. Franz decided that ignoring this woman was not a good idea, reminding himself to include her. He also suspected the elderly housekeeper was silently assessing him. She stood tall and mute by the door, her hands thrust into the pockets of a starched white apron, a paisley turban on her head, making her look like an African queen. Franz could feel her eyes boring through the side of his head. "I spent a year in jail in Philadelphia." Franz gave a penitent nod. "That's the skeleton in my closet."

"Why did you punch the man?" Malinda asked matter-of-factly.

"Because he insulted my mother," Franz replied. "And truthfully, miss, I was well into my fourth or fifth tankard of ale." He lowered his eyes to the floor, ashamed of his youthful folly. "I've since become quite temperate."

"What did the man say to you that prompted the punch?" Malinda exhibited more curiosity than compassion.

"Pardon my language, miss, but he called my mother a 'German peasant and a whore.'" There was an awkward silence in the room. "My mother grew up on a farm in Bavaria. By all accounts, her own included, she *was* a German peasant." He glanced up at Malinda, stiffening slightly. "But she most certainly was not a whore."

Malinda looked at him sympathetically. She was predisposed to hire Franz Mueller. To her mind, her Uncle Ebenezer was sad and lonely, an opinion ratified by Esmeralda. After his mother's death, he had withdrawn from the world. He dutifully kept up his medical practice, but in the evenings and on Sundays, he was a recluse. Esmeralda had told her how much Dr. Cabot benefited from having Malinda, Susan, and Eb in residence. Adjusting to the noisy chaos of a full house of young adults was a healthy stretch for him. But there was no assurance they would stay forever. The Muellers might bring some energy to the household.

Esmeralda had met Henry at the previous interview. The boy seemed self-contained for a five-year-old, well able to entertain himself. It would be good to have a child around the house again—for all of them. Dr. Cabot had no monopoly on mourning the loss of Mrs. Cabot. And Henry was a sweet boy with unruly hair, knobby knees, and a missing front tooth. More to the point, he was a motherless child. How could they turn him away?

During this second interview, Esmeralda kept her eye on Henry. Sitting on a chair by the window, his blond head bowed, Henry was oblivious to the negotiations. He perused the illustrations in the book Malinda had pulled from the bookshelves. The interview was winding down when Esmeralda realized that Malinda was trying to catch her eye, seeking her opinion. Her face impassive, the elderly woman gave a slight nod. As far as she was concerned, Malinda could hire Franz Mueller.

"I believe you and my uncle have agreed on the terms of the offer already," Malinda said. "My approval was all that was lacking. I'm satisfied." Dr. Cabot smiled, happy that the two women who ran his life supported his decision. "Henry's welcome too. We'll sort out his schooling. Maybe he can learn to groom the horses with you. But I'd like to suggest, Mr. Mueller, that we give your employment here on Elm Street a one year's probation." Dr. Cabot peered over his glasses at his niece but said nothing. "That way, one year from now, we can all frankly assess whether the arrangement is working out."

"That seems fair." It was clear to him who ran this household. Franz smiled to himself. It was a good thing he had been married to a strong, opinionated woman for seven years and was accustomed to feminine direction. Dr. Cabot's niece, and, more than likely, the silent, formidable beturbaned servant at the door, would be his true bosses on Elm Street.

"All right then." Malinda began to gather her skirts, signaling the end of the interview.

"There's one more thing," Franz Mueller added with hesitation. "We have a family cat. I'd like to bring her with us. She'd stay in the carriage house and stable, of course." Henry's ears perked up at the mention of his beloved pet. "She's a good mouser, and horses are afraid of mice." This last nugget of information was a myth, but Franz made the assertion with fabricated authority, banking on the ignorance of Dr. Cabot and Malinda Wells.

"A cat?" Malinda raised her eyebrows. "Did you say a cat?"

"Yes." Franz's voice softened. "The truth is my son Henry's attached to her. He's lost his mother. And his home. Another loss— well, I'd hate for that to happen. She's a biddable cat. You'll never even know she's here." This last nugget of information was a bald-faced lie.

Dr. Cabot and Malinda exchanged a knowing look. The fog was lifting from the bog. Eb had failed to mention the cat, but his sister and uncle understood—with no words being exchanged—that the cat played a major role in bringing the debtor Franz Mueller and his boy to Elm Street. Ever since Eb's arrival in New Haven, he had been lobbying for a cat, a suggestion met with rejection by the entire household—Dr. Cabot, Malinda, Susan, Esmeralda, Mrs. Potts. Cats are not proper pets. A dog, perhaps, but a cat, never. Certainly not in the house. Esmeralda's paisley turban was shivering a perceptible 'no.'

"Please, miss." Henry put the book down, approaching the velvet settee where Franz was seated. He hid timidly behind his father's arm. "We can't come without Mrs. Tittles." His slight lisp was exaggerated from the recent loss of his front tooth. He poked through the crook in his father's arm, peering up at Malinda. Unlike his blue-eyed father, Henry's eyes were dark brown, undoubtedly a legacy from his dead mother, and welling up with tears. Even the practical, businesslike Malinda Wells, who was not at ease around children, could not refuse him.

"Don't you worry, Henry." Malinda's words were clipped but not unkind. "If you promise to keep Mrs. Tittles . . . Is that your cat's name?" Henry nodded, still clinging to his father's arm. "Well, then, if you promise to keep Mrs. Tittles in the carriage house and the stable, you may bring her with you." Esmeralda's shoulders sagged perceptibly. She could not compete with a lisping boy with tears ready to roll down a soft, downy cheek. The cat was coming to Elm Street too.

"I promise, miss," Henry lisped. Franz Mueller looked visibly relieved. Henry tugged on his father's sleeve and whispered audibly, "Papa, I need to use the privy."

"I'll take you, son." Esmeralda approached the settee, stooping over to offer the boy her weathered hand. "We'll make a trip out back to the privy first, and then you must come into the kitchen to meet Mrs. Potts. She might have a cookie for you."

"A cookie?" Henry's face lit up. "What kind?"

"Molasses." Esmeralda led the boy out of the room. "At least that's what my nose is telling me."

Letter to Martha Lewis from Rebecca Harding, Wethersfield, April 2, 1821

Dear Martha,

This is great news about your brother's engagement! Did you see this coming? What do you think of Miss Hannah Ward? She's from Kent? Did Jack meet her through the brothers' grocery connection? What does your mother say? I'm full of questions. Jack's certainly of an age to marry. I hope he doesn't quit the studio. Charles and your father can't manage without him. I'm having a hard time thinking of Jack Lewis as a married man! Please tell me all.

So, two more maps in the competition? I can't wait to see the one of Litchfield. I hope you'll find an outlet for your artistic abilities when you leave school. Perhaps your father's studio could expand 'portrait' to include a geographic portrait of one's county, state, river, or woods.

I've started to look for a new position. The Ogre is even more insufferable since I spoke at the town hall meeting. He called me into his office and told me it was 'presumptuous and promiscuous' of me to speak in public before an audience of mostly men. I reminded him that the Committee on Education had requested my presentation, which did nothing to dilute his ire. It's hard to go to work each day, knowing that my headmaster hates me. If it weren't for my students—and I do love them—I'm not sure I could stick it out.

This attitude of The Ogre—he's not alone in his beliefs—infuriates me, Martha. What's the good of educating women if we're only allowed to speak up at home? I understand we must play a role in educating the nation's citizens. I stand wholeheartedly behind Mrs. Willard's views and those of other enlightened female educators. But a woman should feel free to speak in a public arena, particularly when she's been asked to. The Ogre makes me fume. I'm looking for work—again.

One teaching position is at the Morris Academy. You may remember that I applied there last spring. Since then, its founder, James Morris, has died. Miss Pierce writes that he was starting home from a trustees' meeting of his Mission School in Cornwall and felt an attack of his 'strangury' coming on. He knocked on the door of a friend and announced he had 'come to die under his roof.' A few hours later, he did! Imagine how his friend must have felt, Martha, to open his door to an uninvited guest whose stated purpose was to drop dead—and then who followed through.

As you know, schools often don't survive the deaths of their founders, but Mr. Morris had the foresight to marry Rhoda Farnam, a second wife, thirty years his junior, once the head of the Ladies' Department. Mrs. Morris has stepped into his role quite seamlessly. Miss Pierce is her friend and reports that she is hiring teachers for next year. Miss Pierce has put my name forward. I fear The Ogre will give me a scathing review. Still, his desire to be rid of me may inspire him to wax eloquent on my behalf. The parents at the Wethersfield Academy who support me, and there are quite a few, have offered to write letters of recommendation on my behalf. Maybe those will outweigh any invective from The Ogre.

I've mixed feelings about the Morris Academy. It's co-educational. But South Farms is close to you and your family, Charles, and my friends at Miss Pierce's. I'd still be far away from Eb, but away is away. Catharine Beecher wants to start her own female academy, perhaps in Hartford, but lacks funding. Miss Pierce predicts I might someday work with Catharine, but her school has yet to come to fruition. The same is true of Mrs. Willard's in Troy, New York.

I hear from Eb often. I moan and groan about The Ogre. He does the same about copying too many documents. He's been lecturing to Samuel and Oliver in the morning and is working on a second article. I credit this Samuel Taylor for inspiring Eb to write—more importantly, to rewrite. I used to beg Eb to edit his prose, but nagging comes better from a respected colleague. And no, Martha, our letters have not increased in heat or passion, but we're coming to know each other better. That counts for something.

You ask about Lizzie. She doesn't write often, which worries me. I fear she's avoiding mention of her beau. She has given her heart to this Samuel Townsend, who is inconstant and disinclined to choose a profession. Her mother and I are both concerned, as is Mrs. Cox.

I must go. I'm tutoring Caroline and Anna on math pedagogy this afternoon. The experiment with the reading lessons for the younger girls was a great success.

Keep me posted on Katherine and Thomas, and send details about Jack's engagement. Eb will want to know about both as well. Send my love to your family. I miss you!

Yours affectionately,

Rebecca

"Your father and I shared this tiny attic room at Rufus Henderson's." Ned Haines was holding forth to Malinda, Eb, and Samuel in the Elm Street dining room. The stars had finally aligned, and the supper party for the employees of Haines & Haines transpired. As host, Dr. Cabot sat at the foot of the table, and as hostess,

Malinda reigned supreme at its head, Ned Haines to her right, Eb to her left, Samuel Taylor next to Eb, and Susan, Nathan Haines, and the two Redfield brothers distributed on either side. Esmeralda silently moved in and out of the room, removing plates, bringing hot rolls. She wore her black serving dress, brought out for the occasion, with a stiff white apron, her turban replaced by a crisp white hat.

The white linen tablecloth and napkins were also on display, along with Mrs. Cabot's best silver and crystal. The table was laden with plates of food prepared by Mrs. Potts—a pork roast, a meat pie, sweet potatoes mashed in butter and brown sugar, roasted red potatoes, beets, sweet corn, and pickles. Everything glimmered from the candles in the two pewter candelabras at either end of the table. For a centerpiece, a vase of pink Japanese cherry blossoms nestled among the dishes, severed from the tree in front that was blooming.

It was a chilly evening in early April. Both Susan and Malinda wore short-sleeved empire dresses and light woolen paisley shawls. The event had taken several months to pull off due to Ned Haines's busy schedule. After his last arbitration in Albany, Ned promised Nathan he would stay put in New Haven until the end of the summer. The law practice was overflowing with work, and Nathan was stressed. Ned's younger son from his second marriage, Eddie, just seven years old, also suffered from his father's absences.

"I wouldn't have survived the apprenticeship without William Wells." Ned continued to regale Malinda, Eb, and Samuel. "It was your father who set our course of study, not Rufus Henderson. Will used to give me short lectures on the law. I'd sit at the dilapidated little desk we shared up in the attic and take notes." Ned Haines put his glass of wine down on the table. "Your father was a gifted teacher."

"He was?" Eb had never heard this before. He was afraid to make eye contact with the other two. At the other end of the table, the Redfield brothers were jousting with Susan Graham over whether a woman could be a scrivener. Having a good hand herself, Susan mounted a spirited defense on behalf of her gender. None of them heard what Ned Haines said about his father being a gifted teacher. Only Samuel and Malinda.

Eb found himself unexpectedly moved. For his entire life, he had never manifested a single desirable trait of his father's. Family lore maintained that his older brother had fallen heir to all of William Wells's sterling attributes. Eb was an inferior version of what a Wells male should be. His traits came solely from his mother's side—his short stature, his nearsightedness, his interest in books and Latin, his love of birds and flowers, and his impractical nature. Secretly, Eb used to wonder if William Wells really *was* his father. Hearing that his father used to give law lectures to another apprentice—something Eb secretly did now at Haines & Haines—filled him with unexpected pride.

"Attorney Henderson didn't give us the time of day," Ned Haines continued, "but Will used to read *Blackstone*, synthesize it, and repackage it into something more palatable." Ned smiled, harking back to the halcyon days of his youth. "I envy you going to the Litchfield Law School, Eb," he mused. "I don't know why I didn't send Nathan. It's a much better way to study law. More systematic."

"My father believed the traditional apprenticeship system was woefully lacking," Malinda chimed in. "He always told us so."

"He was right, of course." Ned Haines shook his head. "I feel remiss. You know, about your brother and Samuel." He looked pointedly across the table at Eb and Samuel. "I've been out of the office so much this year. Nathan's been working at such a fevered pitch. It's been hard to find time to instruct you boys."

"They copy documents. A lot, I believe." Malinda lifted her eyebrows in an expression bordering on disdain. Eb was horrified. She was close enough for Eb to give her a swift kick beneath the table, but her gown softened the blow. With a blink, Malinda registered the fraternal protest, but as is often the case with older sisters, she ignored him.

"Well, yes, I believe that's true," Ned Haines admitted. He glanced down the table at Nathan, who was engaged in earnest conversation with Ebenezer Cabot. This gave Ned Haines permission to respond—he could be frank with this disarming young woman. "We've had so much new business this year. The Panic seems to be over. New Haven's shipping has taken off with these new routes to the West Indies. But it means we have too much work. I wasn't expecting that when I took on the arbitrations. It's been tough on Nathan."

"I've learned a lot about the writs from copying them, sir." Eb hoped to steer Malinda away from further criticizing his boss. "Copying's part and parcel of any apprenticeship," he added, almost apologetically.

"And Eb has a good hand." Samuel made this irrelevant comment in a panic to move the conversation to safer ground. He had met Eb's sister for the first time that evening, but her reputation preceded her. It was clear to everyone that Malinda Wells was about to improve someone or something.

Malinda began her proposal. "A business, even a law practice, must be nimble. Responsive. When circumstances change, you must change. Reallocate your resources." She placed her hand gently on the arm of Ned Haines. "Or so it seems to me, Mr. Haines." Ned Haines adjusted his glasses. He appeared startled—and pleased—by the unexpected touch of a feminine hand. "Perhaps your law practice needs to hire more scriveners. One, at least. Or even two?"

"You think so, Miss Wells?" Ned inquired. Esmeralda appeared silently at his elbow, bearing a sterling silver bread dish full of hot rolls. He took one. "Tell me more."

"What matters most is what *you* think, Mr. Haines." Malinda flashed him a dazzling smile. Even her mortified brother thought so.

Eb was always in awe when Malinda turned on the Southern charm. "You've said so yourself. You worry that Eb and Samuel are copying too much, and with your absences, your managing partner is buried in work. You admit there's too much work for the current staff to handle." Malinda watched Ned tear off a bit of his roll and butter it. "Isn't that a wonderful thing, Mr. Haines?" Malinda spoke his name in her most honeyed, Southern intonations. "To need more staff because your law practice has too much work?" With a sideways glance, she gave him another smile, this one more private. "That's the price you pay for being so successful."

"Yes, well, I suppose so," Mr. Haines said, his face coloring slightly. "We've done well, thanks to Nathan."

"I hear you're a skilled arbitrator." Malinda continued to lay it on thick. "Do you like the work?"

"I do," Ned Haines replied. "It's new for me. Arbitration has kept me occupied since the death of my wife."

"I'm so sorry for your loss," Malinda said demurely, lowering her eyes. She again moved her hand over to Ned Haines's arm and exerted a warm squeeze, letting her hand linger for a few seconds before discreetly removing it. "That must have been hard on you, with your younger son only five at the time." Malinda let out a delicate sigh. "Eb and I lost our mother too. Last summer. To yellow fever."

"Yes, Eb told me. I too am sorry for your loss."

"What was your mother like?" Malinda leaned over slightly in Ned's direction, close enough for him to catch a whiff of—what was it? Lilacs? Or lavender? For the next few minutes, Ned Haines extolled the virtues of Anne Hubbard Haines, who had been in her grave since 1790. Malinda, Eb, and Samuel listened to tales of her many lost children, her strength of character, the way she made Ned feel better about the way his ears stuck out. Eb tried to imagine what a little Ned Haines might have looked like in the Connecticut colony before the war, with sugar bowl ears, pulling on his mother's apron strings. He must have outgrown those ears, Eb thought. Sitting across from him—this distinguished gentleman of almost sixty, with silver hair and matching glasses, trim and erect, dressed in a well-tailored black suit and brocade vest, his ears well-positioned on either side of his head—Eb's imagination failed him.

The rest of the evening went smoothly. His sister—much to Eb's immense relief—did not try to improve Haines & Haines with any more unsolicited advice. Malinda Wells had an innate sense of when to speak up, when to retreat, and when to ask a man about his mother. Dessert was served. Mrs. Potts had outdone herself—two hot fruit pies, one cherry, and one apple, with fresh whipped cream to put on top. Everyone sampled both.

Coffee, tea, and hot chocolate were also served at the end of the supper. The hot chocolate was a new recipe for Mrs. Potts. Everyone speculated about what spices she might have added. Cinnamon and cloves, surely. But nutmeg? Ned Haines thought he tasted vanilla. Ted Redfield came out of his shell to insist the brew contained the slightest hint of chili. He had needed a dollop of fresh cream on top to cool his mouth.

Dr. Cabot perused the smiling faces at his dinner table. He listened to the knives and forks clinking on the porcelain plates, Esmeralda's soft pattering around the table, the idle chatter about the cool weather, the blooming jonquils and forsythia, the economy, the carriage on order, the new coachman, the clinic, the law office, and mothers of yore. He was pleased to see his old friend Ned Haines again, to make the acquaintance of his son, Nathan, and to meet the young men Eb worked with in the scriveners' room. The soft light of the candles made everyone look well-fed, happy, and healthy. Dr. Cabot patted himself on the back. *My idea for a supper party was a good one, although he missed his mother.*

Dr. Cabot gazed down at his niece, sitting upright, surveying the table, making sure everyone was served each kind of pie, helping Esmeralda take orders for coffee, tea, or more hot chocolate. Malinda's doing an excellent job at playing hostess, Dr. Cabot thought. She looks so much like her mother. He felt another pang of sadness. He would never see his younger sister again. Abigail Cabot Wells would be so proud of her daughter. To see how beautiful, how poised, how competent she was at the head of his table. And charming. Ned Haines seemed to be enjoying her company.

"That's just how my sister is," Eb explained to Samuel Taylor in the law office the next morning. The two young men were engaged in a postmortem of the evening before, the Redfield brothers not having yet arrived. "I apologize. Malinda can't keep her nose out of other people's business."

"It's fine, Eb." Samuel smiled, thinking Eb might be the pot calling the kettle black. "I had a great time. It's the best meal I've had since leaving home. And I was happy to meet your family, to see the house on Elm Street. It's far grander than any home I've ever set foot in. The silver service, the crystal glasses, the white linen, the way that imposing Esmeralda magically appeared at my elbow with another hot roll."

"I'm glad you enjoyed yourself." Eb smiled at Samuel, remembering when he too was in awe of the elegance on Elm Street, something he now took for granted. "But I apologize for my sister. There's no stopping her. I was worried she'd go further."

"Not to worry," Samuel replied. "We both know—you can't control sisters. The thing of it is, Malinda was right on the mark about the office. Hiring a new scrivener is just what we need."

"Of course she was." Eb let out a long sigh. As her younger brother, Eb had been on the other end of Malinda Wells being 'right on the mark' all his life. It could be tiring.

"And that Susan Graham. She's a beauty," Samuel said slyly, looking across the scrivener's table at Eb. "You failed to mention that to me altogether."

"Well, I suppose she is." Eb blushed, not knowing what to say. His shyness around his old playmate had not abated. He had managed to cope with Susan Graham, and his uncomfortable feelings for her, by avoiding them altogether.

"Do you think she's more beautiful than your Miss Harding?" Ever since the night they had shared a rickety bed in the tavern, stranded by a snowstorm, Samuel and Eb had shared confidences.

"She has a different kind of beauty," Eb replied honestly, hoping the heightened color in his face had drained. "Rebecca's a smaller woman, with less physical vitality than Susan. Her face too is paler, more angular, but more classically beautiful than Susan's." Eb brought his analytic abilities to bear. "I've always told my friend Charles—Rebecca favors a male Dark-eyed Junco. Surely her beauty's more understated," he added awkwardly, "but I might not be the best judge."

"Well," Samuel confided, "Elizabeth Wainwright's face wasn't 'classically beautiful,' but it used to buckle my knees. How you feel about a woman colors your assessment of her beauty."

"I suppose that's true." The real problem was that Eb did not know how he felt about Rebecca Harding. Or Susan Graham, for that matter.

The two Redfield brothers burst into the room, expressing appreciation for the supper party, how much fun it had been, and how good the food was. The quartet chatted noisily for a few minutes, their sentences trespassing on one another's, disputing whether Mrs. Potts's apple pie was better than her cherry. Once again, the gentle giant Ted Redfield had an unexpectedly firm and vocal opinion on the matter. Eb was on the verge of mounting a vigorous defense of the liberal use of cinnamon in an apple pie when they heard the front door to the law office open and close with a decisive thud.

Nathan Haines was on the premises. Time to get to work.

The week following the supper party on Elm Street, the senior partner of Haines & Haines trudged daily from his home on Chapel Street to the law office on Fleet Street. Ned Haines put in long hours, helping Nathan catch up and plowing through a backlog of correspondence. Ted Redfield sat across the desk from him, taking meticulous notes.

Back in the scriveners' room, Ted tacked a parchment onto the wall on which he had written a long list of Ned Haines's stock phrases. These Ted used when answering letters. 'I am in receipt of your letter of _________ regarding __________.' 'We are in accord that _________.' 'I beg to differ with you on one point, however. It appears to me that ____________.' 'My client is willing to ____________.' 'My client refuses to ____________.' 'It is my hope that we can reach an amicable and mutually satisfactory disposition of this matter.' 'If we cannot reach agreement on this matter, my client will have no choice but to litigate.' 'Please send me the following _________ posthaste.' 'Please note that your bill for last month's services is now past due.' 'Please give my warm regards _________ (to your family).' The list went on and on.

Answering correspondence was repetitive. The letters all fell into distinct bins in Ted Redfield's mind. Collecting debts, drafting a lease, negotiating a contract, writing a will, threatening litigation, seeking payment for legal services. Ned would communicate the substance of what he had to say while Ted took notes. From his stock of 'Ned Haines' phrases, Ted would craft a response. Later in the day, Ned reviewed the letters, signed most of them, and sent back a few for correction or expansion. Together, the two men worked through a mountain of correspondence. When Ned asked Ted how he managed to condense his thoughts into just a few sentences, Ted replied with a grin, "I'm the one who must copy the letter, so I like to keep them short."

But for Ned, correspondence was tedious. It was also physically demanding. At fifty-nine, sitting at his desk, hour after hour, was difficult. His lower back ached, his toes felt imprisoned in his boots, and his right knee needed oiling. He felt like an old man. Ned also missed his work in upstate New York. Arbitrations were exciting and intense. They required him to listen closely, make judgments on the spot, and respond to unpredictable situations with no script in hand. Answering mail at Haines & Haines was not exciting and intense. It was dull.

After Ted Redfield had taken notes on the letters, Ned Haines would swivel his chair around, stretch his legs, and daydream about Malinda Wells. He could not get Eb's sister out of his mind. He was held hostage by the image of Malinda sitting at the head of the table on Elm Street, dressed in a gray nubby silk dress, her hair neatly captured in a bun, her gold necklace sparkling in the candlelight on her smooth white neck, her paisley shawl, almost diaphanous, wrapped around her firm arms that seemed carved from alabaster, the graceful manner she orchestrated the meal, her lulling Southern accent. Malinda Wells was quite lovely. Why should he not invite her out?

Ned knew the answer. He was too old for her, the same age her father would have been had he not died of malaria. Ned had also been married and widowed twice. Each of his wives had given him a son, almost three decades apart. Ned was in law practice with his older son, Nathan, but his younger son, Edward Jr., was just seven years old. A leftover, grieving boy could be regarded as a liability, Ned knew. Some might also claim he had a bad track record with wives.

The first Mrs. Haines died of consumption. Ned Haines had loved her—surely, he must have, although he did not remember. Their relations were dutiful and cordial, not vexed with the heat of passion. The marriage had been more of an alliance of two wealthy New Haven families than a romance. They were of an age. She was in the market for a suitable husband when Ned was in the market for a suitable wife. Their backgrounds matched. Both attended the right schools and the right church, and their doting parents egged them on. So, they married, set up housekeeping in a solid two-story brick house on Chapel Street, and promptly produced Nathan, their one and only child. The first Mrs. Haines was fiercely loyal to Ned, supporting him in their family life and his work. They had been married for more than twenty years when she died in 1808. Nathan had already graduated from Yale and was apprenticing with another law office. Ned mourned her death as if he had lost his best friend, which he had.

Then, in 1812, Ned Haines married again. His second wife, Fanny, embodied youth and vitality. Only a few years older than Nathan, the second Mrs. Haines was in possession of a gorgeous smile that revealed a set of brilliant, straight, ivory teeth. She had a long, handsome face, a head of luxurious dark blonde hair, her small white breasts much on display from the necklines of her empire waist dresses. She laughed easily and often. Fanny's sexual allure was like a magnet to the repressed metal of Ned Haines, a much older, wealthier man who could offer her a home, social status, and perhaps a baby. At thirty, Fanny was a reluctant spinster.

The couple met at a supper party, not unlike the evening Ned had just spent on Elm Street. Ned fell hopelessly—and later, he wondered, foolishly—in love with Fanny. She was intelligent enough but utterly lacking in depth. Her education at a fashionable school for girls had not taken hold, except in the ornamental arts. Fanny doggedly cranked out one pillow slipcover annually, embroidered with daisies one year, roses the next. She looked lovely, sitting by the fire, her embroidery hoop balanced between her well-manicured hands. She could also play at least five pieces on the piano and was an excellent dancer. Her greatest appeal for Ned when he first met her—then almost fifty—was how young he felt to have Fanny on his arm. Right after their marriage, Ned was ecstatic over sharing a bed with her, a luxury he had never experienced before. That ecstasy lasted for the honeymoon period and then lapsed into something more akin to a pleasurable routine.

As time wore on, Ned Haines had to acknowledge, if only to himself, that his new wife was not that interesting. Fanny had no curiosity. She read little. She found politics boring. She did not keep up with current affairs and showed no interest in the work at Haines & Haines. If Ned and Nathan were discussing a complicated case, Fanny would excuse herself from the room. She refused to learn even the most basic terms to keep up with their legal banter. And while Fanny possessed a giddy quality—she still laughed easily and often—his jokes often whizzed right by her.

With no politics, no current events, no books, no problems at Haines & Haines to mull over, the couple had little to talk about. Ned sought out intellectual stimulation at the Unitarian Church he had just joined. Oddly enough, he still missed his first wife. While he may have felt no passion for her, she was always interested in his work and sometimes made helpful suggestions. His first wife also read aloud to him each night by the fire, mostly novels. They had been reading *The History of Tom Jones, a Foundling*, in her final illness. Because she was so weak at the end, Ned had to read while she lay gravely ill, upstairs in bed. Ned often privately yearned for his first marriage during the early period of Fanny's reign. Marrying a woman who did not read had been a grave mistake. He would never do that again.

But things improved between Ned and Fanny after Edward was

born. Their mutual affection for the boy provided them with a hook to hang their conversations on. Ned took greater delight in his second son than the first time around. He barely remembered what Nathan was like as a baby. Ned had been a young father, too busy establishing a law practice to notice the daily, minute changes that happened to a newly minted human being. But coming home each night to Fanny's infectious enthusiasm, her daily commentary on Eddie's every smile, his every gurgle, his every mangled word, made Ned happy. Eddie became the center of their domestic universe, and Ned came to love Fanny in a new way. When she died in childbirth, his grief was genuine. The baby, a girl, had not survived either. For a fleeting moment, Ned had cradled his dead daughter in his arms, swaddled in a white cloth, a perfectly formed, perfectly still, light blue baby doll. She was buried with her mother.

But what about this Malinda Wells? She was a different creature from Fanny altogether. She held herself upright with a resolute confidence, perhaps even an austerity, that Ned was both drawn to, and slightly afraid of. When Malinda spoke, she chose her words with care. She seemed fluent in legal language and knowledgeable about her brother Eb's work. She was savvy enough to deftly critique his article on the 'Act of God' clause in leases, forcing perceptible steam to pour out of her younger brother's ears. Eb, Malinda, and Samuel had quibbled over whether it was pretentious to include a Latin phrase such as *'Actus Dei nemini facit injuriam'* in a newspaper article. The author and his editor argued it was not, but Malinda had stood her ground.

And Malinda Wells was a reader, keeping up with current events. She could talk about the books of Fielding and Goldsmith, the new canal, the uptick in shipping with the West Indies, the debate on the Missouri Compromise, the secession of Maine from Massachusetts, the Latin root of the word 'delicious' with respect to Mrs. Potts's pies, and why she did not approve of this new word, 'scrumptious.'

All these topics, she could hold forth on. Best of all, her observations came wrapped in a velvety Southern accent that mesmerized Ned Haines. Eb's accent had become diluted from having been up north for a while, but his sister—she still sounded like a proper Southern belle. He liked it.

It puzzled Ned Haines. How could Malinda Wells be so sharp without the benefit of any formal education? He knew nothing about the lack of educational opportunities for women in the South during Malinda's youth. William Wells was not financially able, or perhaps not inclined, to spend the money to send his daughter up north to a female academy. Ned Haines was a much richer man than Malinda's father, and people who have a lot of money often cannot imagine the lives of those who do not.

Ned Haines was also unaware of Malinda's exposure in the schoolroom on East York Street to the many tutors in mathematics, rhetoric, and Greek, engaged to ensure Eb did not flunk out of the boys' academy. Most importantly, Ned had never met her mother. If he had known Abigail Cabot Wells, Ned would have appreciated how many years under her tutelage might produce a young woman with a wide range of interests and an ambitious vocabulary. An educated woman who read books and newspapers and understood the law.

Why should Malinda Wells not accept his invitation? Standing in his dressing room, getting ready for bed, Ned peered into the mirror. He knew of other young women who had walked out with men the same age as their fathers. After all, Fanny had married one. Given the risks of childbirth, these May–December couples were not unheard of in their social milieu. He was a man of wealth and status, after all. Was their age difference such a barrier?

"Certainly not," Ned Haines said aloud to no one, scrutinizing his image in the dressing room mirror. "I'm aging better than my old friend Ebenezer, who's thick around the middle and bald." He sniggered. "Although Ebenezer's got more hair than poor Nathan." Ned smoothed his own hair with satisfaction. "Mine's still full, but silver. Some would call that distinguished." Ned turned to the side and contemplated his profile. "I'm fit and trim." He leaned toward the mirror and patted his face. "I might still lay claim to being handsome." Ned nodded to his reflection with approval.

The next morning, Ned Haines wrote a note to Malinda Wells—not one drafted by Ted Redfield, but in his own hand—inquiring whether she would like to join him on a carriage ride the following Sunday afternoon. If she sent a reply with a polite 'no, thank you,' he would have his answer. If Malinda believed he was too old for her, the matter would be quashed in a quiet, dignified fashion. Ned reached for his nightshirt, humming to himself. Nothing ventured, nothing gained.

"We never talk anymore." It was a late April evening, two weeks after the party. Eb Wells and Susan Graham found themselves unexpectedly alone in the library. During supper, Dr. Cabot and Malinda had been notified of an emergency, an elderly patient who thought she was having a heart attack. Franz Mueller had scurried across the Green to rent one of William Lanson's carriages and a couple of horses. Franz and Henry had already moved into the carriage house, but the new carriage was on order, the horses not yet purchased.

This was Franz Mueller's first emergency call. He left Henry sipping hot cocoa at the kitchen table while Esmeralda and Mrs. Potts washed dishes. The patient was a demure spinster who lived alone, and Dr. Cabot thought she would feel more comfortable if a female assistant accompanied him. Malinda had volunteered, leaving Eb and Susan alone in the library. Eb saw no way to flee without giving offense.

"I don't know why, but you've been avoiding me." Susan peered out from behind her paisley shawl, which she had drawn across her face. She was curled up in Dr. Cabot's wingback chair, her long legs dangling over the arm. Her light brown hair was casually thrown up on top of her head, held captive by a single tortoiseshell comb. Even though it was April, the house was still chilly, and Mr. Potts had made a fire for them in the library. "And you've been ignoring me," she added.

"I am most certainly not avoiding you," Eb retorted, hanging on to his book. "I've just been busy at work." He could think of nothing else to say. He *had* been avoiding Susan since early December but would not admit to that. The 'ignoring' part of her indictment depended on one's point of view, he supposed. In some ways, Eb had never paid so much attention to Susan Graham, although she would have no way of knowing that. "And I'm not ignoring you either."

"You're prevaricating, Eb." Susan gave him her crooked smile. 'Prevaricate' was a favorite vocabulary word they used to bandy about in the schoolroom on East York Street, along with 'mendacity.' Eb returned a fleeting smile in recognition of their shared history. "It makes me sad." Susan had waited weeks for this conversation. Their estrangement upset her. Eb was her oldest friend. She had missed him during the last two years when he was up in Litchfield, and she had practically memorized his letters home. "I know people grow apart, but this is something else. Ever since you arrived in December, you've barely even spoken to me."

"That's ridiculous." Eb feigned exasperation, but his heart pounded in his chest. "We eat breakfast and supper together every day. We talk about the weather, the news, the clinic, my work— you know, all the things going on. And we share this fire in the library almost every evening." He gestured to the fire with a sweep of his hand. "We speak all the time. And as for avoiding you, it's impossible to avoid anyone in this household. We live in such close quarters." This was not true. The house on Elm Street was large, with many nooks and crannies. "Besides, Susan, I'm at work most of the time. How could I be ignoring you?"

"Oh, come on." Susan sounded aggrieved. "I'm talking about when you're here on Elm Street. Sure, we eat meals together and sit by the fire. And yes, I'm included in general conversations, but you never speak directly to me. You address yourself to Malinda, or to Dr. Cabot, even Esmeralda and Mrs. Potts. Everyone but me. You don't even look at me." Susan lowered the paisley shawl from around her face. "You know I'm telling the truth, Eb Wells."

"I don't accept that," Eb stammered. "I don't know what you're talking about."

"All right then, when was the last time you asked me a question?" Susan swung her legs off the arm of the chair and leaned forward. "You could just ask me how I was doing," she began. "How are things going in the clinic, Susan? How do you like following Malinda around all day, with nothing of your own to do? Or how about asking me about my mother? How's Lottie, Susan? Are you missing her too much? How about your own mother?" Susan shook her head in disbelief. "We've never even talked about your mother's death, Eb. It was terrible. I was with her then. Malinda and I never left her side. I still miss her so much." She was silent for a while, staring studiously at the fire, regaining her composure. Eb was tense, his fingers frozen around his book, not knowing what to say.

Finally, Susan started up again, her voice with an edge of protective sarcasm. "Really, it's not so hard, Eb. You could have looked at me, just once, and asked, 'How are things going?' Four words. That's all you needed to say. Five months, and not a single question addressed to me. I know everything about you. All about your work, your friends, your writing, your frustrations with the law, and Haines & Haines. I even know everything about Rebecca Harding." Susan was almost done with her indictment, but her sarcasm had faded. "But you know nothing about me. You could have asked me something. Anything." Her voice now sounded both angry and hurt. "I can only assume you don't care." She leaned back, lifted her feet off the floor and into the air, and folded herself back into the chair.

"That's ridiculous," Eb retorted. "Of course, I care how you're doing." He glanced over at her, curled up in the chair. The light from the fire lit up her familiar face, and he let himself linger there for a moment, her long nose that turned up slightly at the tip, her wide mouth that was currently unsmiling. Even in her mad—and sad—incarnation, she looked beautiful to him. Another long, awkward silence followed. Eb too averted his gaze to the fire. He knew she was right. He deeply regretted having diminished her. Still, Eb had no idea how to continue this conversation. No matter which direction he headed in, he was going to screw things up.

Eb took in a deep, deliberate breath. "So, how are you doing?" His voice wobbled.

No answer from Susan.

"Are you missing your mother?" Eb plodded on with a warranted sense of doom. It had never crossed his mind that Susan might be missing her mother. And why wouldn't she be? After all, he missed his own mother. Eb felt a rush of shame. Susan was grieving the loss of Abigail Wells too. His mother had helped raise Susan since she was a toddler, and Susan had been by her bedside when his mother was dying, something Eb was unable to do. He realized something else shameful—a more global culpability. For months, he had been tied in such a knot over his feelings for Susan Graham. Not once had he ever thought to ask her how she might be feeling.

Eb wondered if Charles would accuse him of 'objectifying Susan.' All those winter nights, he had thrashed around in his bed, trapped in a tangle of sheets, tortured by thoughts of her. And what were those thoughts? Eb cringed. Those thoughts had been mostly about her mane of hair, the taupe color of her wide mouth, her smooth, soft skin, the outline of her legs beneath her skirt. He had been thinking about Susan's body.

Eb Wells considered himself a kind and good man—a judgment shared by almost everyone. But he did not like the widening gap between the kind and good man he believed himself to be—or at least aspired to—and his recent behavior toward Susan Graham. Somehow, Susan herself had gotten lost in the middle of his obsession with her. He had another dismaying flicker of insight. Being obsessed with a woman was not about the woman at all. It was all about him.

"I don't feel like talking about it." Susan pulled her shawl back up to hide the bottom of her face. "Not if I need to prod you with a hot poker to talk to me." She pulled out a book from under her shawl and opened it. "I'm going to read now," she said, bringing the conversation to a resounding close. There would be no appealing her decision. She had regained her composure and shut the door to her heart. "I hereby relieve you of the burden of having to talk to me."

"Yes, well, all right," Eb muttered. He picked up the book on his lap and ran his finger across the leather binding. "I am sorry, Susan," Eb said in almost a whisper, not looking up at her. "If you felt ignored." He felt terrible but did not know what else to say. Eb kicked himself. How could he be so brilliant at moot court and so totally inept at talking to women?

"Just read your book, Eb," Susan said with a sad sigh, nestling into the chair. "Don't give me a second thought."

Eb opened his book and pretended to read. He was grateful when his uncle and Malinda returned within the hour. The old woman had just suffered from acute indigestion, not a heart attack. Susan moved back to the velvet settee, where she and Malinda settled down together, covering themselves with a quilt. Dr. Cabot took off his shoes and sank down into his wingback chair. The room was once again filled with cheerful, aimless conversation. Esmeralda would be in shortly with a pot of tea, and Henry would be carrying—very carefully, Esmeralda admonished—a plate of molasses cookies.

By the middle of May, Eb Wells was lecturing to three avid law students several mornings a week—Samuel Taylor, Oliver Redfield, and, lately, Donald Hawkins. The lectures were held in the scriveners' room at Haines & Haines before business hours, each student leaning over a scrivener's desk, furiously taking notes. Eb lectured from the front of the room, allowing Donald to sit at his desk. In the back, next to the scribbling Oliver, Ted Redfield slumped over his desk, his head resting on his crossed arms, eyes closed, ostensibly snoozing. The light in the room was dim to avoid using any Haines & Haines lamp oil for unsanctioned lectures. It was early enough in the day that neither Ned nor Nathan Haines knew what was happening.

Donald Hawkins was a new addition. Samuel regularly corresponded with Donald's brother, Francis Hawkins, the former apprentice from Haines & Haines. Last year, Francis had moved to Haddam to establish a law practice of his own, but his younger brother, Donald, was still in New Haven, apprenticed to another attorney. As was often the case, Donald's supervision was woeful. To address this lack of instruction, Donald had been attending lectures in the early morning hours at the law office of Allen Lowery, Esquire. After Lowery's lecture, Donald would scurry on to work, his employer none the wiser. That had been his routine all winter.

Allen Lowery, Esquire, had gone to Yale with Nathan Haines. Lowery now ran a proprietary law school out of his office. His 'law school' was not unlike Tapping Reeve's in Litchfield, although on a much smaller scale. He had half a dozen full-time 'apprentices,' and Lowery ran a law practice during the day. A handful of other unaffiliated young men, struggling apprentices at other firms, attended Lowery's lectures, seeking a more coherent legal education—or any legal education at all. Donald Hawkins was one of those who paid on a per diem basis.

Allen Lowery had never attended Tapping Reeve's law school but was familiar with the model. His wife had been a student at Miss Pierce's female academy, and by virtue of a failed romance, had substantial knowledge about the operation of the Litchfield Law School. Lowery had also procured from an estate sale, for a handsome sum, a full set of Litchfield Law School notes. In his New Haven law office, Lowery had built an impressive law library and was constantly on the hunt for more law books. He permitted other members of the New Haven bar to use his law library—for a hefty fee. Everything was for a hefty fee at the office of Allen Lowery, Esquire.

And Donald Hawkins paid a hefty fee for the lectures. He was struggling financially. Samuel Taylor had written to Francis about the new hotshot apprentice at Haines & Haines who gave outstanding law lectures—for free. Francis Hawkins had written back, asking whether his younger brother might attend. Donald would pay for the privilege, although maybe he could be given a discount, as a quasi-member of the Haines & Haines family.

Eb and Samuel discussed this request at great length. Samuel Taylor, as senior apprentice, was guarded. It was one thing for Eb to lecture to those who worked in the inner sanctum of Haines & Haines. How did that differ, Samuel argued, from William Wells lecturing to Ned Haines in Rufus Henderson's attic? But the comparison failed once Donald Hawkins was permitted to attend. He was an apprentice from another law office, a factual distinction that could not be ignored. About one thing, Samuel was adamant. Eb could not charge Donald for his lectures. Not without the permission of Ned and Nathan Haines.

Eb agreed. Ned and Nathan must be informed if Eb were to get paid. It was their law office, and Eb worked for them. They might want a share of Donald's fee. But what was the harm in letting Donald attend for free? Eb was already preparing the lectures. One more student did not matter. And he did not teach to make money. Eb gave the lectures because Samuel and Oliver were his friends, as was Ted, even though he slept through most of them. Both Samuel and Eb had met Donald Hawkins and found him amiable and amusing. Eb saw no reason not to invite him.

Samuel Taylor still had reservations, but he yielded. The terms of the compromise were as follows: Eb would receive no fee. The lectures must take place before the official workday. No Haines & Haines supplies, including lamp oil, would be used. And finally, Samuel insisted Donald must be the first, last, and only outsider, coming in under the aegis of his brother Francis, a well-respected former apprentice. Samuel felt certain he could justify all this to Nathan and Ned Haines when they found out. And they would find out. It was just easier to ask for forgiveness than permission.

Despite their lengthy deliberations about whether to let Donald Hawkins attend Eb's lectures, neither Samuel nor Eb gave any thought to what Allen Lowery, Esquire, might have to say.

"She's a beauty, all right." Franz Mueller stroked the chestnut horse with a body brush. "Her name's Ruby." Susan Graham leaned up against the horse stall in the stable below the carriage house on Elm Street. It was a warm day in May. The stable was redolent of hay and the resting bodies of tired horses, a combination of smells unfamiliar to Susan, oddly sweet and summery.

Franz was dressed in brown pants and a white shirt with the sleeves rolled up, his blond hair recently cropped close to his head for his new role as coachman. He deftly slid the brush over the top of the horse's body, following the pathways of her coat. "That fellow is Hank." He tilted his head in the direction of the stall next door. Through the slats, Susan could see the flank of a larger, darker brown horse, waiting to be groomed. She could hear Hank chewing and munching, his teeth creating a percussive rhythm as he methodically worked his way through his allotment of hay.

"Why did you change brushes?" Susan's mission for visiting the carriage house had been to discuss Henry's lessons, but the horses had captured her attention. William Lanson had delivered them just this week, and everyone in the household was curious about the new equine inhabitants. Henry was in the kitchen inside the main house, on a break from his studies. He had begged Susan to let him accompany her out to the stable, but she had steered him toward Mrs. Potts with a promise of milky tea, perhaps a cookie. She needed to discuss his studies with his father. Alone.

"That one's the dandy brush," Franz replied. "After I've used the curry brush to loosen up the bits of dirt, loose hair, and the like from the roots, I use the dandy brush to remove the debris. Ruby's always been a stable horse, though, so I only needed to use it a little. She's already clean."

"Doesn't it hurt?" Susan looked down at the stiff-bristled dandy brush, propped up against the slats of the stall.

"The dandy brush isn't supposed to hurt if you do it right. She's good with it on the big muscles, you know, the back, the hindquarters, but in other places, you've got to have a light touch." Franz patted Ruby. "She likes this softer body brush a lot more. A horse ought to enjoy her grooming." He stroked Ruby's chestnut shoulder with an affectionate, approving touch. "It's a nice time, I think, for horse and human. A quiet time. A way to get to know one another and build trust."

"Do you think Ruby's feeling pleasure?" Susan peered sideways at the horse's face. Ruby stared back at her with a large, brown, inscrutable eye, too lulled by the stroking movements of the brush to muster curiosity. Susan had never been this close to a horse before. "You know what I mean. Is she happy right now?"

"I think so." Franz regarded the horse's passive face. "I don't know this horse yet, Miss Graham, so I'm learning how to read her myself." He stroked Ruby again and called her 'such a beautiful girl' in his steady, baritone voice. "But I think she's enjoying her grooming. Most horses do."

"How's Henry going to reach up that high?" Susan pointed to the top of the horse. The plan was to teach Henry how to care for the horses—to earn his keep as a stable boy.

"He's too small right now, but I might build him a stool." Franz did not look at Susan, intent on brushing Ruby. "I've got him shoveling manure, putting down fresh hay, making sure the horses have water. That's enough for now. But I'll teach Henry how to groom a horse. Like my father taught me." Franz bent down and deftly lifted Ruby's left front leg, examining her hoof. "You can see Ruby's used to having her leg held a certain way. She's a sweet girl and has been well taken care of." Franz put Ruby's leg back down and went back to running the body brush over the lower part of her body.

Franz did not speak for a while, seeming to be in a trance, concentrating on the growth patterns of Ruby's chestnut hair, ensuring he aligned the body brush in the right direction. Susan stood silently in the stall, watching Franz move slowly from the front of the horse to the back. He was tall, and she liked the way Franz's arms emerged from his rolled-up shirt sleeves. In contrast to the white cotton, his arms were brown and sinewy. His hands were muscular, and square at the base of the thumb, so different from Eb's hands, which were small, almost dainty.

"So, what did you want to ask me?" Finally, Franz straightened up and looked directly at Susan.

"Henry's having trouble sitting still." Malinda had assigned Susan the task of instructing the now six-year-old Henry Mueller. When the two women came to New Haven, Malinda had taken over the clinic's administration, but Susan's role was ill-defined. Esmeralda and Mrs. Potts performed all the housekeeping tasks that Susan used to do back in Savannah. Whenever Dr. Cabot or Malinda asked for Susan's assistance, she always obliged. But she never felt free just to jump in. There was no 'jumping in' when Malinda Wells ran the show. Malinda always had a master plan, and Susan knew better than to interfere. But waiting for her marching orders, day after day, often left Susan unoccupied. This leisure gave her time to monopolize Dr. Cabot's wingback chair in the library and read. Susan loved to read, but at the same time, she felt disconnected from the hustle and bustle of the household. Everyone under its roof had a purpose, and Susan had none. She was a woman who liked to work, and for a while, she had no work to do.

Like Susan, Malinda Wells was a firm believer in people keeping busy. As head of the household, she decided, quite rightly, that Susan should be the one to help Henry with his studies. That had been her plan all along, although Malinda had neglected to mention this to her companion. But Susan did not protest and readily took on Henry's education. She was secretly pleased. It gave her a job to do and relieved her from being at Malinda's unrelenting beck and call. Besides, Henry was a sweet boy, and now she had an excuse to talk to his father.

"Henry and I have been studying in the library all week." Susan looked up from the hypnotic task of grooming the horse, remembering her errand. "But after an hour or so, he gets ants in his pants." Henry and Susan worked at the large French writing table each day, doing math and improving his handwriting. But even though the boy was tractable—or meant to be—Henry wriggled in his seat all the time. Susan also found him staring off into space when he should be doing his work.

"Ants in his pants?" Franz looked over the horse's back at Susan. He found himself appreciating what a handsome young woman she was, lithe, full-figured, athletic-looking, with a slightly off-kilter face. Her mouth was too wide, her sloping nose too long, but the overall effect could be charming. Franz was not afraid of Susan Graham as he was of Malinda Wells, although he found the Southern drawl of both sometimes confusing, as did they his German accent. "What does this mean—ants in his pants? He has insects in his clothes?"

"It's just an expression," Susan said with a playful laugh. "It means he can't sit still."

"Oh, that." Franz smiled. "Well, that's just Henry. If he's really interested in something, he'll sit still forever. But if he's bored—well, the ants show up." He moved over to the other side of the horse and resumed his brushing. "His mother used to teach him." Franz disappeared behind Ruby's flank. "So, he's not had any learning since she died. I make him read with me at night, but Henry's forgotten how to sit at a desk and learn—or sit still, so it seems."

"He's a smart boy." Susan was not just being diplomatic. Henry Mueller had galloped through the books dragged down from the attic by Mr. Potts. "He can already read parts of the Bible."

"He used to read the Bible with his mother." Franz righted himself. "My suggestion is this. Have Henry study in the morning for a few hours, and then let him come out here and work with me. Or if I'm busy, give him a break to play with Mrs. Tittles. Have a bite to eat."

Susan had noticed the calico cat on her way to the stable, sound asleep in a spot of sun right outside the door. Mrs. Tittles had found ways to escape the carriage house in defiance of the boundaries laid down by Malinda Wells. The cat liked to be outside, and lately, she had taken to wandering in the yard between the main house and the carriage house.

"Then, after lunch, bring Henry back into the house for more study," Franz continued. "When he starts to squirm, release him again to do something physical. That's what my wife used to do. Break things up. Or do as you did today—take him to Mrs. Potts and bribe him with tea and cookies. Hot chocolate, if it's around. I should've told you this earlier, Miss Graham." He gave her a broad grin. "I'm familiar with the ants."

"All right." Susan smiled back at Franz. "I'll give him breaks. And bribe him." She noticed, not for the first time, that Franz Mueller had bright blue eyes, like sapphires, no, maybe more like aquamarines. Just as with the horses, Susan had never been this close to a pair of blue eyes before. She found it difficult to look away from them, feeling a sudden flush of warmth move up her body to her neck. Perhaps it was time to return to the main house.

"Mr. Mueller . . ." Susan stammered, turning to Franz, who had disappeared again behind the horse. "Don't worry. Henry's doing fine. He just gets distracted."

Franz stopped to consider his son's situation. Whitneyville had been all Henry knew, but their happy home had cratered when his mother died. Now the boy was living in a carriage house in New Haven, an appendage to a more complex, densely populated household, with three free Black servants, an elderly doctor, a young lawyer apprentice, his imposing sister, and her companion. Everything was strange and new. He no longer had a monopoly on his father's attention. Returning to his education was bound to be a rocky transition. Little Henry Mueller was on overload. And Susan and Henry had not yet hit their stride—the boy was still not at ease with her.

"Maybe it would be good if Henry and I both learned how to groom the horses," Susan said, the idea just coming to her. "You know, do something active together, get to know each other better." Susan inhaled a whiff of hay and horse sweat. Learning how to groom a horse could be fun, away from the formality of the main house, out of reach of Malinda's polite, but firm, requests for her time and attention. Susan liked to be physically active, to inhabit her body, move around, bend over, stretch her limbs, take deep breaths, even sweat—pleasures frowned upon for 'proper' young ladies. Besides, Susan smiled secretly to herself. She would rather be out here alone with Franz Mueller. And Henry, of course.

"We'd need Miss Wells's permission." Franz cocked his head toward the main house. He knew by now that nothing happened on Elm Street without the approval of Malinda Wells. "I'll let you tend to that."

"Okay. I'll ask Malinda. I don't think she'll mind. Not if it would help Henry." Susan grinned, giving Franz a wink.

To Franz Mueller, Susan Graham's face suddenly looked stunning, not at all off-kilter. He was more than charmed. Franz felt dizzy from this unexpected flash of beauty. He could not speak. He could not move.

Without saying goodbye, Susan returned to the main house, wondering what it would feel like to be Ruby, the new chestnut horse on Elm Street. To be stroked by Franz Mueller's strong, competent hands. To be told she was 'such a beautiful girl' in his steady, baritone voice. To have him move slowly over her, working from front to back.

CHAPTER 3

Grumbling

The summer days grew longer and longer. The evening sky glowed with the pinkish-yellow light belonging only to early June. The leaves of the magnolia tree behind the house on Elm Street were thick and leathery, lustrous, and dark. The two horses, Ruby and Hank, were tethered to their outside posts next to the carriage house, eating hay, shifting from one leg to another, lingering outside in the soft summer air. It was later than it seemed. The solstice would soon be upon them. With the extended daylight, Eb sat patiently on the back porch steps, waiting for a visit from Mrs. Tittles. It was his window of opportunity with the calico cat. Eb knew Henry and Franz would be in the kitchen in the main house after supper.

Mrs. Potts and Esmeralda figured out that Franz and Henry were subsisting on Franz's 'cooking'—porridge, sausage, bread, and cheese. With Dr. Cabot's permission, Mrs. Potts had started to serve them an evening meal in the kitchen, along with Mr. Potts and Esmeralda. The servants ate supper together, whatever Dr. Cabot's family was eating that night, after the dishes from the dining room were cleared. This way, the two women knew that Henry would get at least one good meal a day.

Henry and Esmeralda battled fiercely over his dislike of vegetables, just as he had done with his mother. Henry rejected the premise that green beans were necessary. Why bother with carrots, beets, parsnips, or lettuce, for that matter? If it came out of the ground, Henry Mueller had no use for it. But Esmeralda understood the power of a bribe. If you eat your beans, you get your cookie. If you don't, you won't. Mrs. Potts backed her up.

Henry had grown fond of Mrs. Potts and Esmeralda. With the innate sense children have, he understood these two old ladies were taking care of him. The growing fondness went both ways. Esmeralda and Mrs. Potts were pleased to look after Henry. He was all knobby knees and elbows, a gap in his front teeth, his wild blond hair difficult to manage, his sad brown eyes a reminder of his mother, who had left him so abruptly and traumatically. Most importantly, Henry was a child. It had been decades since a child had lived in—or next to—the house on Elm Street.

At first, the free Black servants were wary about inviting a white German widower to break bread with them. But Franz Mueller did not share their reluctance over the racial mix. It was true that the German neighborhood of his childhood in Philadelphia had been racially intolerant, but their customers at the laundry in Whitneyville had been immigrants and free Black laborers. Franz had learned to be comfortable with all kinds of people. Here in New Haven, Dr. Cabot had introduced him to the free Black entrepreneur, William Lanson, and the two men had become friendly. Lanson helped Franz purchase a carriage on Brewster Place and sold him the two horses. When Esmeralda invited the Muellers to eat supper in the main house kitchen, Franz was grateful, not apprehensive.

Franz Mueller knew he was riding on his son's coattails. He

also understood the two old ladies were taking care of Henry—that Henry felt at home in their kitchen, even with skirmishes over green beans. Franz too felt drawn to the warmth of that kitchen. He enjoyed the company at the end of the day, particularly talking things over with Mr. Potts. Anthony Potts, a tall, thin, dark-skinned man with a white beard, inclined to be under his wife's thumb, was thrilled to have another man at the table.

For years, Anthony Potts had eaten supper with his wife and Esmeralda, the conversational topics being dictated by the two women. But Franz Mueller's presence expanded the agenda. Anything in the weekly newspaper the servants shared—one week old, handed down from Dr. Cabot—was fair game. The two men often lingered after the meal, talking over the news and watching the two women clean up while Henry did his homework. Things were working out at the kitchen table on Elm Street. Mrs. Potts was happy to have more people to cook for, and Franz Mueller was savvy enough to lavish her dishes with praise.

Their evening comradery gave Eb his chance with Mrs. Tittles. His routine was to check in with the calico cat right after supper. It was impossible to commune with her if Henry was around. When Henry was not in the library with Susan, or out in the stable with his father, he was fussing over Mrs. Tittles. Franz took good care of the cat too, just as he did with the horses. Mrs. Tittles's dance card was full, with little room for Eb's attentions. But right after supper, the absence of the two Muellers gave Eb his chance to court her.

Mrs. Tittles was not a biddable cat—if such a creature existed. She ignored all efforts to banish her from the back area and was even found begging at the kitchen door. Franz tried to keep her inside the carriage house as promised, but he was too busy to be vigilant all the time. And Mrs. Tittles was crafty. Whenever the woman with all the hair and the boy showed up, the cat seized the opportunity to slip out the carriage house door. Upon their arrival, cheerful greetings and noisy chatter filled the entryway—a flurry of interactions that did not include her. Mrs. Tittles could easily escape.

Esmeralda confessed to Eb her fears that Mrs. Potts was sneaking the cat scraps from the kitchen. Why else would the animal be begging at the kitchen door? In the beginning, Mrs. Potts insisted that cats were the devil's pets, and the black ones were the worst, although Mrs. Tittles's white fur under her orange-and-black splotches was in her favor. But a month or two later, Mrs. Potts opined that Mrs. Tittles seemed free of satanic influence. The old cook was giving in. Then Esmeralda caught Mrs. Potts saying 'good morning' to Mrs. Tittles—as if she were greeting a person. Mrs. Potts was not the only one. Esmeralda had seen Mr. Potts lean stiffly over and stroke the animal's head. Now the calico cat routinely appeared at the kitchen door, with a look of undeniable expectancy. All this, Esmeralda relayed to Eb with a worried expression. In his opinion, Mrs. Tittles was behaving very much like a cat, not something Esmeralda wanted to hear.

On that summer evening, Eb sat still, like a rabbit in the grass, on the back porch steps. Finally, Mrs. Tittles crossed the yard to greet him. He rubbed around her tired neck and under her chin. While watching her ears closely for permission, he stroked her fur all the way down to her tail. In a soft, lilting voice, Eb told Mrs. Tittles all about his day at the law office, inquiring after her day as well. Had she caught any mice? How were things going with the other mammals, the big ones, Ruby and Hank? Tomorrow, Mrs. Potts was baking a chicken. Would she like a tidbit from the table? Mrs. Tittles tolerated Eb's petting. She was wary, needing more time to assess Eb's worthiness, but she was warming up to him. Eb still missed Sir Winston, but having a daily encounter with Mrs. Tittles was salve to his wound.

*Letter to Eb Wells from Rebecca Harding, Litchfield,
June 12, 1821*

Dearest Eb,

Your last letter was forwarded to me here in Litchfield. Yes, it was difficult to say goodbye to Mrs. Cox, but made easier by her leaving for the summer. Elizabeth is to come for Penny's wedding and will accompany her grandmother back up to Boston. Mrs. Stafford's trying to convince her mother to move in with them. It might be a good idea, but I don't think Mrs. Cox wants to leave Wethersfield. She's happily ensconced in her home and shows no interest in going. Mr. Samuel Townsend has also returned to Boston to court Elizabeth, I'm sorry to say. Mrs. Stafford's quite distressed.

I was sad to leave my students too. Many of the girls cried, even a few I thought were indifferent. The teachers gave me a farewell party out behind the school. We had sandwiches, tea, and a golden cake with lemon icing. It was very festive, a day in late May, warm and inviting. We put our chairs out under the maple tree. Mr. Hitchcock stood up for a toast, spouting platitudes and perfunctory comments about me—mostly about my 'enthusiasm.' When someone goes on about someone's 'enthusiasm,' it usually means he finds her unworthy of more laudatory praise. The Ogre's lukewarm accolades were tempered by glowing ones from my colleagues. I'll be so glad to have Asa Hitchcock in the past tense. Miss Pierce warns me that Asa Hitchcock will never go away. He'll be waiting for me at another school in another incarnation. I must learn how to deal with him.

So, you have another student for your secret law school! I'm surprised to hear about your enthusiasm for teaching. I hear far more about your lectures than your work at Haines & Haines. Are you aware of that? Remember this, Eb, no one's forcing you to practice law. A legal education is never wasted. It deepens your knowledge of the world—and teaches you discipline.

I'm sorry Nathan Haines discovered you arranged for your uncle to hire the debtor. I can't say I was surprised at his anger. It was a big-hearted move, but you can see how Nathan might be upset. If the bank's managers were to learn you had given aid to an opposing party, they might not be pleased. At least the laundry was sold, the bank made whole, and the managers never found out. You were lucky this time. I'm glad Nathan's dressing-down was not too harsh, but I can see his point of view.

I detected in your last letter concern over Malinda's growing affection for Mr. Haines Sr. What is your objection, other than his age? You must give me a better accounting. I thought you held him in high regard. What does your brother John think of this budding romance?

It's wonderful to be back at Miss Pierce's, up in my old room on the third floor. Martha visits every evening. During the day, Miss Mary Pierce and I crank out letters of admission. The Litchfield Female Academy is still in session. Next week is the reception for the ornamental arts. Martha has two more maps in the competition. It's likely her map of Litchfield will win something. She spent all spring on it, roaming the streets of the town, ensuring the bottom of her petticoats got caked in mud. Her mother wasn't happy. Nothing new there.

I met Jack Lewis's fiancée this week out at the Lewis cottage. Hannah Ward is pretty in a wholesome way, the daughter of an apothecary in Kent. They met through the grocery connection. Ruth thinks she'll be a good influence on Jack, who's a veritable tornado of energy. Hannah is calm and deliberate. She and Martha get along well enough, although frankly, I don't think Martha likes the idea of Jack marrying anyone. She's a lioness when it comes to protecting her men—Charles, her father, her brothers.

I heard Thomas Bradford finished the course and left for Charleston. Have you had news of him? I know he's a poor correspondent. Katherine Montgomery is still here at Miss Pierce's and hints at an engagement in the offing. Martha thinks not. She may know more than we do since Charles tells her everything. Charles and Thomas studied together up until the day he left, and Charles is less optimistic about a marriage proposal than Katherine. Poor Katherine. Another failed romance.

I should hear from Mrs. Morris this week. There's an opening in the female division, upper level. I'd have to get lodgings in South Farms. It's too far to go each day from Litchfield, although I plan to visit often.

How are things going with little Henry? Is he adjusting to his studies with Susan? And what about your romance with Mrs. Tittles? Is there any reason for me to be jealous?

I must be off. I promised Mary Pierce I'd be down first thing in the morning. We're matching up accepted students with boarding houses. Our goal is to place ten young women by the end of tomorrow. Much work to be done. Hoping you are well. Write soon.

Yours affectionately,

Rebecca Harding

For the past several months, Malinda Wells had spent her Sunday afternoons with Ned Haines. She was surprised to receive his invitation after the supper party in early April. Ned Haines's placement next to her at the dining table had been her uncle's idea. As hostess, Malinda's job was to 'be charming' to Ned Haines—her younger brother's boss. Dr. Cabot knew she was up to the task.

'Being charming' was in Malinda Wells's repertoire. She was, after all, a young woman from Savannah. Her Yankee mother had not taught her how to be charming, lacking the skill herself, although she did possess charm. But to be in possession of charm and to 'be charming' are different qualities altogether. To 'be charming' is an active enterprise, requiring a knack for manipulation and comfort with subterfuge. From an early age, Malinda evidenced these attributes by nature, not by nurture.

It must be remembered that Malinda Wells was a purposeful woman. She knew how to accomplish her goals with nudges, strategic retreats, the soft touch of her hand on an arm, a gentle appeal to reason and emotion. Malinda accepted that her sphere of influence was limited. The only way for one of her ideas to come to fruition was to persuade a man—a powerful one if possible—that it was his. Malinda would tacitly give him stewardship of her idea, let him air it in public, spend some money on it, and yes, eventually, claim it as his own. If the idea turned out to be a bad one—well, there was always the woman to blame.

Malinda's solidarity with the gentler sex—her mother, Susan, Susan's mother, Esmeralda, Mrs. Potts—required a more down-to-earth, frank style of management. Her 'being charming' was reserved for her dealings with men, at least men who were not her brothers. Eb resisted her, and John dismissed her altogether, believing her to be a childlike, childless woman, not to be taken seriously. Malinda held no sway with either of them. This phenomenon had frustrated her all her life. She often wondered, did 'being charming' work only on men of a certain age, or was it just doomed to work on brothers?

But Malinda's 'being charming' was highly effective on men a generation above her. Early in life, she had learned to wrap her father around her proverbial little finger. Her uncle was also susceptible, having been charmed by Malinda's grandmother all his life. (Perhaps the skill *was* inheritable and had skipped a generation.) 'Being charming' also worked on Ned Haines, Malinda had observed at the supper party.

When Malinda received Ned's invitation the following week,

her first instinct was to say, 'Ned Haines is too old for me.' He was the age of her father if he had lived, just shy of sixty. But then she remembered the trim, still handsome gentleman, sitting at her right hand, listening attentively to her at the party. Ned Haines may have worn spectacles, but could not be faulted for that. Eb wore them too. Ned's frames were silver, matching the silver in his hair, and his dark eyes locked on hers, from directly behind the lenses. He did not look out of his spectacles like an old man, the way her uncle did, swooping his head up and down like a crane, hoping the optical correction would travel with his attention. Her Uncle Ebenezer looked his age, a little paunchy, a little stooped, and a lot bald, with his large old-man ears. Ned Haines gave off another aura altogether—that of a much younger man.

And Malinda was impressed by him. Ned Haines seemed intelligent, thoughtful, well-read. He appeared to be kind and solicitous of his sons and employees. He was also in possession of social standing and wealth. As head partner of a prosperous commercial law practice, his affluence was equal to her uncle's and far exceeded that of her father. Most importantly, Malinda had enjoyed talking to him. What do I have to lose by taking a carriage ride with him? she thought. It was not as if she was flooded with invitations. At almost thirty, she had never been invited to anything. So, she agreed, and thus began the courtship of Malinda Wells and Ned Haines.

Having grown up in the eighteenth century, Ned was traditional in his pursuit, buying her flowers, taking her out for meals at elegant hotels, walking arm in arm with her along Long Wharf. Ever since her maiden maritime voyage, Malinda was thrilled to stand next to the sailing ships tied up with massive ropes at the harbor, with their curved wooden sides and tall square-rigged masts. Ned Haines was knowledgeable about shipping. He would point out what cargo was being loaded on or off, where this ship was headed, or had just come from—Boston, Philadelphia, New Orleans, Port

Royal, Bridgetown. Malinda loved all the activity down at Long Wharf, the smell of tar, and the sea. She absorbed everything Ned told her like a dry sponge.

After leading a narrow life in Savannah, circumscribed by her home and a few city squares, Malinda Wells's world was expanding. Every Sunday, Ned talked Malinda's ear off. They discussed the symbolism of *Frankenstein*, the settlement of the Northwest Territory, and the future of the free Blacks who would sail across the Atlantic to form a new colony on the west coast of Africa. (Malinda knew all about the American Colonization Society from her brother's moot court last year.) Ned also filled her in on his arbitrations and revealed how difficult his younger son had become since his mother's death. He bemoaned his growing dislike for the practice of law, his dependence on Nathan, his frustration with Nathan, his guilt over the law practice turning his apprentices into scriveners, and his disapproval of slavery, while acknowledging his wealth depended on it.

The slave trade was illegal in Connecticut, and only a handful of their clients still owned slaves, advanced in age. But goods produced by slave labor in the South and West Indies, such as cotton, indigo, sugar, rice, and tobacco, flowed into the port of New Haven, not to mention the exportation of agricultural goods—timber, meat, vegetables, cheese, and onions to feed the slaves down South. Their commercial, shipping, and manufacturing clients profited from slavery, even if they would not say so. It was a truism, Ned told Malinda. Lawyers thrive when their clients thrive. The booming business along the Atlantic coast led to more contracts, leases, and lawsuits. Everyone was making money off the backs of enslaved people, north and south, including Haines & Haines.

Malinda tried to take in everything Ned Haines told her without judgment. She also understood he was lonely. Ever since the death of his second wife—perhaps, oddly enough, since the death of his first wife—Ned had no one to talk to. It was flattering to be the confidante of this older, powerful man. Malinda listened intently, always on the lookout for opportunities to make things better. A pragmatist, she concentrated on things she could change. While she abhorred slavery, she felt helpless to bring about its end. The problems with Nathan and Eddie, she also could not solve, at least not for now. But Ned Haines's complaints about his workplace? Haines & Haines called out to her for improvement.

Why not promote Oliver Redfield to the position of apprentice? Why not hire one or two additional scriveners and let the apprentices assume more responsibility? Why not give Ted Redfield carte blanche to administer the office, relieving Nathan of the many ministerial tasks he had no flair for? Why not expand the law library and dedicate space for the apprentices—remove them from the scriveners' room? That way, the tasks of apprentice and scrivener might not so easily merge in the future. Perhaps Ned should retire from day-to-day legal practice altogether and devote himself to arbitration. Why don't they consider hiring a second junior attorney, or two? What about Samuel Taylor? Or even Eb? Both would soon take a bar exam and be admitted. Malinda did not know if Eb even wanted such a position, but Samuel might jump at the chance. Samuel had a promising legal mind. At least, that was her brother's opinion.

Malinda was, as always, full of good ideas. The courting couple spent endless hours talking. Within a few weeks of Sunday carriage rides, cut off from the world in their own private soundscape of the clop clop clop of horses' hooves on the streets of New Haven, Ned and Malinda began to feel comfortable with each other. To her relief, Malinda discovered she could drop the full-time efforts to 'be charming.' She could save those skills, and the energy it took to employ them, for some time in the future. Malinda Wells was not done 'being charming' to Ned Haines, but it ceased to be her dominant modus operandi. She was also relieved that she found most of Ned's jokes funny. Nothing wore on Malinda more than having to pretend to be amused when she was not. When Ned made a clunky pun, she was at liberty to roll her eyes and groan.

Ned was genuinely interested in her suggestions, discussing their pros and cons. He would never say so to Malinda—and could barely admit it to himself—but something in Ned was attracted to her dictatorial disposition. Being told what to do by Malinda Wells excited him, sitting next to her in the carriage, within range of the delicate scent of lavender soap that arose from her body. Ned loved to look at Malinda when she talked about improving his law practice. Her bright eyes—eyes that belonged to a raptor—would shine even brighter. Her pretty, round face would turn a healthy, glowing pink. Sometimes, she became so enthralled with a new idea that she would grab his upper arm and lean into him, lingering there a few seconds longer than was necessary. He was not sure whether he was feeling the pressure of her breasts or her corset—and wanted so much to answer that question.

Ned was in the thrall of her Southern drawl. He loved the way she wallowed in her vowels, the way she said 'I' like the eye of a storm that went on and on forever. On Sunday nights, Ned would lie in his bed alone, eyes closed, listening in his mind's ear to Malinda's mellifluous voice and quaint Southern expressions. Ned Haines had come to this conclusion. He would very much like to share his bed with Malinda Wells—which, of course, meant matrimony. He had married before and would do so again—if Malinda Wells would have him.

"I'm bored, Samuel." Eb had just proofread his most recent article on the virtues of vagueness in drafting wills. It was the end of the workday, and he and Samuel were in the scriveners' room. The Redfield brothers, the new scrivener, and Ned and Nathan Haines had already left for the day. Eb was waiting for Samuel to finish copying. The plan was to visit the tavern next door for a pint of ale before heading home. "This article was of interest to me six weeks ago." Eb looked glumly down at the fourth draft. "I cared about it, for one morning in mid-May, between nine a.m. and noon, the day we were drafting Mrs. Ellsworth's will. But now? I can't muster one iota of enthusiasm."

"You always feel that way at the end of an article." Samuel's tall, lean frame was bent over his scrivener's desk. He was concentrating on finishing up a contract and looking forward to his pint of ale.

"Yes, that's all well and good for you to say," Eb muttered, pulling at a few locks of errant hair. "You're not the one who's got to answer letters about something you wrote two months ago." He crossed his arms on his desk and laid his head gingerly in the crook of his elbow, making sure not to dislodge his glasses. "Just yesterday, I had to drag out my 'Act of God' notes to answer a question some lawyer from Simsbury put to me. This fellow must be behind in his reading. He's probably perusing my article out in the privy. Or using it for paper out in the privy. Perhaps both." Eb's voice was muffled from talking into the desk. "Honestly, Samuel, I no longer care about the 'Act of God' clause."

"You should feel flattered people write you letters." Eb Wells was gaining a reputation as a writer on legal subjects. His articles had appeared in the New Haven *Connecticut Journal* and the *Connecticut Courant* in Hartford. Recently, Samuel had placed one of Eb's articles in *The Providence Gazette*.

"I suppose." Eb lifted his head from the desk, glancing at Samuel's last-minute edits of his most recent manuscript. He pushed the draft one inch closer to Samuel. "I'd like to write about something that matters. And do something that matters." Eb shook his head. "I'm not sure my future here is so bright."

"That's ridiculous." Samuel blotted the last paragraph at the bottom of the page. "You're doing substantive legal work now. Ned and Nathan value your legal acumen. We can take a bar exam soon." Samuel was pleased with the recent changes in the law office. Ned Haines had hired a new scrivener, a sallow older man, experienced, quiet, agreeable, with a fast, formal hand. Oliver Redfield had been promoted to apprentice. For now, Eb had yielded his desk to the new scrivener since Eb was spending most of his time in the law library. Eb's, Samuel's, and Oliver's copying of documents had been greatly diminished. "Your future here's bright."

"Yes, but just look at the work I'm doing." Eb thought back on all he had accomplished that week at Haines & Haines, a dreary litany. "This week, I drafted a shipping contract to move a huge load of Connecticut cabbages to Philadelphia. Then I started an eviction of a bankrupt tailor and his wife, filed a writ to sue a shipper over a cargo of sugar cane from Antigua that rotted before it got here, and enabled a mean old man to disinherit his son who wants to marry a Quaker."

"And your point is?" Samuel put the flourishing touches on the contract he was copying. He too had assisted on those matters.

"My point is . . . well," Eb stammered, searching for the right words to say. "I mean, is that all there is to the practice of law? Sending cabbages out to sea? Recouping rotten sugar cane? Throwing people out on the street? Drafting a will to thwart true love?"

"Yes, in a way." Samuel smiled, the gap between his front teeth showing. "I'll grant you, this week's work wasn't thrilling, but we moved commerce along. We made sure debts were paid and helped a merchant recoup a business loss. I'm not so proud of disinheriting the son, mind you, but those other things, Eb, they're the bread and butter of our law practice. Of most law practices."

"I know," Eb groaned. "And when I say my future 'here' doesn't look so bright," he said, gesturing around the now empty room, "I don't mean 'here' here. My 'here' is more metaphorical—not just the office of Haines & Haines, but the 'here' of practicing law." He passed the manuscript back to Samuel, who had begun to tidy up his table, closing the ink bottle and wiping off the pens for Ted to clean in the morning. "Those edits are fine, by the way."

"Maybe another type of law practice would suit you better," Samuel suggested. "Why not write to your old mentor, Judge Reeve? See what he says. Perhaps a firm with fewer commercial clients." Samuel took off his apron and dipped his hands in the wash basin that Ted had left out for him. "Some other kind of legal work—less transactional. Maybe trial work, something to put your oratory skills to use. Don't give up on the law yet."

"I'm even sick of writing these articles." Eb had fallen so deeply in love with the law at the Litchfield Law School, it was hard to imagine how the romance could fizzle. But in proofreading his most recent article, his eyes had glazed over. It might be technically sound, but it held no interest for him whatsoever.

"Why don't you come with me tomorrow night to hear Moses Brown speak?" Samuel suggested, wiping his hands on the towel that Ted had left neatly folded beside the wash basin. "On abolition. Maybe that would inspire you. You'll be reminded that the law can be a vehicle for social change. More than just moving cabbages around or rotten sugar cane." Moses Brown, a famous abolitionist who had founded Samuel's university, was visiting New Haven. "Brown's speaking at the home of one of the Friends."

"Moses Brown?" Eb knew about him from Samuel. "I'd love to come. Thank you." He placed the manuscript on top of Samuel's desk. "And thank you for helping me edit this dreary tome on testamentary dispositions." Eb ran his hand through his auburn hair, trying to set it right. He straightened his vest, pulling his white shirt down. "You must excuse my incessant grumbling. I don't want to tax our friendship." Eb looked up at Samuel through his gold-rimmed glasses and gave him a wan smile.

"No problem." Samuel grinned. He had to admit Eb Wells looked tired, disheveled, and disheartened. "Now, let's get out of here. I'm dying of thirst." And the two young men headed off for the tavern.

"A cat indoors isn't such a terrible thing, Esmeralda." Eb and the housekeeper were having a cup of tea in the kitchen on Elm Street. It was a warm, gray Sunday morning in late June. Mr. and Mrs. Potts were at church in the Dixwell Avenue neighborhood. Sunday breakfast for the family was confined to hard-boiled eggs, toast, and tea, all served by Esmeralda. She did not attend church regularly, despite being a God-fearing woman.

The year before, when Eb was on break from law school, he would roam into the kitchen for a morning chat with Esmeralda and Mrs. Potts—and for tea and pie. He was leading the leisurely life of a law student. Now he had a grueling work schedule, and Sunday morning was the only day Eb could at least visit with Esmeralda. Since coming to New Haven, Eb had stopped attending church. In Litchfield, it was impossible to miss church without public censure, but this was a big city. No one noticed or cared if you did not show up, and Eb needed a morning to sleep in.

"And cats keep mice at bay in a kitchen." Eb was talking up Mrs. Tittles. The bold cat had added the kitchen to her daily route, with the consent of Mrs. Potts. It turned out Harriet Potts had indeed been sneaking the cat tidbits of meat and cheese. For her offerings, Mrs. Tittles rewarded Mrs. Potts, first with head bumps on her ankles and later with purrs of gratitude. Mrs. Potts relented and opened the kitchen door. Henry was over the moon when Mrs. Tittles gained entry, although he understood she had her limits. The calico cat was not allowed to jump onto any surfaces or beg at the kitchen table. The former rule, she obeyed, but the latter, Mrs. Tittles broke routinely.

"I know they catch mice, and I do regret having a row with Harriet." While Esmeralda was the housekeeper on Elm Street, it was understood that the kitchen fell under Mrs. Potts's jurisdiction. The two old friends had argued about Mrs. Tittles, and Eb was trying to smooth things over. "It was her call to make," Esmeralda admitted, her accent tinged with the West Indies. She glanced across the table at Eb. He might be a promising 'almost' attorney, but lounging around in his Sunday morning 'at home' clothes, his auburn hair tousled, Eb looked barely sixteen.

"Old friends disagree sometimes." Eb thought about his estrangement from Susan Graham, who now almost never spoke to him. "But really, Esmeralda, having a cat in the kitchen can be beneficial. And Mrs. Tittles is a gentle beast." That was an outright lie. Eb wondered if he ought to soft-peddle Mrs. Tittles's docile disposition. He wished he were lobbying for Sir Winston, who had a lot less attitude. There were cats, and then there was Mrs. Tittles.

"The truth is, Eb . . ." Esmeralda carefully settled her cup back down into the saucer. The old woman moved with an innate dignity and was scrupulously polite. Malinda had once said the world would be a better place if everyone had Esmeralda's manners. "I'm afraid of cats. My mother told me a terrible story. From when she was a girl back in Barbados on the plantation."

Eb already knew some of Esmeralda's history from their morning chats the year before. Esmeralda Smith—she bore the name of her white father—was born in the early 1750s in southern Connecticut, the daughter of a slave from Barbados. Esmeralda and her mother worked on a small plantation near Lyme. With fifty slaves or so, unlike the Southern plantations with their single cash crops of rice or cotton, Connecticut's plantations grew produce, raised livestock, made cheese, cut wood—all for their main market, the Caribbean colonies.

Sailing from Barbados, Esmeralda's mother and grandmother were purchased off a ship in the port of New London to work in a plantation dairy. Later, after the grandmother died, Esmeralda's mother was invited to become a house slave in the master's house, even though the family did not reside on the plantation. But the master came frequently to supervise its operation, and another invitation was soon issued to Esmeralda's mother—to sleep in the master's bed. While a version of love grew between them, no one could claim their sexual union was consensual. Esmeralda's mother was chattel, and as such, the master could do with her as he saw fit.

But the master was genuinely fond of Esmeralda's mother. His affection also protected her from overtures by the overseer, something she was grateful for. When she gave birth to Esmeralda, the master was delighted. He doted on the infant. This parentage accounted for Esmeralda's light skin. Esmeralda had fond memories of her father, who always brought her sweets when he came to the plantation. When the master died of measles, he emancipated both her mother and Esmeralda in his will, giving them a small bequest, based on 'his affection and solicitude for their welfare.' The master's wife and children protested, but the lawyer faithfully executed the will, preparing the deeds of manumission and delivering the bequest.

"What kind of a plantation did your mother work on in Barbados?" Eb did not know much about Esmeralda's mother. "Was she born there?"

"Yes, she was," Esmeralda replied. "That plantation grew sugar cane. My grandmother and great-grandmother, they were stolen from their home somewhere on the west coast of Africa. The two of them, a mother and daughter, were grabbed together, captured in nets, chained, and taken to the Castle." Esmeralda shook her head. "And then shipped to Barbados."

"How old was your grandmother when she came over?" Eb did not know how to characterize the hellish journey from the west coast of Africa to the Americas. He knew better than to call it a voyage, or even a migration. How to name the forcible transport of enslaved people, stacked up on pallets for weeks, with dirty water and rancid food, lying in their own filth, being treated worse than cattle? What was the right word for that?

"I think my grandmother was twelve or so when she arrived," Esmeralda answered. "Her mother—my great-grandmother—died from the bloody flux on the ship coming over. The food was rotten, and folks got sick. The story was, the sailors would come through every morning, down below, and pull out the bodies of the slaves who'd died the night before. My grandmother was crying when they took her mother's lifeless body away. The poor child had been hanging onto her mother all night long, even after she'd passed. The sailors just stacked the naked dead bodies up on the deck and tossed them overboard." Esmeralda sighed. "That must have been true because all the dead disappeared. That's what happened to my great-grandmother. After that, my grandmother—she was just a girl—was all alone."

"So, what happened to your grandmother then?" Eb shuddered at the image of naked bodies being tossed into the sea, sinking beneath the surface to a watery grave. This part of Esmeralda's history he did not know.

"When my grandmother got to Barbados, she was sold in Bridgetown to work in the sugar cane fields. She did that for a while, but someone figured out she was smart. They used to say slaves with Arab blood in them were clever. Anyhow, my grandmother started to work up in the big house. She must've been about thirteen or fourteen by then. During that time, she was still living in the slave quarters. That's where my grandmother met her husband," Esmeralda continued. "My grandfather was from the Yoruba people. A tall, dark-skinned man, with three lined carvings on each of his cheeks. He was kind and intelligent, so I hear, well-favored by the master. My grandfather worked in the stables and took care of his best horses." Esmeralda shook her head and sighed. "Mother used to say that the master in Barbados loved those horses more than his wife and sons."

"So, your grandmother was allowed to have a husband?" Eb was not certain how a person with no legal status could marry. It entailed consent, agency, and the ability to make a contract.

"They weren't married as such, but in the eyes of the slave community, they were husband and wife. Then my grandmother got in the family way. Now, mostly, having a child wasn't welcome on a sugar cane plantation, not if the girl worked the fields. Those slaves cutting cane were disposable. No need to take care of them, feed them well, take them to the doctor if they were sick. It was just cheaper to let them die and replace them. There was always another boatload coming, ready to be worked to death, down at the port of Bridgetown." This, Esmeralda said with bitterness. "A girl in the family way, working the fields, meant labor lost. But it was different for my grandmother because she worked in the big house. The mistress was fond of her, at least at that time. A midwife was called when she had her baby."

"So, that baby was your mother?" Eb was getting confused with all the generations.

"Yes, she was," Esmeralda replied. "After my mother was born though, the mistress made my grandmother come live up in the big house for good. Said she couldn't bring her baby with her. The mistress didn't want a crying infant in the house. So, she left my mother in the slave quarters to be raised by her father and his mother. She was well-loved and cared for, though. And on Sunday afternoons, my grandmother could go out to the slave house and visit her."

"How did your grandmother and mother get to Connecticut?"

"When my mother was about ten years old, she was pulled out of the fields to come up to the big house to work with her mother.

She had to leave her father and grandmother in the slave house, but it was a good thing for her. You know, to get out of the fields. She slept up in the attic in the same bed as her mother. Mostly, the two of them worked in the kitchen." Eb was concentrating hard on Esmeralda's story, trying to keep the mother and the grandmother straight—the great-grandmother, he was sure, had died at sea. "But about that time, problems were brewing for my grandmother. She was almost thirty then. A tall, handsome woman, still very attractive." Esmeralda laughed. "I don't suppose you can imagine that, Eb."

"No, I can." Esmeralda once told Eb that she favored her grandmother, although a lighter version. He could imagine her grandmother had been a beauty. "So, what happened?"

"Well, the problem was the master's oldest son. His name was William, and he was slated to marry a fancy, rich white girl from Bridgetown, but he grew fond of my grandmother instead. Making eyes at her all the time, following her around the house, that kind of thing. I never did hear it went further than an attraction. But the mistress of the house saw what was going on. She wasn't having any of it." Esmeralda gave Eb a sardonic smile. "The mistress wasn't going to have any slave children around the house who looked like her son William. It might have jinxed his marriage, so she arranged to have my grandmother sold."

"What about your grandfather?"

"Well, my grandfather begged the master to be sold with his wife, even though there was no assurance they'd be kept together once they got to America. They were selling her to a slave trader whose ship was going up north. A lot of slaves from Barbados and the West Indies were shipped up north after being down there for some time. My grandfather figured that's where they were headed."

"But the master said no." Eb made a good guess. "Because he didn't want to lose the man who was good with his horses."

"Exactly," Esmeralda said with a sigh. "It was a tragedy for that couple. They loved each other a lot. Everyone said so, but that's the way it was, Eb. Still is. Folks who own slaves don't care about keeping people who love each other together. Husbands and wives, parents and children. They don't care, not if it doesn't suit them."

"And what about your mother?" Eb asked. "She was just a girl. What was going to happen to her?"

"Well, my grandfather tried to convince the master to sell his wife and daughter together. He was afraid my grandmother would die of a broken heart if she lost her daughter. Plus, after my grandmother was sold, he was afraid the mistress would return my mother to the fields. Working the sugar cane fields in Barbados ate people alive. My grandfather believed they'd be safer going up north together to be sold as house slaves." Esmeralda got up from the table and ambled over to the breadbox. She moved stiffly, having sat at the kitchen table for too long. "The mistress in Barbados finally let the master sell the two together, my grandmother and mother. My mother was about eleven years old then. She was coming into her sullen teen years, not answering the mistress, that kind of thing. She probably wasn't all that useful. Besides, maybe the mistress took a long look at my mother, about to get her first blood, and realized this girl herself might be trouble coming down the pike. More bait for her younger sons." Esmeralda returned to the table with a plate bearing two leftover biscuits. "Want one?"

"Sure." Eb looked around.

"I'll get the butter," Esmeralda said, reading his mind. "So that's how my grandmother and mother came here to Connecticut. They were shipped to New London and sold together to work in the dairy on our old plantation near Lyme, but my grandmother died of a lung complaint. Those slave houses were unheated." Eb knew the rest of the story but did not want to interrupt her. "The master came down to the dairy one day and saw my mother there, churning butter, just fifteen, and moved her up to the main house to 'keep house,' but really to sleep in the master's bed when he came to visit. Here's a nice ripe strawberry to pick, he must've thought. Being a pretty, young slave girl's a peril, Eb." Esmeralda reached for the butter. "It was then, and it is now." Her face was sagging, her voice weary.

"So, I think I know the rest of the story." Eb shied away from the old woman's sadness. "Your mother had the master's child—that's you. Years later, when the master died, he emancipated you and your mother in his will. You were maybe fifteen years old yourself by then." Esmeralda was curious to hear Eb's version of her story. "You and your mother moved to New Haven, where there was a large free Black community. You both found work, but your mother took ill and died. Eventually, right before the war, you were hired as an assistant housekeeper in the household of Dr. and Mrs. Cabot on Elm Street." Eb squeezed Esmeralda's rough hand across the kitchen table. "And here you are, more than forty years later, still taking care of Mrs. Cabot's son, and eating a biscuit with me, Mrs. Cabot's grandson."

"That's pretty good, Eb." Esmeralda flashed him a big smile. "You remember all that, do you?" She had grown fond of Eb, and increasingly of Malinda, and she adored Dr. Ebenezer Cabot. Esmeralda had never married. The Cabots were her family now and had been for many years.

"But let's get back to the cat," Eb urged the elderly woman gently. He wanted to know how this story related to Esmeralda's row with Mrs. Potts over Mrs. Tittles in the kitchen. "Where do cats fit into this story?"

"Ah, well." Esmeralda slowly chewed her biscuit. "My mother used to tell me a story of what happened on the plantation down in Barbados. You know, when she was little, before she went up to the big house."

"It had to do with a cat?" Eb was mystified.

"It did." Esmeralda grew solemn, putting down her butter knife. "There was this punishment the masters used down there called 'cat hauling.' If a slave was disobedient or wasn't doing his work to the overseer's satisfaction, they'd take off his shirt and pants in front of everyone and fasten him face down on the ground. Then they'd take this big old fierce tom cat, and they'd swing this big old cat around in the air by the tail and haul the cat down the body of the slave. All the way down his backside. The cat would be screeching and digging his claws into that man's flesh. He'd tear him from his shoulders all the way down to his buttocks." Esmeralda's eyes filled with tears. "My mother saw that happen a few times. She said people would rather be whipped than have the 'cat hauling.' Those deep cat scratches got all swollen and red, and you might run hot. You could even die of it. 'Cat hauling' was ten times worse than the whip. That's what people said." Esmeralda swiftly wiped the one tear that escaped down her cheek with the back of her hand. She did not want Eb to see her crying.

Eb sat at the kitchen table, unable to move or speak. The horror of Esmeralda's story immobilized him. A long, sad silence fell over the kitchen table. "Oh, Esmeralda," Eb finally said, reaching over to squeeze her hand again, fighting back his own tears. "I'm so sorry. That's a terrible punishment for someone. And for a young girl to witness. It was brutal. Cruel. I can understand how being around a cat might make you uncomfortable."

"Well, it's not just that." Esmeralda seemed embarrassed by Eb's solicitude, but grateful he had heard her story. "People I knew on the plantation, even up here in Connecticut, they always said cats were in league with the devil." She straightened herself up at the table. "Harriet always thought so too, but now, well, she's changed her mind." Esmeralda's indignation contemplated a revival, but then subsided. Resignation was setting in. "I guess Henry loves this Mrs. Tittles. And now Mrs. Potts likes her. Franz too," she added. "I never really thought the cat was taking orders from Satan. That struck me as a wrong notion. Besides, she's not a black cat."

"It's an adjustment, I know." Eb had been shocked the first time he sat down and saw Mrs. Edwards's old orange-and-white cat, warming his haunches by the kitchen fire. A dirty old cat, sitting in the same room where he was eating? But Eb had been so wrong. Sir Winston was a clean animal, even fastidious, cleaner than most of the law students. "You'll get used to Mrs. Tittles, Esmeralda."

"I suppose." Esmeralda did not sound convinced.

"But about your story." Eb looked at Esmeralda kindly. "It's a horrible story—a cruel treatment. An indignity as well. But don't you see, the punishment of 'cat hauling' was also terrifying to the cat? To grab it by the tail, spin him around in the air, and drag him down another terrified creature's back? The cat was in acute distress too. You could tell that from his cries, his screeching—isn't that what you called it?" Eb looked down at the kitchen table. "You can see that, can't you? The tomcat was in pain. That he was being tortured as well?"

"I do see that, Eb," Esmeralda said quietly. "I'm trying to accept a cat as one of God's creatures. For Henry's sake. And Harriet's too. If it matters so much to them." She sighed. "Harriet's going to have a tough time convincing Malinda."

"Could I bother you for another cup of tea?" Eb looked down at his empty teacup. The elderly woman got up from the kitchen and patted him briskly on the shoulder.

"Anything for you, Eb." She headed for the fire, where the copper kettle had freshly boiled water. "I'd like another cup too." Amidst the clatter of teacups, and a second visit to the breadbox, this time for a couple of cookies, Esmeralda called out to Eb, "Harriet told Miss Malinda, like you said, the cat's a good mouser. She's sure to see value in that."

Eb thought about Esmeralda's story, not only the cat hauling, but the tragedy of her entire family, dispossessed of their homes, their liberty, their families, their lives. The violent history of their captures, terrifying sea journeys, forced labor, torture, untreated disease, rape and sexual predation, the separation of husbands and wives, the inability to protect their children. Eb loved the old woman who lumbered around the kitchen, preparing their second pot of tea. It broke his heart that Esmeralda Smith—and her ancestors—had endured such hardships through no fault of their own.

The stirring words of Moses Brown came to mind, the abolitionist he had heard speak the week before. As promised, Samuel Taylor had taken him to a Friend's house to listen to the old man talk on a variety of subjects, agricultural experimentation, the Antiquarian Society, and his lifelong crusade against the slave trade. Brown had described the inhumane treatment of African slaves—a fitting backdrop to Esmeralda's horrific story. For more than a year, Eb had not heard a word spoken in public on behalf of abolition. He and Samuel spoke privately about it, as did his uncle, reading the paper in front of the fire, his slipper dangling from his big toe. But Moses Brown, an old man in his eighties, stood before a group of people and spoke out with such eloquence and passion. He inspired Eb. Here was a white man who used his privilege and education to take a stand against slavery.

Listening to Esmeralda's story, and to Moses Brown, Eb felt a subtle shift in his heart. He made a solemn declaration to himself: I will no longer write for people whose sole concern is to preserve their status, power, and wealth. No more articles on devious contract clauses or mean-spirited testamentary dispositions. In retrospect, Eb's first article lobbying for a homestead exemption in debtor's law was on the right track. From here on out, he would only write on behalf of the poor, the enslaved, and the disenfranchised—to advocate for those rendered silent by various systems of oppression. And it might be time to leave Haines & Haines.

"Would you like a cookie?" Esmeralda asked with a wide grin. "I'll never tell. Harriet won't be here for another half hour." Their clandestine breadbox raids were a time-honored Sunday morning tradition. Mrs. Potts pretended to protest, but her outrage upon her re-entry into the kitchen was a ruse. Esmeralda always found two biscuits on a plate and a couple of cookies tucked away in the furthest recesses of the breadbox.

"On the Fourth, Papa's going to take me to the parade, and then we're going down to Long Wharf to see the tall ships." Henry Mueller's eyes sparkled as he relayed their holiday plans to Susan Graham. He banged his feet against the leg of the French writing desk, eager for his lesson to be over. "There's going to be a twenty-one-gun salute from a cannon." His permanent front tooth had come in, although now he was missing another on the other side, so his lisp lingered. "Kaboom, Kaboom!"

Susan was instructing Henry in the library on Elm Street. It was a late June morning, and a soft summer breeze came in from the direction of the Long Island Sound. The room was cool and dark. The library's ceilings were high, and Mr. Potts had opened the windows and propped the door open, creating cross ventilation. Henry was ostensibly practicing his writing. "Then Papa's promised to take me to the icehouse, so I might try some ice cream." Henry looked up from the writing desk. "Miss Graham, are you even listening to me?"

"Yes, Henry, of course." Susan stood at the window, her arms crossed over the bodice of a floral calico dress, her hair tossed casually on top of her head, anchored by a tortoiseshell comb. Taking a break, she gazed out the window at the busy traffic on Elm Street. She watched horse-drawn carriages, bringing people to and from appointments, carts hitched to single horses, toting hay, potatoes, hemp sacks of flour, and glass containers of fresh milk. Mrs. Potts was outside buying apples for a pie from the fruit wagon. Still dressed in her white cooking apron and cap, the cook stood outside the wrought-iron gate, chatting with the vendor, picking through the bin for the perfect apples for her pie. A mongrel dog passed by on a mission. The sky was a brilliant robin's egg blue except for a few wispy white clouds, way up high.

It was a beautiful summer morning. Susan wanted to be outside, or even better, back in the carriage house with Ruby and Hank, passing the time with Franz. She had grown fond of the horses as she learned how to groom them. But poor Franz was out in the carriage with a determined Malinda, on the hunt for six new chairs for the clinic's waiting room. This was the type of project Malinda Wells could stretch out for hours—even days. She was looking for just the right six chairs, the right size, the right style, the right color, at just the right price. No room for compromise. The quest would tax Franz's patience, Susan predicted.

"I hear you can get different flavors," Henry went on, daydreaming about the upcoming holiday. "Papa says they even have one with strawberries in it."

"Yes, I've heard that," Susan said from the window. Malinda had told her about the new icehouse on Water Street, near Long Wharf, recently opened by a local tavern owner, who planned to operate only during warm weather, serving iced lemonade and punch, desserts, and a variety of ice creams. "Miss Wells says you must eat the ice cream right there at the icehouse—on the spot. They have benches there. Otherwise, it melts straight away." Ned Haines had taken Malinda there several Sundays ago. Malinda and Susan used to go out together in New Haven on Sunday afternoons, but now that Ned and Malinda were courting, their companionable jaunts had come to an end. But Susan did not mind. It gave her time to go out with Franz and Henry.

"But then again, maybe I should start out with vanilla. Papa says the icehouse follows Thomas Jefferson's own recipe—cream, eggs, sugar, crushed vanilla beans, ice." Henry leaned on his elbow. "It's a classic recipe, Papa says, from France. He promises we'll go again. Later in the summer. Then I could try the strawberry." Henry sighed. "I can't make up my mind. What do you think?"

"What do I think?" Susan turned around from the window and looked at her small charge, his straw-colored hair sticking up in several different directions, his feet dangling under the desk from a chair too tall for his legs. For a second, Henry Mueller reminded her of a young Eb Wells, perched on a chair in the schoolroom on the second floor of East York Street. Susan had known Eb when he was about Henry's age and remembered his own set of dangling legs, the hushed concerns about why 'he's not growing taller.' She had stuck up for Eb then, telling him to pay no mind. What mattered was the size of his heart, not how tall he was.

Susan felt a stab of sadness about her estrangement from Eb. Ever since their heated conversation in the library in late April, she and Eb had hardly spoken, except for aggressively polite banter at the dining table. By confronting him, she had meant to clear the air, but somehow the conversation had gone awry. Susan had been far sharper with Eb than she intended. Once she began to commit her feelings to sentences, she surprised herself with how hurt she had been by Eb's behavior toward her. Without warning, that hurt turned to anger. Like a planned prairie fire that had gotten out of hand, Susan had inadvertently scorched the earth between them, killing cherished living beings and useful, lovely weeds she had not meant to set ablaze. The encounter had not gone well.

Susan Graham suspected Eb still cared for her—too much, and not like a sister. His responses to her accusations were all lame. He was defensive. He denied having been avoiding and ignoring her, despite all evidence to the contrary. His excuses made no sense. His painful silences, his acute discomfort with the conversation, his inability to look her in the eye, his pitiful attempts to reconcile with her—his behavior spoke volumes to Susan, even if he had said nothing.

And yet, Susan did not know for sure what those feelings were. Maybe she was reading Eb wrong. Susan and Eb had grown up together in the nursery on East York Street, and later, in the schoolroom. She thought she knew him well. But Eb was different now. He was no longer the boy he was in Savannah, but a grown man, an 'almost' attorney in New Haven. When they were children, Eb wore his emotions on his sleeve. Now he hid them in the vest pocket of his well-tailored suit, along with *The Detritus*, which was also now hidden, close to his heart and inaccessible. Without a declaration from Eb, Susan would say nothing. She did not want to embarrass herself by blurting out the wrong intuition. Instead, Eb and Susan stood on either side of the ravaged, burned-out landscape she had created, engaged in a silent war.

"Yes, what do you think?" Henry emphasized the soft, shattered 's' at the end of the 'yes.' "Should I begin my relationship with ice cream by ordering vanilla?" Henry beamed at Susan. He had just correctly used one of his vocabulary words from yesterday. He hoped she would applaud him. Susan Graham was a great lover of language, and the little boy had discovered a way to make her smile—by playing with words in a clever fashion.

"Your relationship with ice cream?" Susan laughed as she made her way toward the writing desk. "That's very good, Henry." She ran her fingers lightly through his wild blond hair, urging his cowlicks to move in one direction—with no success. "I like that expression very much."

"Thank you." Henry tried to hide his pleasure at her praise. "But what do you think?"

"About what?" Susan sat down next to Henry and looked into his big brown eyes. This is such a nice child, she thought, so funny and sweet. She considered Malinda's disastrous meeting with Eddie Haines last week, Ned's second son.

A year or so older than Henry, Eddie had behaved poorly to Malinda, aloof and ill-mannered, and his father had been chagrined. Her first exchange with Eddie caused Malinda consternation. Perhaps Eddie's sullen attitude meant Malinda was not good with children, she had fretted to Susan. What if that were true? (It might be, Susan thought.) How would Ned feel about that? What if Eddie's approval, Malinda continued, was a hidden condition in any contract with his father? (It might be, Susan thought again.)

"Miss Graham?" Henry tried to get her attention, wiggling in his seat as only a frustrated six-year-old boy can do.

"What do you mean, Henry?" Susan gave him one of her crooked, beautiful smiles.

"About whether I should get vanilla or strawberry," Henry said with exasperation in his voice. "Do you think it matters?"

"No, Henry." Susan tried to take his inquiry seriously. This choice was weighing on his mind, and the boy had sought her good counsel. "It doesn't matter, but I think you should choose the flavor that interests you the most, which seems to be the strawberry." Susan settled into her chair next to him and crossed her ankles under the table, preparing to resume a posture of pedagogy. "Then," she added, "on your second foray to the icehouse, you can order the vanilla to compare. I imagine the recipe will be the same, and your father has promised a second visit before the summer's out."

"Yes!" Henry exclaimed. "I was thinking just the same thing." The little boy looked shyly over at Susan. "Are you coming with me and Papa on the Fourth?"

"I hope to." Susan blushed slightly. "Your father has invited me, but it depends entirely on what Miss Wells is doing." Everyone was making plans for the holiday. All the servants—Franz, Esmeralda, Mr. and Mrs. Potts—had been given the Fourth of July off. Mr. and Mrs. Potts had invited Esmeralda to attend a fair at their church. Franz and Henry were going to the parade and down to Long Wharf.

Eb and Samuel Taylor had plans to go to a picnic with some of the Friends. Dr. Cabot intended to stay home, read Scottish history, and revel in his solitude. Susan had not yet heard from Malinda.

"I'm waiting to hear what her plans are for Independence Day," Susan explained to Henry. "If Miss Wells needs me to accompany her somewhere, I'd have to go with her."

"Why?" Henry swung his feet back and forth under the table in agitation. "Why can't you just come with me and Papa? Why do we always have to wait around to see what Miss Wells wants to do?" Henry behaved respectfully to Malinda Wells under paternal edict, but she scared him. Henry liked his teacher, Miss Graham, a lot better. He thought maybe his father did too. "I want you to come with us." His lower lip quivered ever so slightly.

"Well, I'm her companion, Henry." They had covered this ground before, but Susan understood his frustration—and shared it. "But I suspect Miss Wells will be out with Mr. Haines on the Fourth," she added with a smile, "and if that's the case, I'll gladly go out with you and your father, at least for some of the day." Susan was careful to phrase her response with precision and conditionality. Henry must not construe it as a promise. She did not want to disappoint him. "But we'll have to wait and see. Miss Wells has not yet revealed her plans."

"Good." Henry took this to mean she would probably be joining them. "And what are you going to have?"

"What am I going to have?" Susan was puzzled by his question.

"You know, vanilla or strawberry?" Henry said this with impatience. Again, Miss Graham did not seem to appreciate the pressing matter of the day.

"Vanilla," Susan said with certainty. "I do love strawberries too, Henry, but it's the Fourth of July. I like the idea of trying out Thomas Jefferson's recipe. In honor of his writing the Declaration of Independence."

"Oh. I hadn't thought about that. Maybe I should start out my relationship with ice cream by ordering vanilla after all." Henry looked deflated.

"Well, either way, you're getting ice cream. Let's talk about this some more later." Susan picked up the pen that Henry had put down on the writing table and handed it to him. "But for now, let's get back to your writing." The boy dipped the pen into the inkwell. The two bent their heads over the writing desk, watching his majuscule letters appear on the pages of his commonplace book. He was writing, over and over, the word 'ice cream.'

A warm gust of air suddenly blew into the room from the window. Susan took a deep breath. As soon as the hour was up, she would take Henry out for a walk on the Green. It was a shame to waste such a lovely summer day.

It was not the first time Nathan Haines had found it necessary to speak privately to his apprentice, Eb Wells. The first time, Eb had given assistance to an opposing party, a debtor of one of their banking clients. From his father, Nathan learned that Eb had arranged employment with his uncle for the German widower from the bankrupt Mueller's Laundry. Thankfully, the bank had not discovered Eb's assistance, and the foreclosure went without a hitch. But a client expects his attorney to act in *his* best interests, Nathan explained to Eb as gently as he could, not in the best interests of the opposing party.

During this first conversation, designed to instruct Eb on the importance of maintaining professional boundaries, Nathan had also learned that the German's skill with horses had 'come up over tea.' He had almost fallen off his chair. Why were Eb and Samuel having tea with the debtor? 'Because he invited us to,' Eb had replied with unmistakable naivete. Eb went on to explain himself further. Without employment, in the face of eviction, Franz and Henry Mueller would have become homeless. Franz could have been sent to a debtor's prison, Henry to an orphanage. From his first article, Nathan knew how strongly Eb felt about the need for a homestead exemption in the state's bankruptcy laws. But hiring Franz Mueller was not the solution, Nathan tried to explain. He had the distinct impression that Eb Wells was disagreeing with him, even though he said nothing.

Eb had sat across from Nathan's desk, his hands resting on his lap, listening intently to what Nathan had to say, staring at him through his gold-rimmed glasses. But there were no nods of understanding, no embarrassed glances at the floor, no indicia that Nathan's message was getting through—or that Eb accepted responsibility for any wrongdoing. Nathan had been worried about this attitude ever since Eb's first article. He had lobbied his father to stop Eb from publishing any more, pointing out that the article was distinctly pro-debtor. Eb had argued for the removal of valuable collateral available to banks and other creditors—important clients of Haines & Haines. But his father disagreed.

Ned Haines thought censoring Eb's writing was premature. He wanted to wait and see if Eb published any more articles, to give him a chance to find his voice. And Eb's later articles had not been political. Instead, Eb had offered valuable suggestions on how to deftly draft leases, contracts, and wills. The young man's outrage at the injustices of bankruptcy law seemed to have been an anomaly. No more legislative agendas. His father had warned, 'Don't go about solving a problem until you actually have one.' How many times had Nathan heard that before?

So, this was the second occasion Nathan Haines felt compelled to have a private talk with his apprentice. Nathan found Eb in the law library and asked him to step into his office for 'a little chat.'

Once Eb sat down, Nathan closed the door.

"One of my colleagues from Yale contacted me yesterday." Eb regarded Nathan with a mixture of curiosity and anxiety. "Allen Lowery. He's an attorney here in New Haven, over on Grove Street. You might know the firm. He's running a small law school out of his office."

"Yes, I've heard of Mr. Lowery's school." Eb was relieved. The transgression was giving the law lectures. Samuel had predicted Nathan would find out, and Eb was prepared to defend himself.

"Yes, well, Lowery was upset. He's lost one of his fee-paying students to a new lecturer at Haines & Haines." Nathan looked pointedly at Eb, who returned his gaze. "Those lectures are given by you, Eb. Do I have that right?"

"Yes, sir," Eb did not flinch, looking steadfastly at Nathan. "We do have a study group. Before office hours. And I do organize the lectures. I prepare them the night before, during off hours."

"And did you not think it a good idea to let my father and me know about these lectures?" Nathan looked across the desk at Eb. "It was awkward to have them brought to my attention by an outsider. How do you think I felt, having someone like Allen Lowery tell me what's going on inside my own law practice?" Nathan's jaws were working. His pale face seemed even paler.

"I'm sorry that happened, sir," Eb stammered. "We didn't think we were doing anything inappropriate. It's just a study group. You know, for the apprentices, me, Samuel, and now Oliver."

"I hear four men attend the lectures." Nathan persisted. "That's what Allen Lowery's spies reported to him."

"Well, sir, Ted Redfield attends them as well, but only because he and Oliver come to work together. Ted sleeps most of the time," Eb continued in his defense. "Lots of apprentices do this, sir. They get together and study the law after hours. It's no different from what your father and mine did. If you remember, my father prepared lectures from *Blackstone* to help your father study."

"So, who's the fourth person then, Eb?" Nathan ignored Eb's reference to their fathers' old study group, many years ago. That Nathan's father had been the student, not the teacher, rankled him. He suspected Eb meant to rub that in.

"Donald Hawkins, sir," Eb responded. "The younger brother of Francis Hawkins. You remember Francis?"

"Of course I do. He apprenticed with us for four years." Nathan had great respect for Francis Hawkins, who had been hardworking and obedient, much like Samuel Taylor, and increasingly, Oliver Redfield. None of these others needed to be spoken to privately, not like this Eb Wells. This was his second problematic apprentice from that fancy Litchfield Law School. The first one believed himself to be above the lowly task of copying a contract, and when he finally relented, his handwriting was abysmal. He had to be fired. "Francis is up in Haddam now," Nathan added. "Starting his own law practice."

"Yes, well, Francis asked Samuel if it would be all right if his younger brother Donald came to our study group." Eb tried to reconstruct his lengthy negotiation with Samuel Taylor. "Donald couldn't afford the lectures at Lowery's. They were very dear. And since Donald was the brother of a former Haines & Haines apprentice, we felt he was part of our law practice family." Nathan stared at Eb from across his desk, his jaws clenched and in motion. "We haven't used any lamp oil, sir. I lecture in the dark, and we haven't charged Donald any fee." Eb concluded his defense. "We didn't think it would be appropriate to take money. Not without your permission."

"I suppose I should be grateful you gave Haines & Haines any thought at all," Nathan said with rancor. "Didn't you realize this might cause difficulties—inviting a former student of Lowery's to the lectures, without charging him a fee?" Nathan crossed his arms and glared at Eb. "It was your failure to charge a fee that upset Allen

Lowery—that and the theft of one of his law students."

"I don't follow you, sir. I'm sorry for stealing his student, but what difference does it make to Mr. Lowery whether Donald did or didn't pay me?" Because Eb was not interested in making money, he did not understand those who were.

"Because if you're offering this service for free," Nathan explained impatiently, "it makes it difficult for someone like Lowery to charge for his services." Nathan recalled how angry his old Yale colleague had been the day before. Several of Lowery's students had challenged the recent hike in his teaching fees, arguing they had heard Haines & Haines on Fleet Street was offering lectures—far better lectures than Lowery's—for nothing. A few had threatened to take their business elsewhere.

"But I wouldn't ask Donald to pay, sir," Eb responded. "He's the brother of Francis Hawkins. Plus, Samuel and I agreed. No more outsiders. Donald would be the sole exception. And there've been no others."

Eb did not reveal to Nathan Haines how many inquiries he and Samuel had received from other apprentices who wanted to attend his lectures. Donald Hawkins had improvidently sung Eb's praises at a nearby tavern to an entire tableful of apprentices from other law practices. That one liquid incident of indiscretion spread the news far and wide. Donald's *Ode to Eb Wells* was like throwing a pebble into the still pond of the New Haven apprentice community. News of Eb's excellence as a teacher was still reaching shores far away. Eb stuck to his agreement to 'no more outsiders' but was sympathetic to these requests. Donald Hawkins was not the only one having to choose between buying a pair of boots or paying for lectures from someone like Allen Lowery. Donald's feet were wet and cold all last year.

"I'm going to have to ask you to disinvite Donald Hawkins from the lectures," Nathan Haines announced, not wanting to address the niceties of the arrangement that Samuel and Eb had agreed upon.

Nathan needed to maintain cordial relations with Allen Lowery. Not only was Lowery a fellow Yale alum, but Nathan negotiated contracts with him—two warriors protecting the interests of their clients—a banker, a manufacturer, or some other prosperous business concern. Granting Lowery this favor tipped the balance of power in Nathan's direction.

Nathan continued with his edict. "What you and the other apprentices at Haines & Haines do on your own time is your business, although I would prefer your study group meet in the evening. Most of the 'for fee' lectures for apprentices take place in the morning. Evening sessions make it look more like a traditional study group."

"I don't mind giving the lectures in the evening, sir," Eb replied. "We could all go out to the tavern afterward. But cutting Donald out doesn't seem fair. He gets almost no supervision in his apprenticeship. Think of it, sir. He must pay for the privilege of working for free." Eb paused, trying to come up with a solution. "Could he still come to the evening sessions?"

"No," Nathan said promptly. "That isn't going to happen. Not here at Haines & Haines."

"May I help Donald privately in my own home then, on off hours?" Eb pressed. "Without charging him? A friend helping a friend?"

"I suppose so," Nathan said reluctantly, knowing he lacked the power to enforce a 'no.' "But no more lectures in the morning at Haines & Haines. You may use the scriveners' room for a study group at night, or the library. I don't care which. And light the lamp, for goodness' sake. No need to be in the dark." Eb started to get up from the chair. "And no outsiders at all."

"Is there anything else, sir?" Eb asked Nathan, his face impassive.

"That's it for now, Eb," Nathan said briskly, trying to give him a smile. He regretted being so heavy-handed with Eb Wells, who was, by far and away, his best legal researcher, his best drafter, and one of his most talented scriveners. Haines & Haines had never had such a big legal mind under its roof before. Nathan also knew, without ever attending one, that Eb's lectures were excellent, far better than anything Allen Lowery had to offer. Eb was filling in the instructional vacuum his father's absences had created. Still, at least Nathan could report to his old colleague from Yale that the impromptu law lectures happening at Haines & Haines, for no fee, had come to an end.

But I must remember, Nathan spoke sternly to himself. Eb Wells is *not* like the other apprentice from the Litchfield Law School. He is the son of William Wells, an old family friend who had attended college and apprenticed with Nathan's father. Eb is also the nephew of Dr. Ebenezer Cabot, another Yale colleague of his father's and a respected New Haven physician.

Nathan must tread lightly. Eb Wells had a small cadre of guardian angels hovering over him. Then there was the most powerful angel of them all—a woman in possession of a seductive Southern accent and smooth alabaster skin that exuded the sweet smell of lavender soap. Eb Wells was her baby brother, and his father was in love with her. These were facts to reckon with.

Letter to Eb Wells from John Wells, Charleston,
July 15, 1821

Dear Eb,

Thank you for your letter. I'm sorry if I alarmed you about Eliza's health. She did have a bad bout of summer fever, but is fine now. The girls too are well and miss their Uncle Eb and Aunt Malinda.

I agree with you about allowing Lottie Graham to stay on East York Street. Her presence in the house keeps it safe. I'm comfortable charging her no rent and making no claims on her proceeds from the boarders. Lottie was so good to our mother, and Malinda may want to move back to Savannah after her visit up north. It's best not to sell the house right now. I'm going down to Savannah next month for some depositions. I'll speak to Lottie then.

Speaking of Malinda, she writes she's been walking out with Ned Haines, taking carriage rides with him on Sundays. Is this true? What is our sister thinking? Allowing herself to be courted by such an old man? Ned Haines started at Yale the same year as our father. He must be almost sixty, and Malinda is just thirty. Should we be encouraging this courtship? Malinda has never had a beau before. Eliza worries that her inexperience will make her vulnerable to predation. Since Haines is the senior partner in the law practice, he can't be after her money. Does he have children from his second wife? Malinda didn't say. I'd hate to see her sacrifice herself—to become a governess for someone else's child and a nursemaid to an old man. I don't know this Mr. Haines. What do you think of him? Does it worry you that his wives have all died? Please assess the situation and let me know if you think we should intervene. Malinda may need the protection of her brothers.

On another subject, should we reconsider the stipend we're paying Susan Graham? Malinda sounds busy with the clinic and now Mr. Haines. Malinda writes that Susan is spending her days educating the child of the new coachman. Is this true? Our uncle has written about renovating the carriage house, about the new carriage, the coachman, and his son. This is all fine, but I'm puzzled as to why our family is undertaking this boy's education. Susan's employment is for the benefit of our sister as her companion. I suspect this is all Malinda's idea—a way to keep Susan occupied. Malinda cannot bear for anyone to be idle. But I must confess, from a distance, I don't understand the labor Susan has been put to. Please let me know your thoughts on this as well.

I am happy to report that Thomas Bradford arrived from Connecticut at the end of May. Your assessment was on the mark, Eb. He's hardworking and able, adept at finding practical solutions. Thomas corresponds with the young woman you walked out with last year in Litchfield, Miss Montgomery. Eliza teases him mercilessly about matrimony. He's been coming to our house for supper once a week. The women in my family find him very handsome. The girls make a great fuss over him, particularly Amanda, who thinks Thomas is 'rugged.'

I'm glad you've been substantially relieved of your scrivener duties. No one is supposed to 'enjoy' their apprenticeship, Eb. It's a period of servitude, taking on tasks no one else wants to do. I hope you'll stick out the year at Haines & Haines. It won't be long before you can be admitted to a bar. Hold out until then. If transactional work is not to your liking, try another kind of practice. Perhaps land law? Or trial work? I'm sure your beloved Judge Reeve will encourage you to diversify as well. Malinda sends me your articles about the law. I read them with great interest. Don't give up on the law, not just yet.

I must go. Please extend my warmest regards to Malinda, our uncle, and Susan as well. I hope to hear back from you soon, particularly about Malinda. My worries about Susan are of less concern. I don't mean to appear stingy. You know that I consider her a member of the family.

All the best,

Your brother,
John

"I love how fast the weather changes in the summer," Rebecca Harding said, her arm linked in Martha Lewis's. The two friends walked back to the Litchfield Female Academy along the Goshen Road. It was a Sunday afternoon in early August. Within an hour, the heat of the day had dissipated, and the sky had turned a menacing, roiling gray. A slight wind stirred up. The leaves of the maple trees along the road were rustling, the white pines whispering. A summer squall was on its way. Rebecca and Martha had been chatting about the pros and cons of Jack Lewis's fiancée, Hannah Ward, whether boiled eggs were entirely satisfying, and the weather.

That morning, Rebecca had attended services at the Litchfield Congregational Church with Martha's family and joined them afterward in their cottage for a cold midday meal. Martha's mother, Ruth Lewis, had baked a peach pie the day before, and Rebecca obliged her by eating two pieces. Ruth was distressed by how thin and pale Rebecca had become during her first year of teaching. Her battles in Wethersfield with The Ogre had taken their toll.

"Your mother's trying to fatten me up." Rebecca laughed, taking off her sun hat and pulling out the fastener of her bun at the nape of her neck. She let her dark hair fall to her shoulders. The sudden drop in temperature was refreshing.

"You couldn't be fat if you wanted to," Martha said with a chuckle. Now back in Litchfield for almost two months, Rebecca had put on some much-needed weight. Her cheeks had regained color from their long walks, and the purple half-circles under her eyes had faded. Both Rebecca and Martha were lodging with Miss Pierce over the summer. Rebecca had returned to Litchfield to help Miss Mary Pierce admit the fall class at the female academy, and Martha was hired to make promotional materials for the school. Miss Pierce had asked Martha if she also wanted to board for the summer.

Martha was happy to do so. She could evade the many domestic tasks her mother had saved up for her. She also delighted in spending time with her friend Rebecca. If Rebecca received an offer to teach at the Morris Academy, she would be moving to South Farms at the end of the summer. South Farms was not far away. But while Rebecca would come to Litchfield often, the two friends would not have the luxury of roaming the Litchfield hills in the afternoons or reading novels together at night.

"How do you think Charles seems?" Martha asked.

Rebecca was frank. "A little tense. I fear working in Mr. Fuller's law office taxes him." Charles Godwin fell ill during his first year of law school, requiring an extra year to complete the course. Now that he had done so, Charles spent mornings apprenticing at the probate practice of Theodore Fuller, Esquire, on South Street in Litchfield, and afternoons working in the portrait studio with Martha's father. Charles was not hale and hearty to begin with. He was so tall and thin that Eb used to call him the 'Great Blue Heron.' "He looked exhausted to me," Rebecca admitted.

"True." Martha sighed with resignation. "I'm not sure Charles has the constitution for the law." It was Martha who had persuaded Charles to promise to complete his law studies, apprentice with a local attorney, and be admitted to the bar. He was a man who kept his promises, sometimes to the detriment of his health and happiness. "I may have to accept that. His mother and father too. He deserves credit for trying." A silence fell between them.

"I thought the whole idea was to find Charles some quiet corner of the law." Rebecca observed Martha's grave face. "So that he could feed your children who don't exist yet and pay for your fine clothes." Rebecca teased Martha gently, trying to coax a smile from her. Martha wore a new, pale lime-green cotton frock, complementing her green eyes and coppery red hair, currently piled up under her straw hat. "Like that pretty dress."

"I'll have you know, I paid for this material myself. From my map money. Mother made the dress, of course." Martha had been commissioned by Mrs. Tallmadge, a wealthy woman in town, to make a map. Last year, Charles had painted her portrait, but she had seen Martha's map of the town of Litchfield at Miss Pierce's exhibition and wanted one to hang in the foyer of her stately home. For this, Martha had been paid handsomely. She smoothed the new dress down, wrinkled from sitting so long at the kitchen table. "Charles didn't contribute one cent."

"That's great, Martha." Rebecca envied her friend's ability to make beautiful things. Being a teacher yielded fewer tangible results—a flash of understanding on a student's face, a whispered word of gratitude from a worried parent. Often, Rebecca felt like she was throwing pebbles into the ocean. "What does Charles say about his apprenticeship? He talked about miniature portraits today, but I didn't hear one word about the law."

"Not much. You know how Charles is. He's not inclined to complain. He may erupt once a year, but he doesn't grumble daily." Martha stopped for a moment to admire a towering foxglove. In the summer, she always kept a lookout for this proud plant when walking this way. Its hardiness made Martha suspect the vigilance of an unseen healer, a woman who understood herbs and medicinal plants. She admired the purple trumpet-shaped blossoms, with their speckled lips. "Maybe that's just how men are," Martha added absentmindedly.

"Not all men." Rebecca thought about Eb's letters from Haines & Haines. Eb *was* inclined toward daily grumbling, instead of annual eruptions. Rebecca felt certain everyone on Elm Street had also received an earful. "I don't think anyone would ever accuse Eb Wells of being a stoic." Pulling on her arm, Rebecca urged Martha to leave the foxglove and step up their pace. "Come on, let's go. I smell rain."

"Eb and Charles are different that way," Martha said as she yielded to Rebecca's entreaties.

"I'll have to admit. . ." Rebecca considered her own behavior. "I too grumble daily. My letters about The Ogre last year were as indulgent as Eb's. I suspect it's a matter of temperament," she declared. "Not if one is male or female. Perhaps daily grumbling lets out a little steam slowly to ensure eruptions don't occur."

Rebecca found herself suddenly intrigued, although she could feel her 'teacher voice' coming on, an affectation Martha had no patience for. Rebecca must write Eb about her grumbling analysis. Eb would develop a theory, perhaps a formula on how many daily grumbles it took to stave off one ill-advised eruption. To herself, Rebecca added another layer of analysis. He who is inclined to grumble needs someone to grumble to. She grumbled about The Ogre to Eb. Eb grumbled about Nathan Haines to her. There is a grumbler and a grumblee. But a third party is involved, a silent partner who knows nothing about the grumble—he who is grumbled about. It reminded Rebecca of third-party beneficiaries in contract law.

"Maybe so," Martha said. "I hadn't thought of it that way, but I guess you are sort of a grumbler."

"Complaining comes from being passionate about something." Rebecca fanned herself with her hat, still deep in thought. "Think about me and Eb. I was outraged at The Ogre's backward views on female education. Eb was incensed by unjust bankruptcy laws and the exploitation of apprentices. We're both idealists. When reality fails us, we grumble."

"Should I worry about Charles? That he doesn't grumble about work?" Martha glanced over at her friend, an apprehensive look on her face.

"Of course not. Charles is passionate," Rebecca hastily added, not wanting to sound critical. "At least about his art. Just not so much about the law."

"Are you looking forward to seeing Eb?" Martha asked. Haines & Haines always closed for two weeks at the end of August. Eb was coming up to Litchfield for a visit, staying with Mrs. Edwards.

"I am," Rebecca said with restraint. She was both excited about seeing Eb and dreading it. Their romantic relationship was new and tentative. She worried Eb would find her a disappointment in the flesh. Or worse, maybe Eb might seek clarity about where they were headed.

"Charles is so looking forward to seeing him," Martha said. "Me too. Mother's planning a big Saturday supper one week he's here." She slid her arm back into Rebecca's, and they walked without talking for a while, listening to the wind and the rustling leaves. Martha broke the silence, sounding tentative. "Mr. Fuller tells Charles there's to be a will contest. A client of theirs just died and left his farm and all his money to his housekeeper, or his wife. I'm not clear which. His estranged brothers are contesting the will. That means a trial. Mr. Fuller says he'll need more help, and Charles doesn't want to work full-time." The two young women neared the edge of town. A few dense raindrops had started to fall. "Mr. Fuller's talking about getting another apprentice to help prepare for trial. Maybe part-time."

"I see," Rebecca murmured.

"The truth is, Rebecca," Martha continued with hesitation. "Charles isn't up to the demands of a trial, even as second chair. It's too much exposure for him."

Watching a trial in a county seat like Litchfield was like going to the theater. A juicy trial drew spectators from all over northwest Connecticut and all walks of life. The courtroom would be packed with law students, female academy students, gentlemen, their wives, farmers, workmen, free Blacks, even children. The proceedings in the courthouse would be reported on, discussed, and argued about in taverns, boarding houses, and hotels, over kitchen tables, in stables, in mills, in the streets of small towns, across pillows, and under blankets in the dark. A trial was a spectacle, something to behold—and talk about.

The Litchfield courthouse stood on the Green, its white walls, grand pillars, and spire giving it the appearance of a Congregational church. Much like a minister, the judge sat in the front of the courtroom on a raised dais, dictating to the attorneys down below who sat at tables on either side. There was a hierarchy to the seating in the courthouse. The more elite members of society sat up front in comfortable chairs, the farmers behind them on pine benches. Younger attorneys, female academy students, and law students took over the gallery, while under the gallery stood the furnace and iron workers, the teamsters, the farriers, bakers, and wheelwrights. Everyone flocked to the courthouse to watch Litchfield's famous 'fighting bar.'

Trials were held during the March, September, and December sessions of the Superior Court. When court was in session, trial lawyers—the celebrities of their day—convened from all over the state, staying at the United States Hotel, the Catlin House, the many boarding houses in town, or with friends. Trial work was the most performative aspect of the practice of law, and being in the spotlight was part of the job. Martha knew Charles would hate it. When he first came to Litchfield, Charles had suffered from crippling shyness. Even though he had emerged from his shell, the public scrutiny of a trial would panic him.

"Charles took the job with Mr. Fuller because he does probate work," Martha continued. "Mostly, he stays in his house and writes wills for people. We all thought it would be a peaceful place for Charles to practice."

Rebecca nodded, remembering the deliberations over where Charles might do his apprenticeship.

"But it turns out even a probate practice has its share of litigation. But a trial? Sitting second chair? It's too much for Charles."

"You're right." Rebecca put her hat back on her head as they approached the female academy. "I don't see Charles being up for that, even sitting at Mr. Fuller's elbow."

"It sounds to me"—Martha cast a sly look in Rebecca's direction—"that trial work might be something your Eb would be good at." She was always plotting ways to get Rebecca and Eb together. "Doesn't it?" Martha had a point. In law school, Eb had been a stellar advocate in the moot court. A match between Eb Wells and Oliver Hull had guaranteed a packed house. Eb thrived on the intense preparation, the challenge of thinking on his feet, the excitement of the heated exchange, and all the attention.

"It does, Martha," Rebecca said thoughtfully. "Eb might be very good at that." The two women stopped talking. They had arrived. Miss Mary Pierce peered anxiously out the door of her sister's house on North Street, watching the storm arrive, enjoying the dip in temperature. She waved to Rebecca and Martha, beckoning them to come in out of the rain. The threatening sky was finally ready to yield its harvest. Rebecca and Martha waved back. They would resume this conversation later.

*Letter to John Wells from Eb Wells, New Haven,
August 10, 1821*

Dear John,

Sorry not to have gotten back to you sooner. Things are so busy at work. We were all relieved to hear Eliza's summer fever was not serious.

Regarding Mr. Ned Haines. Yes, Malinda has formed a romantic attachment to him. I too worry that he's too old. He'll be sixty soon. But apart from that, Ned Haines is an honorable man. He's well-respected in the New Haven legal community and has been a good employer to me. He's a Yale graduate like yourself, of considerable wealth, and always treats Malinda in a respectful fashion. Uncle

Ebenezer thinks highly of him. It's not his fault his wives seem to die on him. You were right, though—there is a son from the second wife, just seven years old. Malinda finds Eddie sullen, but I point out to her that he's lost his mother. It can't be easy for him, and he might resent his father's affection for someone new. But I agree—Malinda might be left to raise the boy on her own, if Ned predeceases her. She refuses to discuss this, reminding me that she's not a child whenever I point out the perils of her situation.

Honestly, John, do we even have the power to stop such a marriage? You speak of intervening. How could we do that? Who would Ned Haines ask for permission to marry her? Our uncle? You, her older brother? If you refused to give permission, what legal effect would that have? You're the trustee of her bequest from Mother's estate—does that provide any leverage? At present, I am not in favor of any intervention. Malinda seems happier than I've ever seen her.

As for Susan Graham, you were also right. It was Malinda who assigned Susan the task of educating Henry, the son of our uncle's new coachman. Henry is six years old and the pet of the entire household. Esmeralda, Mrs. Potts, Susan, our uncle, me, even Malinda in her own way—we all dote on him. I fear Susan is forming a romantic attachment to his father, Franz. To be fair, Franz Mueller strikes me as an honorable man, although I believe he was once in prison. Still, he treats Susan respectfully. Even though Susan is busy with Henry, she still serves as Malinda's companion. The two spend a great deal of time together, and Malinda needs a friend right now as she figures out her future. I think we should continue Susan's stipend and not interfere with the work Malinda has assigned to her. I hope you'll agree. We are in accord on Lottie, by the way.

I'm glad to hear things are working out with Thomas Bradford. I hope you and Eliza support him in his temperance. Thomas has strengths in the practical realm, something you would never have gotten from me, I assure you.

Thank you for your advice on my apprenticeship. I'm not sure I can stick it out at Haines & Haines. I keep having run-ins with Nathan. I've received an inquiry from Mr. Theodore Fuller, a Litchfield attorney. My friend Charles Godwin has a part-time apprenticeship with him, and Mr. Fuller's looking for another part-time apprentice for perhaps a year, or even less, whatever time it takes to prepare for a trial. His work is mostly probate, but a will contest is coming down the pike. We have a two-week break from work, and I'm going up to Litchfield for a visit. I may meet with Mr. Fuller then, as a courtesy.

I should warn you, John. I have an opinion piece coming out in the *Courant* next week criticizing the American Colonization Society. It's not likely that the views expressed in a Hartford newspaper will make it down to Charleston, but I thought I'd give you a heads-up.

Please extend all my love to Eliza and the girls. Pass a scrap of meat under the table to Monroe. Give my regards to Thomas Bradford, the world's worst correspondent. Tell him to keep Eliza guessing about his plans for matrimony.

Yours with affection,

Eb

CHAPTER 4

Getting the Sack

Eb lounged on the back porch steps of Elm Street, enjoying his evening visit with Mrs. Tittles. Henry sat inside at the kitchen table, glowering at six untouched Brussel sprouts. Mrs. Potts had baked ginger cookies that morning, but he would not get one until he ate his vegetables. Esmeralda and Mrs. Potts stood at the dry sink, chatting and washing dishes. Mr. Potts sat across the table from Henry, his nose in last week's paper, trying to ignore the nightly domestic drama over Henry and his vegetables. Franz Mueller was out in the carriage house, feeding the horses, cleaning their stalls, preparing them for their night's slumber.

It was twilight. Now that it was mid-August, darkness came more quickly. The cicadas began to chitterrrrrrrrrrrrrr chatterrrrrrrr-rrrrrr from the branches of the trees. When the sun went down, Eb could feel a hint of autumn in the air. He rubbed the calico cat under her chin, and in return, she gave him a throaty purr. Eb was relieved that Mrs. Tittles was now welcome in the kitchen. When the cold weather came, she would be snug and warm. Mrs. Tittles had already made a conquest of Mrs. Potts, who was her source of cream and tidbits of meat. But Esmeralda Smith was now her favorite. How could the calico cat be so perverse, Eb wondered, to be enamored of the one person who disliked her the most?

Mrs. Tittles followed the old housekeeper around, butting her head up against Esmeralda's ankles. At first, Esmeralda had shooed her away. But Mrs. Tittles was unrelenting. When Esmeralda wiped the last dish dry and sank into her chair by the kitchen fire, Mrs. Tittles was right there, ready to curl up at her feet. Esmeralda tolerated her presence. Eb was impressed by the inroads Mrs. Tittles had made with Esmeralda, especially in light of the 'cat hauling' story.

Noticing Susan Graham coming out the kitchen door, Eb waved at her from a distance, and she waved back. She approached Eb and Mrs. Tittles on the back porch steps.

"Hi, Eb," she said. "Mrs. Tittles." She looked down at Eb, who was stroking the cat. In the murky twilight, Eb looked many years younger than his twenty-three years. She felt nostalgia for the Eb Wells she used to know in Savannah. She had loved that boy and missed him.

"Susan." Eb gave her a curt nod. Susan and Eb had barely spoken since their confrontation in the library last April. Susan had slammed the door shut on any further communication, and it had remained closed. Eb emerged from that conversation feeling ashamed. Susan had called him out on his thoughtless behavior toward her, and Eb had lacked the courage to explain himself. Now it was too late. She was romantically involved with Franz Mueller.

"Are you on a nocturnal errand?" His question came out sounding snide, full of innuendo. Eb tried not to be petty about Susan's interest in Franz Mueller. It was the least he could do. Over the past few months, Eb had excoriated himself for having reduced Susan to a female body. He did sometimes still think of her at night, conjuring her up in his mind's eye, the supple way she moved, the shape of her legs beneath her calico skirt. But these fantasies were diminishing the more Susan had her eyes on Franz.

"I'm going out to help Franz with the horses," Susan answered evenly, ignoring Eb's tone of voice. "Henry is engaged in warfare over Brussel sprouts. I don't have the stamina for that. I thought I'd come out to the stable. Help Franz."

"You're spending a lot of time with the horses, Susan." Eb looked up at her from the steps. It was growing dark, and he could not make out the features of her face, just the outline of her lithe body, standing there, one hand on her hip, the other in her skirt pocket.

"Franz has taught Henry and me how to groom them." Susan spoke in a steady voice, refusing to take Eb's bait. "We take breaks during the day to tend to the horses. I help out. That's all."

"That's very generous of you," Eb said, again with a sarcasm he could not seem to stifle. "I'm sure Mr. Mueller appreciates it." He emphasized 'Mr. Mueller,' mocking her intimacy with the coachman.

"It isn't a matter of generosity, Eb." Susan turned in the direction of the carriage house. "I love the horses." Eb said nothing but watched her melt into the evening shadows as she made her way across the yard. He looked down at the calico cat. Mrs. Tittles was annoyed to no longer be the center of his attention. He gave her a long stroke almost down to her tail. Her ears went back. Eb watched Susan disappear into the stable.

"You're my best girl, Mrs. Tittles," Eb crooned to the cat. "And the only woman in my life who isn't complicated." He laughed ruefully to himself, thinking about his upcoming visit to Litchfield. There he would see Rebecca Harding for the first time in almost a year—a thought vaguely terrifying to him. He also considered the plight of his older sister, entangled with a man twice her age, encumbered with a sulky child. Or of Susan Graham—who would barely speak to him—in love with a German widower. A handsome, blond German widower, not afraid of horses, and much taller than Eb. He reached the beginning of Mrs. Tittles's tail, and the calico cat turned around and nipped the side of his hand. That is what he gets for ignoring her ears. "Ouch." Eb rubbed the side of his hand. "I'm sorry, Mrs. Tittles. I disrespected your boundaries." He petted her cautiously on the head. Even the female cat in his life was complicated.

Eb was looking forward to his trip to Litchfield. He needed to consult with Judge Reeve about his future and discuss his love life with Charles Godwin—who always changed Eb's perspective. Eb also sought advice from Mrs. Edwards, who gave him valuable insights into women. He would be staying in his old attic room in her boarding house. Best of all, Mrs. Edwards's orange-and-white cat, the protector of the attic's hanging sausages, drying herbs, and aging cheeses, would sleep at his feet. Eb smiled to no one in the dark. Sir Winston, now there's a fine fellow who would never nip my hand.

From across the yard, Eb could see the silhouettes of Susan and Franz through the open stable door, each brushing Ruby on either side. Together, the two worked in silence, attuned to the flickering ears of the horse, and the movements and moods of the other. Occasionally, Franz must have said something amusing because Eb could see the profile of Susan's head, tilting ever so slightly backward, one of her signature gestures, not quite a laugh, but rather a smile, expressed through her entire body, as well as her face. Eb loved that gesture of Susan's. He felt a profound sadness he could not express. Susan and Franz looked like a couple, and he, Eb Wells, was sitting outside alone in the dark. Even Mrs. Tittles had left for the carriage house.

"I'm so proud of you, Rebecca." Ruth Lewis and Rebecca Harding sat at the kitchen table in the Lewis cottage. Breakfast was laid out on a blue-and-white checkered homespun tablecloth. It was late summer, but this morning's air was cool enough to make Ruth's hip joint ache. She was relieved to sit at the table, talking to her daughter's best friend. Rebecca's dark brown hair was tucked behind her ears, falling around her shoulders, and she was wearing Martha's robe. The two women were alone. Benjamin Lewis and Charles Godwin were out in the portrait studio. Jack Lewis was in Kent, visiting his fiancée's family. Rebecca had gotten up early, lured into the kitchen by the smell of sizzling bacon, leaving Martha sound asleep in bed. "Teaching jobs are hard to come by."

"I know," Rebecca mumbled through her toast, smothered with butter and jam. She had just been offered a one-year contract as a tutoress at the Morris Academy. "I'm lucky to get the job."

"You'll have to get lodgings in South Farms, I suppose." Ruth Lewis got up to refresh the teapot with boiling water. "It's too far to be going back and forth every day, particularly in the winter. But I hope you'll return to Litchfield on Saturdays. That way, you can come to church with us on the Sabbath."

"I'd like to." Rebecca wiped the sides of her mouth with her cloth napkin, removing the butter residue. "But my room at Miss Pierce's has been let for this year." Miss Pierce had warned her of this eventuality when Rebecca had arrived last June with her trunk, hoping to be offered the job at the Morris Academy. "The incoming class at Miss Pierce's is large this year, with more local boys than ever." Rebecca poured cream into her teacup, anticipating more tea. "A new teaching assistant will be in my third-floor room. She's from Augusta, coming the first week of September."

"Oh dear." Ruth Lewis hung the kettle back up on the iron, returning to her seat at the table. "Martha must be disappointed."

"We both are," Rebecca admitted. "But we've been expecting it, and we've had a lovely summer together. Besides, even though Martha boards with Miss Pierce, she always comes home to you and Mr. Lewis on Saturday and Sunday. And Charles, of course." On the few occasions Rebecca had joined Martha at the Lewis cottage, they had shared Martha's bed—an unsustainable arrangement. The bed was narrow, and Martha snored. "So, even if I had my room at Miss Pierce's for Saturday and Sunday, Martha wouldn't be there. We'd be ships in the night."

"Then you too must come home to us at the end of each week, my dear," Mrs. Lewis said promptly, taking the pitcher of cream from Rebecca's hand. "I'll clear out Robert's old room in the back. When Charles came to us, Jack moved the studio office into Ben's old room, but we've been using Robert's for storage."

Ruth Lewis thought about that back bedroom with horror— and delight at its possible excavation. No bigger than a cupboard, the room was packed with things no one wanted or needed. Broken snowshoes, frames for profiles that had not worked out, Ruth's abandoned knitting projects, mismatched boxes and lids, Martha's out-of-style hats she no longer wore. Somewhere beneath all that mess was a cot and a small nightstand. If Ruth carted the junk away, Robert's old room might make a suitable nest for Rebecca Harding.

"Oh, that's so kind." Rebecca's face was flushed. "But I wouldn't want to impose."

"Nonsense," Ruth Lewis said without missing a beat. "We've made room for Charles. We can make room for you too." Since his illness during law school, Martha's fiancé had lived in the portrait studio behind the Lewis cottage. "Martha would love it. We all would, Rebecca." Ruth squeezed Rebecca's hand. "Benjamin and I would love for you to come to us at the end of your teaching week. For Saturday and the Sabbath." She repeated her offer with deliberation, seeing Rebecca flustered.

"I'd give you a boarding fee." Rebecca knew Charles Godwin paid for his room and board. "For the two nights a week."

"Yes, well, you could do that if you'd like, but it's really not necessary."

"No, I'd like to," Rebecca said hastily. "It would make me feel easier." She knew Ruth Lewis adhered to a strict household budget and counted her pennies. Rebecca's salary was not substantial at the Morris Academy, but she had money left over from the summer stipend. Paying for her week's end boarding was affordable.

"Well, that's settled then." Mrs. Lewis put her teacup down. "Rebecca, you're like a second daughter to me." She looked over at Rebecca, thinking how different this slender, pale waif of a girl was from her own boisterous Martha. "You're an honorary member of the Lewis family, and always welcome here, no matter the circumstances."

"Thank you, Mrs. Lewis." Rebecca was suddenly overcome with emotion. Her entire family was buried in Wethersfield on Hungry Hill. Her own mother died in childbirth when she was eight, and her father died of blood poisoning when she was twelve. Her two baby brothers died in infancy. After her father's death, she was forced to live with her only living relative, a great-aunt who lived in Hartford—a dutiful, dour woman, who was relieved when Rebecca departed for the Litchfield Female Academy, never to return. Rebecca Harding had been an orphan for so long that Martha's mother offering her honorary membership in the Lewis family, and a place to come at the week's end, brought tears to her eyes. "I'd love to come here for the Sabbath."

"And that way, you could see Eb each week too, if he takes this job with Mr. Fuller." Ruth got up and made her way to the breadbox in search of shortbread, having hidden some of last week's batch for a rare episode of solitude.

"Yes," Rebecca murmured, reddening slightly. "I could." She gave Mrs. Lewis a weak smile. Eb Wells would be in Litchfield soon, to visit her and all his friends, and possibly for a job interview. "If he comes back to Litchfield."

"I think we need some shortbread to celebrate," Ruth Lewis said with a triumphant smile, bringing out a small parcel from the bread-box, wrapped in muslin. "There's just enough for you and me," she said slyly. "Let's have it now before Martha wakes up."

"Good idea," Rebecca said, her dark eyes glistening. She was not disposed to conspire against her best friend, who lay slumbering in her bedroom, sprawled on her back, her mouth wide open, drooling. But if the plan had something to do with Ruth Lewis's shortbread, Rebecca Harding had no scruples.

Eb Wells's article against repatriating free Blacks to Africa came out in the second week of August 1821. It expanded on his ideas from his last moot court argument at law school, more than a year ago. The article was published in the New Haven *Connecticut Journal,* the *Connecticut Courant* in Hartford, and the *Providence Gazette.* Through his mother's connections, Samuel also placed it with *The Christian Watchman* and the *Baptist Register.*

Just the year before, the first group of free Black settlers, funded by the United States government, had set sail to Sierra Leone on the west coast of Africa. The American Colonization Society (ACS) had sponsored the fledgling colony. Eb asked his readers to consider the fairness of sending away members of valuable free Black communities. They had homes and livelihoods in this country, with roots as deep as many white families who claimed to be patriotic Americans. Almost eight thousand African-descended men had fought in the War for Independence, others in the War of 1812. Most free Blacks opposed the 'Back to Africa' movement. They identified as Americans and did not want to be uprooted from their homes—to be sent into exile to a continent they no longer belonged to.

The proponents of the 'Back to Africa' movement were strange bedfellows—a handful of abolitionists and slave owners from the South. The abolitionists in favor of the American Colonization Society argued that free Blacks would never be free from discrimination in America. Their 'amalgamation' would never happen. In Africa—the land of their ancestors—they could fulfill their potential as human beings and spread Christianity to the heathens. For these abolitionists, the repatriation of free Blacks to Africa was regarded as a humanitarian effort.

Eb did not dispute their good intentions but quarreled with their assumptions. Why should we assume that 'amalgamation' would never happen? Or that free Blacks sent back to Africa could fulfill their potential as human beings? Why do we discount the contributions that free Blacks have already made to this country? Why not support them here, in America, where they have lived for decades, sometimes centuries, where they have fought in our wars, raised families, and built homes and businesses?

The other proponents of the 'Back to Africa' movement were white Southern plantation owners like Jefferson, Madison, even President Monroe, men whose livelihood depended on slave labor, who feared slave insurrections and race wars. Free Blacks posed a threat to the big plantations by assisting runaway slaves to escape to freedom. Many free Blacks were also leaders in the burgeoning anti-slavery movement. Ministers in free Black churches argued for emancipation from their pulpits, and free Black communities started schools, educating their children, giving them tools to fight oppression. Many free Blacks were vocal in their opposition to slavery, writing and speaking about its moral depravity, fomenting dissent. Without these leaders in the free Black community, who would be the champions of enslaved Africans? One way to silence them would be to ship them back to colonies in West Africa. Let them denounce slavery from the west coast of Africa, an ocean away. The Southern planters who supported the 'Back to Africa' movement shared no interest in helping free Blacks meet their full human potential. Their goal was to keep enslaved Africans in chains.

Eb's article against the 'Back to Africa' movement caused quite a stir—throughout New England and at Haines & Haines. He knew it would sound the death knell of his employment, but he no longer cared. His time at Haines & Haines was almost over—no matter what he did or did not do. If Eb sneezed in the wrong direction, Nathan was ready to sack him. He may as well go out with a flourish, writing about something he cared about. Eb might also be able to finish his practicum up in Litchfield. He had received a query letter from Charles's employer, Mr. Theodore Fuller, Esquire, who needed a second part-time apprentice.

Eb liked the idea of moving back up to Litchfield. More than anything, he would not have to witness the happiness of Susan Graham and Franz Mueller, something he dreaded. He would also be near all his friends—Rebecca Harding, Charles Godwin, Martha Lewis and her family, Judge Reeve and his wife, Mrs. Edwards, and of course, the cat Sir Winston. Trial work might be more appealing to him. How much worse than Nathan Haines could Theodore Fuller be? An impending job offer in Litchfield had given Eb the courage to publish his anti-slavery tract.

Samuel Taylor tried to talk Eb out of publishing the American Colonization Society article. It was suicidal—Eb would surely lose his job. But Eb would not be deterred, so Samuel dutifully edited the article and found publishers for it. They both knew that as soon as it appeared in print, Nathan Haines would lower the axe. Samuel admired Eb's integrity, even though he would miss him at Haines & Haines. Still, things at the law practice were so much better. The new scrivener was working out well. Samuel and Oliver were doing substantive legal work. Eb had shown them how to study on their own. Besides, Eb Wells would always be his friend. And it was agreed. Samuel would continue as Eb's editor and agent, even if he left the New Haven area.

The morning Eb's article appeared in the New Haven *Connecticut Journal,* Nathan Haines went to work early, called Eb into his office, and promptly fired him. This Nathan did without consulting his father, who was up in Albany on an arbitration. Nathan suspected his father would want no part in sacking Eb Wells, an event that might wreak havoc with his father's love life. From Malinda Wells, there would be hell to pay.

Before pushing him out the door, Nathan castigated Eb. It was totally inappropriate for an apprentice at Haines & Haines to publish a radical article against the institution of slavery. Eb knew the law office's stance on political neutrality. Too many clients of Haines & Haines had vested interests in perpetuating the peculiar institution, the shippers, manufacturers, businessmen, and purveyors of agricultural products to the West Indies. An anti-slavery stance was a luxury only a few could afford, up north, as well as down south. The law practice of Haines & Haines could not be seen to support abolition, or anything close to it, not even by a mere apprentice. Eb had once again failed to recognize his professional responsibilities. This last transgression was too glaring for Nathan to ignore. Nathan's harangue went on and on. Eb would have to go.

Eb felt a flush of embarrassment at his dismissal, then a flood of relief. The axe he had been watching, hovering just inches above his head, had finally fallen. But when Eb returned home to Elm Street, only an hour after he had left for work, he had to face his sister. When she heard what had happened, Malinda Wells was furious. It was one thing for Eb to be disenchanted with his work at Haines & Haines, to seek employment at another law practice—but no one summarily dismissed her baby brother. No one sent him home from the law office before noon with all his personal effects thrown haphazardly into a small wooden box. No one.

Malinda Wells took great pride in her family's reputation. Her father, her older brother John, and soon Eb, were all known to be fine lawyers. They were to be treated as professional colleagues, not mere employees. No one had ever had the audacity to fire a Wells. Malinda blustered and grew red in the face. She would not countenance this unceremonious sacking of her brilliant brother, no matter the reason.

For over a week, Ned Haines had received daily, affectionate letters from Malinda Wells at his hotel in Albany. Then a brief letter from his son Nathan arrived, explaining that he had fired Eb Wells, and why. Ned understood the reasons for Eb's dismissal. He had to support Nathan in this decision. After all, Ned had turned over the management of the staff to Nathan, a job he no longer had any interest in. Nathan had done what he thought was best for the law practice. Ned might have done the same thing, although he would have done it differently. Even so, Ned Haines secretly admired Eb's stance on the 'Back to Africa' movement. And it made Ned sad to let him go. That was the difference between father and son.

As it was, the whole affair broke Ned Haines's heart. Letters from Malinda Wells stopped coming. He languished in Albany for two weeks with no word from her. When he returned to New Haven, a terse note from Malinda waited for him. Haines & Haines had treated her brother in a harsh and unprofessional manner. She no longer had any interest in seeing him.

"I found her." Franz Mueller burst through the back door of the kitchen, breathless, his German accent exaggerated, no doubt by emotion. "She's fine." Mrs. Tittles had been missing for two days. Everyone—Franz, Henry, Mr. and Mrs. Potts, Susan, Eb, even Esmeralda—had searched for the cat high and low. "She was burrowed down in the straw in a corner of the stable." Franz gave Esmeralda and Mrs. Potts a meek smile, unsure how his next announcement would be received. "And she's got two kittens."

"I told you she was expecting, Harriet." Esmeralda gave Mrs. Potts a triumphant nod as she entered the kitchen, juggling a few empty plates from the breakfast buffet. "But I thought there'd be more than two."

"There were," Franz said in a rush, glancing over his shoulder to see if Henry was in his wake, "but two were dead." He lowered his eyes to the floor, adding quickly, "I had to dispose of them before Henry found out." Franz looked up and gave Esmeralda and Mrs. Potts a sad shake of his head. "But the two left are hardy and sweet as can be."

"And how's our little mother doing?" Mrs. Potts wiped her hands on her apron. "Could I bring some cream out to her?"

"She seems just fine," Franz said, "but I'm sure she'd like the cream. I think she's hungry but doesn't want to leave her babies."

"You must come and see the kittens, Mrs. Potts." Henry came rushing through the back door, all excited, his blond hair standing on end, going every which way. He had been worried sick when Mrs. Tittles had disappeared and thrilled when his father had found her—with the bonus of two tiny kittens, their eyes closed shut, no bigger than two fat mice. "One of them looks just like Mrs. Tittles but with less white. The other one's black and white."

"I'll be out in a minute, Henry," Mrs. Potts said, "to bring some cream for Mrs. Tittles." She came over to the boy and gave him a quick hug, trying to calm down his hair with her hand. "Esmeralda and I will come calling."

"I wouldn't pick the little ones up yet, my boy," Esmeralda warned. "Not until they're a bit older. Let Mrs. Tittles take care of them." Esmeralda had never raised a litter of kittens before, but she had helped a mother dog whelp her puppies—the principles must be the same.

"All right," Henry said with a reluctant sigh, itching to play with the kittens. "Is Miss Graham here? I've got to tell her."

"She's still eating breakfast," Esmeralda replied. "Go into the dining room and tell her."

"And Eb? Is Eb around?" Henry wanted Eb to be the next to know. The boy understood he had to share Mrs. Tittles with Eb— and now the kittens. It was an unwritten condition of his father's employment. Eb would be so excited to hear the news. "I want to tell Eb."

"Eb left for Litchfield early this morning," Mrs. Potts answered kindly, filling a bowl with fresh cream. "Mr. Lanson's cousin took him to the stagecoach. He'll be traveling up north with a new servant." This, she said with a wink to Esmeralda. Just as he had done last year, Eb was helping to transport a fugitive slave to Waterbury. William Lanson had arranged it. For one leg of an unknown Black man's journey, Eb would pretend to be his Southern master. Both would disembark in Waterbury; Eb would spend the night at a clergyman's house, traveling alone the following day to Litchfield. The runaway slave would then travel undercover further up north to Canada.

"But Eb must be told," Henry urged, not digesting the information. He took off for the dining room. "I can't wait to tell him." And the boy disappeared into the house to spread the good news about Mrs. Tittles and her kittens.

"I simply can't believe my brother John." It was a muggy Sunday afternoon in late August. Malinda Wells and Susan Graham were walking across the New Haven Green. The day before, Malinda had received a letter from her older brother in Charleston, warning her off a marriage to Ned Haines—a man the age of her father. The letter was sent before Eb was fired from Haines & Haines, before Malinda had broken things off with Ned. John Wells knew nothing about either. Malinda was still ablaze with anger over Eb's sacking. This letter from her brother blew a blast of air on the flames.

"John gave me a veiled threat. You know what I'm talking about. I read you the whole letter." Malinda repeated yesterday's rantings. "He implies I'll lose my estate money if I marry someone he doesn't approve of." She was short of breath, trying to keep up with Susan, whose legs were longer. Besides, her fiery indignation needed oxygen to burn. "It's not like I'm seventeen."

"I still don't think John can do such a thing." Susan also repeated herself. She and Malinda had gone over all this the day before. John's letter could not have come at a worse time. Malinda Wells had been a mess of raw emotions all week. Eb had been fired from Haines & Haines. In a fit of anger, Malinda had severed her relations with the Haines family—her suitor, Ned, included. This had all occurred in one week, against the drama of the missing cat. That mystery, at least, was solved, but Malinda was a wreck.

"He doesn't have the power," Malinda said emphatically, continuing to rant. "Plus, he made it sound like he and Eb were on the same page. I would expect this high-handed treatment from John, but from Eb?" Malinda's eyes filled up with tears again. She had been crying all week. "That would be too cruel, to have both my brothers gang up on me."

"It's hard to know what Eb's thinking these days," Susan mused, mostly to herself. "But honestly, Malinda, it doesn't sound like Eb. He would never get in the way of your happiness." She checked herself, remembering Malinda had dismissed Ned Haines. "I mean, if your being with Ned is what would have made you happy."

Susan was sad about Malinda's breakup with Ned. Malinda had been acting like a woman in love, something Susan thought she would never see. Over the summer, Malinda's pretty, round face had taken on a shade of light pink from the sun, no longer a pale ivory. Her dark eyes were shining. She had been spinning plans for a rosy future. Strangest of all, she had taken to engaging in endless, cheerful chatter—so unlike the deliberate, taciturn Malinda of yore. Like removing a corset, Malinda had loosened the strings that held her together. Now, she had pulled on them in anger, tighter and tighter, drawing herself back in. Susan was sad to see this contraction.

"I wish Eb were here to explain himself." Malinda too was uncertain whether Eb deserved her wrath. Eb had left for Litchfield on what would have been his break from work—had he not been fired. "But you're right. It doesn't sound like Eb. He wouldn't make threats about who I could or couldn't marry—should I want to marry anyone." Malinda sniffled. "I know he and John exchange business letters I'm not privy to, but I can't believe Eb would say anything bad about Ned, aside from his age. About Nathan, yes, but not his father."

"His age seems to be the only problem John has with Ned," Susan pointed out. "John's letter said that Eb held Ned Haines in high regard. Dr. Cabot too. Everyone does."

"Well, I don't understand why Ned's age is anyone's business but mine," Malinda snapped. "If we were still together, that is." She was silent for a moment, then added for emphasis, "Which we are not."

"And then there's Eddie," Susan added cautiously. John was worried Malinda might be stuck raising Ned Haines's son by his second wife—his second dead wife—a boy with whom Malinda had no rapport. "John's concerned about him too." To Susan's mind, John's letter had just sounded worried. John Wells could not help himself. He was a lawyer and always struck the same tone, in writing or in person, no matter the subject. John approached his sister's love life as if it were a business transaction. No soft words to cushion the blow, just cold, hard facts. "If Ned were to die before you do—which seems likely—Eddie might become your problem."

"You're one to talk about having a 'problem' child," Malinda said curtly, referring to Susan's growing attachment to Franz.

"Henry's different," Susan retorted. "He's not a problem. He's an easy child. More to the point, Malinda, Henry's father is thirty-four years old and not likely to die soon." Susan knew it was unkind to compare Franz's youth to Ned Haines's senectitude, but she could not help herself.

"Doesn't it bother you, Susan," Malinda said in a careless manner, "that Franz Mueller is just a coachman?" She was in such a state of distress, her usual consideration for the feelings of others had vanished. "An immigrant. Uneducated?"

"Franz had eight years in school and is fluent in two languages." Susan rose to his defense. "He's got a good trade and is hardworking. And Franz isn't an immigrant. He was born in Philadelphia—the son of immigrants perhaps, but a loyal American." Susan abruptly withdrew her arm from Malinda's and hugged her own elbows. "So, no, it doesn't bother me that Franz is 'just a coachman.'" She turned her gaze away from Malinda to the edge of the Green, focusing on its row of white churches. "You must remember, Malinda, I don't come from a long line of distinguished lawyers." Susan's voice had taken on an uncustomary chill. "I'm the daughter of your mother's housekeeper. My father was a wheelwright."

"Oh dear," Malinda said softly, retaking her friend's arm. "I've been so tactless. All of that's true, of course. I was wrong to ask such stupid questions." Her eyes filled up with tears again. "I'm just so unhappy. Maybe I wanted you to be unhappy too." A tear began to fall down her cheek. Malinda brushed it away and looked down at the ground. "I wasn't being fair to Franz." A long, awkward silence fell between them. "The truth is I'm envious of you and Franz," Malinda finally said. "You seem so happy together, always talking and laughing. And Henry adores you. You're so good with children." Malinda did not lift her eyes from the ground. "But that's no excuse for my harsh words. I'm so sorry, Susan." Another tear escaped down Malinda's cheek. "I can't bear your being cross with me." She let out a small moan and looked up. "Not right now."

"It's all right," Susan said in a comforting voice, knowing Malinda meant no harm. "I understand." And the two women linked arms again, continuing their walk across the Green, each immersed in her own thoughts about the future.

Rebecca Harding had been in South Farms all day. The term at the Morris Academy was about to begin. On Mrs. Morris's recommendation, Rebecca had contracted for room and board with the Barnard family. The Barnards lived in a large, rambling farmhouse on the north side of town. Mrs. Barnard, a husky, red-faced woman who minced no words, had handled the negotiation. Breakfast was served promptly at half past seven and supper at six. No special food requests would be entertained, but if Miss Harding liked, Mrs. Barnard could prepare a lunchpail for her, just like her children.

The Barnards sent their three oldest children to the Morris Academy, two boys and a girl. The walk from their house to school was short and pleasant along a country lane, currently lined with fading Queen Anne's lace. Rebecca's room in the Barnards' attic looked comfortable enough, larger than her room at Miss Pierce's. She would have privacy, although she noted the lack of a fireplace. Still, the cot was positioned next to the stone chimney that would radiate some heat. Rebecca thought fondly of her large, gracious bedroom in Mrs. Cox's stately brick house on the Wethersfield Green, with the matching chintz Martha Washington chairs, her own roaring fire, started each winter evening by Mrs. Cox's obliging servant. Now she was back in the Northwest Hills of Connecticut, living in a stranger's drafty old attic with no fire, no servant, no elegant chintz chairs.

Earlier in the day, Rebecca and Mrs. Morris had met to discuss her curriculum. Rhoda Morris was still in mourning, wearing a simple black dress with puffy sleeves that dovetailed down into long, snug cuffs. She was businesslike and upbeat, greeting Rebecca heartily in her morning room, offering her some tea. Rebecca realized that she had never once shared a cup of tea with Asa Hitchcock. If The Ogre were to reincarnate at the Morris Academy, it would not be in the body of Mrs. Morris—and she supposed he would have to die first.

Mrs. Morris discussed the books Rebecca would be teaching from. *Murray's Grammar Exercise Book*, the *Classical English Letter-Writer or Epistolary Selections*, *Webster's Elements of Useful Knowledge*, and Bunyan's *The Pilgrim's Progress*. Rebecca was in possession of all four books, although she inwardly groaned to learn Bunyan was on the list. She considered the allegory *The Pilgrim's Progress* too dark, too dense, too desperate for children. To Rebecca's way of thinking, no child should ever know about the *Slough of Despond*, the boggy swamp that devoured Christian and Pliable in their own doubt, fear, lust, and shame. Besides, the book had been a favorite of Asa Hitchcock's, obligating Rebecca to despise it.

Rebecca's classroom would range in size and age. Some students were committed to attend each full thirteen-week session, while others would drift in and out. This was nothing new to Rebecca. The population in female education always waxed and waned, even at Miss Pierce's. Some teaching beyond rhetoric was required, although Agnes Thatcher would be covering math. Both tutoresses must pitch in for geography. Mrs. Morris felt certain Rebecca would excel at that, being a graduate of the Litchfield Female Academy, where geography was given high priority. Rebecca made a mental note. Martha Lewis should join her again as a guest speaker, just as she had done in Wethersfield—to share her expertise in making maps.

Teachers were expected to attend church services on the Sabbath, setting an example for their students. Still, Mrs. Morris predicted Rebecca would travel four miles each Saturday afternoon to Litchfield. She assured Rebecca that attending the Congregationalist church on the Litchfield Green would suffice, as many of their students were members of Lyman Beecher's congregation. For an extra fee, the Morris Academy arranged transport after the Saturday half-day to take the Litchfield students home for the Sabbath, returning them to South Farms early Monday morning in time for classes. Rebecca was relieved to hear she could join them. Church attendance was part of any teacher's job. But her ability to attend church in Litchfield meant Rebecca could go to the Lewis cottage on the Sabbath, where all her friends were—and maybe Eb Wells.

During her interview, Rebecca noticed how attractive Mrs. Morris was, with her curly brown hair, sharp features, deep-set intelligent eyes, and a slight cleft in her chin. A former student of the Morris Academy, Rhoda Farnam had been the head of the Ladies' Department from 1810 to 1815, before becoming the second wife of the school's founder, James Morris. She had married him in her late twenties when he was in his early sixties. Before his death, she bore him two children, a daughter and a son.

Rebecca assumed Rhoda Farnam's retirement from teaching in 1815 had been forced upon her by becoming Mrs. Morris. But now that James Morris was dead, no one thought it unseemly for her to become the preceptress of the school. An experienced educator and now an unmarried woman, she could step into his shoes. Perhaps more to the point—she would bear no more children unless she remarried. Rebecca was still trying to come to terms with the rule that female educators must be unmarried.

Rebecca and Martha had long conversations about marriage that summer at Miss Pierce's. Now that Martha was engaged, they talked often about pregnancy, childbearing, and motherhood. All three were dicey for women. Rebecca's own mother had died in childbirth and lost two baby boys in infancy. Ruth Lewis, Martha's mother, had four living children, but had suffered two miscarriages. Eb Wells's mother had successfully given birth to five children but had lost two little girls before they reached the age of two. Ned Haines's younger second wife had died giving birth to a stillborn daughter. Then there was the elegant Mary Godwin down in New Haven, Charles's mother, who only had one child and was barren thereafter.

Charles's mother's story appealed to Rebecca the most. Putting aside the thorny problem of her teaching career, she was not up to raising a large family. Rebecca had witnessed the toll it took on young mothers, many her own age, to be pregnant year after year, taking care of small children, their noisy demands, their constant state of hunger, all those noses to be wiped and hind ends to clean. She could imagine pleasure in educating her own hypothetical children, but their day-to-day care held little appeal. Rebecca's mother died too early to teach her the domestic arts, and upon her death, her father hired a housekeeper. But watching Ruth Lewis, Rebecca knew what women did to maintain a household—cooking, baking, cleaning, washing clothes, carding wool, spinning, weaving, knitting, sewing, putting up preserves, churning, making candles, tending to the sick, feeding animals if there were any. None of these activities interested her. Not with so many books to read.

Running a household was one thing—but being pregnant? Martha and Rebecca had heard rumors about the discomforts of pregnancy. Hemorrhoids, swollen ankles, nausea, loss of teeth, heartburn, intense fatigue. The grave risks of delivery were also known to them. Excruciating pain, labor lasting several days, death from breech births, uterine ruptures, perineal tears, bleeding to death, and the most common cause of maternal death—childbed fever. Marital love was a dangerous business.

And before that summer, Rebecca Harding had been in the dark about marital love. Because she had lost her mother, no other woman had pulled back the veil on the mysteries of conception. Certainly, her austere Great-Aunt Gertrude in Hartford was not up to the task. Consequently, Rebecca had only a vague notion of what happened in the marital bed or how it resulted in pregnancy. But Martha Lewis had grown up almost in the country on the edge of town. Some years, her mother had raised pigs and sheep, and springtime acts of procreation were familiar to her. Ruth Lewis also considered it her maternal duty to educate her only daughter on the facts of life. Martha had been told all about the physical realities of love, even though she and Charles had not yet experienced them—at least not all of them.

The tables were finally turned, and Martha taught Rebecca. On the third floor of Miss Pierce's at night, Martha passed on everything that her mother had taught her about sex, pregnancy, birth, and motherhood. What Martha did not know, she and Rebecca speculated about with whispers of excitement and apprehension. Rebecca was grateful to Martha for filling in these crucial gaps in her knowledge. Before their frank conversations, Rebecca understood what kissing Eb Wells meant emotionally. Now, under Martha's gentle tutelage, she understood what it meant physically. The kiss was just the beginning of things, Rebecca was amazed to learn.

This new information shed light on why academies insisted female teachers not marry. Marriage led to marital love, which led to pregnancies and children. Rebecca now understood the sequencing of events. How inappropriate would it be for students to see their teacher in the 'family way' in such a public setting? Her pregnancy would imply sexual activity. It was better that she be sent home until the baby was born, but confinement meant leaving school in the middle of a term. That would be disruptive. And once the baby arrived, who would take care of it? Martha had described lactation in detail, how the breasts would double in size and manufacture milk for the baby's nutrition. How could a teacher re-enter the classroom with a mewling infant latched onto her breast? The marriage bar rule made more sense to her now, but it was still a harsh reality. Marriage meant that her future as an educator would be over. Rebecca Harding would sink into her own *Slough of Despond*.

It wasn't fair, Rebecca thought, as she rode home on a farmer's cart back to Litchfield, how Rhoda Farnam had to give up teaching to become Mrs. Morris. A man could marry and continue to be an educator. A woman could not. Not only that. The allocation of labor in the reproductive process was inherently inequitable. The man's contribution was such a fleeting, puny, paltry thing compared to her own monumental sacrifice. The woman could pay the rest of her life for one night of love—or five minutes, Martha had opined, at least with sheep and pigs, and maybe some men, her mother had told her, grinning.

These were the thoughts going through Rebecca's mind as the farmer's cart entered the southern border of Litchfield. A few stalwart cicadas were still engaged in twilight chatter, but daylight was dwindling. Crows were caw, caw, cawing in the fields. Rebecca smelled smoke from the chimneys of the cottages they passed on the side of the road and a slight whiff of mold from the first falling leaves. The air felt cool and damp once the sun slipped behind the undulant hills. No doubt about it—summer was almost over. She would have to dig out her shawl from the bottom of her trunk. Rebecca also thought about her upcoming evening with pleasure. Martha, Charles, Jack, and Mr. and Mrs. Lewis would be waiting for her at the Lewis cottage for the Saturday evening supper. Martha's mother was baking a shepherd's pie. Rebecca hoped a fruit pie would be on the table too. Apples would soon be ripe.

And Eb would arrive in a few days. Rebecca still did not know what to say to him, or how she should behave. After exchanging letters for almost a year, she felt she knew him better, but he remained a stranger in many ways. She suspected Eb sought clarity about their relationship, something she felt ill-equipped to provide. But when she thought about seeing Eb's face, sitting next to him, his eyes locking with hers through his gold-rimmed glasses, his small, delicate hand reaching for hers, her stomach flipped over. Would he hold her hand, she wondered, or kiss her again? She hoped he would. She hoped he would not.

"So, when Susan confronted me in the library . . ." Eb Wells looked up at his friend Charles Godwin. "About how I'd been avoiding her, ignoring her, I just clammed up. I didn't know what to say." Charles and Eb sat outside on the bench behind Tapping Reeve's house in Litchfield. They had just taken lunch with Betsey Reeve, along with a dozen clamorous law students. Mrs. Reeve was happy to see Eb again. She would accelerate her plans for autumn soup if he promised to come to supper one night this week. Was butternut squash still his favorite? The old judge had excused himself for his postprandial nap.

The two friends were catching up. Charles had finished his matinal duties at Mr. Fuller's law office. Most days, he would make his way out the Goshen Road to work in the portrait studio, but Eb's visit to Litchfield was a treat. Benjamin Lewis had urged Charles to take some time off to visit with his friend. Eb had not yet met up with Rebecca and was discussing the complexities of his love life.

"So, would you say you botched it?" This was the first time Charles had heard of Eb's infatuation with Susan Graham. He knew of her existence, of course. Charles was familiar with the bare bones of Eb's family history, that Susan had been raised in the Wells household in Savannah. Charles also knew that Susan had come up to New Haven to be a companion to Eb's sister Malinda, in flight from yellow fever.

"Yes, Charles," Eb said emphatically. "I did. I botched it." Eb leaned back against the bench and took note of Mrs. Reeve's somewhat disheveled garden. Weeds were mixed in with her blooming flowers, offending Eb's sense of order. Wood sorrel had no place growing rampant under the dahlias about to bloom. He loved Betsey Reeve, but her talents were culinary, not horticultural. "Susan really called me to task."

"What was the nature of her complaint?" Charles had a history of receiving confidences about Eb Wells's love life, through the initial Rebecca-Eb platonic phase, the ill-fated era with the Southern belle Katherine Montgomery, and now the more recent, ambiguous Rebecca-Eb iteration. Charles wanted to understand this 'Eb-Susan' situation better.

"She said I didn't treat her like a friend," Eb said with a sigh. "That I never asked her any questions. You know, how she was doing, if she liked New Haven or missed her mother, that kind of thing." Eb thought back on his awkward and painful encounter with Susan last spring. He removed his gold-rimmed glasses and cleaned them on the sleeve of his white shirt. "I didn't even ask if she was mourning my own mother's passing." He put his glasses back on, hesitating. "She was there when my mother died, Charles, and I never asked her anything about it."

"Well, none of that sounds like you." With his long fingers, Charles stroked his sandy-colored whiskers. "Above all, you're a kind man. Solicitous of others."

"Yes, well, I failed with Susan." Eb gazed out at the sloping expanse of green grass. A couple of law students were having an intense conversation in the back of the garden, jousting with each other over some aspect of Judge Gould's lecture. They must be first years, Eb thought, not recognizing them. He felt a pang of envy. He would do anything to be back in law school, arguing some niggling point of law on Tapping Reeve's lawn. That was the problem with life. You never knew when you were in the middle of the 'good old days' until they were over.

"Go on." Charles nudged his friend from his reverie.

"Susan was right." Eb resumed his story. "I acted as if I didn't care about her. I was thoughtless." He gave Charles a sideways glance. "Do you remember when you were first smitten with Martha? You worried you were more enthralled with her luscious mouth than with Martha as a person?"

"I do remember the 'luscious mouth' discussion." Charles grinned. "Well, I still find Martha's mouth luscious." Charles tried to remember how he had felt when he first met Martha, but the emotions were difficult to conjure. He and Martha had moved too far along and were now engaged to be married. "But that's only one of her many finer attributes."

"Well, I'm not the man you are, Charles, I'm ashamed to say. I wasn't thinking about Susan's finer attributes at all." Eb was embarrassed to confess all this to Charles, whose moral sense was more highly developed. "I was thinking about how beautiful she had become. How interested I was in her crooked smile. Her breasts. Her thick mane of hair. Susan's hair is light brown. Although in the summer, it gets streaked with blonde." Eb added this tidbit of gratuitous information.

"Her breasts?" Charles scratched the back of his head in a gesture of curiosity, perhaps wonder. "Is there something about her breasts I should know about?" His voice was a little squeaky. Charles had to admit it—he wanted to hear more.

"Well, somehow, over the years, Susan acquired this beautiful cleavage." Eb sighed. "Honestly, I don't know when that happened. It must have been when I was away at college, but I never noticed them when I came home." Eb thought about this for a minute. "Perhaps it's the fashion of these new dresses. Have you noticed how they emphasize a woman's breasts? A man hardly knows where to rest his eyes." Eb laughed suddenly. "I find myself staring studiously at Susan's forehead, lest my eyes slip down to take a gander." He let out a snort. "It makes me cross-eyed."

"How would you say they—I mean, how do Susan's breasts compare to Rebecca's?" Charles was curious to hear how his friend would reply—and curious in general.

"I don't know how to answer that, Charles." Eb considered the question with solemnity, raking his fingers through his auburn hair. He intended to get a haircut in Litchfield, Mr. Grimes having moved up here from New Haven. "Rebecca's more modest in her dress, for one." Eb thought about the question longer. "And she's slenderer than Susan, slighter, less round in some places. Maybe I don't think about her breasts as much as I do about Susan's."

"I see." Charles lifted his eyebrows ever so slightly. "So, what happened after Susan accused you of not treating her like a person? Did you tell her how you felt?" Charles tried to think of a way to put this discreetly. "That you were attracted to her?"

"I did not," Eb muttered. "It didn't seem right to say anything. Susan's always been like a sister to me, and my feelings were distinctly not those of a brother." Eb cast his eyes to the ground. "I was having impure thoughts about her. Do you know what I mean, Charles? At night?"

"Yes, I understand." Charles too could have impure thoughts about a woman at night, although thankfully, he now noted to himself, they were about his fiancée. "And where does Rebecca Harding fit into this story?"

"That's another reason the whole thing's inappropriate," Eb said wearily. "Here I was, corresponding with Rebecca. I didn't want to be untrue to her. I wanted to tell you about it, Charles, but I couldn't. I didn't want to put you in an awkward position with Martha. You know, to burden you with this knowledge. Rebecca and Martha are such close friends."

"Yes, well, that's true." Charles looked like a contemplative heron, staring at a pond, deep in thought. "But you and I are close friends too. I wouldn't have said a word. And your secret's safe with me now, Eb. We men need to stick together."

Eb breathed a sigh of relief. He had been worried Charles would think less of him for being attracted to one woman—who was like a sister to him—while corresponding with another. Charles also might have told Martha, who would most certainly have told Rebecca.

"And what *are* your feelings for Rebecca?" This was not the first time Charles had asked his friend this question.

"I don't know." Eb shook his head. "Rebecca and I were becoming more than friends right before we left Litchfield, if you remember. That was wonderful." Eb had given Charles a detailed description of their few stolen kisses last summer. "And we've been writing several times a week since then," Eb continued. "But I wouldn't call our correspondence passionate. I'm not sure why. We act more like dear friends."

Eb thought about how much he had relied on Rebecca's advice this year, her good counsel about his work at Haines & Haines, and her encouragement about his teaching and writing. He too had tried to support Rebecca in her work. But Eb had come to realize that he needed her far more than she needed him. Rebecca possessed a sturdiness of temperament that Eb lacked.

"I continue to rely upon Rebecca. I tell her everything."

"Do you tell her that you love her?" Charles crossed his long legs, trying to get comfortable on a bench made for shorter people. "I don't mean to intrude. I'm just trying to get the lay of the land."

"No," Eb admitted. "I don't tell her. I'm not sure I really know what love means." It was difficult to pinpoint his feelings for Rebecca Harding—to figure out where she belonged in his life. "I respect Rebecca more than any other woman."

"Respect is surely a part of love," Charles said thoughtfully. "An integral part. But there's more to it than that." He rolled his eyes at Eb. "You know what I mean."

"Well, I know what it feels like *not* to love someone. I didn't love Katherine Montgomery. I'm sure of that." Eb gave a weak smile, shrugging. He avoided looking at Charles, who had warned him off Katherine long before they broke up. "Okay, I'll admit it, I was quite taken with her for a while."

"Ah, well." Charles thought it best to let the subject of Katherine Montgomery fade away without further comment. It was not the finest chapter in Eb's book.

"And I might love Rebecca. But the truth is, Charles, I have no idea how she feels about me."

Charles lifted his eyebrows imperceptibly. "And how about this Susan Graham? Do you think you love her?"

"That's a complicated question," Eb replied. "You've got to remember. I grew up with Susan. We were best friends when we were little. Our history goes way back. So, yes, I've always loved Susan, but more like a sister."

"And how would you characterize this new set of feelings?" Charles was back in investigatory mode. "Your attraction for her?"

"Lust," Eb said without thinking. Suddenly, he realized that was what it was—an overlay of lust on top of a long-standing, quasi-sibling relationship. "I'm ashamed to admit it, Charles, but that's the truth. It's lust."

"Does Rebecca know how you've been feeling about Susan?"

"No," Eb answered swiftly. "I could hardly bring myself to tell even you."

"And these feelings you've had for Susan—are you still having them?" Charles wanted to gauge how dire the situation was. For a man deemed ill-equipped for trial work, he could execute a mean direct examination. "At night, I mean. Those impure thoughts."

"A lot less so than before," Eb answered, surprising himself.

That was a truth he had not yet embraced. Susan was much less on his mind. "I think she's in love with Franz Mueller, my uncle's new coachman. I told you about him. He was a debtor of one of our clients."

"So, Susan's being romantically involved with someone else has diminished your ardor?" Charles continued his interrogation. "Would you say that?"

"Yes, I suppose so." Eb noted Charles had shifted to cross-examination—that was a leading question. Maybe Charles was right. His lustful feelings had turned to resentment toward Susan for having chosen the handsome, and much taller, German widower. As usual, talking to Charles Godwin changed his perspective. "That might be true."

"And do you feel angry with her for her interest in the coach-man?" Charles had read Eb's mind. He could be merciless in his pursuit of understanding.

"Yes, a little," Eb admitted, thinking about what he had just confessed to. "That's not really fair to Susan, though," he concluded. "It's not like she was presented with a choice to make—Franz or me."

"Because she didn't know how you were feeling?"

"Yes," Eb replied. "At least I didn't tell her. But she might have guessed. Susan can be uncanny that way. She can read my mind." Eb had no evidence for his intuition that Susan Graham might know how he felt about her—but the thought still stuck with him. "Susan might have figured things out." Eb shook his head, looking over at Charles. "Honestly, women are an utter mystery to me."

"Me too," Charles chuckled. "I've only had one love in my life, and she still confounds me."

"So, what do you think? Do you think I should tell Rebecca about Susan?" Eb asked, anxious to have Charles's counsel. "I've been feeling so deceitful. I've shared everything with Rebecca, but so far, not this." Eb was scheduled to meet with Rebecca soon. She had been teaching in South Farms before, which had suited him. It gave him time to talk things over with Charles.

"No, Eb." Charles shook his head, wagging his long index finger for emphasis. "I don't claim to know much about women, but in this instance, I'm on solid ground. Absolutely do not tell Rebecca."

"But isn't that being dishonest with her?" Eb frowned. This was not the answer he expected from his high-minded friend, so conscientious about honesty.

"Perhaps, but sometimes it's more honorable to be dishonest." He stopped and listened to himself. "No, wait, let me restate that." Charles uncrossed and recrossed his legs again, searching for the right words. "Okay, I'll try again. There can be honor in failing to disclose everything—if the intention is to be kind."

"I'm shocked, Charles Godwin." Eb teased his friend. "You who were raised with Quaker values. What would your mother say?"

"She would say I was giving good counsel. What's to be accomplished by telling Rebecca?" His tone changed, and Charles gave Eb no chance to answer. "Look, you're feeling guilty. That's all. You want to confess. I want to suggest that confession is to make yourself feel better. But it won't make Rebecca feel better. I guarantee that."

Eb squirmed uncomfortably, thinking Charles might be right.

"To tell her would devastate her." Charles looked down at Eb. "And it could destroy all that is good between you. You need to take care, Eb."

"I don't know, Charles." Eb again cast his eyes on the wood sorrel, growing rampant beneath Mrs. Reeve's dormant dahlias.

Charles sat still while Eb thought things over. He could count on one thing about Eb Wells—he would analyze absolutely everything. When Eb continued to sit in silence, Charles adopted a more soothing voice, feeling he had been too harsh. "Listen, my friend, don't be so hard on yourself. Sometimes, these things just happen. Men get infatuations with women that go nowhere. It probably happens to women too." Charles poked his bony elbow into Eb's upper arm in a gesture of affection. "My guess is it happens more frequently when the person you're lusting after isn't available. The lure of forbidden fruit. Someone almost like a sister."

Eb said nothing. He had not been expecting this last insight. The notion of Susan Graham as forbidden fruit had not occurred to him.

"Look, Eb, this thing with Susan doesn't need to be consequential. It's water under the bridge. Nothing happened. You never declared yourself, and she's involved with someone else. Just let it go. And don't tell Rebecca." Charles repeated this with solemn emphasis. "Promise me that."

"All right, Charles. I suppose you're right." Eb blew out a long sigh. "But it feels strange holding things back from Rebecca."

"Well, I don't know much about women," Charles said with a knowing smile. "But I have learned this from my time with Martha. You don't always say everything you're thinking." He shook his head. "Sometimes it's best not to. Often."

"Eb?" The face of a young boy peered around the corner of the house, interrupting their conversation. It was T.B. Reeve, Judge Reeve's grandson, who lived with his grandparents. He was now almost twelve years old, and the boy had shot up since Eb had seen him last. His chubby, round little boy face was now leaner, foreshadowing the man he would become. "Eb Wells? I heard you were here!" T.B. plopped down onto the end of the bench, Charles and Eb scooting over to make room for him. "How long are you staying?" he asked with a great, toothy smile. "I've got so much to tell you!"

The three of them sat chatting on the bench for a while—the tall, long-limbed Charles Godwin, his legs crossed; the much smaller Eb Wells, his hands folded in his lap, smiling over at the boy through his gold-rimmed glasses; and the twelve-year-old boy, still exuberant with the energy of a child, despite his proximity to adolescence. They gossiped about T.B.'s classes at the female academy, the new law students slurping soup at his grandfather's table, Betsey Reeve's latest recipe for strawberry-rhubarb crumble, and the glorious toad who had taken up residence in her haphazard garden. Eb Wells leaned back on the bench and let the warm sun envelop him. It felt good to be home.

"We don't brush a horse's tail like that." Franz Mueller and Susan Graham were grooming the horses in the stable underneath the carriage house quarters. It was dark and cool inside. Outside, it was a warm late August afternoon. Franz had just scolded Susan for taking a brush to Ruby's tangled tail. Susan was on a break from teaching, and Henry was in the kitchen, helping Mrs. Potts bake bread, begging for tidbits of yeasty, unbaked dough.

"I was just trying to untangle this knot," Susan said in exasperation. "It's a devil." She stood in the stall behind Ruby, who remained still, enjoying the ministrations of her humans.

"I know. But brushing it will just thin out her tail over time." Franz had already explained to Susan how to use a wide-toothed comb to disentangle a horse's tail. "I told you that before."

"I'm sorry." Susan sounded disheartened. "I forgot."

Franz heard her discouragement. "I'm sorry I snapped at you," he said, not looking up. The only times Franz exhibited ill-temper with Susan, or with his son, were over acts of carelessness with the horses—their grooming, their food, the cleanliness of their stalls. He was also solicitous of Mrs. Tittles, and now the kittens. Above all, Franz Mueller took the welfare of his animals seriously. "I know you were trying," he added quietly, having glanced up to see Susan's crestfallen face.

"It's all right." Susan tried to muster a smile. She withered when Franz got high and mighty over his horses. "It's just there're so many things to remember." She leaned over to pick up the wide-toothed comb, returning to Ruby's tail. "A part of me just loves to brush someone's hair. I still brush Malinda's at night," Susan confessed, letting Franz catch a glimpse of her intimate life with her longest friend. "My poor Malinda."

"She does seem very sad." Everyone on Elm Street knew about Eb's getting fired from Haines & Haines, Malinda's outrage, and her abrupt severance from Ned Haines. "I do understand Nathan Haines's position though." Franz and Mr. Potts had discussed the situation over apple tansey the evening before. While Anthony Potts appreciated Eb's advocacy for the free Black community, he must have known his article was too political for the law firm. Franz agreed. "Eb was taking a risk."

"Well, I'm sure Eb knew what he was doing." Susan agreed with Malinda. She too thought Eb's termination was harsh. Eb had worked hard at Haines & Haines, and he had single-handedly taken on the education of the apprentices—even though he was himself one. "I don't think Eb really cared if he got fired or not. His work at the law practice wasn't really working out."

"Then why is Miss Wells so upset?" Franz shook his head, trying to understand Malinda's anger and why she felt compelled to break things off with Ned Haines—a highly favorable liaison, in his opinion. "Eb's the one who got fired, not his sister. I thought she loved Ned. Why would she toss him away like that?"

"Sure, Nathan fired him, but Ned didn't exactly come to Eb's rescue, did he? For Malinda, Eb can do no wrong. She registers his every achievement as if it were her own. That means when Eb fails—I think we can agree getting fired is a failure—she feels it acutely."

"That doesn't strike me as healthy. Eb's an adult. He needs only to account to himself, not his older sister."

"That's easy for you to say, Franz Mueller," Susan retorted, defending Malinda. "You're a man. Malinda's an intelligent, resourceful woman. She has few opportunities to make her mark." Susan did not look at him, staying focused on the knot at the bottom of Ruby's tail. "It's not so unusual, Franz, for a woman to pour herself into the achievements of a husband, a father, a brother. Malinda's very proud of all the Wells lawyers and their distinguished careers. When they're disrespected, she feels disrespected."

"I see." Franz thought back to his wife, now buried in the Whitneyville cemetery, how irked she had become when their male laundry customers ignored her—how invisible she felt—she, the brains of the operation. Franz was familiar with complaints about women's lack of agency and sympathized. "And what about you, Susan Graham? How are you going to make your mark?" Franz took a break from brushing Ruby's side and looked intently down the horse at Susan.

"I'm not as ambitious as Malinda." Susan continued to scrutinize the unyielding knot in Ruby's tail. "I'd like to learn how to ride a horse. Maybe even drive the carriage someday." She glanced up and gave Franz a challenging smile. "And I do like to be useful. I enjoy teaching Henry. It makes me happy when he does well." Franz smiled back. Susan added softly, "Honestly, Franz, Henry's such a sweet boy. Your wife must have been such a good mother. You're wonderful with him too. I don't mean to say you're not, but I feel her influence on him." Susan looked back down at the knot, which was beginning to loosen. "Sometimes I feel she's here with us."

"You do?" Franz stared at Susan with amazement. He felt the presence of his wife all the time—even after he and Henry moved to New Haven—but never dared to mention it to Susan, fearing she would think he was crazy. Or be jealous.

"Yes," Susan answered quietly. "I think she's still worried about you and Henry."

"Ah, well, yes, she would be," Franz admitted, not wanting to commit himself to a phantasma. "She left us so abruptly. One day, she was here, washing clothes out in the backyard, singing lieder over the ironing table, baking bread, letting Henry eat tidbits of dough—his little worms—and two days later, she was gone." Franz had not talked to anyone about the death of his wife before. He was relieved to do so now.

"Was she pretty?" Susan was curious but feared the answer.

"She was."

"Prettier than me?" Susan asked softly.

"No, not prettier than you. But just as pretty, in a different way. You and Johanna are alike in many ways." Franz veered away from comparisons of beauty. "She was a strong woman, even obstinate at times. A hard worker who enjoyed being outdoors. It was important for her to feel useful too. And of course, Johanna loved Henry." Franz gave Susan a knowing nod, confident about what he was going to say. "Just as you do."

"I do love Henry." Susan was too shy to look up at him. "You know I do." Johanna. Johanna. She had never heard Franz say the name of his wife before. Johanna, Johanna. Susan said the name to herself several times, without making a sound. It was a lovely name, with open vowels to linger in, and double n's that lingered on her tongue for a while. It surprised her when Franz pronounced the first syllable of his wife's name as 'Yo,' but she would do so as well, whenever Susan communicated with her, which was often. "Why didn't you have more children?" Susan looked up briefly at Franz from the horse's tail. She had always wondered why Henry was an only child. She realized it was none of her business, but she wanted to know.

"We'd hoped for more." Franz suddenly became shy. "But God had other plans. For some reason, Johanna could not become with child after Henry."

"Would you like to have more children someday?" Susan's voice was thin, almost reedy. She kept her eye on the horse's tail.

"I would like that, Susan." Franz flashed her a brilliant smile from the side of the brown horse. "If I could have them with you."

"That's a good answer, Franz." Susan looked up and returned his smile—the same crooked smile that drove some of the men on Elm Street crazy. "Maybe that's how I'll make my mark."

In the din of the stable, Franz's hair was the color of the straw Ruby stood on. He was tanned from the summer's carriage rides, usually with Henry and Susan. He looked so appealing, standing beside the horse, grinning at her, his blue eyes shining, a grooming brush in his hand, the muscles in his arms taut, his white shirt slightly damp with perspiration. Susan's knees felt unreliable and weak.

A peaceful calm radiated between them. The sweet smell of horse sweat rose up from Ruby, who snorted a warm, wet sigh of equine happiness. Susan had undone the knot in her tail. Already groomed, Hank chomped on his hay in the adjoining stall, shifting around on the straw that whispered softly beneath his feet. They continued their work in the stillness of the late summer afternoon. Susan smiled at Franz occasionally across the horse's back. He smiled back at her. The couple in the stable were coming to an understanding.

"So, I must say, Eb," the old judge said in an even voice, "I agree with Mr. Haines about the debtor." Judge Tapping Reeve, the founder of the Litchfield Law School, was assessing Eb's situation, distressed to hear that he had been fired from his first professional position. "Better not to have taken tea with him. Or to have offered him a job." As promised, Mrs. Reeve had invited Eb to supper. Eb and his mentor sat in the candlelight at the Reeves's dining room table on South Street, waiting for Betsey Reeve to emerge from the kitchen with dessert. It was early evening, but the sun's setting rays already fell on the garden and the law school building in the side yard. It was late August. Outside, the cicadas had lapsed into an eerie silence.

"Yes, sir." Eb looked abashed.

"It's not uncommon for a young lawyer to get confused," the old man said kindly. "You're a generous person, Eb, with a big heart. Your actions were well-intended." He wagged his finger gently. "But in the future, you must keep a professional distance from the opposing party. Even when there's a cat in the bargain," he added slyly. Judge Reeve looked across the table with his large, orb-like eyes, the candlelight lighting up his silver hair that fell on his shoulders in the old style. Eb sat meekly on his chair, ready to accept any criticism that came his way. He had decided to reveal to Judge Reeve everything that had transpired between him and Nathan Haines, even the embarrassing parts.

"Yes, yes, I understand that now, sir. It won't happen again," Eb muttered, considering how hiring Frank Mueller had backfired in another way—how he had stolen Susan Graham's heart.

"As for your second transgression, the study group, you should have told your boss what you were up to," the judge continued. "But I don't see much harm in it. You weren't taking money from this young man or allowing others to join."

"Yes, sir." Eb hated exiling Donald Hawkins from the lectures, but had been tutoring him privately on Elm Street. The old study group still got together once a week—Eb, Donald, Samuel, and the Redfield brothers—for a pint of ale at the tavern. Eb still thought Nathan had been mean-spirited.

"But this matter of your article, the one critiquing the 'Back to Africa' movement. That's more complex." Judge Reeve smiled at his wife as she entered the room, an energetic, big-boned woman in her middle forties with a stoneware bowl in the crook of her arm. "I've gotten in trouble for publishing unpopular opinions myself. I was indicted for libel once for criticizing President Jefferson. It came to nothing, but still, it seemed to me then, and now, I ought to be free to speak my mind."

"I feel that way too, sir." Eb nodded. "Slavery is immoral and violates my core beliefs. It's my duty to speak out."

"If we look at it from Nathan Haines's perspective, I suppose he thought he was protecting the interests of his clients. And Haines & Haines." Judge Reeve peered intently across the table. He had only known Eb Wells for two years, but in the interim, Eb had changed. When he first arrived in Litchfield, fresh out of college, Eb had been an insecure, disheveled boy. That boy was gone. Eb Wells presented himself differently now. He sat up straight in his chair, dressed in a well-tailored dark brown suit and crisp white shirt, evincing an underlying confidence he had lacked before. Eb was now a serious young man, no longer apologetic for taking up space in the world. Judge Reeve shook his head. "But I wouldn't have fired you for publishing that article. In my opinion, Nathan Haines did the wrong thing. Lawyers should speak up on matters of injustice."

"That makes me feel better, sir," Eb said with a slight bow.

"But what about the father? The one who apprenticed with your father years ago? Mr. Haines Sr.?" Judge Reeve was struggling to see what could be salvaged from Eb's rupture from Haines & Haines.

"I think if Ned Haines had been in town," Eb replied, craning his neck to see the contents of Betsey Reeve's stoneware bowl, "things would have happened differently. He's a Unitarian who'd be more sympathetic to an abolitionist cause." Eb shifted uncomfortably in his seat. "And I don't know if I told you, Judge Reeve, but Mr. Haines Sr. is courting my older sister."

"Yes, so I heard." Eb had told Mrs. Edwards everything about his sister's romance, who in turn had passed the story on to Betsey Reeve, her good friend, who in turn had informed her husband. Gossip moved along at remarkable speed along well-traveled pathways in Litchfield. "Who else knows about the firing?" Judge Reeve probed further. "Besides your family, the others at the law practice, the apprentices, and the like?"

"I don't know, sir. Maybe no one. The legal community in New Haven shuts down at the end of summer. Haines & Haines is closed for two weeks. I got fired right before their customary break."

"Well, that's good then," Judge Reeve said. "You should contact the father as soon as you return to New Haven. Explain everything to him. Tell him you've found a position up here in Litchfield to finish off your practicum. I think you'll get an offer." Judge Reeve had recommended Eb to Theodore Fuller, Esquire, whose office was several doors down on South Street. "See if you can find a more honorable way to seal off from Haines & Haines." The judge's eyes lit up as his wife sank a spoon into the bowl bearing this evening's dessert, the new and improved strawberry-rhubarb crumble. "And you must endeavor to get a good recommendation from him."

"That's right, Eb." Betsey Reeve stood beaming over the two men, dishing the dessert into three porcelain bowls. She still wore her apron—no need to get dressed up for Eb Wells, who was practically a member of the family. (T.B. had already eaten his portion and was upstairs reading a book by his allotted candle.) "Getting the axe will follow you around the rest of your life." She patted Eb on the shoulder with her broad, capable hand. "We can't let that happen to you." With a decisive maneuver, she placed the bowl of warm, sticky, sweet glue before him.

"Yes, ma'am," Eb said obediently, picking up his spoon. He could not wait to try the juicy concoction of mashed strawberries, cooked rhubarb, oats, butter, cinnamon, and brown sugar, baked in Betsey Reeve's beehive oven. T.B. had leaked the ingredients to him from furtive scrutiny in the kitchen, but he did not know their proportions. Mrs. Reeve had brought out a bowl of fresh cream to drizzle on the top. If the crumble was as delicious as T.B. touted, he must ask for the recipe to take to Mrs. Potts.

"Listen to my wife." Judge Reeve gave his wife a grateful smile. "She knows what she's talking about." He too looked at the dessert with relish. "And after we devour this delicious crumble, Eb, we're going to discuss how to handle your interview with Mr. Fuller. I have a few suggestions. I'll need you to listen closely." Eb gave the old man a grateful smile. "Now, pass me the cream, if you please."

Ned Haines lay in his bed, staring up at the ceiling. He had just returned home to New Haven after several weeks in Albany. His back hurt, his eyes were blurry, and his bones were tired, the marrow inside feeling stiff and dry. Ned could not fall asleep, even though he was exhausted.

The arbitration had been taxing, not legally, but emotionally. A partnership was breaking up. For the past decade, the company had successfully transported agricultural goods back and forth from Schenectady to Albany. But the Erie Canal was scheduled to open in a couple of years, an east-west navigable waterway between the Hudson River and Lake Erie, connecting the Atlantic Ocean to the Great Lakes. In anticipation of the canal, one partner petitioned for a dissolution of the partnership, predicting the failure of their business. It was not an unreasonable speculation, Ned Haines thought, though premature. The reluctant partner—a volatile man with a bulbous nose—opposed the dissolution of the partnership, disagreeing on the impact of the canal. After listening to more than an hour of 'yes, it will' and 'no, it won't,' Ned was forced to declare the issue 'unresolvable at present.' Since the canal was not yet complete, the arbitrator would entertain no more discussion on its impact.

Regardless, the reluctant partner continued to bring up the canal, and Ned had to tell him—sternly and repeatedly—to forget about the canal. 'The canal doesn't matter—your partner wants out.' Their original agreement provided that the partnership could be dissolved 'upon request of either partner.' Our task here, Ned had told them, over and over, was to bring the partnership to a peaceful end. 'You must cease operations. You must pay off your debts and divide the assets in an equitable fashion.' Ned knew that he had the power to end the partnership by fiat, but it was not his style. He always endeavored to help the parties reach a mutually satisfactory agreement, to the degree possible. His approach took more time, but it made him a popular and well-respected arbitrator.

The parties had clearly soured on each other months, if not years, before. The reluctant partner felt betrayed, but after several days of dealing with him, Ned came to understand why someone would want to divorce him. He wheedled, whined, and indulged himself in occasional outbursts of anger. His bulbous nose turned purple and red. Sometimes, he cried, disconcerting everyone.

In the early days of the settlement discussions, Ned had to call the arbitration to a halt, asking the parties to separate and regroup, returning when both men were ready to get down to work. This strategy failed miserably. The reluctant partner continued to come back to the table in a state of heightened distress. The proceedings had almost reached a standstill, so Ned decided to power through. For days, then weeks, the three men hunkered down together in a stale, windowless room while one of them raged and wept. The ordeal was enough to desiccate the marrow of anyone's bones.

Every night, Ned returned to his hotel in Albany, drained. Every night, he looked for a letter from Malinda Wells behind the hotel desk where his key was stored. For the first ten days, he was rewarded. Malinda wrote him daily, cheerful, funny letters, relaying the inconsequential comings and goings on Elm Street, letting him know how much he was missed. Then one day, the hotel clerk handed him another letter, this one from Nathan, bearing the news that he had fired Eb Wells. From that day on, there were no more letters from Malinda.

At first, Ned worried Malinda was having second thoughts about raising Eddie. Their first encounter had not gone well. Eddie had grown sullen and silent when Malinda entered the front parlor. The boy had positioned himself across the room, facing the velvet loveseat with his back to her. Malinda had plied him with predictable questions that he answered with grudging monosyllables. How were his studies going? Fine. Did he like studying Latin? No. Why not? It's stupid. (This was the only sentence Eddie uttered.) Would you like to come with your father and me to get ice cream one day? No. Ned intervened at that point, ordering his son to be more polite. Eddie growled a 'No, thank you' and fled from the room. Ned was flustered and made for the door to follow his son, presumably to chastise him, but Malinda shook her head. 'Let the boy go.' Pressuring him would do no good.

Ned could tell Malinda was not at ease with children. She had little experience, there being no children in Malinda's feminine enclave in Savannah. Susan Graham had lived there for years too, but she was different. Over the many Sundays of fetching Malinda from Elm Street, Ned had observed Susan with the coachman's son, Henry, who was only a year younger than Eddie. But unlike Malinda, Susan had an easy, frank way of interacting with the child. She was open and friendly, but clearly in command. Even with the tractable Henry, Malinda could be brittle. This did not bode well. The coachman's son was a well-mannered, cheerful child, poised among adults. If Malinda found Henry Mueller a challenge, Ned noted, things might not go that well with his moody, difficult, sometimes rude, son.

Eddie had not started out life sullen and silent. He was once full of life and ready to laugh. Eddie and Ned used to have a warm relationship, but after Fanny's death, things changed. The boy's mother had showered him with so much love and attention, no one could take her place. In her absence, things fell apart. Now, Ned felt stiff and awkward around Eddie and no longer knew how to be easy with him, his poor, grieving boy.

Ned hired a tutor, a college man, who engineered Eddie's education to prepare him for a boys' academy. Nathan, who lived in lodgings nearby, tried to be kind to his half-brother, but he spent most of his time working at the law office. Besides, Nathan had almost thirty years on Eddie—a chasm too great to close. The housekeeper on Chapel Street was a stern woman who tolerated children only because they were necessary for the perpetuation of the species. The cook, at least, was fond of the boy. She was warm and paid attention to Eddie when she could, but she was often busy in the kitchen. No one could break through the armor Eddie had donned since his mother's abrupt and untimely departure.

When he was home, Ned spent evenings with his son. At present, father and son were chugging their way through Defoe's *Robinson Crusoe*, a book Ned thought too adult for Eddie, with its portrayal of slavery, escapades with cannibals, and pursuit by famished wolves. But Eddie wanted to be a castaway, and pirates thrilled him. Reading at bedtime was their only intersection of intimacy and pleasure. Sadly, Eddie would not let Ned tuck him in or kiss him goodnight. Eddie's grief grieved Ned, but he was at a loss for how to make things better. Disappearing to upstate New York all the time did not help. Ned knew this, but the arbitrations kept him from sinking into his own grief. He kept abandoning the boy, but at least he came home. Eddie's mother had left them forever.

And now, with the loss of Malinda, Ned had a new grief of his own. The problem had not been Eddie after all. Nathan had hinted in a letter that maybe Malinda's silence was due to Eb's dismissal. Ned did not fault Nathan for firing Eb, although the manner of firing was not Ned's style. In a fit of pique, Nathan had just lowered the guillotine, giving no thought to the impact on Eb's reputation or dignity. Preserving the dignity of an adversary, Ned had learned, was the foundation of any negotiation—a subtlety his son Nathan might not be capable of.

If Ned had been in New Haven the morning the article came out, he would have found a way to ease Eb's departure. After all, Eb Wells was a young man at the beginning of his professional career. It was understandable—and expected—that he would make mistakes. His legal work was excellent, and he had single-handedly undertaken the education of the apprentices. Furthermore, his father had been an old friend of Ned's, his uncle a colleague from his Yale days. Perhaps more to the point, Ned was in love with Eb's older sister. Nathan did not have to be so harsh, so black and white.

Ned also felt guilty about not being there. He had broken his promise to Nathan to stay in New Haven all summer, but with the new scrivener, Oliver's promotion to apprentice, and Ted's taking on the administration, the law practice was running smoothly. The office was closed for the last two weeks of August. Why should he not accept the arbitration in Albany? It would generate income—money he might need for a wedding. Looking back on those wretched weeks in Albany—trapped in a stuffy room with two unhappy, entangled people—Ned should have stayed home. The Albany arbitration came at a much higher price than imagined. Not only had Nathan fired Eb, but Ned too had gotten the axe—this time by Malinda Wells.

Ned was feeling the loss of her acutely. He had grown accustomed to having Malinda at his side, to discuss legal matters and the management of his law practice. She listened to him with discrimination, asking probing questions. She was shrewd, and he trusted her judgment. She read books and kept up with current events, an avid consumer of the newspaper. And Malinda was always surging toward the future, full of proposals and plans to disrupt the status quo. Ned often had difficulty keeping up with her, but found himself swimming happily in the frothy waters of her wake.

But it was more than that. They had fun. Their Sunday afternoon outings always turned into adventures. Ned and Malinda had been reading *Gulliver's Travels* together. Inside the carriage, his arm linked in hers, he liked to call her 'my little Glumdalclitch'—an oxymoron, Malinda pointed out, since by definition, a giantess was not 'little.' Ned ignored her, loving the way the syllables hummed behind his teeth. Malinda was more astute about Swift's allegory than he was. Ned was embarrassed to admit that, with all the pirates and being cast ashore, he sometimes confused Swift with Defoe. This was a sign, he told her with a wry smile, of his impending senility. Ned let Malinda tease him about being her 'much older man.' Malinda assured him with a warm, secret smile, leaning up against him, that she did not think of him 'like a father.' Not at all.

Ned missed the pressure of her arm in the carriage. He missed her dutiful low moans at his occasionally clunky jokes. He missed the crow's feet around her sharp eyes that deepened when she smiled, her smooth, pretty, round face, the rustle of her silk skirts, her dark hair pulled into its bun, the scent of lavender soap that rose up from her skin—and oh, how he missed her heavenly Southern accent. Ned had felt young and vital around Malinda. Now she was gone, and he felt like a broken old man.

All these things, Ned Haines thought about, lying in his bed, and he wept. Malinda had returned all his letters. He did not know if he could bear this latest loss. Eb was up in Litchfield for a visit, but he would be home soon. Ned would meet up with him and make things right. No matter what it took, Ned Haines was going to win Malinda Wells back.

"Don't get me wrong," Theodore Fuller told Eb Wells. The law office of Theodore Fuller, Esquire, was on the first floor of his house on South Street in Litchfield. "Charles Godwin has the makings of a fine probate lawyer."

Theodore Fuller was a man of forty-five years. While his vest had been stitched only the year before, he had recently put on weight. His wife was learning how to bake from their neighbor Betsey Reeve, and his vest buttons strained around his middle. Mr. Fuller's hairline had receded, exposing a high forehead and a set of reddish-brown eyebrows that ended with a flourish toward his temples. Eb thought he had the look of a startled female Hooded Merganser. He recognized Theodore Fuller's face immediately from his law school days, having seen him on South Street, at the courthouse, at church, on the Green. Litchfield was a busy commercial—and legal—hub, but not so large that Eb would not know at least the face of every lawyer in town, if not his name.

"Charles has such a pleasing manner with my elderly clients. Particularly the old ladies." Theodore Fuller was a gregarious man, inclined to ramble on. He leaned back in his chair and smiled at Eb. "Probate work requires the right personality, shall I say, temperament." Eb gave a perfunctory nod, having no idea what he meant. "Writing a will is a delicate matter," Mr. Fuller continued, unprompted. "No one really wants to sit down to talk about his or her death. And then to have to pay for the privilege. That adds insult to injury!" Mr. Fuller laughed. "But Charles sails through these difficult conversations. He's a shy person, but comfortable with life's fleeting nature. Somehow, he puts everyone at ease, don't you know, Mr. Wells."

"Yes, well, that's true." Death had become one of Charles's favorite topics of conversation ever since his illness, now over a year ago. "I'm certain Charles has a good manner with all your clients."

"He does." Mr. Fuller righted his chair and looked across the desk at Eb. "But Charles is committed to a part-time apprenticeship. He pursues his art in the afternoon. That's fine, just fine. That was our agreement, don't you know. But one of my cases is surely going to trial. It should be settled, but these two brothers want their day in court." Mr. Fuller absentmindedly pulled down his vest, which was riding up at the sides. "I don't try a lot of cases, but I've done a few in the probate court, and even the Superior Court. I tried one there two years ago. It almost killed me. Mrs. Fuller wasn't happy to hear about this trial, I can tell you that." Theodore Fuller let out an audible sigh. "A trial can be very exhausting. And time-consuming. It takes hours and hours of preparation. You've got to do a thorough investigation, develop a theory of the case, get all your documents in order, prepare your witnesses. The day or two in the courthouse is just the tip of the iceberg."

"I can only imagine," Eb said, being unable to imagine.

"So, here's where you might fit in. Charles doesn't want to give me any more hours, and he's got no interest in sitting second chair. An apprentice can, don't you know. The second chair doesn't file an actual appearance with the court—you need not be admitted to the bar, although by the time the case makes it to trial, you might be, but at any rate, it's still a very active and public position." Mr. Fuller shook his head, remembering his last will contest. "You know what it can be like in Litchfield when trials are going on. Attorneys come from all over to try cases. The whole town's likely to show up." He let out a laugh that sounded almost desperate. "All of Litchfield County, even. That wouldn't suit our Charles."

"Yes, sir." This time, Eb knew what he was talking about. Charles, Thomas Bradford, and he had attended many trials at the courthouse while they were in law school. He was familiar with the circus-like atmosphere. And he also knew his friend Charles well.

"I need someone comfortable being in the public eye. Someone who can think on his feet. I asked Judge Reeve if he knew any recent law graduates who might fit the bill. He immediately thought of you." Mr. Fuller leaned back in his chair, his hands resting on his ample stomach. "With your moot court experience and all."

"How many hours a week would you need me, sir?" At Haines & Haines, Eb had often put in fourteen-hour days. He felt as if he had already logged a year's worth of work in his seven-month tenure there. One reason Litchfield was attractive to him was its slower pace. Eb wanted a less grinding schedule.

"I think half days will suit," Mr. Fuller responded. "That way, you and Charles put together will make up one full apprentice." His reddish-brown eyebrows knitted together. "Is that enough hours for you? I was thinking you might've already put in a year's worth of hours in New Haven." He looked worried, anticipating disappointment. "Of course, when we're on trial, it will be full time, and then some. But as for now, I'm not sure I have a full day's work for you."

"No worries, sir," Eb assured him. "Part-time is perfect." This would free up some time for his writing. Samuel Taylor had lined up a couple of newspaper articles for him to work on. "I've got some writing of my own to do."

"There's just one more thing I need to ask you, though." Mr. Fuller seemed hesitant, ignoring the comment about Eb's writing. "I detect from your accent that you're from the South. I've got a good ear that way. That's what Mrs. Fuller says, don't you know. Does my good ear deceive me, Mr. Wells?"

"It does not." Eb's Southern drawl may have faded from his two years up north, but it would never completely disappear. "I was raised in Savannah and attended Franklin College in Athens, Georgia. Why do you ask, sir?"

"Well, we represent the estate of a man who lived out Bantam way. I won't go into the details right now, but I always found him to be a good man. Maybe not an easy man. I didn't know him well, but he was always all right with me. But he was known to drink a bit." Mr. Fuller meandered. "Some in town would say he was a bit eccentric, don't you know. And his relations with his family were not always good." Eb listened intently, wondering what any of this had to do with his being from the South. "This gentleman lived alone and was estranged from his two younger brothers. One of them lives now in Harwinton, the other in Granby."

Mr. Fuller took a deep breath and slowly exhaled. "When I say our client lived alone, that isn't quite accurate. Our client had a housekeeper who lived under the same roof as him for years. Well, now, when we drafted his will, he referred to this woman as 'his wife,' and I surmised they lived together as man and wife—except they weren't married. What would you call that, Mr. Wells? In a state of concubinage?" Mr. Fuller laughed nervously to himself, not expecting Eb to answer.

"And he's left his property to her in the will?" Eb hardly went out on a limb. It was a will contest, most of which were started by disgruntled relatives. In this instance, a housekeeper would not usually be considered the 'natural object of the testator's bounty,' although certainly a wife would be. "I'm guessing that's what the will contest is all about. The two brothers want to take the property from her."

"Precisely." Mr. Fuller gave Eb a nod of respect for having sur-mised the situation. "But there's one other complication. This woman who lived with him for all those years, and took good care of him, this putative spouse—this concubine, if you will, his servant . . ." Theodore Fuller hesitated. "Well, she's a free Black woman."

"I see." Eb's eyebrows went up ever so slightly. The case was suddenly becoming more interesting.

"With your being from the South and all." Mr. Fuller stam-mered around and then said, "Well, I'm not sure how you'd feel about representing her." Eb sat still, waiting for Mr. Fuller to finish. "It just wouldn't suit if you were opposed in any way to a free Black woman inheriting property. I'd need to know your heart was in it. You must know what I mean."

"I do understand." Clearly, neither Judge Reeve nor Charles Godwin had fully described him, at least not his political leanings. Eb wondered how much to reveal about his background. "But you've no need to worry, Mr. Fuller. While I grew up in the South, my parents were from Connecticut. My mother was against slavery, and I've taken an abolitionist stance myself in several public settings." Eb looked him straight in the eye. "I can assure you, sir, that representing a free Black woman poses no problems for me." Eb did not add that just this week, he had assisted a fugitive slave en route to Canada, not wanting to blow his cover.

"Ah, well, yes, that's good, that's good." Theodore Fuller seemed relieved. "And what exactly is the status of your current apprenticeship, if I might ask?"

"That's unclear at present." Judge Reeve had coached him the night before to be vague, insisting that *until* Haines & Haines's senior partner had weighed in, Eb's firing by Nathan should be considered conditional. Upon his return from Albany, Ned Haines might very well override Nathan's actions, or at least approach Eb's departure differently. Eb continued with his script, speaking with studied deliberation. "I believe I'll be leaving before my year is out, sir, but we're working out the details." Eb had practiced the sentence over and over the night before, with Sir Winston playing the role of Mr. Fuller. "I'd like very much to return to Litchfield," he added, "to help you out with this trial." This too was part of the script dictated to him by his elderly mentor. By now, even the old orange-and-white cat knew these canned sentences by heart.

"Well, I'm happy to hear that." Mr. Fuller beamed. This Eb Wells had come well-recommended by both Tapping Reeve and Charles Godwin. Even James Gould thought highly of him. That Eb had worked closely with Charles before was a bonus. Charles was an odd duck, and Eb could jump right into the pond without making any waves. "Would you mind if I corresponded with your current employer?" Theodore Fuller's ferocious eyebrows moved up his forehead in query. "I wouldn't want it said I stole you away from another attorney, without his knowledge or consent."

"That's no problem." Judge Reeve had insisted that Eb assent to this inevitable request. "If you wouldn't mind, though, sir, would you send your letter a few days after I leave to return to New Haven? I'll be here in Litchfield for one more week. That way, when I return, I'll have a chance to speak with my senior attorney first." Eb took off his glasses and rubbed them on his sleeve, his signature gesture of anxiety. He hoped Mr. Fuller did not register his distress. "I wouldn't want Mr. Haines to hear about this before I had an opportunity to discuss it with him in person." More dictated and memorized script from Judge Tapping Reeve.

"Yes, of course, of course, Eb. All very proper." Theodore Fuller took a ledger from his desk drawer and dipped his quill pen into the well. "Let's see now, one week's time plus several days to give you a chance to speak with your employer." Theodore Fuller perused his calendar. "How about two weeks? I will send a letter indicating my interest in having you join me up here in Litchfield in two weeks' time, to help me prepare for trial. I'll ask for a recommendation at that time. Just a formality, don't you know. You come highly recommended by the Litchfield bar, but your current employer will expect it. Will that suit?" He peered up at Eb.

"Yes, sir." Eb breathed a sigh of relief. Judge Reeve had steered him carefully through this first set of steep rapids. Before talking to his mentor, Eb had given no thought to a recommendation from Haines & Haines. He was a novice when it came to crossing bridges without setting them on fire, but he was learning. "That would be just fine, sir."

"Assuming they'll release you," Theodore Fuller said, checking out the next page of his ledger to see what was coming up on his calendar. "Let's say you might start work with me on October 1st? Would that give you sufficient time to arrange the move? You might want to spend some time with your family before coming back up to Litchfield."

"Yes, sir." Eb smiled. "October 1st sounds good to me."

"Good, good." Theodore Fuller wrote something down in his book. "And where do I send my letter?"

"To Haines & Haines." Eb provided him with the Fleet Street address of the law practice in New Haven. "And would you mind addressing the letter to Mr. Edward Haines, sir?" Theodore Fuller was leaning over his ledger, carefully entering the address. "He's the senior attorney there. It would be most appropriate to send your inquiry to him." More instructions from Judge Reeve—to keep the request from Theodore Fuller from falling into Nathan's hands.

"Yes, yes, of course. Proper, very proper." Theodore Fuller carefully wrote down Ned's name and returned the quill pen back to its holder. He stood up and offered his hand to Eb. "I'm very hopeful this arrangement will work out." He gave Eb a wistful smile. "It's a quieter life in the Litchfield hills, don't you know. You're probably used to more action than we get up here. I hope you won't miss all the excitement of a fancy New Haven law practice." Theodore Fuller's eyes glistened as he thought about his one trip to New Haven when he was a much younger man. How exciting it had been to walk through the bustling city streets, with its big buildings, many churches, large university, elegant horse-drawn carriages, vendors hawking their wares, and along Long Wharf, all those tall ships headed to parts unknown. Litchfield, in comparison, was bucolic and mired in the last century. "With all those shipping contracts and business litigation. I worry you might be bored here in our little town."

"No, sir, I know Litchfield well. I've many friends here," Eb said with a smile. "And I'm looking forward to working with you on a trial. I've never done one before."

"Well, trial by fire, that's what they say, isn't it?" Mr. Fuller laughed and wiggled his reddish-brown eyebrows up and down. "Let me see, this trial would be your trial by fire. Oh, I wish I could do something witty with that. We must get Charles to work on it. He's so clever with words, our Charles."

"That he is, sir." Eb Wells shook Mr. Theodore Fuller, Esquire's hand. He was going to like this man.

Letter to Eb Wells from Susan Graham, New Haven,
August 24, 1821

Dear Eb,

I hope this letter finds you well and that you're enjoying your visit to Litchfield. I wonder how things are going with Miss Harding? Or your interview with the attorney? We await news upon your return. I hope this letter arrives before you get home.

You're probably surprised I have written to you. Malinda doesn't know. I beg you not to mention this letter to her. I just wanted to tell you about some happenings here on Elm Street in the past week. That way, you can give thought to them before you return.

First, your brother John has written Malinda a stern letter. He warned her off marrying Ned Haines. He worries about Ned's age and the prospect of raising Eddie on her own. Would John refuse to consent to the marriage? Or withhold her estate funds if she defied him? Can he even do that? His letter also suggests that you agree with him. Is that true? I didn't think it sounded like you. But fair warning—your sister might be upset with both of you.

This brings me to my second point. Malinda has broken it off with Ned Haines. She did this over the way Nathan Haines fired you. She refuses to see Ned or accept his letters. Ned writes every day—I assume to plead his case—but she returns his letters unopened. In my opinion, this is a sad turn of events. I believe Malinda loves Ned, and he loves her. Honestly, Eb, she wouldn't be the first woman to marry an older man. Eddie will come around. Can you talk to Malinda? Or to Ned? Intercede in some fashion? You owe it to her.

Third, I wanted you to know that Franz Mueller and I intend to marry sometime this fall. I wasn't certain if this news would upset you in any way, but I wanted you to hear it from me. After the wedding, I'll be moving into the carriage house. We need to discuss later my status as Malinda's companion.

Speaking of Henry, this brings me to my fourth point. He wants you to know that Mrs. Tittles had two kittens, one black and white, the other a calico. Mrs. Potts has made a bed for the three of them in the pantry off the kitchen. She's worried that in September, the nights will be too cold for the kittens. Esmeralda pretends to be dismayed by kittens in the pantry, but I have seen her peering over them. They're so tiny—they look like little blind rats.

It's been a whirlwind week. I don't expect or want an answer from you. I beg you not to let Malinda know about this letter. She wouldn't be happy with my meddling.

Yours,

Susan

"So, you're feeling good about taking this job?" Rebecca and Eb walked arm in arm up North Street toward Mrs. Edwards's boarding house, chatting in a cheerful, desultory fashion. It was the day before Eb was to return to New Haven. The couple had seen each other almost every day of his visit.

"I am." Eb had been making plans for his return to Litchfield in October. He would take lodgings again with Mrs. Edwards. Unfortunately, his attic room was spoken for, but Charles's old room on the second floor—much larger and nicer—was available.

Eb wanted to know whether Sir Winston would be granted visitation rights. After all, the second-floor room harbored no sausages, no cheeses, no herbs drying from the rafters—and hence no mice. Mrs. Edwards assured him that Sir Winston was free to roam the boarding house at will. The old orange-and-white cat would seek out Eb Wells anyhow. No use in trying to keep them apart. "I'll be happy to be back with Mrs. Edwards."

"And Sir Winston." Rebecca smiled.

Rebecca and Eb had grown easy with one another, as they used to be in the old days before romance was in the air. They joked about their first year on the job—Rebecca's struggles with Asa Hitchcock, and Eb's with Nathan Haines. They discussed politics and shared book recommendations, although Rebecca was characteristically way ahead in reading. Eb told her about attending Moses Brown's talk, getting fired, Malinda's rupture with Ned Haines, Susan's engagement to the coachman, Mrs. Tittles's new kittens, how having a cat was necessary for his spiritual life. Rebecca told Eb all about her new lodgings, the curriculum at the Morris Academy, her little Sabbath nest at the Lewis cottage, her uncertainty about co-education, her apprehension about teaching in a new school. But so far, their future together had not been on the agenda.

Eb had asked Mrs. Edwards whether he might use her garden behind her house on his last afternoon, privacy in Litchfield being at a premium. His request came as no surprise. In the morning, after her other boarders had departed for Miss Pierce's and the law school, Eb lingered behind to talk to Mrs. Edwards—and have more tea. She knew everything about his love life. The backyard was at his disposal.

"I'm so upset about Malinda," Rebecca was saying. "She sounded so happy with Mr. Haines Sr."

"Yes, yes," Eb said, not paying much attention. They were getting closer to Mrs. Edwards's boarding house. The garden in the back had been the site of their first kisses, and he was feeling nervous.

"You must do something," Rebecca urged him, not for the first time. "Your getting fired is no good reason to call things off. Talk some sense into Malinda or reach out to Ned Haines. You owe it to her."

"I never asked her to break ties with Ned." Eb had heard this from Susan too. It was not clear to him why he 'owed' Malinda anything. "It was foolish of her."

"Well, in a way, you do owe it to her. She's upset because of what happened to you."

"But I'm the one who got the axe, not Malinda." Eb wished his sister did not identify with him so much. Over the years, this was a long-standing grievance of his. "She never gives me any room to fail. Just once, I'd like to make a mess of things without taking Malinda's feelings into account."

"I understand that," Rebecca murmured. "I'm just saying . . ."

"All right, yes. I'll see what I can do. I'll talk to Malinda and Ned when I get home. Try to make things right. You know I will." Eb may have been annoyed, but he did want his sister to be happy. "I need to see Ned as soon as I get home anyhow." Eb hesitated, not wanting to hear Rebecca's opinion on his getting fired one more time. "You know, about the firing. The new job. Otherwise, I won't be able to work for Mr. Fuller."

"Well, that's the bed you made for yourself, Eb Wells. Sometimes you act impulsively." Rebecca did not mean to sound hard-hearted, but at times, Eb's judgment was lacking. She squeezed his arm and softened her voice. "Don't get me wrong, your transgressions come from your generous heart, or your sense of justice. Writing that critique of the 'Back to Africa' movement, helping the debtor and his son." Rebecca forgot Eb's third misdemeanor—or was it a felony? "But you're almost a lawyer now, Eb. You must act like one."

"Yes, well, I suppose that's so," Eb muttered under his breath.

"That's more or less what Judge Reeve said too." They walked along in silence until they arrived at the boarding house.

"I hope things work out with Mr. Fuller." Rebecca began to sound nervous herself. "It would give us some time to get to know one another better. Not just through correspondence."

"Yes." Eb led Rebecca to the hidden bench in the verdant back-yard, full of bushes and tall sycamore trees, with their smooth gray trunks and peeling bark. Mrs. Edwards's flower garden was minimal, with one valiant rose bush next to the house, already done blooming. Eb liked the wild greenness of the setting—and its seclusion. "Have a seat, Rebecca."

"You come too," she said in a comforting way, sitting down on the bench and patting the seat beside her. Her desire to calm him down resulted in her own calm. It had always been so between them. "Sit here, won't you?"

Eb sat down and slipped his arm through hers. He could feel her warmth next to him. Rebecca looks so pretty today, he thought. The summer sun was always kind to her, lending her face a pale pink. No, a peachy pink. She was dressed in a simple gray dress, her gold locket dangling from a chain. Her bun had become loose, and a stray lock of dark brown hair curled against her neck. That neck looked tantalizing to him—and naked. He felt an urge to kiss her.

"So, Eb," Rebecca began. "We've been writing to each other for over a year."

"Yes," Eb replied, repressing his urge. He did not want to be accused of being forward, of thinking of kisses instead of treating her like 'a person,' of not listening to her. "That's true. I've enjoyed our correspondence. Really, Rebecca, your letters have meant a lot to me this year. I want you to know that."

"Me as well," Rebecca said. "What a tumultuous year we've had. My first year of teaching went well, except when it didn't, and your first year as an apprentice went well, except when it didn't." She laughed. "Honestly, we're a pair. Do you think we'll get the hang of things? Maybe in our second year?"

"I'm not sure." Eb had left Haines & Haines over a week ago and felt nothing but intense relief. He missed his friends at the office, Samuel Taylor and the Redfield brothers, but not the work. Certainly, Eb did not miss Nathan Haines, lurking around, ready to find fault with everything he did. "It's a bit discouraging," Eb confessed. "I loved law school so much, but I'm not sure about the practice of law. I wouldn't say I love it."

"You need to give it another chance. Maybe trial work will suit you."

"Yes, that's what everyone says. Judge Reeve. Samuel, even my brother." Eb sighed. "They all say I shouldn't give up too soon." He glanced over at Rebecca. Her eyes were on him, her face turned toward him. "And what about you? Even struggling with The Ogre, do you still love teaching?" He raised his eyebrows over the gold rims of his glasses and watched for any changes in her face.

"I do," Rebecca said with a blush, recognizing they had now wandered off the map—into the uncharted territory of their relationship. "It's harder than I thought—the preparation, dealing with the parents, what to do with the girls who were forced to be at school." Rebecca missed the intimacy of her schoolroom at the Wethersfield Academy, where her students, perched on wooden benches, their faces expectantly turned up to her, were excited for the lesson to begin. She could see them so clearly in her mind. "But I do love teaching, and I miss my girls, even the indifferent ones." Rebecca experienced a rush of love for her students. "I just hope this second year will be easier."

"And how are you feeling about our being together?" Eb felt clumsy, blundering into the topic abruptly, unable to find a gentle way to introduce it.

"It's hard to say," Rebecca replied, her voice sounding calm and self-assured. "If I were to be with a man, I would want it to be you." She looked over at Eb with a constant gaze. "Really, Eb, only you. I think we're good together. We're both bookish. We value the same things. I love to be with you, to write to you—to get your letters." It looked as if she was going to reach out and stroke his face, but she did not.

"But it still comes down to the 'if I were to be with a man,' doesn't it, Rebecca?" Eb felt a sudden surge of anger, surprised by the force of his emotions. Rebecca was still pushing him away, while at the same time gesturing for him to come forward. Just seconds before, he had wanted so much to kiss her. But now, he was not so certain.

"Yes, Eb." Rebecca kept her voice steady. Perhaps Eb's question, right before their discussion, on whether she still loved teaching, had not been strategic. The eager faces of her students were still looking up at her in her mind's eye. "I don't make the rules, you know."

"I know you don't," Eb snapped, his anger not receding. "But I'm wondering if I might have to wait forever."

"I wouldn't want you to," Rebecca said softly, looking down at the ground. She was not prepared for his anger, even though she understood it.

"Because maybe I could find someone else," Eb blurted, no longer choosing his words with care. He was still smarting from the sting of Susan's news about her upcoming marriage to Franz. "I did have an interest in someone else this year, Rebecca, and I did nothing about it." Then he added, "Now it's too late. All because of you." Eb did not know why he said it. He knew that his failure with Susan was due to his own lack of courage, and Rebecca had no hand in that.

"You did? Someone else?" Rebecca sounded genuinely surprised—and hurt. "Who, Eb?"

"Susan," Eb replied. "Susan Graham."

"I thought you told me she's going to marry the coachman?"

Rebecca's face no longer looked peachy pink. She had not anticipated the conversation to take this turn. Never in her wildest dreams did she imagine the housekeeper's daughter, Susan Graham, posed any threat. Eb was fond of her, she knew, but only like a sister.

"She *is* going to marry him," Eb said glumly, knowing he had done exactly what Charles Godwin made him promise he would not do. He had told Rebecca about Susan, and now he did not know how to handle the fallout. "But earlier this year, well . . . Susan had changed a lot since I last saw her." Eb stumbled blindly forward. "You know, she was even more beautiful than before, and . . ."

"Even more beautiful?" Rebecca was now pale, almost white, her voice no longer calm or self-assured. She looked as if she had been slapped. "That's why you were interested in her—for her beauty?" She took her arm out from Eb's and crossed her chest with it, grasping onto the opposite elbow with her thin, delicate hand. "I suppose she's more beautiful than I am," Rebecca said with a bitterness that surprised them both. She shrugged her slender shoulders. "Who wouldn't be?"

"Not at all, Rebecca," Eb stammered, looking over at her. Rebecca's dark brown eyes were full of tears about to brim over. She did look beautiful to him just then, perhaps because he had just wounded her. "Yours is a different kind of beauty than Susan's, that's all."

"I see," Rebecca said stiffly, not wanting to cry. She would not give him the satisfaction of her tears. "Please, go no further. You need not explain."

"And nothing happened, Rebecca." Eb's voice shook. He had not prepared himself to veer off in this direction. Now that he had, the conversation had taken on a life of its own. He had no script and felt out of control. Where was Charles Godwin when he needed him? Eb cringed. Charles had expressly warned him not to indulge in this revelation. There was nothing else to do but careen forward.

"But something could have happened." Eb immediately regretted the words, but they just came tumbling out. "I'm ready to love you, Rebecca, if you would let me, but you don't."

"You're 'ready' to love me?" Rebecca looked over at Eb, feeling her own surge of anger. "What does that even mean?" She pulled on her necklace chain. Her tears had disappeared, and her face was flushed with fury. "You never say anything to me about love in your letters. How am I expected to know how you feel?"

"Well, you don't say anything to me about love in your letters either." Eb felt unjustly accused. He knew he had mangled things by telling her about Susan, but Rebecca bore half the responsibility for the coolness in their correspondence. He may have been right—but sometimes being right does not matter. At the very least, his observation was poorly timed.

"Well, I guess that sums it up, doesn't it, Eb?" Rebecca said with an unrecognizable chilly crispness in her voice. "I don't know why you're worried about waiting forever for a woman you don't yet love." She stood up suddenly. "For a woman you don't find beautiful." And with that, Rebecca Harding stormed out of Mrs. Edwards's backyard, leaving him all alone on the bench.

Eb took off his glasses and rubbed them furiously on the sleeve of his white shirt. He was unsure what had just happened, but it was not good. Not good at all. He sat there alone for a while in the dense green foliage, cursing himself.

That evening after supper, Mrs. Edwards and Eb shared a pot of tea in the kitchen of the boarding house. The servant Maggie and Mrs. Edwards's daughters had already gone to their rooms. The law students had all vanished to prepare for Saturday's oral examination, Miss Pierce's students to study. The glowing logs of the dying fire gave off a lambent light. Mrs. Edwards asked Eb how his meeting with Rebecca Harding had gone that afternoon. She had noticed that Eb seemed quiet and withdrawn.

"It didn't go well, Mrs. Edwards," Eb said with a deep sigh. He sensed he had lost something precious that afternoon, even though he did not fully understand what it was. "I think I did something terrible."

After Eb told her the entire story, Mrs. Edwards agreed. He *had* done something terrible. The two talked for a long time, with Sir Winston curled up on the stone hearth between them, wheezing and warming himself by the fire, waiting for Eb to go up to bed. Mrs. Edwards told the old cat in no uncertain terms that he would just have to wait. She needed to explain a few things to Eb Wells. A few things about women.

CHAPTER 5

Détentes

"Dr. Cabot named him 'Domino.'" Henry and Susan sat at the French writing desk in the library on Elm Street. It was an early September day with no need for a fire. Henry had written 'Domino' for the third time in his commonplace book, and Susan had asked him why. "It was his idea. Last night. Dr. Cabot named him Domino because he's a black-and-white cat."

Henry looked sideways at Susan, not sure she understood. Because he was now six years old, Henry often felt smarter than his teacher. His father was going to marry her, and that made Henry happy. Franz Mueller had sought his son's permission before asking her, and Henry had said an emphatic 'yes.' His own mother's face had begun to fade in his memory, and he could tell how happy Miss Graham made his father. Henry loved her too.

"And you say Dr. Cabot invited the kitten to come into the library with you?" Susan was wide-eyed. "While you played dominoes?" Even the bold Mrs. Tittles had never crossed the threshold of the library. Dr. Cabot had let it be known he was not fond of cats, but Esmeralda and Mrs. Potts had informed him they needed a mouser in the kitchen, allowing Mrs. Tittles, and now her small brood, to sleep in the pantry. He would tolerate that—not that he had any choice in the matter. Even Malinda had assented.

"Well, he didn't exactly 'invite' the kitten in." Henry did not make eye contact with Susan. The truth was the boy had been carrying the black-and-white kitten around in his jacket pocket. The kitten liked to snuggle up in the dark space, close to the warmth of Henry's torso. Sometimes Henry carried both kittens, one in the left pocket, the other in the right. But on this occasion, only the black-and-white kitten had accompanied him to the library, having fallen sound asleep. "He was in my jacket, but once Dr. Cabot found out he was there, he asked me to show him—for a 'physical examination,' he said."

In all his sixty years, Dr. Ebenezer Cabot had never been in the presence of a kitten. Domino, as he was now called, was a poised little cat—confident he would be oohed and aahed over wherever he was. That had been his experience to date. Both he and his sister were the darlings of the kitchen on Elm Street. Dr. Cabot stared at the kitten on Henry's lap, teetering, unsure of his footing on the little boy's knobby knees. He was charmed by the kitten's pert black face, his white bib, his white whiskers, his white mittens, his luxurious black pelt, the defiant way his little black tail stuck up in the air.

"The kitten was waking up, so I gave him to Dr. Cabot to hold. Domino was all 'wobbly and wiggly.'" Henry gave Susan a secret smile. 'Wobbly and wiggly' was what Susan called Henry when he could not settle into his chair to study.

"And Dr. Cabot held the cat?" Susan shook her head, having a difficult time imagining the scene.

Henry nodded. "He did, and Domino took right to him. He purred and purred, so loud, I could hear him from the other side of the game table."

At first, the black-and-white kitten let himself be held limply in Dr. Cabot's hands, dangling his spindly legs onto his wrists and rumbling his pint-sized motor against the palm of his hand. Peering through his spectacles, the doctor had inspected the kitten from his black pointed ears to his pearly pink splayed-out tiny toe pads. The little cat struggled to be released from Dr. Cabot's hands. Once set free, the kitten proceeded to nestle down into his lap, turning himself around and around, settling in for a nap, right in the crevice of Dr. Cabot's thighs. The doctor tentatively stroked the kitten's back, feeling his delicate, hollow backbone, his little birdlike shoulders. The kitten purred and purred.

Dr. Cabot appeared befuddled but told Henry to turn the tiles over and start the game of dominoes once more. Throughout both rounds—Henry won the first, but not the second—Dr. Cabot was careful not to move, even when drawing from the boneyard. He kept his legs squeezed together, and eventually, his feet went to sleep. After all, he did not want to disrupt the kitten's nap.

When Dr. Cabot saw the letter in the stack of household mail in the foyer, he recognized his old friend Ned Haines's handwriting. His niece had returned many of his letters in the last two weeks, but this one was addressed to 'Eb Wells.' Because he did not want Malinda to return this letter too, Dr. Cabot took it upstairs, leaving it for his nephew on the dresser in the bedroom adjoining his. Eb would be back from Litchfield soon. Maybe Ned Haines had proposed a meeting with his nephew—he hoped so.

Dr. Cabot watched with great interest all the comings and goings and the ups and downs of the young people under his roof. Their lives were so turbulent, so exhausting. His own existence moved peacefully through the days at a glacial pace, with no changes in status or inclination. But with Malinda, Eb, and Susan, something was always happening to one of them. They fell in and out of love, worked hard, acquired new friends, made colossal mistakes, lost jobs, got new ones, reached new heights of happiness and depths of despair. They went down to Long Wharf to see the tall ships, took walks on the Green, had pints of ale with friends in taverns, and tried all the flavors of ice cream offered in the new icehouse on Water Street. Each one embraced New Haven in his or her own way. His young people crawled into the carriage he had provided them with and roamed the city, looking for adventure. For Dr. Cabot, New Haven was just the stratum of granite he was embedded in—not a place to explore.

The only thing new in Ebenezer Cabot's life these days was a small cat named Domino. Now at night, the black-and-white kitten sometimes slept on top of the doctor's bald head, moving back and forth from the warm cat bed in the pantry to Dr. Cabot's cozy room upstairs, treading the stairs softly on his little padded feet. Esmeralda balked at first, but quickly yielded. It was Dr. Cabot's house, after all, and anything that brought joy to Ebenezer made Esmeralda happy. He had been so lonely after the death of his mother, and the little cat seemed to comfort him. No one else in the house paid much attention. But for Ebenezer Cabot, Domino's arrival in his life was monumental. The old doctor had opened his heart, and the little cat sauntered right in, his black tail sticking straight up in the air.

About the impending marriage of his niece's companion and his coachman, Dr. Cabot was also pleased—and he hoped the couple would stay in the carriage house. Franz Mueller was an excellent coachman and an asset to his medical practice, treating his patients with kindness and respect. He got along well with Mr. and Mrs. Potts, and Esmeralda approved of him. And Dr. Cabot had grown fond of the confident, outspoken Susan. Franz Mueller would make a good husband for her, just as he made a good father for Henry.

Most of all, Dr. Cabot wanted Henry Mueller to stay on Elm Street. The doctor and the boy had become fast friends. They played dominoes at night—checkers and chess would come later when Henry was older. Sometimes, Henry shadowed Dr. Cabot on routine house calls. Maybe Henry would himself become a doctor, he would say to the boy, trying in vain to smooth down Henry's defiant tufts of blond hair before entering a patient's home. Dr. Cabot hoped Franz and Susan would choose to stay indefinitely. The ruckus of family life could take place under the roof of the carriage house, but the family would be nearby. It was a combination of solitude and company that suited him.

But Dr. Cabot was distressed over his niece's rupture with Ned Haines. True, at first, he had been dubious about the liaison. In private, he had complained to Esmeralda, who had her own reservations. Both held Ned Haines in high esteem. Ned was an honorable, well-respected lawyer in New Haven, a man of property and education, and an old family friend. But speaking of old, Ned was as old as Methuselah—the same age as Dr. Cabot, and Malinda's father too if he had lived. And then there was the problem of the difficult son. But seeing Malinda so happy with Ned, the qualms of Dr. Cabot and Esmeralda were eventually put to rest.

After all, it would not be the first such May–December match, or perhaps, Ebenezer Cabot chuckled, July–December. His niece was in love. This was a diagnosis Dr. Cabot felt confident to make. All the symptoms were there—Malinda's humming in the morning, her readiness to smile, the color in her cheeks, her endless, excited chatter about what she and Ned were going to do next Sunday. Then Eb was unceremoniously fired from Haines & Haines, and Malinda abruptly cut ties with Ned.

After that, she collapsed. Malinda did not eat or sleep well, and for days, she barely left her bedroom. She refused to come down for meals, and when Mrs. Potts prepared trays for her, laden with food, Malinda returned them hardly touched. She delegated her clinic duties to Susan, citing malaise, permitting Susan entry into her bedroom only when necessary. She was besieged with intermittent headaches that forced her to lie down and draw the drapes.

After examining her, Dr. Cabot could find no medical reason for her suffering. Malinda was pale, losing weight, and her previous good cheer had given way to a gloomy melancholy. Dr. Cabot was worried. He once had a patient years ago, a young woman who was jilted by her lover and went into a precipitous decline. No matter what ministrations her family and Dr. Cabot provided her, his patient had died of a broken heart—not a medical diagnosis, but the reality. He was haunted by that experience, and this time, the patient was the beloved daughter of his beloved sister. He could not let Abigail down. Things must be set right.

For these reasons, Dr. Cabot was relieved to see the letter for Eb from Ned Haines. Maybe Eb could straighten things out upon his return from Litchfield. Dr. Cabot was aware that his nephew was inclined to meddle—a propensity he did not always approve of. But in this instance, a judicious meddle was just what the doctor ordered.

"I can't abide losing Malinda. I find our separation unbearable."

Ned Haines looked across the rough wooden table at Eb Wells. They had each ordered a tankard of ale at Beers Tavern at the corner of College and Chapel. Upon Eb's return to New Haven, a note from Ned was waiting for him on his dresser, inviting him out to Beers. The tavern was cool and dark. It was a September afternoon, but Indian summer had brought unseasonable heat. Because it was the middle of the day, after lunch hour, the two men were alone. The room was empty and quiet, except for two employees in white aprons who were wiping down the tables in expectation of a crowd later. It was a good place to talk.

"I know you're unhappy, sir." Eb looked over at the distinguished older man sitting across from him, with tousled silver hair and a haggard face. "And I have to say, Malinda's unhappy too." Eb did not want to tell Ned Haines how alarmed he was about his sister. When he returned from Litchfield, Malinda had lost weight and gone pale. Plagued by headaches, she had withdrawn into her room. "She was just so angry about . . . well . . ." Eb stammered.

"About Nathan's sacking you. I'm truly sorry about that, Eb. If I'd been home, things would have unfolded differently." Ned shook his head, contemplating once more how much the arbitration in Albany had cost him. "I can assure you that."

"I doubt the end result would have been different," Eb said in a studied, even voice. "Nathan's been furious with me for some time. The ACS article wasn't our first difference of opinion."

"I'm well aware." When Ned returned from Albany, Nathan had filled him in on all of Eb Wells's myriad transgressions. "Nathan has an unfortunate tendency to keep score."

"Well, I was wrong about befriending the debtor." Eb jumped in, wanting to get this part of the conversation over. "I do apologize. I didn't fully appreciate the distance an attorney must keep from the opposing party." This was another scripted line from Judge Reeve— who thought an apology was due to Ned Haines on this count. "I am sorry, sir."

"No harm done, Eb," Ned said graciously. "We all learn by doing. I made more than a few mistakes myself when I was first in practice." He gave Eb a gratuitous wink. "You'll get the hang of it."

"I don't apologize though, sir, for tutoring the other apprentices, or for including Donald Hawkins." Eb ran his fingers nervously through his new haircut. "Samuel Taylor and I thought of Donald as a member of the Haines & Haines family. He was Francis Hawkins's brother—it was Francis who made the request. We studied before the office opened, and I took no payment for the tutoring. And we let no one else join the study group." Ned listened to Eb intently. "I don't see, sir"—Eb took off his glasses for an unnecessary polishing with his shirt sleeve—"how this differs from the sessions you and my father had in Rufus Henderson's attic. Back when you were apprentices."

"I can see why you might think that." Ned nodded. "And you're right. Nathan and I do think highly of Francis Hawkins. If I'd been asked, I would've agreed that Donald could attend your sessions as well, for no fee. But you should have run this by Nathan. That would have given him a heads-up. That way, when an outsider like Allen Lowery approached him, he wouldn't have been caught unawares."

"Honestly, sir, we didn't think to tell him." Eb was reminded that Judge Reeve had said the same thing. He tried to recall the negotiations with Samuel Taylor. They had talked about the inevitability of Nathan finding out, but not whether they should inform him.

"You need to understand something about your supervisor." Ned chose his words with care, looking around the dark, cavernous room for eavesdroppers, but no one else was there. "Nathan doesn't always feel secure. He was embarrassed in front of Allen Lowery, an old colleague from Yale. Someone he respects. It looked like Nathan didn't know what was going on at his own law practice—and he didn't." Ned continued with caution, trying not to disrespect his son. "That embarrassment is what fueled his anger with you." Eb listened to Ned Haines closely, beginning to understand why he might be a skilled arbitrator. "If Nathan had known what you were doing, his response to Allen Lowery—and you—would have been different. Do you see what I'm saying?"

"Yes, sir. That never crossed my mind." Eb had a faint memory of Nathan mentioning his embarrassment in his reproach, but it had not made an impression on him. "I'm sorry, sir." Eb looked Ned

Haines in the eye. "That we didn't inform you and Nathan about the study group. And about Donald." Judge Reeve had not scripted that line. It was an apology that welled up in Eb spontaneously.

"Not a problem, Eb, but it's a good lesson to learn," Ned said kindly, "to imagine how the other person might be feeling. To me, it's the one lesson every lawyer needs to know. And the one lesson no one ever teaches you."

"I've been known to be somewhat obtuse in this area, sir," Eb said, feeling chagrined. "Particularly with women."

"Oh, well, don't ask me for help there. Still, in my experience, women are much better at this than we men are," Ned said with a wistful smile. "Their mothers teach them to consider the feelings of others. We men are stunted this way, not because it's our nature. It's our upbringing. We're permitted to think only of ourselves because we're men. But we could learn how. We just lack the training."

"Really?" Eb felt a flicker of hope. These days, he experienced feelings of global sadness that crept up on him unawares. It happened every time he encountered a new idea. Ned Haines had just made an interesting observation, and his first response was to share it with Rebecca. But now she was gone, and it was all his fault. Eb wanted to believe he could improve at love—and restore relations with Rebecca. "You think I could learn how to do that? Imagine the feelings of others?"

"I do think it's learnable." Ned leaned back in his chair, thanking the tavern owner who had just brought their ale. "I've had to develop the skill in arbitrations. I make it my business to see both sides. You and I are trained as lawyers to do that with arguments and competing ideas. But no one ever teaches us how to do that with feelings. An effective arbitrator must imagine what each party sitting in the room feels. To get the parties to do the same." Ned took a long drink of his ale. "It's tricky. I don't always succeed. I couldn't get through to one of the men in my last arbitration. Reaching an agreement was a nightmare. I finally had to step in, something I'm loath to do."

"I see. Do you have any suggestions about how I might improve?" Eb asked this tentatively, thinking about Rebecca.

"Well, let me think." Ned took another long drink of his ale. The warm weather had generated a thirst he had been unaware of. "Try this. The next time you're in a difficult situation, ask yourself, 'How is what I'm about to say or do going to be experienced by this other person?'" Ned laughed. "I know that sounds easy, but I assure you, it's not."

"So, what do you think Malinda's feeling right now?" Eb ventured, wanting to steer the conversation toward his mission. "About my being fired?" He also wanted to see if Ned Haines was as good as his word—whether he had any grasp on why Malinda had come unhinged.

"I think she feels shame about your being fired—summarily axed." Ned let out a long, heartfelt sigh. "Listen, Eb. For most of her life, Malinda has loved you more than anyone in the world. I know that. Anything that happens to you, happens to Malinda." He seemed to accept this long-standing sibling enmeshment without rancor. "The boundary between the two of you is not that well maintained."

"I try to maintain it," Eb grumbled, not arguing with Ned's assessment. "But Malinda can't. Or won't. It's been a source of friction between us for years. And to tell you the truth, sir, I feel no shame about being fired. Only Malinda does." He shook his head adamantly. "And I wish she wouldn't."

"Well, that's probably so, Eb," Ned said in a gentle voice, "but you can't control the way your sister loves you." Eb gave a weak smile, recognizing that Ned Haines had just said something else wise.

"And she loves you too, sir," Eb said abruptly, without thinking. The opinions of John or his uncle or Esmeralda—or Eb—did not matter. The only thing that mattered was how Malinda and Ned felt about each other. We ought to support them if they were in love and wanted to marry. Those were Eb's thoughts later that day when he had time to collect them. But more than anything, Eb wanted Malinda to be happy. He was worried sick about her. He could not bear a thin, pale, sad, withdrawn, headache-riddled Malinda in perpetuity. "We need to fix things between you."

"I couldn't agree with you more." Ned looked sad but determined. "But I have to say this, Eb. Your return to Haines & Haines isn't going to happen. I can't override Nathan on this. I would have spoken to you about the article myself. Our clients won't countenance your views. For them, it's untenable for their own lawyer to argue against slavery—not when they've got so much invested in it." He shook his head. "Personally, I admire your courage. I even share your views on the ACS, but Nathan's right. We have a law practice to protect, which means remaining politically neutral. At least in public."

"I understand all that." Eb had returned his glasses to their rightful position and looked squarely across the table at Ned Haines. "But the truth is, sir, I'm probably not suited for political neutrality. Not on this issue. The pressure just builds up in me, and I must speak out."

"So, that's the bottom line, isn't it?" Ned Haines picked up his tankard and took another long swig of the cold brown brew, relieved that the worst of the conversation was over. "Haines & Haines wasn't a great fit for Eb Wells, and vice versa." He wiped the foam from his upper lip with his handkerchief. "But listen, your work's been excellent—you're the sharpest legal mind we've ever had in the office. You get along well with everyone, Nathan notwithstanding. Our clients all like you. And we greatly appreciate your pitching in with the other apprentices. You're an outstanding teacher, a real chip off the old block." Ned looked across the table at Eb, who blushed from all this praise. "Your father would be so proud of you."

"Thank you, sir," Eb said quietly, not knowing what to say next.

"So, let's do this." Ned seemed to have already formed a plan, perhaps before he even walked into the tavern. "My recommendation is that you write a formal letter of resignation. In it, say you want to leave for professional reasons, to pursue this opportunity up in Litchfield. To get some trial experience. Of course, we'll give you a stellar recommendation." Ned paused, looking over at Eb. "I've already received Mr. Fuller's letter of inquiry about you."

"And what about Nathan's sacking me?" This was just the scenario Judge Reeve had been hoping for. Not for the first time, Eb wondered how he could ever repay Judge Reeve for rescuing him from this fiasco at Haines & Haines.

"We'll wipe it off the slate, I think. Of course, I'll need to talk Nathan into that," Ned said matter-of-factly. "But no one will be the wiser. Your future won't be ruined. Nathan will be getting what he wanted—to have you gone from the law practice." Ned knew he was going to have to struggle with Nathan over Eb's 'stellar recommendation.' But he was a man fighting for his future happiness. It was a battle Ned Haines was determined to win. If he had to pull rank, he would.

"I think that would mollify Malinda." Eb thought over Ned's proposition. "She really is most unhappy without you, sir."

"Listen to me, Eb Wells," Ned Haines said with a big smile. "I intend to marry your sister. You'll have to stop calling me 'sir.'"

"Yes, sir," Eb sputtered, lifting his tankard to his mouth for the first time. Ned Haines had guzzled his ale, but Eb had been so tense, he could not imagine swallowing. Now, the cold yeasty liquid slid down his throat. It tasted so good and quenched his thirst. Eb suddenly realized he was taking in air again with ease. He had not noticed that for the past month, he had been holding his breath.

"And Eb," Ned added, "you and Nathan must make peace. If things work out between me and Malinda, the two of you will belong to the same family."

Eb stared in disbelief across the rough wooden table at Ned Haines. It was the first time this fact had been brought home to him. Nathan Haines would be in his life forever.

Letter to John Wells from Eb Wells, New Haven, September 20, 1821

Dear John,

By now, you've received Malinda's announcement of her engagement to Ned Haines. Consider yourself lucky, John. You missed all the drama of this past month. Malinda was incensed over something that happened at my work. She broke it off with Ned but was miserable without him. She fell into a deep melancholy, not eating or sleeping, and was plagued with headaches. Uncle Ebenezer and I were worried about her health. You too would have been worried, I know. I'm relieved they've reconciled. Malinda's on the mend.

I've come to appreciate Ned Haines. He's both kind and wise, and devoted to our sister. Honestly, Malinda will gain both financial and social advantages from the marriage. At thirty, she'd resigned herself to spinsterhood, to sleeping in a bedroom in one of our homes—yours, mine, or Uncle Ebenezer's. This marriage to Ned Haines gives her a chance to have a home of her own, perhaps her own children. We must honor her decision, John. Please give the couple your blessing. It would mean the world to Malinda.

You've also heard the news about Susan Graham and the coachman? After they marry, she'll be moving into the carriage house. Uncle Ebenezer will benefit from having Franz Mueller and his family on Elm Street, particularly his son Henry. Now that Malinda and I are both moving out, our uncle might be lonely, although he now has a constant companion, a kitten named Domino. One is never truly alone with a cat around. About Susan, Uncle Ebenezer has asked if she can work for him in the clinic as administrator, for a salary. Malinda insists she'll be 'in and out' of Elm Street, but he thinks it's best not to count on her. Should we consider terminating Susan's stipend as Malinda's companion? She'll have another source of income by that time. There's talk of sending Henry to school, perhaps next year, so she'll soon be relieved of her teaching duties. How does that sit with you?

I've resigned from Haines & Haines and accepted the part-time apprenticeship position up in Litchfield. I'm going to help with the trial preparation for a will contest and sit second chair. Mr. Fuller seems amiable, and the case is of interest to me. I look forward to boarding with Mrs. Edwards—you still have her address? I start work on October 1st. I'll return to New Haven for Malinda's wedding and the holidays. I assume the journey is too far for you and Eliza to attend the wedding.

I must be off. There's much to do here before I leave for Litchfield. Malinda's forcing a new suit upon me for the wedding. Our sister has returned to her usual bossy self, ordering everyone around, and making lists of 'Things to Do' for each one of us. It is nice to have her back in all her dictatorial splendor.

Give my love to Eliza and the girls. Please pass a tidbit to Monroe under the table for me.

Yours with affection,

Eb

PS Please also send my regards to Thomas Bradford. Tell him of my news. Any movement on the Katherine Montgomery front?

Malinda not only resumed her courtship with Ned Haines but also accepted his marriage proposal. Her brother had worked things out with Haines & Haines to her satisfaction. Eb was permitted to resign honorably to seek a new apprenticeship in Litchfield. She wrote to inform her brother John of her engagement to Ned, presenting it as a fait accompli, refusing to ask for permission. Malinda and Susan decided on a double wedding—in the parlor on Elm Street with a sit-down supper afterward. Ned Haines would ask an old family friend who was a justice of the peace to officiate.

Both couples preferred not to marry in a church. Neither Malinda nor Susan had been raised in a church in Savannah. Malinda's mother and Dr. Cabot were nominally Congregationalists, but the former was dead, the latter indifferent. Franz Mueller had already been married in a Lutheran church in Philadelphia. That was enough for him—the less fuss, the better. Ned Haines's commitment to Unitarianism was nascent, and he did not feel ready to marry within that congregation. He had two church weddings under his belt, both more extravagant than the modest plans of his intended third wife. Ever practical, Malinda argued the money would be better spent on renovations on Chapel Street. Ned readily agreed. If Malinda was happy, Ned was happy.

The double wedding was set for the third week of December—close to the holidays. This would give Eb several months at his new job before he had to travel back down to New Haven. Ned also needed time to redecorate the rooms upstairs on Chapel Street, space dedicated to Malinda. The ghosts of former wives had to be exorcised. Malinda and Ned wanted a few months for Eddie to adjust to the idea of a stepmother. Once the engagements were announced, Susan suggested they get Eddie and Henry together. Maybe the two couples could take the boys out on an adventure. Susan offered to coach Malinda on how to relate to a seven-year-old boy. Having another child around as a buffer would surely help.

Many decisions needed to be made. Mrs. Potts had to settle on her menu. After the ceremony, supper would be served in the dining room. The guest list had to be kept small. There would be twelve adults and two children: the justice of the peace, Ned, Eddie, Malinda, Nathan, Susan, Franz, Henry, Dr. Cabot, Eb, Samuel Taylor, the Redfield brothers, and the new scrivener. (Malinda insisted it would be impolitic to leave him out.) They could fit all the adults around the mahogany table if Mr. Potts crawled up to the attic and unearthed the leaves. Where the boys would eat was still up in the air. Mrs. Potts planned to hire her niece and husband to assist with the serving and cleaning up.

Esmeralda would oversee everything—with Malinda's supervision. The housekeeper insisted on new drapes in the parlor. The old ones were put up by Mrs. Cabot twenty years ago, she complained to Dr. Cabot, not a suitable backdrop for such a joyous occasion. Malinda and Esmeralda picked out a celery green satin with a matte finish. Both Susan and Malinda needed new dresses for their weddings. Would Henry need a suit? Probably, yes. Dr. Cabot, Franz and Eb certainly did. Eb would have to hurry over to the tailor on the other side of the New Haven Green before he left for Litchfield. The final fitting could happen in December. Dr. Cabot, Franz, and Henry had more time.

John Wells wrote to his sister, offering his warmest congratulations. Regrettably, he and his family would not be able to attend the wedding, the travel to and from Charleston taking more than a month. His law practice was too busy to leave unattended, and the girls were both in school. He hoped Dr. Cabot would do the honors of giving Malinda away. A wedding gift for Ned and Malinda would be coming from England, hand-picked by his wife, Eliza. Malinda hoped it might be a china set like Eliza's, the one with roses and gold edges.

Dr. Cabot was pleased to give Malinda away, and Susan intended to ask Eb to do the honors for her. Both Susan and Malinda hoped Eb would invite Rebecca Harding down from Litchfield or from Wethersfield, wherever she spent her holidays, assuming Mr. Potts could locate the leaves for the dining room table. A thirteenth person might make the seating arrangements lopsided, Malinda admitted, but it would be good to have another woman at the table.

Eb made no commitment to inviting Rebecca to the wedding, muttering he would 'think about it.' He and Rebecca had not communicated in any fashion since she had rushed out of Mrs. Edwards's backyard that awful day in August.

"I hope you're comfortable at the cottage, Rebecca." Martha gathered her green cape around her. A wispy pale mist rose from the hills on the horizon, promising a chilly autumn evening. It was late September in Connecticut, and the leaves were turning various shades of orange, yellow, and red, muted by the lateness of the day and the long slant of the sun's rays. The two friends were on a walk after the cold Sabbath meal with Martha's family, seeking some privacy. Now that Robert's old room in the back was ready, Rebecca was staying at the Lewis cottage after her teaching week. Martha was home from Miss Pierce's for the Sabbath. "My mother's happy to have you," Martha added. "She misses me."

"I love my little nest." Rebecca also gathered her long black cape around her, feeling the chill. "But your mother's determined to teach me how to cook. I didn't know cooking lessons were part of the bargain," she added with a smile.

"She can't help it. My mother has no patience for a young woman who can't cook. Probably because she failed so miserably with me." Martha glanced over at Rebecca, whose dark hair had begun to curl from the mist. "She's a bit like you, Rebecca. She loves to teach."

"It won't hurt me to learn my way around a hearth." Rebecca did not want to admit that last Saturday, before Martha arrived at the cottage, she had baked bread under Ruth Lewis's tutelage—and enjoyed it. And the day before, Ruth had enlisted them both in the kitchen to make the Sabbath meal, instructing Rebecca on how and why she was doing each step. She knew her audience well. If a lesson was in the offing, Rebecca Harding would be there, even if the topic was 'making mustard.' Rebecca now knew how to soak the black and brown mustard seeds overnight, why salt and vinegar must be added, plus a little honey for Benjamin Lewis, to sweeten him up, Ruth added with a wink.

"I never thought we'd see the floor again in that back room." Martha caressed some faded goldenrod as they walked along the Goshen Road. "It's been full of junk ever since Robert left. My mother was in heaven, tossing out all that old stuff. Daddy loves to hang on to things." Ruth Lewis had thrown herself into a tizzy, preparing the room for Rebecca. Once the room was clear, Benjamin put up some shelves. That way, Rebecca could leave a nightgown, her Sabbath clothes, boots, and toiletries, and not have to pack a big bag every Saturday. Ruth even made curtains for the little window that no one had seen for a decade. Although no more than a glorified cupboard, Rebecca's snuggery at the Lewis cottage was far cozier than her lodgings in the drafty attic at the Barnards'. Still, she had been right about the stone chimney. It radiated heat. Maybe winter nights in South Farms would not be unbearably cold.

"Have you written your letter to Eb yet?" Martha broached this subject with trepidation. Rebecca had revealed all the details of the last disastrous encounter with Eb to her. While Martha had firm opinions about what Rebecca should do, she was determined to hold her tongue. Charles had begged her to stop meddling—to let Eb and Rebecca find their own way. "Like you thought you might?"

"No," Rebecca replied somewhat tersely. "Not yet." The two

walked along in silence, Martha struggling to keep quiet. Finally, Rebecca spoke. "I've been thinking. I may have been unfair to Eb. I'm always telling him to be honest with me, but when he gets up the nerve to tell me something difficult—well, I punish him."

"Those kinds of conversations are always hard." Martha wondered if innocuous sentences of empathy constituted meddling. After all, she had to say something in response to Rebecca's confession.

"My vanity was hurt," Rebecca said quietly. "I just heard him say something about Susan Graham's beauty, and I flew off."

"I'm certain she's no more beautiful than you are."

"Right." Rebecca gave a wan smile, glancing over at her friend. Martha was stunning, a petite beauty, with her luxurious coppery red hair, high cheekbones, and upright bearing, daring the world to challenge her. Rebecca knew her own beauty would never compare. It was just a fact. Martha Lewis sometimes brought the purposeful strides of men—of all ages—to a halt. Rebecca Harding did not.

"And Eb didn't say Susan Graham was more beautiful than you. He just said your beauty was of a different type."

"I know, I know." Rebecca had gone over her conversation with Eb many times in her head, and several times with Martha. "I'm just vulnerable on that subject, I guess. I've always felt like an ugly cygnet. One who never grew into her proper swanhood."

"Well, that's just silly," Martha said. "That may be how you feel, but it's not how others see you. Everyone thinks you're lovely, and so smart. You're at least as smart as those Beecher girls. And my mother says you're much prettier than Catharine." Martha referred to Catharine Beecher, the oldest daughter of Reverend Lyman Beecher and a luminary at the Litchfield Female Academy. It was not saying much.

"Catharine has the face of an intelligent, good-hearted woman," Rebecca replied diplomatically. She respected her colleague Catharine Beecher and wanted to cut short Martha's usual incantation—Ruth had said it first—that it was a shame Lyman Beecher's 'houndlike face had shown up on a female child.'

"I suppose." Martha stopped on the side of the road for a moment to admire a patch of purple asters with bright orange centers. "We're always told beauty doesn't matter. It's inner beauty that counts. And physical beauty fades away with time." Martha flicked her coppery red hair back over the hood of her cloak, her green eyes sparkling, even in the low, late afternoon autumn light. "Charles tells me he'll love me always, even when I'm covered in wrinkles. Maybe tooth-less too." Martha flashed her friend a smile, showing off her straight white teeth.

"Some of us have more physical beauty to fade than others," Rebecca said dolefully. "I wish I didn't feel that way, but I do." She was quiet for a moment. "It's another form of vanity, I suppose—to worry you're not as beautiful as another." Rebecca suddenly felt a theory coming on, but did not know what to do with it, now that Eb was gone. Her dear friend Martha was not always the person to try them out on. With his philosophical bent, Charles Godwin was up to the task, but he was so busy these days. Rebecca plowed on regardless. "Do you know what I mean, Martha? That the insecure woman who worries she can't compare has more vanity than the woman who's secure in her beauty. The latter is less vain because she knows she's beautiful. Her confidence in her beauty relieves her of vanity. She doesn't have to think about it."

"I suppose so." Martha decided to change the subject, not cer-tain she understood. "But honestly, Rebecca, have you never had a foolish infatuation with someone? It sounds to me like Eb was just stupidly sweet on this Susan for a while," she added impul-sively. "And Susan's getting married in a few months to someone else. Nothing happened." Martha took a deep breath, aware that she was on the verge of interfering. "I mean, really, was that such a crime?"

"Have you ever been stupidly sweet on someone?" Rebecca was happy to turn the conversation over to one of Martha's meandering stories.

"I was once." Martha blushed. "When I was sixteen, a couple of years before I went to Miss Pierce's. Our cousins from Danbury came up for a visit, and I featured myself in love with Adam, my mother's first cousin's son. He was twenty-one back then. Tanned, with broad shoulders and a square jaw. Honestly, I thought he was a bronzed god." Martha reminisced about that summer with a mixture of embarrassment and pleasure. "I'd lie in bed at night and think about him. And when I saw him, my heart would palpitate, my palms would sweat. I loved his curly hair. He had this dimple on the right side of his cheek when he smiled, and he looked so lovely from behind . . ."

"He sounds just like Charles," Rebecca teased. Charles Godwin's sandy-colored hair was wavy, not curly; he had no dimples, and broad shoulders were never going to happen to him. He was tall and slender, and it had never been said that Charles looked 'so lovely from behind.'

"Yes, well." Martha smiled, ignoring Rebecca's comment. "Anyhow, Adam and his wife now run a tavern in Danbury. He's gotten a lot thicker, and he's losing his hair. Honestly, Rebecca, our families got together last summer, and when I saw him—well, I was worried about seeing him. That I'd still find him attractive and feel unfaithful to Charles, but it wasn't a problem at all. When Adam crawled out of that stagecoach, right after his wife and my aunt, I couldn't imagine what I'd seen in him. He's still handsome and all, even with added weight and a receding hairline, but I found him dull. We talked about this and that, but I enjoyed his wife's company far more than his. Bottom line—there were no palpitations, no damp palms. No nighttime yearning for what I couldn't have. *Riens*." Martha liked to show off her French. "Mother says it was just a harmless infatuation. A phase, that's what she called it."

"But you were sixteen," Rebecca protested. "Eb's twenty-three years old."

"I thought we'd agreed that men our age are stunted compared to women. By at least six years." Martha and Rebecca had developed this theory over the summer. It went something like this. A man of nineteen has the emotional age of a boy of thirteen. A man of twenty-one has the emotional age of a boy of fifteen—and so on. That was why young men sought out younger women, being ill-equipped to court women their own age. When they shared their theory with Martha's mother, Ruth Lewis concurred, with the caveat that somewhere in their mid-to-late twenties, most men catch up, the 'good ones,' that is. The differences in maturity evened out, Ruth promised. There was hope.

"I guess you're right," Rebecca mused, not knowing whether she agreed in this instance. "Anyhow, I'm feeling a little guilty. I think I used Eb's confession about Susan to have something to be angry about—so that I could be mad at him instead of the other way around."

"So, you weren't really upset by Eb's fantasies about Susan?" Martha kept her gaze steadily ahead of her, not looking at Rebecca.

"No, I was." Rebecca remembered feeling slapped when Eb had let slip how much more beautiful Susan had become. "It's true. Eb was clumsy and hurtful about Susan. Not considerate or careful with my feelings. But still . . ." She hesitated. "Still, I think it was easier for me to lose my temper over Susan than to deal with the underlying problem—that I keep Eb at arm's length."

"Let me get this straight. You got mad at Eb over Susan, so you didn't have to tell Eb how you feel about him—whatever that is." Martha glanced over at Rebecca. "Am I getting this right?"

"You're getting close," Rebecca said. "I mean, at the time, sitting there on the bench behind Mrs. Edwards's boarding house, I wasn't thinking that. I just felt hurt and lost my temper. But in retrospect, I may have wanted, maybe needed, something to be mad about. Then, when Eb told me about Susan Graham, I grabbed the opportunity. That way, I got to be the victim of Eb's cruelty." Rebecca clarified the analysis for herself. "So, I may have been unfair. By not owning up to my own part in this charade."

"Which is?" Martha furrowed her brows, trying to keep up with Rebecca's evolving analysis. "Your own part?" Perhaps it was time to turn around and return to the cottage.

"My own part," Rebecca said, "is my hesitancy over a courtship with Eb. We've been writing to each other for over a year. Still, I'm neither here nor there. I fear he's losing patience with me."

"Ah, that part." This was an old conversation between them, and Martha had promised Charles she would not meddle. By listening to Rebecca's theory, she thought she had shown remarkable restraint. If they talked further, Martha would have to speak her mind. "I'm getting chilly." She wrapped her green cloak more closely around her. The sun was about to set, and the temperature had dropped precipitously. The hills were now devoid of color except for a purple-blue outline on the horizon. "I think we ought to turn around, to give my mother a hand. It's almost teatime." Martha widened her eyes and grabbed Rebecca's elbow. "No, wait. It's almost pie time."

"Good idea." Rebecca turned on a dime. "I'd forgotten all about the pie." Ruth Lewis had promised to heat up the cherry pie she had baked the previous day. Rebecca had listened to a small lecture on why one must keep the lard in the pie dough as cold as possible before baking. "I hope there'll be cream," Rebecca added, puffing slightly, keeping up with the galloping Martha.

"Not to worry." Martha quickened her pace even more. "If my father is at the table, the pie will be warm—and there *will* be cream." With the promise of good things to come, the two young women hurried toward the cottage.

"It was nice of Mrs. Potts to send in a pot of tea. Some cookies." Her statement was prosaic, but Susan's voice wavered. She and Eb faced one another in the wingback chairs in the library. He would leave New Haven the next day for Litchfield. It was mid-morning in late September, and no fire was lit. The window facing Elm Street was wide open, letting in a brisk autumn breeze, the Indian summer having departed abruptly. At breakfast, Susan had announced her intention to speak to Eb alone. Everyone in the household scattered, assuming she wanted to ask Eb to give her away at the wedding. Esmeralda and Malinda were upstairs in Eb's bedroom, repacking his trunk, disapproving of how he had folded his clothes. Dr. Cabot was in the clinic.

Eb was exceedingly nervous, although grateful his fantasies about Susan had diminished in frequency and urgency since his conversation with Charles. By revealing his dark secret, his nightly torment had almost disappeared. Almost. Whenever thoughts of Susan reappeared, he would repeat this mantra: 'Susan is marrying Franz. Susan is marrying Franz.' But Eb and Susan had not regained their ease with one another. Her engagement had slammed shut another door between them. When she asked to speak to him alone in the library, Eb was afraid Susan would be on the attack, for something he had or had not done. Given their recent history, probably the latter.

"Yes." Eb stirred the cream in the cup of tea Susan had poured for him. "Very nice." He stared down at the plate of sugar cookies but did not feel like taking one. I must be ill, he thought, to turn down a cookie from Mrs. Potts's kitchen. A long, weighty silence filled the room.

"Eb . . ." Susan began in an almost inaudible voice, leaning back in Dr. Cabot's chair, where she liked to sit in his absence. "Why did you tell your brother John that Franz had been in prison?"

"Did I?" Eb was thrown off track. He had not suspected this line of attack and had no memory of having done so. The news of Franz's stint in prison must have been relayed by letter since Eb had not seen his brother for over two years.

"Yes, you did." Susan's voice took on an angry edge. "Don't deny it. You wrote to John and told him that Franz had been in prison. John went on to tell my mother when he was down in Savannah to check up on the house." Susan sat upright in the chair, chewing on her lower lip. She looked down her long, sloping nose at the empty fireplace, her light brown hair piled on top of her head, captured in a tortoiseshell comb.

"Oh," Eb mumbled, feeling a rush of guilt. Perhaps he had mentioned it in a letter. "I honestly don't remember doing that. But I may have."

"Well, you did, Eb Wells," Susan retorted. "My mother wrote me quite upset. She said it was one thing for her only daughter to marry a German widower with a six-year-old son, but a convicted felon? I wrote back and explained to her what happened. How when Franz was young, someone offended his mother, and he hit the man and went to prison. A foolish drunken brawl. I also told her Franz barely drinks at all these days."

"What did Lottie say?" Eb could picture Lottie Graham in dismay, reading Susan's letter in their kitchen on East York Street, her eyebrows knitted, concerned about the man her daughter was to marry. Lottie Graham was an upright, God-fearing woman, and news like that might turn her off someone—like her new son-in-law.

"My mother wrote back and gave us her blessing. She said, 'I don't want to be the only cloud in your clear blue sky.'" Susan gave a rueful smile. "My mother can still turn a phrase. You'd think she was Scotch-Irish or something."

"Yes," Eb said stiffly, relieved Lottie had come around. He knew how much Susan relied on her mother's opinion. "That's good."

"She can't come to the wedding, but she's working on a wedding quilt. One with pinwheel blocks. My parents had one." Susan smiled at the memory. "The boarding house is full these days," she added, apropos of nothing.

"I'm glad she understands." Eb shifted awkwardly in his chair. "If I did let it slip out about Franz, I'm sorry, Susan. I didn't mean to upset your mother."

"Well, no harm done. Mother's accepted things." Susan continued to sit upright in the chair, not her usual posture. She liked to curl up like a cat when reading a book by the fire, but today, there was no fire or book. She had business with Eb Wells. Her anger had abated, but she was not done raking Eb over the coals. "I still don't see why you had to tell John. Or why you thought that was any of your business to relate."

"You're right, of course. I meant no harm. You know I think highly of Franz." Eb was still struggling to come to terms with their marriage. His mantra of 'Susan is marrying Franz. Susan is marrying Franz' had limited efficacy. Maybe he should tell her what had been on his mind—a rash thought, but it might clear the air. "I think I must have been jealous of him. Of Franz."

"Jealous?" Susan looked sharply at him. "Why on earth would you be jealous?"

"Because I thought of you as mine. Or I wanted you to be, at the time," Eb finally confessed, again shifting uncomfortably in the wingback chair. "I was interested in you myself. Ever since I came down to New Haven last December."

"Oh, Eb," Susan said in a soft voice. "I worried that might be the case. Why didn't you just say something?"

"I couldn't say anything, Susan." Eb's face felt hot and flushed. He pulled off his glasses and began to clean the lenses on his shirt sleeve. "I knew it wasn't right. You're like a sister to me."

"And you're like a brother to me," Susan said firmly. "But if you'd told me, we could've talked things out. I would've told you the truth—I could never have feelings for you that way." Susan leaned over and pressed Eb's arm. "Listen, Eb. We were in diapers together. For years, we studied together, we played together. We did everything together." Susan crisscrossed her arms in front of her chest and took a deep breath. "We were just like brother and sister." She looked at him steadily and said slowly, deliberately, "And that's what we are now. That's how I feel anyhow."

Eb said nothing. He could not refute anything Susan said. The truth she spoke was the source of his discomfort all these months—that, and his loyalty to Rebecca.

Susan continued to look intently at Eb. His face was no longer flushed, but ashen, almost as pale as Malinda's. For a flickering moment, Susan saw Malinda in Eb's face, not something she often observed.

"You're so dear to me," Susan went on. "Both you and Malinda. You've been my family all these years. You still are." She continued to look at Eb, whose expression was sad, resigned. "But it would never have worked out." Susan spoke with quiet resolve. "You know what I mean, you and me, romantically."

"I know that now." About one thing, Eb acknowledged to himself, she was right—he should have told her months ago how he felt. That would have given him clarity. Eb would have been embarrassed by his confession, but her certainty would have shut down his feelings. She could never think of him romantically. Never. Of course not. Why would he have ever imagined otherwise? Her sturdy rejection of him was valuable information, Eb told himself. Maybe not what he wanted to hear at the time—maybe not even now—but something he needed to hear.

"And now I'm to marry Franz." Susan continued to sound determined. "I do love Franz. He must never hear a word about this, Eb," she added with some urgency.

"Of course not." Eb regained his composure. He felt much better for having told Susan the truth. Sad, perhaps, but lighter. "There's no need for him to know. It was just a passing fancy."

"Yes, well, I don't even want him to get wind of that," Susan reiterated, sounding serious. "Franz looks up to you. Don't you know that? You saved his life."

"I didn't really." Eb thought back on how much trouble he had gotten into at Haines & Haines for helping Franz out. "I just found him work. Uncle Ebenezer needed a carriage driver. That's all."

"You were caring and kind. You stuck your neck out for Franz and Henry. Who knows what would have happened to them if you hadn't intervened." She closed her eyes and shuddered, thinking of her poor Henry alone in an orphanage or Franz hungry and cold, incarcerated in a debtor's prison. "We're all so grateful, Eb."

"It's nothing." Eb glanced over at Susan. Sitting in his uncle's chair, she looked so sad and so incredibly beautiful to him, but he pushed those thoughts aside, his heart aching. "I'm happy for you, really. I am." It was his turn to reach over, to pat her hand affection- ately. "Franz is a good man. He'll make you a fine husband," he said with false cheerfulness. "And Henry adores you."

"Thank you." Susan gave him a weak smile. "I was wondering, Eb, if you would give me away. You know, at the wedding? My father's dead, and you're the closest thing I have to a brother."

"Of course I will." Eb's voice cracked. He coughed and spoke again, this time with a manufactured, steady calm. "I'll do it." Eb picked up a sugar cookie, pretending to be hungry. He forced him- self to be jovial. "I guess that's why Malinda's ordering me to get a new suit." He gave Susan a rictus smile. "I thought I'd be standing in the back row, not waltzing down the aisle. She doesn't want me to embarrass her in my old moot court suit."

"You guessed right." Susan felt weary, thinking of all the plans

Malinda had made. She would have been just as happy to elope, as she had told Franz the night before. She turned to Eb, speaking in a soft voice. "I don't care what suit you wear. As long as it's you who gives me away."

"That's nice." Eb's eyes began to well up with tears. He fought them back, desperate not to cry, not now. He took refuge in the cookie, closing his eyes and savoring his first bite for a few seconds. It was still warm from the oven, and he could taste the hint of salt— Mrs. Potts's secret ingredient. It's a paradox, he always said to the cook in the kitchen, that a sugar or molasses cookie would need salt. As his tears subsided, he opened his eyes and looked directly into Susan Graham's eyes. She looked tearful herself. "It would be an honor to give you away, Susan." Eb spoke with his own quiet resolve. He leaned over and picked up the plate. "Now, would you like a cookie? Mrs. Potts has outdone herself this morning."

Late that night, Susan Graham lay alone in her bed, under a quilt that Esmeralda had pulled out of the wardrobe earlier that evening. In typical Connecticut fashion, the weather had taken a ninety-degree turn toward winter just that morning. The quilt still smelled sweetly of cedar. Eb was leaving for Litchfield the next morning, and Susan was crying softly to herself in the dark. She wondered what would have happened if Eb had confessed his feelings for her back in December—before Franz and Henry had appeared on the scene.

Susan Graham had loved Eb Wells all her life. How difficult would it have been to turn her love for Eb as a brother into love for Eb as a husband? And where did Rebecca Harding fit into all this? But answers to these questions no longer mattered, she told herself sternly. Susan had declared her love for Franz, and they were to marry. Henry was to become her stepson. When Eb confessed his attraction to her, she had been unwavering in her rejection of him as a potential suitor. She had made it clear. She loved him like a brother only. That stance was only fair to Eb—and to Franz. As a matter of principle, Eb must always believe she could never think of him in a romantic way. Even though that was not true back in December, and not true now. Not true ever.

Timing is everything in love, Susan reflected. She had read many novels and often regarded her own life as having a plot. While not a believer in fate, she wondered why things happened to her when they did. It made her believe in a God, an author constructing her narrative. Character often drives love's course too, Susan thought somewhat bitterly. She dried her tears on the edge of the quilt. Things would have turned out differently if Eb Wells had possessed the requisite courage to declare himself to her early on. Susan was certain of that.

But the fact was Eb Wells had lacked that requisite courage. It was not in his nature to reach out and grab what was his. Nothing could be done about that now—or ever. In three months, Susan Graham would become Mrs. Franz Mueller, the stepmother of Henry Mueller, and Eb Wells would give her away at the wedding. Indeed, he had already given her away.

Without writing or uttering a word to each other, Eb Wells and Rebecca Harding had taken a break from any correspondence or in-person communication. Both felt shattered from their conversation in Mrs. Edwards's backyard on Eb's last day in Litchfield. Eb was furious with himself for spilling the beans about Susan Graham. He had hurled himself headlong into that conversation, like the proverbial bull in a china shop, with no purpose, plan, or exit strategy. As Charles had predicted, his gratuitous, self-indulgent confession had devastated Rebecca. His declaration of love was weak, wishy-washy, and unnecessarily conditional. What man would say, 'I'm ready to love you, if you would let me.' Rebecca Harding probably hated him now. And why not? Eb hated himself too.

Rebecca too was full of regrets. She had overreacted to Eb's confession. Rebecca understood Eb's worry that she would keep him in abeyance for eternity—that he could grow old, waiting for her, giving up opportunities to love someone else. In this instance, that someone else just happened to be Malinda's companion, the only other woman in Eb's life who was not his sister. Susan Graham was not the problem. Rebecca was. She could not express her love for him. He undoubtedly thought she was ambivalent about him—when she was only ambivalent about love. Her declaration of love was weak, wishy-washy, and unnecessarily conditional. What woman would say, 'If I were to be with a man, I would want it to be you.' Eb Wells probably hated her now. And why not? Rebecca hated herself too.

"You've got to learn this first." Susan was giving Malinda advice in the carriage. They were on their way from Elm Street to Chapel Street to pick up Ned and seven-year-old Eddie. It was a cool, sunny Sunday in mid-October. Franz was driving up front, with Henry on the bench beside him, urging on Hank and Ruby. The roads in New Haven were lined with elms, maples, and oaks—a blur of orange and red and yellow leaves as the carriage passed by. Cut off from the world's noises by the thudding clatter of horses' hooves on city streets, the two young women conspired inside the carriage, planning how the afternoon would unfold. The outing was designed to improve Malinda's relationship with Eddie, and Susan had assumed the role of tutoress. "A child is not a project, Malinda."

"Whatever do you mean?" Malinda drew herself up in her seat, a difficult task as the carriage swerved and swayed in the city traffic.

"What I mean is this—don't try to improve Eddie today." Susan did not have time to be tactful, opting for frankness. It was her usual mode anyhow.

"I don't know what you're talking about." It bothered Malinda that Susan had a knack with children, and she did not. She had watched Susan with Henry in the library, bending over him at the French desk, cajoling the boy to do his work. Malinda was envious. Susan was able to be affectionate with Henry but remain in quiet control. But Malinda was no fool. She may envy Susan, but she also admired her—and sought to emulate her. "I've never once tried to improve Eddie Haines. You know that."

"That's only because you haven't had the opportunity," Susan said with her off-kilter smile. "All I'm saying is this. Don't criticize Eddie today. Don't instruct him either, not until you've gained his trust. Not today. Let Ned be the parent."

"Well, what should I do then?"

"Nothing special," Susan replied. "Just be yourself. This is supposed to be a fun day for the boys. Remember, Henry and Eddie don't know each other. Neither one of them has a friend their own age to play with. They'll be awkward around each other at first. Just let them work it out." Susan brushed a crumb from the front of her lapel, not looking at Malinda. "Our only job today is to make sure they're safe and provide a backdrop for fun. That's why we're taking them to the Green and Long Wharf. Maybe to get ice cream later, before the icehouse closes for the winter."

"So, that's it?" Malinda said this with a mixture of annoyance and amusement. She rearranged her bonnet, tucking a lock of hair back where it belonged. "I'm just part of the backdrop then?"

"Pretty much so, on an outing like this. That's the thing with children. Sometimes, you need to be right in front of them. Teaching, reading a book at night, forcing green beans down their gullet, that kind of thing. But more often, you need to be invisible, on the sidelines, watching out for them. Not interfering." She settled back in her seat in the carriage, finished with her long exposition. "I'm just saying, we need to leave Eddie and Henry alone. Let them be boys."

"So, your advice is to back off? We've organized an outing for me to get to know Eddie, and my job is to back off?" Malinda rolled her dark eyes at Susan and shook her head, incredulous.

"My advice is for you to have a good time too. Enjoy yourself with Ned, but don't fawn over him too much. Give Eddie some time to get used to seeing you together. No holding hands, no kisses today." Susan paused, trying to think of other tidbits of advice. "And smile when Eddie looks at you."

"Honestly, Susan, I could have figured that one out for myself." Malinda harumphed, although she was not certain she had smiled at Eddie the first time she had met him. A smile was not Malinda Wells's default expression. Her face in repose was that of a sentry, bearing a watchful, cautious look—not unpleasant, but not smiling.

"I know," Susan said kindly, nudging her friend with her elbow. "Don't worry, Malinda. We'll have fun today. So here are the rules. Don't correct or instruct Eddie. Don't hold hands or kiss Ned. Don't get in the middle of the two boys. And smile when Eddie looks at you."

"Got it," Malinda said with a nod. "Anything else?" She might balk at first, but she could take instruction.

"No, that's it. And keep your expectations low," Susan warned. "Eddie needs to get used to you. And used to seeing you with his father." She thought back to how long it had taken Hank and Ruby to let her groom them. "Little boys are like horses. Eddie will be wary at first, but with time, he'll come to trust you."

"Like Domino?" Malinda was coming to terms with Domino. Against her wishes—but it was his house, after all—her uncle had coaxed the little black-and-white cat not only into the library, but upstairs. Rushing down the hall one day, Malinda scooted the kitten aside with her foot. Domino had lost his balance and hit the side of the wall. She had not meant to kick him so hard. Neither had she realized how light and fragile a kitten could be. Domino was dazed but not hurt. But her Uncle Ebenezer had been angry with Malinda—for the first time in her life. No violence or animosity toward the cat would be tolerated, he told her. Ever. Slowly, Domino and Malinda formed a pact of mutually desired distance. No love was lost on either side, but a grudging respect was developing.

"Well, yes, I suppose, like Domino. But children are more predictable than cats." Susan laughed, as did Malinda. "So, relax. Above all, enjoy yourself. Eddie will like that."

"Susan," Malinda asked meekly, feeling full of dread about the afternoon. "Can I be the one to recommend we get ice cream? And pay for it? Can that be my treat?"

"Absolutely," Susan replied with alacrity. "I've already told Franz he's not to mention it, although I'm not sure we can trust Henry. He's certain to beg and wheedle for ice cream."

"That's fine." Malinda sounded decisive. "Just as long as I get to be the adult who says 'yes.'"

Susan smiled at her friend. "Maybe you're not so dumb about children after all."

"So, here's how it seems to me." Charles Godwin and Eb Wells had just left town and were walking out the Goshen Road, headed for a midday meal with the Lewis family. The morning's work at the law office was over. It was a cool, crisp autumn day. The sky was a brilliant, bright blue, and the trees were ablaze with colors—reds, yellows, oranges, residual emerald greens—almost at their peak of fall foliage splendor. The air smelled musty, earthy, and sharp, redolent of decaying leaves that had already fallen, rustling and crackling under their boots.

Eb was settling into his new life in Litchfield, his work at Mr. Fuller's probate practice, his room at Mrs. Edwards's, Sir Winston curled up on his feet at night. He was adjusting to the slower pace of a smaller town and happy to be among his friends. New Haven and the clamor of the city seemed far away, although Malinda wrote often, mostly with details about the upcoming wedding. Things were going well for Eb, except for his rift with Rebecca.

As the two friends walked, Charles held forth. "The problem lies not with you and Rebecca per se. The problem lies with the marriage bar for female teachers. A structural issue."

"I suppose that's true," Eb admitted. He was hungry. On workdays, Eb and Charles took their midday meal with Mrs. Reeve. The Reeves lived only a few doors down from Mr. Fuller's on South Street. Breakfast and supper, Eb took with Mrs. Edwards, and a cup of tea by the fire after supper. Although it was a Wednesday, Ruth Lewis had asked Eb to accompany Charles to their cottage for a midday meal. Ruth knew about the estrangement between Rebecca and Eb, so inviting Eb out on the Sabbath was not an option—Rebecca would be there. Still, she and Benjamin were fond of Eb and wanted to see him.

Already the middle of October, Eb had been in town for two weeks. He had still not written to Rebecca Harding or tried to see her. The same was true of Rebecca. It had been more than six weeks since their last traumatic encounter. Rebecca and Eb were close geographically for the first time in over a year, but far away emotionally—unless you counted the hours each spent thinking about the other.

"Yes, the rule about no marriage for female teachers." Eb agreed with Charles. "That seems to be our major problem. A structural issue, as you put it."

"Yes, well, that's all I'm talking about right now." Charles held his long arms behind his back. His sandy-colored hair pushed back from his face, he wore his customary brown suit for work. The air was almost chilly. Before he left the Lewis cottage, Ruth had insisted that he take a woolen scarf this morning—the lumpy red one Martha had knitted him last winter. It now hung around his neck. "You and Rebecca have other problems as well. You could use some instruction on how to get along better."

"We get along with each other very nicely," Eb said defensively. "At least until we don't."

"It's the 'until you don't' episodes that are problematic." Charles looked down at his friend. Eb was catching his breath, trying to keep up with Charles's long stride. "You haven't spoken or written to Rebecca for six weeks."

"Yes, well, she hasn't done so either," Eb muttered, having no explanation to offer, hoping Charles would not take him to task for not making the first move. "It seems we're taking a break."

"You're right, though." Charles slowed down, ignoring Eb's last comment. "You and Rebecca do get along on most things. Your work, your ideas, your values, your studies, your sense of humor, and the like, but when it comes to talking about your feelings, you're both a disaster." Eb was quiet, having nothing in his arsenal to defend against this charge. Charles stopped for a moment to enjoy a particular vista he was fond of—a meadow that was now the color of wheat, with a dry rock wall overflowing with orange bittersweet. "But back to this structural issue. Why do you accept this marriage bar for female teachers as if it were written in stone?"

"What do you mean?"

"You're the great challenger of the status quo, Eb Wells." Charles gave his friend a pat on the back. "The outspoken proponent of abolition, the champion of debtors and downtrodden apprentices—why don't you see the marriage bar as a social injustice?"

"Go on." Eb wrinkled his brow, wondering where Charles was headed. They had discussed the marriage bar for teachers before, during their law school days, but not as an issue of social justice. If anyone could sniff out a hidden injustice, it would be a man raised in a Quaker home. Charles had the nose for it.

"This notion of a woman even being educated, let alone entering the teaching profession—well, it's novel. And radical." Charles gestured toward the October sky as if he were engaged in oratory before hundreds. Mostly a shy man, if an idea grabbed him, Charles Godwin could turn into a wall of words. "The women running these female academies—the schools that teach women real subjects: math, Latin, geography, history, something other than embroidery and etiquette—they've started a revolution. Like Miss Pierce."

"Really?" Eb laughed at the thought of the diminutive, owl-like Miss Pierce as a revolutionary. "It's hard for me to think of Miss Pierce that way. No respectable revolutionary wears a little white lace cap."

"Don't be fooled by appearances," Charles said. "Miss Pierce has a vision for female education. She's a missionary of sorts, dedicated to training promising young women—like your Rebecca, perhaps my Martha—to educate the next generation of girls. They're a new breed, these graduates of female seminaries and academies." Charles clapped his hands in the air as if to get his friend's attention. "That, my friend," he declared, "has all the makings of a revolution."

"I wonder where it will lead." Eb considered what Charles had just said. "Do you think women will ever go to college?"

"It's hard to imagine," Charles said with a sigh. "Perhaps for our granddaughters. But let's stick to 1821. You're in love—yes, you are, even though you won't admit it—with a woman who is trained as a female educator. You'd like to marry her. Or at least to court her." Charles hesitated, wondering if Eb was going to quibble with him. "Do I state the case correctly?"

Charles had saved this part of his presentation—since that was what it was—for when the two men were actively walking, not looking at one another. From experience, Charles knew Eb would be more inclined toward frankness if they walked side by side, not facing each other, nose to nose.

"I'm willing to stipulate to the facts," Eb replied guardedly, wanting to hear what Charles had to say.

"Well, I'd like you to consider the injustice of Rebecca having to choose between a profession and a marriage. Marriage is a God-given right. A man in her position would not have to forfeit family life." Charles was revving up. "Probate law has an aversion to restraints upon marriage. Some old people—it may surprise you to know this—try to control the marriages of their children, grandchildren, even their great-grandchildren. From the grave."

"It doesn't surprise me at all. I taught *you* the Rule against Perpetuities, if you remember, under the herbs and sausages at Mrs. Edwards's." Eb grinned wryly at Charles. "And I had to draft a will for a testator who wanted to disinherit his son for marrying a Quaker."

"Really, in this day and age?" Charles registered a slight affront, thinking of his own Quaker mother. "So, you know what I mean. Those kinds of restraints on marriage are considered void as against public policy."

"Which is?" Eb's own research on this issue was shallow. Nathan had taken over the will of the mean-spirited man who refused to have a Quaker in his family. Charles might know more than he did, he grudgingly admitted. "What's the public policy?"

"The promotion and protection of marriage. The law won't countenance interfering with someone's choice of a spouse." Charles raised his voice, hoping to be heard in the back row of his imaginary audience. "And this rule for female educators? It's even worse. It denies them the right to marry at all."

"I hadn't thought of it that way." Eb had regarded the marriage bar as an inconvenience, an impediment to his courtship of Rebecca, not as an issue of social justice. Perhaps Rebecca would like to get married and have children—if not with him, then with someone else. The same might be true of many other female educators.

"Just because Rebecca's a teacher," Charles continued, swept away by the cause of women educators, "why should she have to give up marriage? A husband? Children? It's unfair. A man would not have to do so."

"True." Eb considered this new approach to the marriage bar. He wondered—as always—what Rebecca would think. But mostly, his stomach was rumbling.

"I suggest," Charles went on, "that you and Rebecca challenge this injustice together." Then he fell silent. Eb peered over at Charles, who appeared finished with his rhetorical flourish.

"But Rebecca's always saying she's the one—not me—who'll pay the price for breaking the rules." Eb remembered an earlier exchange on this topic in which Rebecca had excoriated him. "She's bristled before at men of privilege—that would be you and me—for making these arguments on her behalf when we have nothing to lose."

"Well, then, it's up to you to convince her to fight for her basic freedoms. She has the same right to marry as anyone else—without giving up her teaching."

"I suppose." Eb was dubious. Rebecca was not by nature a rabble-rouser. Maybe she should try wearing a little white lace cap to make herself more revolutionary. Eb was about to make this joke aloud when Charles interrupted.

"Another strategy," Charles continued, now with hesitation, changing tactics abruptly, "is to escape the society that's imposing the rule. Most of these new academies are located here in New England. Our region has too many 'Rebeccas,' and teaching jobs are scarce."

"Go on."

"Well, with so few teaching jobs and so many teachers, Rebecca might indeed pay a hefty price for rocking the boat. If she doesn't abide by the rule or complains about its unfairness, her headmaster could just fire her. Replace her with a more compliant young woman. One willing to accept her enforced spinsterhood." Charles was crafting his argument as he went along, Eb could tell. "Connecticut, Massachusetts, New Hampshire, Vermont—all of New England is overflowing with biddable female educators."

"What do you mean by escaping society?" Eb felt a sudden chill and buttoned up his suit coat, envying Charles his woolen scarf. It was a good thing Malinda and Esmeralda had packed his winter coat, with gloves and scarves of his own. "We have to live in society."

"But if you went somewhere where teachers were scarce, the rules might be relaxed. On the edge of the wilderness, for example. The need for teachers would be great, the number of teachers small." Charles glanced over at Eb. "A school would be lucky to get a teacher with Rebecca's qualifications. They might have to accept her as she came—married to you or some other lucky fellow—if they wanted a teacher at all."

"What exactly are you proposing, Charles?"

"Ohio. I'm proposing Ohio." This, Charles said with a dramatic flourish. He had been waiting to introduce this topic to Eb for two weeks. His concern was that Martha's brother Jack would crash into the proposal with his irrepressible enthusiasm—and no warning.

"Explain yourself, my friend." Eb stared at Charles, stupefied.

"Jack Lewis and Hannah are planning to move to Ohio in a couple of years with her church in Kent. They want to go west. All the young couples are doing it, Jack says." Charles was breathless with excitement. "They want Martha and me to join them. Maybe Mr. and Mrs. Lewis too. This won't happen soon. Not until after we're all married, and Martha's done with school."

"Go west?" Eb had never considered such a thing. Samuel Taylor talked about it from time to time in an aimless fashion. Many of the other law apprentices in New Haven also daydreamed of 'going west' over tankards of ale after work. The Indian names of the new states had a ring of glamour to them. Ohio, Indiana, and even Illinois, which had just become a state. Land in the former Northwest Territory was plentiful and cheap. The government encouraged young people to move out there, bring their families, cut down trees, farm the land, and build towns that looked like they belonged to New England. Even to set up law practices—or schools.

"Yes, go west," Charles replied. "Jack promotes a different town almost every month. First, it was Marietta along the Ohio River. Or was it Miamisburg? Another month, we were all moving to Chillicothe. Now he's touting the new capital in Franklin County." Charles let out a good laugh. "Columbus," he said in mocking, stentorian tones. "At the confluence of the Scioto and Whetstone rivers—or the Olentangy as the natives call it. Jack loves to wallow in those Indian names."

"I've never heard of any of these places." It just occurred to Eb that the furthest west he had ever been in the United States was Litchfield, Connecticut, or Athens, Georgia. His grasp of longitude was minimal. Eb would have to consult one of Martha's maps.

"We've got a couple of years," Charles said. "But you know how Jack is. He'll have the group moving to a dozen other places by the time we start rolling in a covered wagon. I keep warning Martha not to get too invested in any Ohio town. If we wait a few weeks, Jack will find another." He laughed. "'Jack be nimble, Jack be quick,' that's what I tell her. We've got a few more candlesticks to jump over before we settle."

"I see." Eb's voice was thin, wondering how he felt about his dear friends moving to Ohio—far away from Connecticut. He had never considered himself pioneer material. And what kind of animal pulled a covered wagon? Oxen? Mules? Horses? Who was going to hold the reins? "Covered wagons, you say?"

"Yes. Covered wagons. Jack's been learning all about them. He's learned a lot. Keeping the wood supple, not letting the wheels dry out and pulling off the metal. That kind of thing. You'd be surprised by how much there is to know." Charles stopped at another bittersweet vine cascading off a stone fence and snapped off a branch for Mrs. Lewis. "Ruth likes bittersweet when the berries are all desiccated," he explained. "Mark my words, this will end up on the table in her hammered copper pitcher."

"Will the men have to drive the covered wagons?" Eb asked apprehensively. He was already finding a host of reasons not to move to Ohio.

"Not all of them. Don't worry, Eb. Jack will take care of everything. He'll be at the reins, literally and figuratively. He's working with the leaders at Hannah's church."

"So, you and Martha are actually considering this?" Eb was surprised he had not heard about Ohio from Rebecca. Almost all information flowed through the Charles-to-Martha-to-Rebecca-to-Eb pipeline, although he had to admit that the pipeline had been clogged lately. "Migrating to Ohio?"

"Well, we're not *not* thinking about it," Charles answered hesitantly. "It's a touchy subject right now. Benjamin Lewis is dead set against it. He's always lived in Connecticut and doesn't see a big market for his profiles, although Jack disagrees with him. And Martha's mother is distraught over the idea of the four of us disappearing into the wilderness. If you just say the word 'Ohio,' Ruth will burst into tears. That's why I'm bringing it up with you now." Charles waved his hand at the horizon, where the Lewis cottage could now be seen. "Martha and I have promised Jack that we won't talk about it at the kitchen table. Not in front of Mr. and Mrs. Lewis. But I wanted you to know about our maybe moving to Ohio. And to let you know that you're invited—both you and Rebecca, as a couple or not. We'd love for you to come, if we go, that is."

"I see." The two friends had reached the path up to the Lewis cottage. The conversation was about to come to an end. Eb's legs were aching. His life in New Haven had been sedentary. He had to get used to country distances again, and keeping up with Charles's long legs was always a challenge.

"I just wanted to give you a heads-up." Charles looked over at Eb, who was solemnly digesting all he had just heard, continuing to worry about who was going to drive the covered wagon. "A move to Ohio might open things up for you and Rebecca. That's all I'm suggesting. The marriage bar for female educators might not be such a barrier out there. On the frontier." Charles put his arm around Eb's shoulder and gave it a gentle squeeze. "It's just one more thing for you to think about as you analyze your situation to death."

"Thanks for letting me know." Eb's thoughts drifted back to food. He was famished. Mrs. Lewis had mentioned a ham steak in her invitation. Would she be making her customary mustard? He must ask Mrs. Lewis to share that recipe with Mrs. Potts. Eb could swear he detected a hint of honey. "Let's go eat, Charles."

The two men approached the cottage. Eb would think about Ohio later.

Letter to Eb Wells from Rebecca Harding, South Farms,
October 27, 1821

Dearest Eb,

I'm going to break this silence between us. I can't tell you how miserable I've been since our last encounter. I hadn't expected to learn about your interest in Susan Graham. I fear I overreacted. Still, you're not always careful with my feelings. We can talk about this later if you're willing. But I do want you to know that I take responsibility for some of your frustration.

Charles approached me with an idea. Would you consider sitting down with Ruth Lewis at her kitchen table? Let her help us have a conversation? It's a novel idea. I rejected it at first. These are our private affairs, after all. But Charles has persisted. He believes that you and I aren't skilled at expressing our emotions. We may be book smart, he says, but inept at talking to one another, at least when the stakes are high. Our history supports his claim.

At this point, we're both orphans. We don't have parents to go to for advice. Ruth Lewis is older and wiser. She knows us both well. We can trust her. She's agreed to sit down with us if we're both willing. Her only goal, she says, is to restore our good relations and help us define our goals. She has no attachment to the outcome. How we end up, Mrs. Lewis insists, can only be determined by you and me.

I hate feeling so cut off from you. I have so much news to tell you about my teaching in South Farms, and I want to hear all about your work with Mr. Fuller. How are things going with Mrs. Edwards and the noble Sir Winston? Also, I want to hear news about everyone on Elm Street. I've missed you so much.

I'll leave it up to you, Eb. I'm willing to let Ruth Lewis assist us in having a conversation. If you don't wish to do so, I'll understand. Please let me know.

Yours with affection,

Rebecca

The initial outing in October with Ned and Malinda, Franz and Susan, and the two boys started out a disaster, but ended a success. After an awkward hour of eyeing each other suspiciously, not making conversation, the two boys were let loose to play. Their instructions were to stay within the line of sight of the adults and not go off the New Haven Green.

Franz had brought his game of ninepins. Henry and Eddie were giddy with their new freedom and took off, the heavy bag holding the wooden pins and ball slung over Henry's shoulder. Ned and Malinda, Franz and Susan, settled on a bench on the edge of the Green where they could keep an eye on the boys. The bench was in the shade of an elm tree that looked like it was on fire, with its rustling orange and red leaves. It was a crisp autumn day. The adults were all distracted and in love, so the boys were on their own.

Across the Green, Henry and Eddie played ninepins. From a distance, it looked like they were getting along. Up close, a battle was brewing. The problem was Henry Mueller, who kept winning. Eddie may have been a year older and taller, but Henry often played ninepins with his father, and his arms were strong from shoveling horse manure. Eddie Haines rarely went outside, and no one ever played any games with him, let alone ninepins. His arms were skinny and weak, and he kept losing.

"It's not fair," Eddie protested to Henry, kicking the grass with his foot. "You keep winning. I can't hit the pins like you do." His long, slender face was red with exertion.

"It is too fair," Henry sniped back, seeing no problem with winning all the time. "I keep winning because I hit the pins better than you do."

"Well, I don't like this game." Eddie swung his leg over the ninepins that Henry had just carefully set up. The pins tumbled to the ground, all higgledy-piggledy, clunking against each other.

"Heh, you. Don't do that!" Henry protested. "I just set them up."

"I'm sick of this game." Eddie's frustration suddenly animated him. He held the wooden ball in his right hand. Looking down at Henry crouched in the grass, repositioning the pins in their precise positions on the Green, for some reason—he could not tell his father why later—Eddie threw the wooden ball hard, right at Henry. His aim was better with a boy as a target. The ball hit Henry's back with a thud.

"Ouch!" Henry called out. "That hurt, Eddie." He turned around and saw the older boy, backing away and smirking at him. Henry reached over, picked up a ninepin, and threw it in Eddie's direction. He had hoped to hit Eddie somewhere on the torso, but the ninepin swerved and hit Eddie on the shin. The sound of bone and wood colliding went clunk.

"Ouch!" Eddie yelled out, grabbing onto his leg. "That hurt too." He made a lunge for the ninepins and picked up two. Henry understood instantly what had transpired. War had been declared. He too reached for two wooden ninepins. From their distance of benign supervision, the two couples could see the two boys on the other side of the Green, shrieking and throwing ninepins at each other.

An elderly man, using a cane, laboriously made his way across the Green and approached the warring children. Waving his cane in the air, he tried to stop the fracas, bellowing, "Stop this now, you boys. You could hurt one another." Then came the words no adult ever wants to hear, reverberating across the Green. "Where are your parents?"

Franz leaped up and made a beeline across the Green. Eddie had just scored a hit on Henry's face—it had smacked the heavy bone above his eye, promising a bruiser.

"Henry Mueller," Frank yelled sharply. Henry swung around and dropped the ninepin he had been grasping. Eddie saw the blur of Henry's father too late. He had already pitched the other ninepin in Henry's direction, which fell squarely on Franz Mueller's shoulder. Eddie stared at him with horror as Franz winced from the hit.

"Oh, no, Mr. Mueller," Eddie called out, his face pale, his eyes wide with both dismay and amazement at having just walloped

Henry's father with a ninepin. "I'm so sorry, sir."

Franz did not even look at Eddie or Henry, just addressing the elderly gentleman. The old man was gesticulating with his cane, sputtering at Franz, upset by the flying ninepins, launched by the woefully unsupervised boys. "We were watching the boys from far away," Franz tried to explain to the old man, pulling Henry to his side by the back of his shirt collar.

"A bit too far away," panted the old man disdainfully, taking off in the other direction, his cane tap, tap, tapping on the pathway as he tottered off.

"That's it now, you two." Franz's tone was sharp. He was embarrassed at being dressed down by a stranger—a stranger who was right. "Go back to where the others are. I'll pick things up." He looked down at Henry, his eyes a steely blue, glowering at his son. "I'll deal with you later, Henry Mueller." Franz sounded threatening, and Eddie hung his head, worried now that his own father would be angry too. Franz's jaw was working as he picked up the scattered ninepins— some of them had landed quite far away—and stuffed them every which way into the bag. Henry and Eddie marched silently back together across the Green, enveloped in a cloud of gloom.

When the boys joined the others, they were inspected for injury. Eddie's shin was just bruised, not broken, and Henry's black eye would be impressive, but no permanent harm was done. Ned Haines, whose teeth were clenched, his temples pulsing, could not believe his son had started the fight. Henry protested that it was not Eddie's fault. Henry had baited Eddie. He always kept winning, and Henry knew Eddie had never played the game. Ned was still angry and insisted they end the outing. Franz concurred, not having overcome his fury and embarrassment. They should take the boys home right now. The boys should be punished. They had engaged in violent, risky behavior. One of them could have shattered a tooth, broken a nose, or lost an eye—or hurt a passer-by. What if a ninepin had struck the old man with the cane, causing him to fall? Henry and Eddie mumbled apologies. Both boys were close to tears.

No, Malinda Wells intervened, putting her hand discreetly on Ned's arm. "We should all try to calm down. The boys are sorry for what they did." Malinda insisted they go down to Long Wharf as planned, stroll around, and find some ice cream. Susan backed her up. The two young women held firm, and after some further ranting at the boys, the ire of the fathers subsided. Malinda and Susan won out, Franz and Ned yielded, and the afternoon resumed its original shape. All four adults were thinking the same thing. Perhaps an alliance between Henry Mueller and Eddie Haines was not such a great idea. But it did not matter what they thought. It was too late now. From here on out, the boys were thick as thieves.

This is how a friendship of many years was forged, throwing pieces of wood at each other on the New Haven Green. The story of *The Battle of the Ninepins* was told many times later in their lives, to their friends at the academy, and later at Yale, to their girlfriends, and eventually to their wives, children, and grandchildren—long after the fathers of Eddie Haines and Henry Mueller were around.

It was an unforgettable encounter. What could be more glorious, more exhilarating, to two boys ages six and seven—a battle to the death? Incurring the wrath of both their fathers? Eddie Haines had hit Henry Mueller's father with a ninepin. Henry had stuck up for Eddie. And one detail was never forgotten either, in every retelling of *The Battle of the Ninepins*. It was Malinda Wells who had advocated for their exoneration—and for ice cream.

"So, let's lay out some ground rules for this conversation." It was a Saturday afternoon in early November. Ruth Lewis, Eb Wells, and Rebecca Harding were gathered in the kitchen of the Lewis cottage.

Ruth sat at her customary place at the table, the other two on either side. Jack was in Kent at his fiancée's. Benjamin had disappeared into the portrait studio to work. Martha had hovered like a hummingbird all morning, hinting that perhaps she should join the session, a suggestion loudly vetoed by her mother, her best friend, and her fiancé. Instead, Charles dragged Martha out of the cottage for a walk. The plan was to reconvene later for pumpkin pie. A warm fire crackled in the kitchen.

Eb looked across the table at Rebecca. It had been almost two months since he had laid eyes on her. He gave her an appraising look—her pretty, angular face, her dark hair pulled back in a bun, her brown eyes, and a moss green dress he was unfamiliar with. She looked well. The job at the Morris Academy must be working out. Rebecca was also eating at Ruth Lewis's table two days a week. Not only was she learning how to cook, but she had put on some weight. He smiled shyly at her, and she reciprocated.

"These are the rules. One person talks at a time. No interruptions. The other person just listens." Ruth Lewis pushed away from her forehead a wisp of reddish gray hair streaked with strands of silver. "And I ask the questions. Is that clear?" She peered to her left and right, looking for assent. Both nodded. "All right then, let's start with you, Rebecca. How do you feel about Eb?"

"In general? Or romantically?" Rebecca looked down at her lap, smoothing the wrinkles that did not exist on her new dress. "I'm sorry," she said, glancing up. "I'm nervous. I feel like this is an oral exam. I'm used to getting the answers right, but I'm not sure what to say."

"I understand. There aren't any right or wrong answers here." Ruth considered Rebecca's apprehension, unaccustomed to seeing her flustered. "No one passes or fails. You may answer the question any way you like. At least to start with. So, let's try again. How do you feel about Eb?"

"All right, then." Rebecca took a deep breath. "Eb's my dearest friend, next to Martha, of course, and Elizabeth Stafford. But they're my women friends. Eb's my dearest male friend. That's different." She looked hesitantly over at Ruth Lewis, who said nothing. "Well, let's see, what else? I care very much for Eb. I respect him. I love being with him. I tell him everything, and he's very supportive of me." She looked down again, straightening her dress. Again, Ruth Lewis said nothing. "And I can't bear it when we're on the outs." This last sentence, she said in a low, sad voice.

"How do you feel when you and Eb are 'on the outs?'" Ruth asked.

"I feel terrible." Rebecca finally looked up, letting herself slide into a pocket of truth. "I have this hollow feeling in the pit of my stomach all the time. I don't sleep well. I feel all alone. I've so many things to tell him, but he's not there. I miss him. I think about him all the time." Rebecca spoke without hesitation and stopped fiddling with her dress.

"Now you, Eb." Ruth shifted slightly to her left. "How do you feel about Rebecca?"

"I love Rebecca." Eb made this announcement in a calm, straightforward fashion. His hands were folded in front of him. He looked across the table at Rebecca through his gold-rimmed glasses. Rebecca stared back at him in disbelief. He did not waver or remove his eyes from her gaze. Rebecca blushed and lowered her eyes again.

Before their meeting with Ruth Lewis, Eb had decided to declare his love for Rebecca Harding—just say the damn thing aloud. In the past, and during their painful hiatus, Eb was always waiting for Rebecca to make the declaration. He had lacked the courage to say he loved her first. Afraid to crawl out on a fragile limb. Afraid of crashing to the ground if she did not reciprocate. But what did he have to lose? Eb had recently risked rejection, and it was not the worst thing. Bruised pride, perhaps a blow to the heart. But by saying nothing, he risked far more. If he continued to bumble and stumble on this path of cowardice, he would surely lose Rebecca too. "That's the truth, Mrs. Lewis. I haven't told her before, but I do love Rebecca."

"Rebecca?" Mrs. Lewis turned slightly. Rebecca looked pale. "How do you feel about Eb telling you he loves you?"

"It's nice," Rebecca said almost inaudibly, gazing at the kitchen table. "I mean, he's never said anything like that before. I never know what Eb's feeling."

"Eb?" Mrs. Lewis looked over at Eb. "Do you hide your feelings from Rebecca?"

"I do," Eb admitted, feeling uncomfortable. He had been determined to declare his love at the outset, but beyond that, he had given little thought to what else Mrs. Lewis might ask. He too felt like he was taking an exam—and was not prepared. "I'm not always forthcoming with her, it's true. I've kept my feelings hidden." Eb had opted to be honest but felt an incredible urge to clean his glasses.

"And why is that, do you think?" Mrs. Lewis continued calmly. "Do you know?"

"Well, I haven't been certain how she'd respond." Eb decided to say aloud what he had been thinking for the past two months. "I didn't want to look foolish if she turned me down. Also, if I told her I loved her, I was afraid she'd feel pressured. She might even run away." He laughed feebly, succumbing to his urge to take off his glasses. He gave them a satisfying rub on the sleeve of his shirt. "I thought . . ." Eb put his glasses back on. "I thought that if I didn't say anything about it, we could go along just as we were. You know, continue to be close. Write to each other, be together all the time." Eb ran his fingers through his auburn hair. "It wasn't a very good strategy. Not sustainable." He paused. "And honestly, Mrs. Lewis, I hide my feelings from myself."

"Well, you're not the first person to do that." Ruth Lewis smiled at him. She turned to Rebecca, changing the subject. "Rebecca, Eb told you this past year, when you were apart, that he'd developed an interest in someone else. How did that make you feel?"

"Jealous." Rebecca looked up sharply, her dark brown eyes flashing with an unwelcome rush of anger. "I wasn't happy about it." She pursed her lips.

"Do you understand how that might have happened?" Ruth Lewis picked up on Rebecca's anger but did not back down.

"But nothing happened." Eb suddenly jumped in. "I told her that." He wanted to clarify that he had never declared himself to Susan, at least not in a timely fashion, and that anyhow, she was destined to reject him. Susan had told him they were too much like brother and sister. This was all new information, wasn't it? He felt hot around the collar. But Mrs. Lewis reached over and grabbed Eb's hand, giving it a warm but firm squeeze.

"Eb, please," Ruth Lewis said gently. "This isn't your turn to talk. I'm asking questions of Rebecca right now."

"Yes, ma'am." Eb sank back into his seat, chastened. Maybe he did not need to tell Rebecca all of that anyhow. Charles would probably say, 'Say nothing more about Susan.'

Ruth resumed her interrogation. "I asked you, Rebecca, whether you understand how Eb might have looked elsewhere to form an attachment?"

"I suppose," Rebecca said with a sigh, her anger waning. "No, of course, I understand." She glanced over at Ruth Lewis and began to play with the gold chain and locket around her neck, but a calm had returned to her voice. "I won't commit myself to Eb because I want to be a teacher. I make it so he can't really court me, but at the same time, I demand he be faithful to me." She hesitated. "I keep him in limbo."

"Does that strike you as fair?" Ruth Lewis's eyebrows were raised, looking like an imperious matriarch. The silver streaks of her hair were shining in the light thrown off from the kitchen fire.

"No," Rebecca replied softly. She stopped playing with her necklace and folded her hands in her lap. "It's not fair."

"May I ask you another question? If there were no rule about female teachers remaining unmarried, how would you feel about Eb? Would you want to court him?" After a pause, Ruth added, "With a possible eye to marriage?"

"Yes, I would," Rebecca said simply. "There's no one else in the world I could imagine being with but Eb." Eb felt a rush of affection for Rebecca. He wanted to jump up from his chair to give her an encouraging hug. This grilling by Ruth Lewis was far tougher on her than on him.

"Then I'm going to propose something," Ruth Lewis announced, folding her hands on the kitchen table. She had to accept that Rebecca Harding, for whatever reason, would not declare her love for Eb Wells. Or could not, at present. No sense in waiting for that to happen. "I'm going to propose an arrangement. A courtship that will last for one year. During that year, you'll be faithful to one another—no more casting eyes in other directions." She gave Eb a stern look, and he shrank down in his chair. "With this caveat. The subject of marriage will not be discussed at all for a full year." Ruth Lewis smiled at Eb and Rebecca. "Not a whisper between you about the future, where the courtship's going. Would you like to hear my thinking?"

"Yes," Rebecca and Eb said in unison.

"Well, it's God's will that you're both back here in Litchfield for the year. Just look at your history. You exchanged a few kisses over a year ago—yes, I know about the kisses—and then you both promptly moved away. When you reunited, you had all of eight days together before you exploded in a huge fight and parted again. A year of courtship will give you time to be together, not as dear friends, but as sweethearts. After a year, the courtship will either succeed or fail. But at least this way, your decision will be based on time spent together—as a committed couple. The ban on marriage discussions will take the pressure off." Eb and Rebecca listened to Ruth intently, not looking at one another. "You should feel free to be physically affectionate, within the customary bounds of courtship." Ruth was almost at the end of her ruling. "But I urge you to express your feelings openly with one another. Whatever those feelings are. Absolute honesty is the mandate." Ruth put her hands down on the table and spread her fingers apart. "A year together will bring you more clarity."

"So . . ." Eb spoke up, not wanting to sound like a lawyer, but he could not help himself. He felt in the presence of a contract. "Just to confirm. The courtship will last for one year. Exclusivity is required. No discussion of marriage is permitted. Affection permitted. Honesty about our feelings. Do we reconvene after a year?"

"Yes, if you like. We can discuss the future at that time." Ruth Lewis recognized in Eb the lawyer's pathological need for certainty. These were small promises she could keep. "And you may come to me any time this year—if you hit a rough patch." Ruth crossed her arms over her apron. "Let me be clear. I'll only discuss the courtship when you're both here. No independent discussions, complaints about the other, private asides about how things are going." She looked to her right and then to her left, and said emphatically, "And no more destructive silences for months on end. You've been given a year. Use the time wisely. If you find yourselves engaged in warfare again, you come here." She gestured around her cozy kitchen. "I'm not going anywhere."

"And will others know of the courtship?" Rebecca wondered how such a formal courtship would sit with her employer, Rhoda Morris, who was counting on her to remain unmarried.

"Yes." Ruth Lewis had anticipated Rebecca's concern. "You must make this commitment to Eb—not to marriage yet, but to the courtship. And it must be public. Others must know about it.

Even your headmistress at South Farms." Ruth hesitated and added, "Eb deserves that from you. If you can't commit to a year-long courtship now—well then, I think it's clear. You'll never commit to marriage later. In that case, you must let Eb go." Ruth could see tears welling up in Rebecca's eyes, but she soldiered on. "Letting Eb go, Rebecca," Ruth said slowly, with a grave look, "means you'd have to stop spending time with him. I'm sorry to have to say this, but it's the truth. Others in town already think you're courting. Eb can't possibly approach another young woman if it looks like the two of you are together." Rebecca's tears had begun to fall silently, but Ruth continued. "You may choose not to marry, Rebecca. We'll all support you if that's your decision." Her tone was warm, but she spoke with determination. "But you can't hold Eb hostage, not in a town like Litchfield, with all those young women at the female academy. Eb Wells would have no trouble finding a wife. Not if the coast was clear."

"Yes, I see." Rebecca nodded. "You're right, of course." Wiping away her tears with a handkerchief she kept in the sleeve of her dress, Rebecca peered up at Eb. He gave her an encouraging look across the table, and she responded with a sweet, shy smile. "I don't want him pursuing some young woman from the female academy." Rebecca shook her head. "He's mine."

"So, we're agreed on the terms of the arrangement?" Ruth looked to her right and her left again.

"Yes," Eb and Rebecca said again in unison. Eb reached across the table to grab Rebecca's hand. Rebecca took it.

"Well, that's settled then." Ruth Lewis covered the couple's joined hands with her own hand and gave them both a broad smile. "Better put the kettle on." She got up from her chair, stiff from her rheumatism. Silently, Ruth patted herself on the back. Rebecca Harding was looking at Eb Wells across her kitchen table with what looked like adoration—that's a good start. But Ruth was a realist.

If this couple could follow her rules, they might succeed. If they couldn't, they wouldn't. Their track record wasn't all that great. "Why don't you two take a walk out to the pines?" Ruth suggested. "Martha and Charles will be back shortly. We'll have to tell them what you've decided, and Martha must desist from matchmaking." She heard stirrings at the back door of the cottage—the shuffling feet of a hungry man. "There's my Benjamin at the door. Looking for pumpkin pie."

After *The Battle of the Ninepins,* Eddie and Henry kept pestering their parents to get together. Neither boy had ever had a friend before. It was all well and good to play ninepins with his father, to study with Susan Graham in the library, to hang out with Mrs. Potts and Esmeralda in the kitchen, to visit the kittens in the pantry. Still, all Henry Mueller wanted to do was play with Eddie Haines. The desire was even stronger in Eddie as Chapel Street was dull compared to the yeasty environment on Elm Street.

During October and November, Franz transported the boys back and forth almost every day. Malinda often went along for the ride, to oversee the redecoration on Chapel Street and spend some time with Eddie, sitting across from the two rambunctious boys in her uncle's carriage. Slowly, over the weeks, Eddie came around on his father's fiancée. He began to feel her presence as a benign despot in their home. The past few years on Chapel Street had been chaotic and sad. The household was rudderless, with no one to give direction to the housekeeper and cook. Now Miss Wells had taken the helm, issuing polite orders in a Southern accent he was growing accustomed to—even liked. It made him feel secure to have her in the house when his father was at work. Maybe after they got married and she moved in, Eddie might let her tuck him in. She smelled good—

like lavender soap. After they got married, she could even read to him if his father was out of town, although they would have to pick another book. *Robinson Crusoe* was a man's book, Eddie argued, and his to share with his father.

Even at age seven, Eddie understood that his father was happy. Ned Haines smiled and laughed when Malinda Wells was around. He made bad jokes and teased them both. And Miss Wells kept things interesting. Whenever she entered Chapel Street, plans were set into motion. Redecorating and rearranging, she steered the household toward the future—a place Malinda inhabited with ease. The miasma that had descended upon the house after the death of Eddie's mother was lifting. A new Mrs. Haines was taking over.

In Malinda's considered opinion, a more thorough rehabilitation of Chapel Street was required. She sent at least six pieces of furniture to the upholsterer. Two area rugs, one in the parlor and one in the morning room, had to be replaced. New curtains were also needed in both rooms, not just in her quarters on the second floor. Malinda chose delicate fabrics, some of them almost diaphanous. Light filled the house as never before. And, of course, Eddie's room needed to be redecorated. It was still done up as a nursery. He was now a boy, preparing for the academy.

At Susan's suggestion, Malinda let Eddie redecorate his room, and the boy chose a wallpaper with a burned orange background. Malinda was horrified. 'It'll be like sleeping inside a rotten pumpkin,' Malinda had groaned to Susan, who urged her to make peace with the rotten pumpkin. Eddie liked it, and she had delegated the decision to him. Above all, Malinda must keep her promises to the boy. That was what mattered.

Ned Haines began to see that his fiancée was going to be expensive. The money he had squirreled away for a fancy wedding was rapidly disappearing. But the house on Chapel Street began to look fresh and inviting—and different. Ned was thrilled.

On cold or rainy days, after his lessons, Henry would lobby to go to Chapel Street to play dominoes with Eddie. If Malinda stayed home, the boys had almost no supervision on Chapel Street, colonizing parts of the house normally off-limits on Elm Street. The smooth oak banister could be ridden, the stairs descended on cardboard boxes. That no limbs were fractured was a miracle. The boys liked to line up all the domino tiles on the wooden floor of the long front hallway, like an undulating serpent, thrilling at the clatter of cascading tiles when one boy—they took turns—tipped over the tile at the head of the line. This clickity-clack glory of cause and effect was repeated with glee, over and over again. They made a secret clubhouse up in the attic. Eddie raided the linen closet and stole two sheets to tack up on the eaves for a white wall of privacy. Sometimes, pirates lurked behind the sheet. On other days, castaways eked out an existence on unknown shores. When the weather was good—it was not yet winter—Eddie would lobby to go over to Elm Street.

On Elm Street, play and work mingled, and Henry and Eddie were more closely monitored. Once their schooling was over, the boys played ninepins in the backyard, shoveled manure, amused the kittens, and assisted Mrs. Potts with her baking. Mrs. Potts made treats for two boys now. She and Esmeralda dispensed hugs all around, the latter's quick and grudging, but hugs just the same. Both boys were enlisted to help groom Hank and Ruby. Franz built two stools to elevate them. Eddie Haines's boots were often muddy, his knees often scraped, and his muscles grew stronger daily. He remembered how to smile.

Everything on Elm Street was in flux. After the wedding, Malinda would move to Chapel Street, beginning her reign as the third Mrs. Ned Haines. Susan would move into the carriage house as the second Mrs. Franz Mueller. Susan's work in the clinic would officially begin. Henry's lessons were up in the air. Susan worried that she could not responsibly serve in the clinic and keep up with Henry's education.

After some discussion, Ned Haines came up with a brilliant idea. Since the two boys wanted to be together, why not have Henry tutored along with Eddie on Chapel Street? Last year, Ned had hired a tutor for Eddie, a Yale student. His task was to prepare Eddie for the boys' academy. That meant Latin and Greek, history, geography, and higher mathematics. The plan was to tutor the boys privately until Eddie was nine and Henry eight. If both boys were proficient, then they could attend the same academy.

Franz Mueller was grateful. He could keep his promise to Henry's mother. Tutoring by a 'college man' would prepare Henry for admission to a boys' academy and perhaps one day to college. While Henry had thrived under Susan's instruction, it was time for him to step up his game. Eddie was older and had already been tutored for over a year. Some concern was expressed over Henry's youth and tendency for distraction, but Henry was keen to be tutored on Chapel Street. He vowed to outdo Eddie in the classroom—no more 'ants in the pants.' Dr. Cabot offered to pay Henry's portion of the tutoring fee. The boy could pay him back by playing dominoes with him on winter evenings.

As the nights grew longer, Mrs. Tittles ventured out of the kitchen to find Henry. Once the entitled cat poked her terracotta nose inside the library, there was no turning her back. Besides, Domino had already claimed the terrain as cat-friendly. Dr. Cabot relented, but Mrs. Tittles could only stay for the duration of the game. Afterward, she must rejoin the lone kitten Dora in the pantry. For that autumn season, Henry Mueller, age six, and Ebenezer Cabot, age 60, played dominoes after supper with three cats, Mrs. Tittles warming her haunches by the fire, and Domino purring on Dr. Cabot's lap. Little Dora finally discovered where the party was. One evening, she had padded silently into the library and curled up next to her mother, a pool of warm, calico fur and pink-padded paws, her little engine whirring.

These evenings provided an island of peace for Dr. Cabot, who grew weary of all the fuss over the weddings. Malinda was in high gear—and she exhausted him in low gear. Susan too was busy, slowly moving her things over to the carriage house. Mrs. Potts and Esmeralda pestered him with questions about this or that. He was talked into a new suit, something he certainly did not need. The money was there to do it all. He did not begrudge the girls their wedding, but he wanted the whole thing to be over. After all this fuss, and things quieted down, Dr. Cabot promised Henry—checkers was on the horizon. Maybe chess in the spring.

"You must be careful not to teach the law." Judge Reeve looked over at Eb with his large, orb-like eyes. The midday meal was finished at Betsey Reeve's. Charles Godwin had left for the Lewis cottage. The law students had all dispersed to the law library to copy over their notes and look up cases. Eb and Judge Reeve sat alone at the empty dining room table, facing the law school. The sky was a luminescent gray. The leaves had all fallen, exposing the bare branches of the trees. It was late November.

"You can't teach law here, Eb," Judge Reeve repeated. "Not in Litchfield." Somehow, the apprentice gossip mill in New Haven had disseminated the news statewide. The law students at the Litchfield Law School now knew that Eb Wells, the moot court star, formerly of Haines & Haines, and current apprentice to Mr. Theodore Fuller, Esquire, was an excellent teacher. In many ways, the law world in Connecticut was a small one. "Not even tutoring. Not even for free," Judge Reeve warned. "James would never forgive you."

"I realize that, sir." Even though Eb no longer fell under the Litchfield Law School's jurisdiction, he must submit to the will of Judge James Gould, its new owner and senior lecturer. A few law students with New Haven connections had asked Eb to tutor them, but he had reluctantly said 'no.' James Gould took a fiercely proprietary stance toward his law lectures. Tutoring the law was just inches away. "But I was wondering, sir," Eb asked his mentor, "what you thought about this other part-time teaching position?" Just yesterday, Miss Sarah Pierce's nephew, Mr. John Pierce Brace, had approached Eb about teaching Latin and Greek at the Litchfield Female Academy. "At Miss Pierce's?"

Latin and Greek were not in the female academy's formal curriculum, although students were permitted to study them after school. But this year, Miss Pierce's academy had enrolled twenty-six boys, and boys required preparation for college. Miss Pierce had heard that a classics scholar, disguised as a law apprentice, roomed at Mrs. Edwards's boarding house. And how did Miss Sarah Pierce know about Eb's expertise? He could only guess—Rebecca Harding or Martha Lewis must have told her. Or both. Eb later learned that it was Katherine Montgomery. Katherine herself was excellent in Latin, maybe better than Eb, but the parents of these boys expected a proper teacher—a college-educated male.

"Mr. Brace assures me I'd only teach in the afternoon after my morning duties with Mr. Fuller." Eb eyed the last piece of bread on the plate. He observed his mentor eyeing it too. "Mr. Fuller says it's fine with him, at least until the trial gets closer."

"Well, you're certainly qualified." The old man reached over and picked up the remaining piece of bread. "Classics was your major course of study at college, wasn't it?"

"Yes, sir." Eb's only claim to fame at Franklin College had been his proficiency in Latin, although his Greek was passable. "I'd need to brush up, but I think I'm qualified."

"And do you like teaching?" Judge Reeve leaned over for the butter dish.

"I do." During his miserable seven months at Haines & Haines, lecturing to his fellow apprentices was the only thing Eb had enjoyed. "What I don't know is whether I'd like teaching boys." Eb had only taught adults who were eager to learn. Law apprentices are like sharks. If you toss them a single bloody, meaty tidbit of information, they will churn around in the sea, thrashing their tails, devouring it with multiple rows of sharp teeth. But Eb had witnessed Susan Graham on Elm Street, struggling to keep a six-year-old Henry Mueller from falling off his chair. "Boys are different, I believe."

"Well, do you like children?" The judge was slathering his bread with the remaining butter. He heard his wife bustling around in the kitchen, sorting out the dirty dishes. She was out of range and not there to chastise him. "That would help, I suppose."

"I'm not sure," Eb admitted. "But I like your grandson, T.B. And there's the six-year-old boy who lives at my uncle's. The coachman's son. I like him too." Eb conjured up the image of Henry, his shock of wild blond hair and goofy smile, dragging a limp Mrs. Tittles across the backyard on Elm Street. On reflection, Eb thought he might like T.B. and Henry more than most people. "I suppose I do like them well enough."

"Well, if Mr. Fuller's amenable," the old judge opined, "it might be a good experience for you, teaching at an academy." Judge Reeve wiped the edges of his mouth, removing all traces of butter, his wife's heavy footsteps approaching. Perhaps she would believe Eb had consumed the last piece of bread and demolished the butter. "You know, Eb . . ." Judge Reeve had given this some thought. "Even though you excelled in law school, it's not written in stone that you must practice law. Lots of my former students—even some of my best ones—have gone on to do something else. The ministry, commerce, politics. A few months ago, I received a letter from a former moot court star who had moved to Ohio. He became a newspaperman. I hear George Catlin is giving up the law to study art. Your friend Charles might become an artist too, although Ted Fuller tells me he's got the makings of an excellent probate lawyer." He laughed aloud. "Now, who would have predicted that?" Judge Reeve beamed at his wife, who picked up unused forks and knives from the table. Betsey Reeve patted her husband's shoulder affectionately as she passed by. "I guess what I'm saying is this. You're not wedded to the law. I'll be proud of you no matter what you do." He gave Eb a benevolent smile and chuckled. "Just because you're good at something, doesn't mean you have to do it."

"Thank you, sir." Eb was surprised to find himself relieved. His own lawyer father was dead and beyond disappointment—but Eb still felt that he had let William Wells down. He had also disappointed his older brother, with his abolitionist views and failure to return to the family law practice. But sitting there in the dining room, over-looking the Litchfield Law School, Eb Wells had an epiphany: he did not want to disappoint Judge Tapping Reeve either. He admired the old man—revered him. "I'll try teaching Latin then, if you think it's a good idea."

"I do." Judge Reeve patted his stomach. "You need to find your life's work, Eb. It's almost as important as finding the right wife." His silvery white hair was lit up from a burst of unexpected sunlight through the window. He winked at Eb. "Your work, your wife—you must feel passion for them both to be a happy man." Betsey Reeve was standing in the doorway, eavesdropping. She blushed, something Eb had never seen before, or even dreamed possible. "So, I say, go ahead. Take the job with John Brace." The old man smiled again and pushed himself from the table. "Why not give teaching Latin and Greek a try?"

"I may do that, sir." Now, Eb regretted not eating that last piece of bread. Oh well, he thought, it's baking day at Mrs. Edwards's. There's always supper to look forward to. Eb excused himself and took off to speak with Mr. Brace at the Litchfield Female Academy.

Judge Tapping Reeve tottered into the house to nap, limping slightly from the gout. Betsey Reeve and her servant swooped down on the almost empty table and finished clearing the dishes.

EPILOGUE

Wedding Day

The joint wedding of Ned Haines and Malinda Wells, and Franz Mueller and Susan Graham, took place on a frigid day in the third week of December 1821. Winter had finally come to New Haven, although thankfully, there was no snow. The parlor on Elm Street, with its new celery green draperies, looked festive, decorated with white satin ribbons. Mr. Potts had set up chairs on either side of the table where the justice of the peace officiated. Mrs. Potts had brought over her sister's African violet to put on the table, with its rich purple blooms and thick, velvety green leaves.

Dr. Cabot led Malinda down the short aisle. She wore a demure peach-colored silk dress, trimmed at the collar and sleeves with ivory lace. Malinda's dark hair was pulled back in her customary simple bun, but around her head, she wore a wreath of braided white ribbons. Eb followed with Susan Graham on his arm. Her dress too was simple, a light blue satin moiré, with an empire waist that accentuated her figure. Susan's thick, light brown hair was braided in a plait that wound around her head, topped with a wreath of white ribbons, which matched Malinda's. As is true of all brides, Malinda Wells and Susan Graham were both beautiful.

Because it was required of them as well, the grooms too were handsome, Ned looking distinguished in his black suit and brocaded vest that brought out the silver in his hair, Franz standing tall in a navy-blue suit that did the same for his aquamarine eyes, his blond hair still rebelling. Eb, Dr. Cabot, Henry, and Eddie all had new suits too. Dr. Cabot's free Black tailor on the other side of the New Haven Green had worked feverishly on the attire of the men in the Cabot wedding party for the past two months.

Henry and Eddie, scrubbed and imprisoned in their new suits, stood by the side of their respective fathers, the latter sandwiched between Ned and Nathan, watching the ceremony with enforced solemnity. Henry had promised Esmeralda and Susan that he would not make googly eyes at Eddie. Both boys had to swear they would not even look at each other. It was a tough promise to keep. Neither boy was accustomed to attending church, and proper comportment at a wedding was not in their repertoire. All things considered, they behaved moderately well.

Esmeralda and Mr. and Mrs. Potts were in attendance, as were the employees from Haines & Haines, and Donald Hawkins. Rebecca Harding and her friend Martha Lewis had made the trip from Wethersfield, where they were staying for the month of December with the elderly Mrs. Cox. Mr. Potts had found the leaves for the mahogany table in the attic. There were fifteen for the sit-down supper after the ceremony. Mrs. Cabot's best china, silver service, and crystal were brought out, polished, and graced the table. Esmeralda had moved the African violet into the dining room as a centerpiece. Eddie and Henry opted to take their meal in the kitchen, where they could eat with their mouths wide open and swing their legs beneath the table. Their suit coats were rapidly shed. The boys promised to stay out of the way of Mr. and Mrs.

Potts and Esmeralda, who had all changed into their work clothes.

Esmeralda donned her formal serving attire, proudly wearing a stiff white cap on her gray hair. Mrs. Potts's niece and husband were also hired to help prepare the plates for serving and any other task Mrs. Potts ordered them to do. There was a blur of people of African descent, rushing back and forth from the kitchen to the dining room, calling out to one another in sotto voce, ensuring the wedding meal for Miss Malinda and Miss Susan went off without a hitch.

Mrs. Potts outdid herself. The supper included clam chowder, stewed oysters, pheasant, venison, crispy potatoes, beets, Indian corn bread, and a pumpkin casserole. For dessert, she had made a traditional wedding fruitcake and an exquisite Washington pound cake with lemons and currants, coated with a sweet white icing. She had also baked a blackberry jam cake, covered with traditional caramel icing. Mrs. Potts remembered how well her hot chocolate concoction had been received last April. It was served along with coffee and tea.

Mrs. Potts also showcased a new beverage, a warm apple cider spiced with brown sugar, lemons, limes, and a smattering of mystery spices. The spices had been tried out, consulted over, and reworked for two weeks in the kitchen on Elm Street. Franz, Mr. Potts, and Esmeralda had all weighed in. Even Eddie and Henry had been enlisted to perfect the recipe. As was their custom, the employees of Haines & Haines speculated about the secret ingredients. Martha was to be the referee. Ted Redfield insisted on a hint of clove. Eb felt certain he detected cinnamon—a guess Samuel Taylor declared pedestrian. Donald Hawkins defended Eb's choice, also voting for cinnamon. Oliver Redfield thought it was possible Mrs. Potts had slipped in the juice of another fruit. Pear perhaps? The new scrivener and Nathan Haines concurred with Oliver, although both thought the twist might be due to two kinds of apple—more appropriate for a beverage labeled 'apple' cider. They quibbled over which ones. Martha Lewis gathered all the comments and tallied the votes. She sat wedged between the Redfield brothers, basking in all the male attention.

"This has been a lovely celebration," Rebecca whispered to Eb, who sat to her right. "I'm so happy to finally meet Malinda, your uncle, and Samuel Taylor, well, everyone."

"I'm glad you can stay a few days." Eb smiled at her. Rebecca wore the same moss green dress from their détente, but she had dressed it up with a loosely crocheted shawl that looked to Eb like a cranberry spiderweb. The elderly Mrs. Cox in Wethersfield had also lent her a pair of garnet earrings that dangled from her ears. Rebecca's dark eyes sparkled in the candlelight. A curl escaped from her bun, adorning her neck. She looks so pretty tonight, Eb thought, this woman I'm courting. She's glowing.

Eb cast his eyes around the table at the other women. His sister sat at the head of the table, smiling serenely at her new husband. Eb's heart skipped a beat—she looked so much like their mother. Eb missed his mother terribly today. He knew Malinda did too. Susan and Franz were teasing one another over a piece of wedding cake. Eb's heart skipped another beat—he allowed himself just one—while he contemplated Susan's beauty, and the happy, easy way she was with her new husband. Martha Lewis sat right across from him, a mermaid rising out of a sea of young men, laughing, boisterous, her mane of coppery red hair worn loosely around her shoulders, her lightly freckled face flushed from the cider. Feminine grace abounded at his uncle's table, but none of them, Eb decided, suited him like his Rebecca. His Rebecca was elegant, delicate—and just the right size for him.

"We're to dine with Malinda and Ned tomorrow, just you, me, and Martha," Eb whispered back. "You'll get to know Malinda better then."

"Yes," Rebecca murmured. "I'm looking forward to it." Eb and Rebecca had both slipped off their shoes beneath the table. Eb surreptitiously scooted his left foot between Rebecca's, and she had wrapped her own feet around his. Eb then added his right foot to the pile. Above the tablecloth, Eb Wells and Rebecca Harding were two separate people, discussing whether the blackberry jam cake would also work with red raspberries. But beneath the tablecloth, with their tangle of toes and caressing stockinged feet—they were one.

Dr. Cabot surveyed the table of chattering, happy, well-fed people, the crew from Haines & Haines, flirting hopelessly with the petite, vivacious young woman from Litchfield; Susan and Franz Mueller, feeding each other cake; Ned Haines, conversing with Nathan and his old friend, the justice of the peace; Malinda's hand on Ned's arm in a gesture of new ownership. Ebenezer Cabot, not for the first time today, felt his eyes sting with tears. His niece was the spitting image of his younger sister, Abigail. How happy his dear sister would have been today, to see her lovely daughter married. It was a great privilege for Ebenezer Cabot—and a pleasure—to have provided two of Abigail's children a haven on Elm Street. A home in Connecticut to call their own. A Haven in New Haven. He chuckled to himself.

Then Dr. Cabot glanced over at his nephew, Eb. The infamous Rebecca Harding had finally made an appearance on Elm Street. She's just a slip of a thing, pretty enough, he noted to himself, and highly intelligent. That much he had garnered from their conversation the night before. Rebecca Harding could give Eb a run for his money. And that was saying something, Dr. Cabot recognized. For all his youthful indiscretions, his foibles, and eccentricities, Eb Wells was a brilliant young man. More importantly, he was kind. Eb smiled over at Miss Harding with a look Dr. Cabot had never seen on him before. I do believe, he thought with a mixture of amusement and amazement, that my nephew is happy. And maybe in love.

The old doctor let out a long sigh. Esmeralda passed through the room, picking up dessert plates and replacing them with new ones. Mrs. Potts was fastidious about that. Her Washington pound cake must not mingle with the blackberry jam cake. New plates were required for each dessert offering, necessitating hasty washing and drying out in the kitchen—even Henry and Eddie were enlisted to help. Dr. Cabot shot a look of gratitude at Esmeralda down the length of the table. Esmeralda smiled back. The old doctor and his housekeeper loved all these young people, their infatuations, their emotional peaks and valleys, their home improvements, their out-ings, their efforts to raise the next generation, and their struggles with each other. Being young took a lot of energy, or so it seemed to Ebenezer Cabot and Esmeralda Smith. But it also took a lot of energy to be around them.

The two old people relished, with unexpressed delight, the thought of having the house on Elm Street to themselves again. A peaceful house where nothing much happened. Dr. Cabot dreamed of long, silent winter nights. A pot of tea, a fire, a game of dominoes with Henry after supper—maybe checkers and chess soon—and then sending Henry and Mrs. Tittles across the backyard to their parents in the carriage house. Ebenezer Cabot looked forward to climbing the stairs of his quiet home, to a hot brick at the end of his bed, and a little black-and-white cat sleeping on his bald head, perhaps at his feet. He wanted to sink into the pillows and read his book on the Battle of Culloden by candlelight. Such were the yearnings of an old man. Small, modest dreams that could—and did—come true.

And what of little Dora, the calico kitten with the white under-tow? Coming into her cathood, Dora had followed her brother Domino upstairs in the big house one day. All on her own, satisfying her feline curiosity, Dora discovered a second set of stairs. Ascending one step at a time, her tiny opalescent nails, scritching and scratching on the wood, Dora found her way up to Esmeralda's quarters in the attic. Before long, Dora discovered that Esmeralda Smith too had a hot brick at the bottom of her bed—perfect for a small calico cat to curl around. The two creatures of God were negotiating a contract of their own.

THE END

Author's Note

This is Book 2 in a four-part series, *The Litchfield Chronicles*. *The Apprenticeship of Ebenezer Wells* takes place between December 1820 and December 1821. The book continues with the lives of four young people featured in Book 1, *The Education of Ebenezer Wells*: Eb Wells, Rebecca Harding, Charles Godwin, and Martha Lewis. Thomas Bradford and Katherine Montgomery move to the periphery, and several new characters step forward. The reader has already met two of them in Book 1: Eb's sister, Malinda Wells, and her companion, Susan Graham. In this book, Eb, Malinda, and Susan live together on Elm Street in New Haven in the home of Dr. Ebenezer Cabot. Samuel Taylor, a new character, is Eb's fellow apprentice at the law practice of Haines & Haines. Another new character is Franz Mueller, the German coachman who comes to live in the carriage house behind Elm Street with his five-year-old son, Henry. Franz becomes Susan's love interest, while Malinda Haines attracts the attention of the much older Ned Haines, the senior partner at Haines & Haines, also a widowed father of a young son.

As I mapped out *The Litchfield Chronicles*, the books would progress chronologically, but I wanted a reader to be able to pick up any one of the four books and follow the story. For myself, I prefer to chug through a series in order, but occasionally, I must deviate from that policy. With Louise Penny's wonderful mysteries, for example, her offerings on my local library shelf are sporadic, and I have been forced to read them out of order. (I have no patience for reserving books. At the library, I need instant gratification.) Louise Penny kindly anticipates that eventuality, providing enough background at each book's beginning for the out-of-sequence reader to get up to speed. I hope to emulate her.

Even for those of us who prefer to read a series sequentially, that background also serves as a refresher. It reminds us of what happened in the preceding book(s) and locates the characters in the current book. In my thumbnail sketches of what happened in Book 1, I address the clueless out-of-sequence reader and the in-sequence reader who needs a recap. If that background information seems clunky, dense, or redundant at times, I apologize.

Romance flourishes in the book, although not always between Eb and Rebecca. A dear friend of mine expressed dissatisfaction with the ending of *The Education of Ebenezer Wells*, complaining that Eb and Rebecca only 'sort of' get together. This friend expected a grand finale worthy of Jane Austen, a tale of thwarted love, where, after pages of torturous misunderstandings, the protagonist and her love interest end up at the altar. But Rebecca Harding's circumstances would not have occurred to Austen. The female seminary movement in England lagged behind that of New England. In Austen's time and place, boarding schools for girls and private governesses focused on basic literacy and the ornamental arts, including music, dancing, and etiquette. Austen would not have been exposed to a female academy like Miss Pierce's, where young women learned substantive subjects at the same level as men. Hence, Austen would be equally unfamiliar with the 'marriage bar' for female educators.

For Austen's young women, only marriage or spinsterhood was on the horizon, as they resided in the homes of their fathers, husbands, brothers, or other male relatives. The female seminary movement in the United States expanded those horizons. My female protagonist, Rebecca Harding, was among the first generation of women to have a professional teaching career. Rebecca had worked so hard to become a female educator. Should we now expect her to swoon and fall into Eb Wells's arms? It would have been a betrayal of her character. My dear friend will have to forgive me for not letting that happen—at least not at the end of Book 1.

The Education of Ebenezer Wells left me with loose ends. Eb's education was incomplete. He was on the brink of an apprenticeship with a commercial law firm in New Haven, his first step into professional life. True, Eb had excelled at law school. However, from experience, even two hundred years later, I know that excelling in law school bears little relation to doing well in law practice. The skill set is different.

Not only that, but practicing law in a commercial firm would inevitably pose problems for Eb. What happens when he is confronted with the tedious, nitty-gritty work of the law? Or law firm hierarchy and the whims of a boss he has no respect for? Worse yet, how will Eb deal with the mandate of political neutrality? Eb Wells was destined to struggle at Haines & Haines. For that reason, I felt obliged to follow him into his first year of work life.

In Book 2, Rebecca was also destined to struggle. Her idealism about female education hits a brick wall when she faces off with her headmaster, Asa Hitchcock. She enjoys her stay with Mrs. Cox, luxuriating in the two-story brick home in Wethersfield, but her first teaching position turns out to be a dead end. Unlike Eb, who blunders through his apprenticeship, Rebecca deftly finds an alternative to the Wethersfield Academy. She is shrewder than Eb, more worldly.

And, of course, Eb and Rebecca struggle romantically, unlike Charles and Martha, who are now engaged and on solid footing. On Elm Street, Eb is consumed by fantasies of Susan Graham. Somehow, he manages to screw up his chances with both women by lacking the courage to tell Susan of his feelings for her, and by revealing to Rebecca his attraction to Susan. In Litchfield, Martha's mother, Ruth Lewis, helps Eb and Rebecca patch things together, at least for a trial courtship of finite duration. But by the end of

The Apprenticeship of Ebenezer Wells, my friend will continue to be disappointed, shaking her head. Eb and Rebecca still only 'sort of' get together.' At least Book 2 ends with a wedding, and a double wedding at that. My friend will have to be satisfied with the marital alliances of Malinda and Ned Haines, and Susan and Franz Mueller.

Malinda and Susan interested me. Their circumstances are more commonplace, with limited horizons that Jane Austen *would* understand. Their contemporaries, Rebecca Harding and Martha Lewis, were among the minority of women in the 1820s with a formal education. Malinda and Susan had no opportunity to study at a female academy, despite being well-educated at home by Abigail Cabot Wells. But both women are intelligent and resourceful, laudable for their willingness to marry a widower with a young boy to raise. Malinda and Susan will stay with us through Books 3 and 4. I also wanted to flesh out the past of Esmeralda Smith, the free Black housekeeper on Elm Street, who stays the course throughout the series with dignity and grace.

I was not quite done with Judge Tapping Reeve either. At the end of Book 1, he left the law school podium, having committed the sin of getting old. The contemporary writings about Reeve in the early 1820s suggest that his forgetfulness had become problematic at the lectern. But being in the classroom is not the only role a good teacher plays, and Judge Reeve emerges in Book 2 as an invaluable mentor when Eb manages to make a royal mess of his first professional position. Eb is smart enough to follow Judge Reeve's sound advice on how to depart Haines & Haines with his reputation intact, allowing him to return to Litchfield to prepare a trial for Theodore Fuller, Esquire.

But Eb is not smart enough to follow Charles Godwin's sound advice about his love life. Charles urges him not to tell Rebecca about his crush on Susan, but Eb loses his temper with Rebecca and spills the beans. I have a deep fondness for Eb Wells, but I keep asking:

how can the man have such a brilliant mind and be such a dolt with women? Eb wonders the same thing. Is there any hope for him? This same question lingers at the end of *The Apprenticeship of Ebenezer Wells*, just as it did at the end of Book 1.

I should warn you. Eb Wells and Rebecca Harding require a great deal of patience. This is what I keep telling my dear friend: Ask not for whom the wedding bell tolls. But if you want to know how Eb and Rebecca's romance turns out, you must read the following two books: *The Trial of Ebenezer Wells* and *The Education of Johanna Wells*. In Book 3, Eb tries his first case in Litchfield, and he and Rebecca make some momentous decisions about their future. Book 4 jumps forward to the summer of 1838 and turns its attention to the next generation, although Eb and Rebecca feature prominently, as do Charles and Martha Godwin. Much of Book 4 takes place in Worthington, Ohio.

Readers often wonder which of the characters in the book were real. The list is similar to that of Book 1. **Here are the actual people who lived in Connecticut or elsewhere who are featured in the book**: Judge Tapping Reeve, his second wife, Betsey Reeve, his grandson, T.B. Reeve, Judge James Gould, Miss Sarah Pierce, her half-sister Mary Pierce, her nephew John Pierce Brace, Rhoda Farnam Morris, the landlady Mrs. Edwards, William Lanson, and by reference, Reverend Lyman Beecher, his daughters, Catharine Beecher and her sister Harriet (later Harriet Beecher Stowe), James Morris, the abolitionist Moses Brown, and the artist, George Catlin. There are first-hand accounts of many of the Litchfield historical figures, particularly Judge Reeve, Judge Gould, Betsey Reeve, Sarah and Mary Pierce, and Mrs. Edwards. I have relied on sources to imagine how they might have comported themselves in the world. All the conversations, however, are fictional.

Beyond those individuals, the other characters are fictional. I make the requisite disclaimer. *The Apprenticeship of Ebenezer Wells* is a work of fiction. All incidents and dialogue, and all characters, except for the above-mentioned historical figures, are products of the author's imagination and not to be construed as real. Where real-life historical figures appear, the situations, incidents, and dialogues concerning those persons are entirely fictional. They are not intended to depict actual events or to change the entirely fictional nature of the work. In all other respects, any resemblance to actual persons, living or dead, events, or locales is entirely coincidental.

There is one exception to the above disclaimer: Mrs. Tittles is unabashedly based on a cat named Sydney, may she rest in peace. I tried to disguise her by changing her furrage, but Syd's entitled temperament was impossible to hide.

Fiction is not the same as history, so I may have gotten some details wrong. I researched the practice of law during the New Republic and the historical context of New Haven, Wethersfield, Litchfield, and South Farms (now Morris). Sources were not always consistent, or there were gaps in knowledge. Sometimes, I filled in the blanks or made minor changes. I apologize for any historical mistakes that I have made. I am not a historian, merely a writer of historical fiction.

I also took a few liberties. During this period, the mail was notoriously slow, slower than depicted, but the narrative flow required those letters to move back and forth with alacrity. I have downplayed the poor hygiene and state of dentistry of the period, but I do not believe I have exaggerated the perils of pregnancy and motherhood. Love was such a risky business for women in the 1820s and continues to be so, even in our times, at least for women with poor healthcare.

I have attached a bibliography including most of my resources. I offer it for anyone who wants to dig deeper, not as evidence of my seriousness as a scholar.

I want to express my gratitude to the staff of the Oliver Wolcott Library, the Torrington Library, and the Litchfield Historical

Society, particularly to its Executive Director, Jessica D. Jenkins, for their kind assistance. I am also grateful to Sharon Rutland, my editor. And, of course, I am always indebted to Avrom, Nan, Kate, Jo, and my beloved cats.

The Apprenticeship of Ebenezer Wells
Bibliography

American Revolution Bicentennial Commission of Connecticut (1976). The Underground Railroad in Connecticut. https://prod.ctda.dgicloud.com/node/281031

Anderson, D. L. & Leonard, S.H. (2004). Grammar of Death: An Analysis of Nineteenth Century Literal Causes of Death from the Age of Miasmas to Germ Theory. *Social Science History, 28* (1), 111-143. https://www.jstor.org/stable/40267835

Appel, A. (2014, Feb. 27). 'King of the Colored Race' of New Haven Revealed. *New Haven Independent.* https://www.newhavenindependent.org/index.php/archives/entry/willian_lanson_revealed/

Andrews, E. (2016, May 3). 6 Early Abolitionists. *History.Com.* https://www.history.com/news/6-early-abolitionists

Archer, M. & Blau, J.R. (1993, August). Class Formation in Nineteenth-Century America: The Case of the Middle Class. *Annual Review of Sociology, 19*, 17-41. https://doi.org/10.1146/annurev.so.19.080193.000313

Blakemore, E. (2017, September 6). In Early 1800s American Classrooms, Students Governed Themselves. *History.com.* https://www.history.com/news/in-early-1800s-american-classrooms-students-governed-themselves

Blumenthal, S.L. (2006). Deviance of the Will: Policing the Bounds of Testamentary Freedom in Nineteenth-Century America. *Harvard Law Review, 119.* https://papers.ssrn.com/sol3/papers.cfm?abstract_id=839387

Bryson, W. H. (1983). The Abolition of the Forms of Action in Virginia. *17 U .Rich. L. Rev.*, 273. https://scholarship.richmond.edu/cgi/viewcontent.cgi?article=1396&context=law-faculty-publications

Bryson, W. H. (1979) The History of Legal Education in Virginia. *14 U. Rich. L Rev.*, 14, 155-210. https://scholarship.richmond.edu/lawreview/vol14/iss1/9/

Bulkeley, A.T. (1907). *Historic Litchfield, 1721-1907; being a short account of the history of the old houses of Litchfield.* Hartford Press.

Butler, N. (2017, April 7). A Woman's Progress in Early South Carolina, Part I. *Charleston County Public Library.* https://www.ccpl.org/charleston time-machine/woman%E2%80%99s-progress-early-south-carolina-part-1

Cabranes, J. A. (1983). Notes on the History of the Federal Court of Connecticut. *57 Connecticut Bar Journal*, 351. https://www.ctd.uscourts.gov/sites/default/files/Notes%20on%20the%20History%20of%20The%20Federal%20Court%20of%20CT.pdf

Clark, G. L. (1914). *A History of Connecticut: Its People and Institutions.* G.P. Putnam Sons.

Connecticut State Library (2000, November). History of Connecticut Newspapers. *Connecticut State Library.* https://ctstatelibrary.org/history-of-ct-newspapers/

Copeland, R.W. (2010, May) The Nomenclature of Enslaved Africans as Real Property or Chattels Personal. *Journal of Black Studies, 40* (5), 946-959. https://www.jstor.org/stable/40648615

DeLuca, R. (2011). *Post Roads & Iron Horses: Transportation in Connecticut from Colonial Times to the Age of Steam.* Wesleyan University Press.

Fall, K.W. (2018). The Enslaved Members of the Davenport Household: Geography, Mobility, and Pre-Davenport House Lived Experiences. *Georgia Southern University, Department of History Public History Graduate Project Reports, 1.* https://digitalcommons.georgiasouthern.edu/history-grad-internship/1

Gaines, P. (2001, April). The "True Lawyer" in America: Discursive Construction of the Legal Profession in the Nineteenth Century. *The American Journal of Legal History, 45* (2), 132-155. https://www.jstor.org/stable/3185365

Galenson, D.W. (1981, June). The Market Evaluation of Human Capital: The Case of Indentured Servitude. *Journal of Political Economy, 89* (3). https://www.journals.uchicago.edu/doi/epdf/10.1086/260980

Gallman, J.M. (1984, Winter). Relative Ages of Colonial Marriages. *The Journal of Interdisciplinary History, 14* (3). https://www.jstor.org/stable/203726

Gilder Lehrman Center for the Study of Slavery, Resistance, and Abolition (2007). *The Emergence of Free Black Communities in Connecticut, 1800-1830. Citizens ALL: African Americans in Connecticut 1700-1850.* https://doczz.net/doc/8751632/1-module-iii--the-emergence-of-free-black-communities-in.

Grant, S. (2002, March 3). Sisters Trace Black Ancestors to 1700s in Litchfield County. *The Hartford Courant.* https://www.courant.com/2002/03/03/sisters-trace-black-ancestors-to-1700s-in-litchfield-county/

Harmon, L. (2008). The Lawyer Scribe: The Litchfield Law School, Laptops, and the Metaphysics of Soul-Searching. *Legal Studies Forum, 32.* https://digitalcommons.tourolaw.edu/scholarlyworks/64/

Hicks, P.D. (2019). *The Litchfield Law School: Guiding the New Nation.* Prospecta Press.

Kilbourne, P.K. (1859). *Sketches and Chronicles of the Town of Litchfield, Connecticut.* Case, Lockwood & Co., Hartford.

Hattery, E., Nguyen T., Baker, A., & Palmieri, T. (2015). Burn Care in the 1800s. *Journal of Burn Care & Research, 36* (10), 236-239. https://academic.oup.com/jbcr/article-abstract/36/1/236/4568894?redirectedFrom=PDF

Hoeflich, M.H. (2013, Summer). From Scriveners to Typewriters: Document Production in the Nineteenth Century Law Office. *Green Bag 2D, 16,* 395-411. http://greenbag.org/v16n4/v16n4_articles_hoeflich.pdf

Hodgdon, D. R. (1937). School Law Review: Marriage of Women Teachers. *The Clearing House: A Journal of Educational Strategies, Issues and Ideas, 12*(1), 55–56. https://doi.org/10.1080/00098655.1937.11474612

Hurst, J. W. (1967, June). Lawyers in American Society 1750-1966. *Marquette Law Review, 50* (4). 594-606. https://scholarship.law.marquette.edu/cgi/viewcontent.cgi?article=2502&context=mulr

Katcher, S. (2006). Legal Training in the United States. *Wisconsin International Law Journal, 24* (1), 335-375. https://wilj.law.wisc.edu/wp-content/uploads/sites/1270/2012/02/katcher.pdf

Kelley, M. (2008). *Learning to Stand and Speak: Women, Education, and Public Life in America's Republic.* University of North Carolina Press.

Kenslea, T. (2006). *The Sedgwicks in Love: Courtship, Engagement, and Marriage in the Early Republic.* Northeastern University Press.

Klebaner, B. J. (1955). American Manumission Laws and the Responsibility for Supporting Slaves. *The Virginia Magazine of History and Biography*, 63(4), 443–453. http://www.jstor.org/stable/4246165

Kilbourne, P.K. (1859). *Sketches and Chronicles of the Town of Litchfield, Connecticut.* Case, Lockwood & Co., Hartford.

Kohl, M. (2014, December 18). "Must a woman…give it all up when she marries?" The debate over employing married women as teachers. *Women's History Matters.* http://montanawomenshistory.org/must-a-woman-give-it-all-up-when-she-marries-the-debate-over-employing-married-women-as-teachers/

Land, J. (2009). Lyman Beecher: Conservative Abolitionist, Theologian and Father. *Madison Historical Review, 6* (2). https://commons.lib.jmu.edu/mhr/vol6/iss1/2/

Lang, J. (2002, September 29). Chapter 1: The Plantation Next Door; How Salem Slaves, Wethersfield Onions and West Indies Sugar Made Connecticut Rich. *Hartford Courant. https://teachitct.org/wp-content/uploads/sites/9/2023/06/The_Plantation_Next_Door_highlighted.pdf*

Langbein, J.H. (2008). Blackstone, Litchfield, and Yale: The Founding of the Yale Law School. In A.T. Kronman (Ed.) *History of Yale Law School: Tercentennial Lectures.* Yale University Press.

Langbein, J. H. (2008). Law School in a University: Yale's Distinctive Path in the Later Nineteenth Century. In A.T. Kronman (Ed.) *History of the Yale Law School: Tercentennial Lectures.* Yale University Press.

Larkin, J. (1989). *The Reshaping of Everyday Life, 1790-1840.* Harper Perennial.

Lepore, J. (2009, April 6). IOU: How we used to treat debtors. *The New Yorker.* https://www.newyorker.com/magazine/2009/04/13/i-o-u

Litchfield Historical Society (ND). The Ledger. *Litchfield Historical Society.* https://ledger.litchfieldhistoricalsociety.org/ledger/

Lockley, T. (2012, Fall). Survival Strategies of Poor White Women in Savannah, 1800-1860. *Journal of the Early Republic, 32* (3), 415-435. https://www.jstor.org/stable/23315161

Mansfield, E.D. (1879). *Personal Memories, Social, Political and Literary Sketches of Many Noted People, 1803-1843.* Robert Clarke & Co.

McKenna, M.C. (1986). *Tapping Reeve and the Litchfield Law School.* Oceana Publications.

McKirdy, C.R. (1976). The Lawyer as Apprentice: Legal Education in Eighteenth Century Massachusetts. *J. Legal Educ, 28* (2), 124-136. https://www.jstor.org/stable/i40110583

McMahon, L. (2009, Fall). "Of the Utmost Importance to our Country:" Women, Education, and Society, 1790-1820. *Journal of the Early Republic, 29* (3), 475-506. https://www.jstor.org/stable/40541858

Milkofsky, B. (2021, January 7). Connecticut and the West Indies: Sugar Spurs Trans-Atlantic Trade. *Connecticut History.Org.* connecticuthistory.org/connecticut-and-the-west-indies-trade

Muney, L. (2014). *Silhouettes in History.* Silhouettes in History. https://www.silhouettesbyhand.com/history

National Park Service (2012, November 12). Connecticut Abolitionists. *National Park Service.* https://www.nps.gov/articles/connecticut-abolitionists.htm#:~:text=Abolitionists%20Lewis%20Tappan%2C%20Joshua%20Leavitt,living%20expenses%20throughout%20the%20trial.

Normer, E.J. (Ed.). (2016). *African American Connecticut Explored.* Wesleyan University Press.

Perlmann, J, Siddali, S. R. & Whitecarver, K. (2017, February 24). Literacy, Schooling, and Teaching among New England Women, 1730-1820. *History of Education Quarterly, 22* (37) 2, 117-139. https://www.jstor.org/stable/369356

Kilbourne, P.K. (1859). *Sketches and Chronicles of the Town of Litchfield, Connecticut.* Case, Lockwood & Co.

Priest, C. (2021) *Credit Nation: Property Laws and Institutions in Early America.* Princeton University Press.

Raposo, J. (2019, January 22). Colonial America was Obsessed with Chocolate that Probably Tasted Pretty Bad. *Munchies.* vice.com/en/article/a3bzy8/colonial-america-was-obsessed-with-chocolate-that-probably-tasted-pretty-bad

Rothman, E. (1984). *Hands and Hearts: A History of Courtship in America.* Basic Books, New York.

Russo, R.E. (2005). Memory and Place on the New Haven Green, 1638-1876. *Yale-New Haven Teachers' Institute, III* (4). https://teachersinstitute.yale.edu/curriculum/units/2005/3/05.03.04/4

Sawula, C. (2017, October 24). Slavery in Revolutionary-Era Connecticut. *H-Slavery.* networks.h-net.org/node/11465/pages/671377/slavery-revolutionary-era-connecticut-topical-guide

Seeley, S. (2016, March 4). Beyond the American Colonization Society. *History Compass, 14* (3). https://compass.onlinelibrary.wiley.com/doi/abs/10.1111/hic3.12302

Seymour, M. (1935, August). *A Lawyer of Kent: Barzillai Slosson and his Account Books, 1794-1812.* Yale Law Library Publications. https://openyls.law.yale.edu/bitstream/handle/20.500.13051/173/YL_05_L61_no2.pdf?sequence=2&isAllowed=y

Siegel, A. M, (1998). 'To Learn and Make Respectable Hereafter':
The Litchfield Law School in Cultural Context. *N.Y. U. L. Rev., 73*,
1978-2028. https://digitalcommons.law.seattleu.edu/cgi/viewcontent.
cgi?article=1644&context=faculty

Sizer, T, & Sachwager, N, Bricklyand N., Schwager, S., Brickley, L., &
Krueger, G.(1993). *To Ornament Their Minds: Sarah Pierce's Litchfield Female
Academy, 1792-1833.* The Litchfield Historical Society, Litchfield.

Snyder, T.L. (2012, July). Refiguring Women in Early American History.
The William and Mary Quarterly, Vol. 69 (3), 421-450. https://www.jstor.org/
stable/10.5309/willmaryquar.69.3.0421

Spooner, M. (2014). 'I Know this Scheme is from God:' Toward a
Reconsideration of the Origins of the American Colonization Society. *Slavery
and Abolition. 35* (4). https://www.tandfonline.com/doi/abs/10.1080/01440
39X.2013.847223

Strong, B. N. (1976). *The Morris Academy: Pioneer in Coeducation, 1790-
1888.* Morris Bicentennial Committee.

Sweet, L.I. (1985, March). The Female Seminary Movement and
Women's Mission in Antebellum America. *Church History, 54* (1). 41-55.
https://www.jstor.org/stable/3165749

Tarr, J.A. & McShane, C. (2008). The Horse as an Urban Technology.
Journal of Urban Technology, 15 (1). 5-17. https://www.researchgate.net/
publication/232907707_The_Horse_as_an_Urban_Technology

Taylor, F.G. & Roberts, A.D. (1977). An Analysis of Shaker Education:
The Life and Death of an Alternative Educational System, 1774-1950.
University of Connecticut. https://files.eric.ed.gov/fulltext/ED138543.pdf

Thornton, T. P. (1998). *Handwriting in America: A Cultural History.* Yale
University Press.

Warren, C. (1911). *A History of the American Bar.* Little, Brown, and Company.

Vanderpoel, E. N. (1903). *Chronicles of a Pioneer School from 1792-1833 Being the History of Miss Sarah Pierce and her Litchfield School.* Cambridge University Press.

Vermilyea, P.C. (2021, November 30). Hidden Nearby: The Morris Academy. *Connecticuthistory.org.* https://connecticuthistory.org/hidden-nearby-the-morris-academy/

Wajda, S.T. (2020, August 17). Eighteen-hundred-and-froze-to-death: 1816, The Year without a Summer. *Connecticuthistory.org.* https://connecticuthistory.org/eighteen-hundred-and-froze-to-death-1816-the-year-without-a-summer/

Wethersfield Historical Society (N.D.) History. Wethersfield Historical Society. https://www.wethersfieldhistory.org/history/

Winans, R. B. (1975, Winter). The Growth of a Novel-Reading Public in Late 18th Century America. *Early American Literature, 9* (3), 267-272. https://www.jstor.org/stable/25070682

White, A. C. (1920). *The History of the Town of Litchfield, Connecticut, 1720-1920.* Enquirer Print.

Woodruff, G. C. (1845). *History of the Town of Litchfield, Connecticut.* Library of Congress.

Whitescarver, K. (1993). Creating Citizens for the Republic: Education in Georgia, 1776-1810. *Journal of the Early Republic, 13* (4), 455-479. https://scholar.google.com/citations?view_op=view_citation&hl=en&user=F8ZW-wAwAAAAJ&citation_for_view=F8ZWwAwAAAAJ:zYLM7Y9cAGgC

Zorn, R. J. (1957, July). The New England Anti-Slavery Society: Pioneer Abolition Organization. *The Journal of Negro History, 42* (3). https://www.journals.uchicago.edu/doi/10.2307/2715935

About the Author

Louise Harmon is a retired law professor, with a JD, a PhD in philosophy, and two master's degrees. She has written numerous scholarly writings and published short stories with *The Legal Studies Forum,* including one on the history of the Litchfield Law School. Her three published books are: *Fragments on the Deathwatch,* Beacon Press; *Cultivating Intelligence: Law, Power, and the Politics of Teaching* with Deborah Post, New York University Press; and *The Education of Ebenezer Wells,* Hot Brick Books. She lives in northwest Connecticut and frequently visits the graves of Tapping Reeve and Sarah Pierce, the two innovative educators who made Litchfield a center of learning during the years of the Early Republic.